Elaborate Lives

A NOVEL

IN LIFE, AS IN FILM,
FIGHT FOR THE ROLE YOU WANT

JAYE VINER

Other books by Jaye Viner

Jane of Battery Park

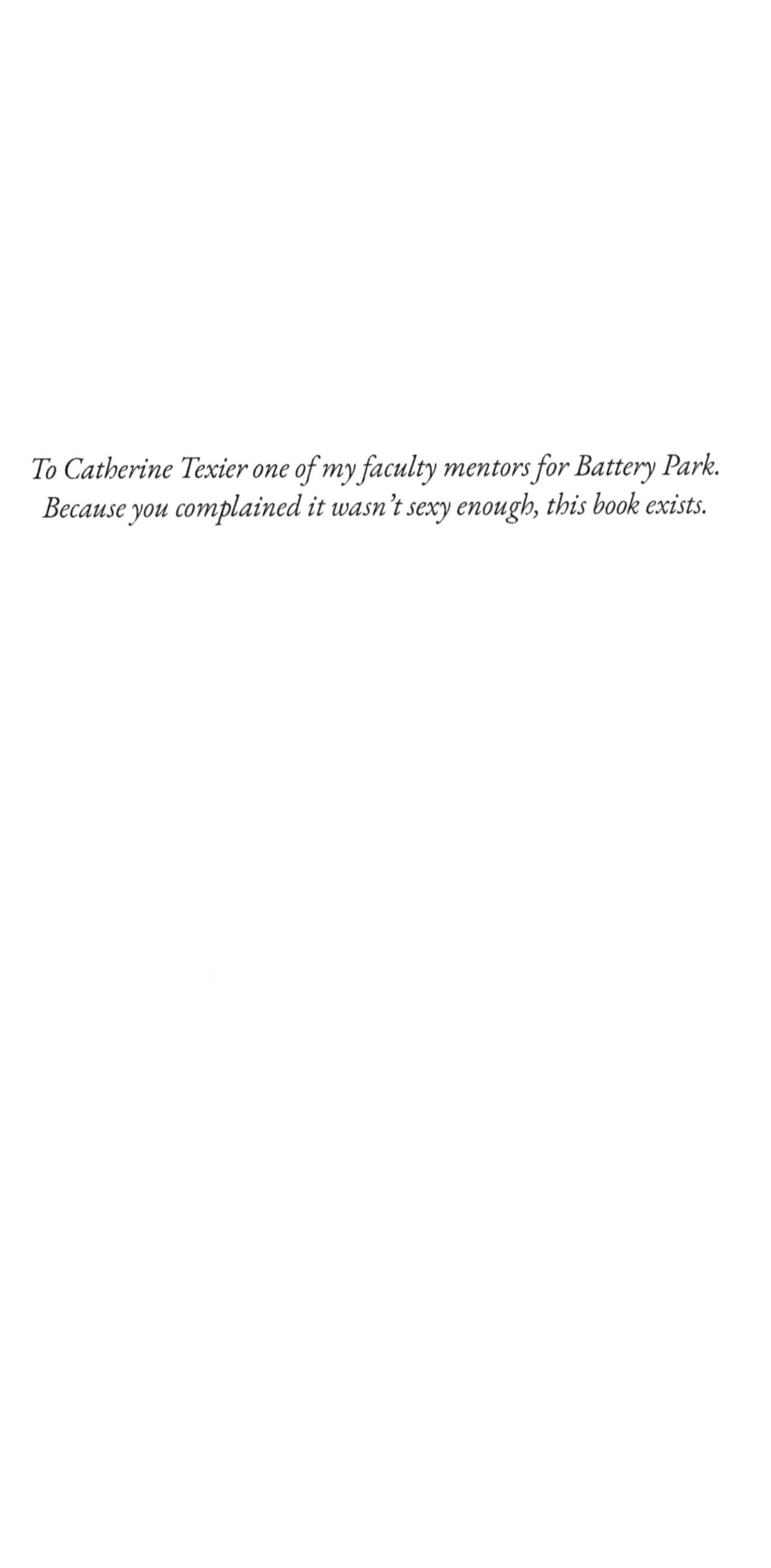
To Catherine Texier one of my faculty mentors for Battery Park.
Because you complained it wasn't sexy enough, this book exists.

Elaborate Lives

"Did I enjoy hurting people? Sometimes. But not simply for the sake of their physical pain. Only if they wanted it. But for someone bent on mastering her given conditions, on inventing herself and her world in opposition to convention, it was an act of supreme defiance."

Whip Smart by Melissa Febos

Content Warning

This novel contains a handful of BDSM scenes and some explicit sex. Readers who are troubled by this content might want to skip Chapter 18 The Statue.

Please note that this novel is a romance novel and thus involves both suspension of belief and fantasy imagination. The portrayal of mental health medicine and its practitioners was well-researched but adapted for the purposes of the story. It is not meant to be an accurate portrayal.

If you or someone you know is struggling with mental health, you can call the crisis emergency line 988, or the National Suicide Prevention Line at 1-800-273-TALK (8255).

Playlist

- Wrecking Ball by Miley Cyrus
- Cosmic Love by Florence + the Machine
- All We Want, Baby, Is Everything by Handsome Furs
- I Wanna be Me by Sex Pistols
- Fake Empire by The National
- Talking Hotel Arbat Blues by Handsome Furs
- Holidays in the Sun by Sex Pistols
- Hooligans by Rancid
- The Phantom Mullet by Five Iron Frenzy
- We Will Fall Together by Streetlight Manifesto
- California Über Alles by Dead Kennedys
- Holiday by Green Day
- There is Nothing Left to Lose by Foo Fighters
- The Middle by Jimmy Eat World
- American Idiot by Green Day
- Never Let Me Go by Florence + the Machine
- Sabrina Suite by John Williams
- Hear You Me by Jimmy Eat World
- And So It Goes Billy Joel

Chapter 1

Stress Relief

It was a quiet night at LA's favorite dungeon, Club D. On stage in the large central room, Club D's headmistress, Anapurr, performed some complicated rope work with a client who liked to be seen. In the audience, a woman known only as the Queen watched from the shadows at the edge of the room, considering what it would be like to be that client, to *desire* visibility.

The Queen wore her usual costume, a black leather corset, stiletto boots, spandex hot pants, custom-made biker's gloves with pads to protect her fingers from long flogging sessions, a silver-linked wristwatch, and a matching low-riding belt with a bedazzled holster for her phone. Most importantly, a latex hood concealed all but her eyes and mouth. She wore garish black lipstick lined with purple, and she'd blacked out all the visible skin around her eyes with kohl.

Club D's social manager, Doan, stood beside the Queen. "See anyone you like?"

The Queen shrugged her bare white shoulders and checked the time on her watch. If she didn't commit to a partner soon, she wouldn't have enough time to finish before work.

"I've got a sub coming on the clock at seven," said Doan. "They would love to take everything you give."

Again, the Queen shrugged. There was something about this night. It felt tired, plagued with the well-worn ache of survival and never enough release. The Queen didn't share these thoughts with

Doan because she didn't want to be cheered up, as she knew Doan would try to do. Instead, she gave a simpler version of the truth.

"I'm tired of being single."

"Unfortunately, I can't help you with—" Doan cocked their head to one side, listening to a message coming through their earpiece. They straightened and looked up at the Queen, eyes glinting in the dim, red-tinged ambient light. "I might have something special for you."

The Queen followed Doan down a hallway of doors painted with a mural of an unknown goddess and her consorts. Most of the doors led to private rooms, but the Blue Room at the far end featured a one-way window with a lounge area set up for an audience. Two couples had staked out claims on the couches. The first gawked like nervous newbies. The second caught the Queen's eye.

The woman lay with her head on the man's lap, not an unusual position in the least, but her head was tilted at just the right angle that the lighting illuminated her face and the side of her neck. Her brown and purple hair had been arranged in a frame at the edges of the light. As the Queen watched, the man brought the woman's hand up and laid it across her chest just so. His head bent over her in concentration as he adjusted the arm, spreading her fingers out so they brushed her collarbone. A pose, the Queen realized, though she wasn't sure for what audience.

The couple looked vaguely familiar, but the Queen couldn't place them in the low light. *Why are they here?* she wondered. They didn't seem like regular D clients.

"This is their fifth time," Doan was saying. "The sub's desires keep elevating. Tonight, looks like the dom can't go far enough."

For a moment, the Queen thought Doan was discussing the couple posed on the couch, then she followed their gaze through the one-way glass to the Blue Room. Inside were two men: one, shirtless in leather pants halfheartedly flogging a second man with a riding crop, the second, kneeling on the floor wearing a collar.

As the Queen watched, the dom threw aside the riding crop

in frustration. "I'm leaving marks. Are you happy? Can we fuck now?"

The sub lowered his head to the floor in an even more submissive posture. "I'm unworthy."

The dom threw up his hands and looked through the window at the unseen audience as though they could save him.

The Queen could. She and Doan exchanged a knowing look, then she walked back to the hallway, knocked on the door, and entered the Blue Room.

"I'm looking for a dirty little man."

The dom's eyes widened with terror as she advanced on him. She pushed him into the bondage chair at the far end of the room and locked his wrists in the cuffs. "What the—"

"Silence! You're not the one I want."

Her heels clicked heavily against the floor as she picked up the abandoned riding crop. It was one of the lightest weights, which meant she'd need to exert more physical effort to inflict the pain this sub wanted. She circled him, letting the crop flick against his hair and trail along his fleshy shoulder.

"I've heard about you," she said. "I'm extremely displeased, and so is your daddy. Aren't you, Daddy?" She looked toward the dom who managed the barest open-mouthed nod.

"I want to do better," said the sub at her feet. "Please punish me so I don't forget."

"I will punish you," said the Queen as she took up a wide stance to the right side of his hip. "You will earn your daddy's love."

She gave him an opening blow to test his endurance. He yelped and settled in, bracing for more. She began her punishment, subjecting the sub's shoulders, butt, and feet to her blows. The Queen was breaking at least three of Club D's rules coming in and role-playing with an unknown party without setting any expectations or even a safe word, but that hardly mattered. Once she was in her rhythm, with the sub's white skin turning red beneath the crop and the tension of a long week draining out of her shoulders, the rules were irrelevant.

A song came to her mind with a steady beat matching her strokes as they vibrated through the air. Her body moved with the beat, an exorcism that drew together all the disparate parts of herself and allowed them to be whole, to sing their own harmony to this current of motion, the passion play of power becoming something truer than what it imitated. That song opened a portal to another place where flesh was a mere object; where obligation, convention, and expectation could be played against each other to unmoor, terrify, and delight.

The song faded as the Queen's arm began to ache. The sub, to his credit, took it all without ever moving his hands from where he'd rested them at the small of his back. This was the sweetest moment, as they both came down from the high, sinking into that delicious oblivion of a body well spent, the seamless moments that rose up from a timeline of fractures to bestow the sweet transmutation of pleasure from pain.

"Go to him," said the Queen. "Beg his forgiveness and his love. Don't release him until he grants it."

The sub scampered across the floor to the dom in the chair.

"Nicely done," said Doan as the Queen returned to the lounge. The four audience members turned to look at her. The newbie couple wore almost mirror expressions of bashful interest. "Is that a service you provide?" the man asked.

"I don't work here," said the Queen.

"We can accommodate all your needs," said Doan quickly. They left the Queen, pulling up a chair to have a business conversation with the couple.

For a moment, the Queen stood alone, watching them, then her attention moved to the other couple. They'd been having a hushed conversation, but as the rhythmic humping from the Blue Room grew in volume, so did their conversation.

"Why not?" said the man. "You might enjoy it."

"But, baby, I don't want to hurt you. I love you."

The Queen pressed her lips together, turning her head just enough to see the couple. The man had his eyes on the couple in the Blue Room, but the woman stared at her man in panicky agitation; the kind that came when you realize the person you're with is profoundly different than what you thought.

They won't make it, thought the Queen.

Neither would the couple in the Blue Room. One of them had tasted a new elixir of life. It would consume him until it burned itself out or became something else. The dom would have to learn to play his role, wait out the infatuation, or be replaced.

She checked her watch. Five minutes to spare. She took a deep breath, then rotated her head around her shoulders to check for residual tension. She debated going over to mediate for the couple. Seeing a display like what she'd put on gave people ideas, made them horny as fuck even when they didn't understand it. She could advise them not to make any rash decisions.

But she didn't really have time for all that. And it wasn't her business. She let herself out the wheelchair-accessible door in the back and walked to her Murano, the car she drove when she was going to Club D. In a silence that still hummed with the song of the scene, she drove to a long-term lot where she parked away from the streetlights, but with her trunk facing the nearest security camera. She peeled herself out of her boots and gloves. From an overnight bag in the passenger seat, she pulled out navy slacks, trouser socks, and sneakers, all from Burberry. She covered the corset with a Tom Ford men's shirt. Experience had shown removing the corset in the car never worked out.

She removed her hood and stowed it along with the rest of her discarded clothes in the bag, which she carried with her to the apple-red Bentley parked at the corner of the lot. As she drove away, she fluffed her long auburn hair out of its French braid, put in pearl earrings, plugged in her iPod, and cranked up the stereo to Florence and the Machine, searching for the perfect song to start the night.

At a stoplight coming off the freeway, two makeup-remover

pads took care of the racoon mask around her eyes and the purple lipstick. She made a note that she was chapped and should increase her moisturizing regime as she pulled into the employee parking lot of Sacred Heart Methodist Hospital, waved her badge at security, then parked. The last piece of her transformation came as she walked towards the hospital, a white doctor's coat with her name embroidered above the pocket: Dr. Larisa de France-Kahn, Psychiatrist. More specifically, she was a third-year, overworked, underpaid resident, who was questioning her life choices every step of the way. The life choices of all three of her lives.

Putting on the coat was like putting on armor, not unlike the way her mother put on Dolce & Gabbana. In the psych ward, every person had the potential to hurt her. For the next twelve hours, she needed to walk the line between compassion, medical expertise, and self-preserving vigilance.

Larisa paused with her hand raised to press the elevator button. *Oh,* she thought. She had, in fact, met that couple from Club D. The man was Quinn VanderVeer, an up-and-coming film director with the rare credential of having grown up in LA. And the woman was an actress, Parish something or other. They'd been together at her mother's New Year's gala.

"This is why I wear the hood," said Larisa, as she swiped her badge for access to the third floor where she would manage the overnight shift of the hospital's inpatient psych ward. It probably wouldn't be catastrophic to be discovered as a psychiatrist who liked bondage—therapists were expected to have weird issues of their own—but it *would* be a kind of a cataclysm to be recognized at Club D as the dangerously single daughter of producer Gunter Kahn and supermodel Suzette de France. She shrugged off the spark of adrenaline at what felt like a near miss.

It's fine, she thought, *they won't be back.*

Even though the couple in the Blue Room had finished and moved to the bar for a celebratory drink, Quinn continued to stare through the window as though the room remained occupied. He could still hear the woman's voice, *I will punish you. You will earn your daddy's love.* When she'd said those words, a fission of energy had shot through him like a live wire. Here was the answer to a question Quinn hadn't even known he'd been asking. A missing piece. Maybe even a solution to the thoughts plaguing him. Not that he wanted a daddy. He needed a daddy even less than he needed Parish melting and simpering as she tried to please him.

What he needed was that woman, an iron rudder that would plunge into the tumultuous currents of his life and steer him straight. A woman who would punish him as he deserved. Maybe then he'd feel ready to direct a major studio production.

"I want to try it."

"You want to whip me?" Parish's eyes widened with mock wonder, her favorite expression for concealing her real feelings.

"No," Quinn hesitated, "The other way."

"Why would I do that?" Parish began to cackle so hard she grabbed her stomach.

"Never mind. You want a drink?" Quinn was on his feet and walking away before she answered. He found Doan at the far end of the hallway, ushering the other couple who'd watched the Blue Room scene toward the stairs which led up to the second floor of private rooms. One of the club's dominatrix waited for them at the top.

He considered this option for a moment before dismissing it. Parish would never share him with someone like that. And Quinn wasn't sure he wanted something just any dominatrix could give him. He wasn't sure about anything except that voice, that woman.

"Hi, sorry." Quinn stepped into Doan's path as they turned from the stairs. His heart pounded in his chest. Was he really doing this? "Did you see where that woman went? The one in the hood? Long boots, bedazzled phone holster."

"She left."

"Do you have her contact information?"

"I can't help you with that."

Right, obviously. Quinn glanced down the hallway, sure that Parish's little head with its perpetually perky ponytail would appear at any moment.

"Can I give you my information and you can pass it along?"

Doan shrugged. "Sure, but don't expect anything."

Chapter 2

BMI ≠ Single

When Larisa gave into her mother's pleading that she come back to LA for residency, she had drawn up a contract for her parents. It stipulated she would give them no more than six hours of her time a month until she graduated and passed her licensure exams. This included time spent on the phone with them, event planning, event attending, personal emergencies, and, for her mother, blind dates. Her father, the favored parent, had talked Larisa into an increase of hours for each year of school. Six became seven, then eight, and would become nine this fall when she started her final year.

This week, they were brunching (two hours), and on Thursday Larisa was going on a date with Greg, a hedge fund manager who was also the son of a woman Larisa's mother had met at her hair salon (three hours, probably less).

"I have a feeling he'll be the one," said Suzette. "He sounds like a darling."

"No man is a darling past the age of five," said Larisa, drawing a smile from her father.

They sat together at one of the raised tables on the periphery of the restaurant's deck on an unusually clear and warm late-January morning. Latices of bougainvillea sheltered them from the people on the street, but not from their fellow diners. Already several of her parents' mutuals from the fashion and film industries had stopped by to say hello. Ashton Carter, last year's top-grossing leading man, had sent a round of mimosas and winked at Larisa when she made the rookie mistake of glancing toward his table. (Excuse: she'd been up all night working.)

"Is he seeing anyone right now?" asked Suzette, pulling out her phone to text her network of wives and personal assistants who always knew the latest gossip before the tabloids went to print.

"I thought you didn't want me marrying into the industry." Larisa cut another knowing glance to her father.

"You can do better," he said.

If I'd done my residency in Minneapolis or some other normal-people city, I might have done better, thought Larisa bitterly.

"Don't make that face," said Suzette. "People are watching. Do you want Greg to think you're a thirty-year-old sour lemon?"

"I'm twenty-eight and I like lemons."

Suzette smiled at her phone screen. "Ashton is single right now. But my source says, we should try a Saudi prince. Just bought a house in the hills, arriving next month."

"No thanks, Mom."

"I agree, too complicated. You're far too difficult for someone like—"

"Look at this, the whole family out together!"

Larisa turned and saw Eddie Sacks, one of her father's old production partners, now a bigwig at Enterprise Studios, approaching their table. Her father rose to shake hands. Eddie pulled him in for a hug instead.

"Look at us old men," Eddie said, as he patted the belly bulge pressing against the front of Gunter's shirt. Gunter did the same to Eddie's larger bulge. Larisa put on a pleasant smile, playing the role of the good daughter, but then her phone began to vibrate against the table. A message appeared that made her snatch it before her mother could read it.

> Club: My Queen, this is Doan. A man saw you last week and wishes to know you better. I gave him nothing, FYI.

Larisa buried the phone in her lap, face burning, heart in her throat. She struggled to hear what Eddie was saying. New production with an untested director. Ulcers. Needs to retire.

"Sounds like your director just needs a good therapist," joked Gunter. "Isn't that the way people solve all their problems these days?"

"But who could I trust?" moaned Eddie. "And half of them are cracks, in it for the money."

"Larisa, do you know someone who could manage Eddie's difficult director?"

Eddie's gaze shifted to Larisa, eyes lighting up. "I remember you were doing something with medicine." His enlightened eyes lingered, tracing her contours and softening with an intimacy Larisa had never gotten used to. She wondered if he was remembering her teen years and the short-lived reality series that had broadcast the horror show of her adolescence to the world on MTV.

"I'm a psychiatrist," said Larisa, drawing her lips into that sour look her mother hated. "That's a type of doctor. And I don't know anyone who sees industry people unless they're the struggling nobodies who no one will listen to because they can't pay, they don't have insurance, or they're homeless."

Eddie blinked. For a moment, Larisa thought her poisoned arrows had landed. But then Eddie smiled. "Well, I like to think once we start filming, he'll settle down."

More vibrations of messages sounded on Larisa's phone. She clenched her hands around the hard plastic shell. *Why the fuck is Doan messaging me?*

Eddie drifted away. Gunter waited until he was out of earshot before shaking his head and saying, "I'm glad I'm away from all that."

"You could come out of retirement and make Eddie look like the ass he is," said Suzette. Larisa felt her mother's eyes watching, wondering about the hidden phone.

"I like managing the guild. I play golf. I give new people their PGA cards. I feel good about myself for a change."

Suzette huffed dismissively and turned her full attention to Larisa. "Your social life is active this morning?"

"It's Jaden and the wedding planning." This wasn't exactly a lie. Jaden was the last of Larisa's sorority sisters to get married. There had been messages on the group chat that weekend. Larisa had ignored most of them, only answering the one that directly related to her.

Jaden: Larisa, how tall are you?

Larisa: 5'11.

Rosa: I'd still kill for those model legs.

Jaden: None of the groomsmen are tall enough for you.

Larisa: I'll wear smaller heels.

Krissy: But then we wouldn't match!

Jaden: No biggie. We'll do a single file processional down the aisle.

Larisa: Don't change anything because of me.

Jaden: No, I think this is better. I like it.

"When is that wedding again?" asked Suzette. "Not March?"

"Cousin Milo's wedding is March. Jaden's is in April."

"Three months," mused Suzette. "You could be engaged by then."

"Let's not plan on that," said Larisa.

"At least a steady, interested party."

"I have PRITE in April, Mom."

"That sounds like a disease. Which reminds me, bring condoms with you on Thursday. Greg's mother says he's not good with details."

On Mondays, Larisa held outpatient talk-therapy sessions to help support patients who had been admitted to the emergency ward and then released. Her nine o'clock was Kara, a teen who had been brought into the ER by her parents for the third time in as many months for refusing to eat. This morning's session was both an exit interview for the ward and an introduction to her judge-mandated therapy sessions. If she and Larisa couldn't make progress, Kara would be indefinitely involuntarily committed for her own safety.

Kara, an emaciated skeleton of a girl, walked circles around the couch in counseling room three. "This isn't going to work."

"We could try it and see if we're surprised," said Larisa.

"I'm never surprised."

Larisa knew how it felt to be world-weary at sixteen, but that didn't make it easier to help her. The only thing that seemed to work in Larisa's favor was being famous. When she'd met Kara that weekend on the third floor, Kara had recognized her from her adolescent reality show, *Drama Queen*, where she'd been an exceptionally skinny teen going through a Hollywood Hills version of high school. There was irony in this, as Larisa felt she was constantly trying to get her instructors and cohorts to forget she was a grown-up reality TV star with famous parents. But with Kara, who everyone secretly thought was a lost cause, Larisa would use everything she could, even if it skirted the lines of ethics and patient-doctor boundaries.

From her bag, Larisa retrieved Kara's cell phone, which had

been confiscated when she'd been admitted Friday night. "Will you share your Twitter feed with me?"

Kara gave her a suspicious side-eye. "So you can tell my parents what's on it?"

"They already know, but that's not the point." Larisa paused. One of the cardinal rules of therapy was to keep a professional distance. Her personal life was not relevant to the client. But the inequality of that dynamic often made clients less likely to trust her, especially kids like Kara who specialized in calling adults on their bullshit.

Larisa came over to the couch with both her personal phone and Kara's. "We'll go back and forth. Until ten till," Larisa pointed to the clock. "Then your mom will be here."

"No cheating," said Kara. "Whatever comes up."

"Alright. But I'm warning you, I haven't looked at my feed in weeks. I've no idea what we'll see."

"Burn my virgin eyes?" Kara grinned, unlocking her phone and expertly navigating to the social app her parents said was the root of all evil. The first image that came up was a model, photo edited, glossy lips parted as she looked down into the camera.

"First thought that comes to mind?" asked Larisa.

"She's so pretty."

"Why?"

"What do you mean, why? It's obvious."

"I don't think she's that pretty. Look, see that line there between the contrast shades?"

"That's contouring."

"Right, but it's not real. And that there? Where's her butt? Everyone has a butt, but hers has been erased."

"It would ruin the line," said Kara.

"Why would we want beautiful women to have their butts erased?"

Kara chewed her bottom lip, thinking hard for a comeback.

"I've met her," said Larisa. "In fact, I think I have a picture of her." Larisa turned her phone away from Kara and went to her photo archive. She was now fully overstepping ethical boundaries of information sharing, but Larisa's heart beat with a quiet thrill. This was a karmic moment. Of all the models, celebrities, and "it girls" who could have shown up on Kara's feed, the woman was the daughter of Larisa's parents' neighbor, a girl Larisa had babysat during a set of episodes for *Drama Queen*. They'd just seen each other for Suzette's New Year's gala.

"This is Jaquelle last month." Larisa turned her phone and showed a picture of the two of them posing with the commemorative New Year's banner behind them. There was full-stage lighting (because her mother never cut corners on quality production), and both were wearing slinky sheath dresses, which gave plenty of exposure to the curves of their bodies. Neither woman was considered the average clinical weight for their heights, but they were far from the airbrushed version of Jaquelle.

Kara studied the picture, then looked back at her phone. "I don't think that's her."

"I promise it is."

"But she's fat."

Larisa knew better than to engage Kara in an argument of definitions about fatness and beauty. She'd been down that road with her parents, school counselors, and several previous doctors.

"So, you don't think she's beautiful here? As her own self?"

"Yes, but . . ."

"But what?"

"But this picture doesn't count. It's secret."

"Because it's not online?"

How do children survive anything these days? wondered Larisa.

"Alright, I'll message Jaquelle. If she says it's okay, I'll post this picture to my socials."

"You're never on your socials."

"So I don't count?"

Kara shifted over to Larisa's Facebook profile. The last post was from Suzette's autumn masquerade the previous October. Larisa didn't recognize the images. The posts had probably come from her publicist's assistant.

"I guess that would be okay."

"Then we'll look at it when you come back next week and see what the comments are like."

"Now we have to look at your Twitter."

Larisa took a deep breath, only slightly exaggerating her fear for effect. Kara rolled her eyes. "What do you have to be scared of? I bet you follow a bunch of boring doctor accounts about how to torture your patients."

The first picture was a tweet from Jaden. The attached picture showed her surrounded by the small army of her event team as she toured the Palisades resort where her wedding would take place.

"She's fat too. Is she famous?"

"Jaden is like me, famous because of her parents. Soon she'll be more famous because she's marrying a Dodgers baseball player."

"I thought baseball players only liked small girls. She's not even wearing makeup."

"The horror," said Larisa.

"You're not funny."

"Let's do another. This time, you aren't allowed to say anything about weight."

"I'll just think it to myself."

"Don't even do that. There's a lot more to a picture than you realize."

Kara heaved a dramatic sigh as she scrolled down her feed. "Why aren't you married?"

The words stabbed into Larisa's side, sending out a spasm that took her breath away. "Not everyone gets married."

"Yeah, but . . ."

Larisa felt Kara about to ask the question *What's wrong with you?* She braced for impact.

Instead, Kara reached over and pinched together an inch of skin above Larisa's hip. "Your BMI doesn't seem horrible. Not great, but some guys like chunky."

"I promise you, I'm not single because of my weight."

Chapter 3

The Breakup

Quinn woke up with a start. Breathless. Too hot. It took him a moment to realize Parish was in bed with him, wrapped around his torso like a leech. They'd fought again last night. He'd locked himself in the bedroom when she'd started throwing things at him.

How did she get in? He lifted his head and looked around. The bedroom door was still closed but the balcony's French doors stood open, letting in dry morning heat that smelled of smoke. He'd been in the house only a few months, but he felt this smell was unusual. A fire alert hadn't come through his phone.

"Parish, wake up."

Mumbling. An even tighter grip on his waist.

Fuck.

He reached for his phone and checked the time. Not even six. Plenty of time before he needed to leave for the studio. Too much time.

"I can't breathe, Parish."

She loosened her grip enough that he could pry her off. There were scrapes on her arms and knees. Blood crusted the tops of her toes where she must have dug into the mortar of the exterior brick wall.

Do not panic, Quinn. She's calmer now.

He rolled out of bed, retreating up against the wall. He braced for Parish to follow and latch onto him again. Instead, she remained curled up, naked in bed, her face puffy from hours of crying. Her big brown eyes blinking at him.

"Get dressed," he said. "I'm making coffee. We're going to talk."

He grabbed a mostly clean T-shirt from the floor and escaped to the hallway where he leaned against the door, hands pressed against the soft gully just below his ribcage, trying to breathe. Diaphragm restriction due to anxiety was not a new thing, but it had become exponentially more frequent since he'd taken the job as director of *The Key* for Enterprise Studios. But this felt different. A new thought raced breathless circles through his mind: *She's trying to suffocate me.*

Finally, a deep breath. It flowed smoothly from beginning to end. The bedroom door solid at his back. The tile floor cool beneath his feet.

He padded down to the kitchen. Coffee first, then a conversation that was long overdue. She'd listen to reason. Neither of them was happy. They'd tried something; it hadn't worked out. Could they just be adults about it? *Remember what you said last night about wanting a normal boyfriend?* he would say. *I'm not him.*

The smell of fire grew stronger as he entered the kitchen. Quinn looked into the adjacent living room to check for more open windows. Instead, he found a charred black husk where his favorite chair had sat. In the midst of it, he could see the melted rubber and tarnished metal of a pair of handcuffs and the beginners' flogger he'd bought after watching Club D's online class, Introduction to Power Exchange Role Playing.

He considered the symbolism of this scene in the plotline of his relationship with Parish. The scene wasn't right. The two picture windows let in too much light. He drew the blinds, then turned on one of the floor lamps, tilting its shade toward the chair. Better. He went back to the kitchen to start coffee.

It was only as he set the double boiler on the stove that the truth of what Parish had done broke through his awareness. She didn't care about symbolism. She hadn't staged a set for him. Their life together wasn't a movie he was constructing scene by scene. She'd charged passionately down a path of destruction and could have burned the house down with him inside.

Quinn stared at the spout of the boiler as condensation began to gather around its metal sides. *This isn't how it's supposed to happen.* He'd chosen Parish because she looked the part. A young, sexy girlfriend went a long way in making a gawky film director look cool. He'd thought she would help deflect attention in public, help him feel less exposed.

None of those things had happened. Parish was insecure, fussy, and distractable. In public, she often wandered off to say hello to people she knew, leaving him alone, flustered, and too easily defensive.

Eddie will be furious, thought Quinn.

Steam poured out of the boiler. Quinn moved it to a cold burner, then took two mugs from the cupboard. Parish still hadn't emerged from the bedroom. Fine. He would wait her out.

At the kitchen table, a battered, faux-wood monstrosity he'd had since his first apartment, Quinn looked up locksmiths. He used the app on his phone to reset the front gate security code, then messaged his assistant, Sid, to come over as soon as he could.

When he'd finished his coffee and Parish remained absent, Quinn began to sift through the kitchen, picking out her things and setting them in a cluster on the counter. Behind him, he finally heard the light brushing of feet. Amazing how gentle she sounded.

"What are you doing?"

"Collecting your stuff."

"Why?"

"You're moving out."

"Why?"

He faced her. She was dressed in another of his discarded T-shirts, which fit her better than it fit him. Her hair hung provocatively around her shoulders, asking him to push his fingers into it, to rub those soft strands between his fingers. Parish was the only rich woman he'd ever dated. As in, she came from money and knew how to groom herself. Her hair had been the first thing he'd loved about her. He'd never known hair could be so soft.

"This isn't working."

"I disagree."

"I want you to leave."

"I'm not leaving." She slid past him and poured herself a mug of the remaining coffee.

A creeping wrongness edged up Quinn's back and raised the hairs on his neck. He'd expected her to cry, maybe yell, but not this blasé calm, as though they were talking about the weather.

"Parish, I'm not good for you."

"Then do better." She peered at the scene in the living room over the rim of her mug. A satisfied smile played across her lips, like she'd already won, like his part in this didn't matter because she knew he needed her.

Quinn knocked the mug out of her hand. The ceramic shattered on the kitchen counter. Lukewarm coffee splattered in all directions as Quinn grabbed Parish's arm and dragged her out of the kitchen, down the hallway to the front door.

Outside, she began to scream at him and kick. Then, out of nowhere, she relaxed her legs and dropped to the cement where she sat like a boulder, immovable.

"I love you, Quinn."

"Parish—"

She tilted her head up, raising her voice as though calling to the neighbors. "I love you. This weird sex thing won't last."

"For fuck's sake, would you shut up."

"I don't care what you want to do to me. I'm staying."

He knelt down, plastering his hand over her mouth. "Listen to me. It's over. It's fucking over."

She bit him.

He slapped her across the face. She fell over, knocking her head on the cement with a soft thunk.

"Parish!" Dread encased him, dense, suffocating. *This is not happening.*

But then she was smiling. Her delicate face tilted up at him with a daring gleam in her eyes. "You're going to regret this."

There was no blood, so Quinn retreated inside. He locked the doors and went through the house gathering Parish's things. In the bedroom, he stopped and screamed into a pillow.

When Sid arrived an hour later, Parish remained laying in the driveway. Quinn watched from a second-floor window as Sid stopped to say hello. Parish waved a fragile little hand in the air for him to grasp. He pulled her up and helped her into his car.

Quinn and Sid had known each other since high school when they'd starting at a distribution warehouse at the same time, trying to make enough money to support their single mothers and Sid's younger siblings. They came from the same place, so when Sid said, "Parish claims you hit her," the shame that rippled through Quinn's bones and threatened to raise the coffee back up his esophagus, was all his own.

"I lost myself."

Sid nodded. "I'll get her some breakfast, see if I can calm her down. Where should she go?"

"I'll text you her parents' address. There's a locksmith coming at ten. Can you be here to make sure both doors and the patio are changed, get the keys from him?"

"Sure thing." Sid closed the distance between them. "You okay to go to work?"

An absurd question. Quinn didn't bother answering.

"Don't let those hot shots push you around. You've earned this."

How did people know when they'd earned something? Was it a process of slowly learning it through the repetition of people telling them? Or did they simply believe so fully in their own enti-tlement that the question of deserving or earning a good thing never crossed their minds?

Even on stage at Sundance, listening to the roar of applause as he won the Audience Award for his first film, Quinn had been sure he'd done something wrong. It hadn't seemed possible so many people could like him or his work.

He didn't deserve to be in charge of a big production. He knew this was true because one of the studio executives had revealed that Eddie Sacks had pressured the studio into hiring him. Why had Eddie Sacks wanted to hire Quinn against the wishes of the studio? Eddie was Parish's uncle. *Maybe he'll fire me,* thought Quinn, as he drove up to Studio City.

The day started with a crew meeting to review the first week's shooting schedule. Easy enough. Quinn retreated behind his shooting script and listened to the production team talk around him. When there was a debate about something, he chose the side that seemed the most reasoned and weighed in. Film school had given him enough of the lingo to have a sense of the basics, but most of the time he had no idea what they were talking about. He'd shot his first two movies on the street with a crew of eight people, who all did exactly what he said in the moment. There'd been no plan, barely a script, two work lights from a hardware store, a rented steady cam, and a boom mic.

From the crew meeting he moved on to costume approval for the extras, then to an emergency conclave about the forecast on Thursday, since they were planning to shoot on location at a cafe in Santa Monica. Rain. Two mid-level executives and Lane, his director of photography—a guy who'd made it clear he didn't think Quinn knew anything about photography—wanted to reschedule.

"We'll shoot in the rain, if necessary," said Quinn. "There's no continuity problem. It's an isolated scene."

"I strongly advise against—"

"Make sure you have what you need," he said, walking away. He was late for the cast's final table read. Quinn hated being late even though he knew it was within his rights as a director to keep his own schedule. Being the last one to enter a room meant everyone had permission to stare at him.

This was exactly what happened as he rushed into the conference room, flustered from the almost-argument he'd had about the rain; his hackles raised because he could still see Lane's doubtful gaze echoing through his mind's eye, as he sat in resentful silence, letting Quinn make decisions he thought were wrong.

Parish's words echoed through his head. *You'll regret this.*

Eddie Sacks sat in a chair at the edge of the conference room with a studio accountant on his left and a mid-level manager on his right. *Does he know yet?* Eddie gave him a small salute. Quinn tried to breathe as he sat down at the table in the circle of actors. The main cast was headlined by Vince Rocks, a star aging out of his prime. He played Walt, a retiring CIA agent who takes one last job stopping a rogue Russian general from acquiring nuclear missile codes. To do this, he recruits a thief to infiltrate the general's circle.

Vince had been Quinn's dream choice, and the studio had made it happen. He told himself he should be grateful. He told himself even experienced directors rarely got the lead they most wanted. This should have made up for the rest.

Australian actor, Sal Peffer, played the general even though his Russian accent was spotty at best. He was known for his role as a gruff but lovable rugby player on an Australian soap opera. But, in the words of the casting director who had gone over Quinn's head to convince the executive producers, "He looks more Russian than most Russians."

The role of the thief turned CIA recruit had gone to a nobody Dutchman named Dansby Vaast. Not a nobody actor, but a nobody civilian. The studio's CFO had plucked Dansby off a European beach, brought him to America and said, "This is the boy," with a finality that defied debate.

Should Quinn apologize for being late? *Just get on with it. Focus. Pretend everything's fine.*

Nothing is fine.

"Let's start from the top," said Quinn. "I want to do each

sequence without pause, then we can discuss any changes. We're not necessarily performing today, but if you want to develop things from rehearsal, that'd be great."

A shuffling of script pages. Tish, the first assistant director, cleared her throat and read the scene heading, "Exterior. Market."

"The key to being invisible is knowing what you should be doing here," said Vince as Walt. He delivered the line with the authority of many years of experience, inviting confidence as he adjusted the prop glasses he'd brought along.

Quinn let himself relax against the back of his chair.

"What are we doing here?" asked Dansby in his Dutch accent. He coughed out a laugh, glancing at Quinn with those bright eyes. His tanned, chiseled face was like a Greek marble come to life. "Let me try that again. 'What are we doing here?'" he said in a passable American accent with a touch of southern drawl.

"We're here to observe that woman, Natalia." Vince nodded his head toward the corner of the conference room. "She might be someone of interest. But that isn't what we're really doing here."

"It's not?" asked Dansby, flat.

"Obviously, we're buying food. That's what one does at the market. So, what are you cooking?"

"Breakfast?" asked Dansby.

"What kind of person cooks breakfast?"

"For my girlfriend who's been sick all week?"

"Good," said Vince. "Now, approach that woman and start a conversation."

An actress named Lizette was playing Natalia. She rolled her chair closer to Dansby and gave him a covert side-eye.

Dansby grinned. "Heya,"

Quinn gritted his teeth. "Stay on script please."

Dansby squinted at his script. "If you've been sick all week, would you prefer hashbrowns or fried potatoes?"

Lizette, as Natalia, pressed her lips together and shrugged, unwilling to reveal she didn't speak English.

"I'm not good at cooking," said Dansby, still flat.

Quinn wished he'd made acting the lines mandatory. Dansby needed practice. But he didn't interrupt. He felt Eddie shifting in the far corner of the room. Was he checking his phone? What time was it? How long had Parish been at her parents' house? What if Sid hadn't managed to deliver her to them?

Several lines passed without his notice. Now Dansby and Lizette were at the checkout. She'd warmed to him. He was working up to the anchor line of the scene, asking Lizette about her homelife in the hope it would reveal a connection to the Russian general.

Quinn watched Dansby smile and blush his way through the lines, half a beat away from laughter, like he thought the exchange was silly. *He's nervous.* Quinn tried to ignore the feeling of wrongness. Tried to put himself in the scene, imagine the blocks, the sounds, the turns, but all he could think about was how Dansby would never be recruited as a spy. He was too pretty, too simple.

He's going to ruin my movie, thought Quinn, not for the first time.

Again, he sensed movement in the corner. Eddie, growing restless. Quinn's pulse surged with a rush of blood to his head, a thrumming in his ears.

He knows.

Before he could stop himself, Quinn was standing, moving across the room. He grabbed Dansby's script and threw it across the table. "Didn't I tell you to work on your lines?"

Dansby shrank back in his seat so far it tipped back and would have fallen if Quinn hadn't grabbed the armrests and pulled it down. "Didn't I tell you to mark the emotional beats?"

"I did. I swear."

"What are you feeling right now?"

"Scared?"

"You're Sam Stocklin from Columbus, Missouri. You're in the grocery store with a Russian spy. What do you feel right now?"

"Excited. I think. Jah, excited, but nervous because I don't want to mess up." Even though Dansby weighed twice as much as Quinn and could've snapped him in half like a toothpick, he put his arms up to protect his face like he expected Quinn to strike him.

It felt too familiar.

Twice in one day.

Quinn stumbled back, then returned to his seat. Silence. So many eyes, looking away or looking too closely, all of them surely seeing the same thing—he didn't belong there.

Chapter 4

Rules of the Game

Another lackluster Thursday night. Larisa would usually be at Club D, releasing herself from a week of hanging onto her future as a doctor by the ends of her acrylics. Instead, she was on her way to Mr. Chang's to meet Greg, who she would spend approximately three hours with before going back to the hospital for her overnight shift.

She went through her usual pre-date mental exercises and reminders.

1. Do not assume it's going badly until it actually is.
2. Do not mention your intimidating degrees.
3. Smile when he brings up *One Flew Over the Cuckoo's Nest*, then change the subject.
4. Do not eat too much.
5. Do not make that face when he brings up children.

The list went to ten, but Larisa's mind wandered to what she was missing at Club D. The possibility of something fresh and revitalizing, that didn't involve an audition for a trophy wife. She thought of Doan's message from Sunday. Quinn VanderVeer wanted to meet the Queen. Larisa hadn't even made up her mind if she'd say yes, but it irritated her that she *could* have said yes tonight if not for this date.

You're doing this because you haven't given up, Larisa told herself. *True love can find anyone willing to be found.*

Greg wasn't likely to be true love, but he was a step toward it. Eliminate one possibility, keep an open mind, and leave space for whoever might come next. It wasn't the best logic, but it was all she had. With Jaden, her fellow, long-standing single soulmate, now getting married, the possibility that Larisa would find what she was looking for felt even more impossible than it had before.

At the beginning of her residency, when she'd moved back to LA after medical school and her mother had launched the bachelor parade, Larisa had still been romantic enough to judge men by chemistry and attraction. She'd started every date preoccupied with the question: Do I find him attractive? After a year of rejecting men out of hand or diving in headfirst only to crash and burn, she knew a yes to that question could easily turn into a no on closer inspection. And a no could just as easily evolve into a yes with added familiarity.

Now, when facing a new potential mate, she asked herself four questions, none of which bothered with passion:

1. What kind of person does he present to the world?
2. Does it match his internal sense of self?
3. Does he have enough going on to keep me interested for the next ten years?
4. Is he flexible enough that I can work and be his wife?

Suzette had promised Greg was smarter than the average man. As if a lack of smart explained why Larisa was what her mother called, "chronically single." As most conversations went with her mother, Larisa had held her tongue and not asked which definition of smart her mother was using or interrogate her on the implication that the real problem was Larisa being too smart; if smart in this sense meant overeducated, opinionated, strong-willed, and generally interested in her independence.

Greg had procured a reservation at Mr. Chow's even though this was unnecessary; Larisa had been dining there with her parents since she was ten (the age old enough to be seen socially in restaurants and not be embarrassing) and was one of those people who could just walk in.

As his second transgression, Greg ordered a bottle of wine without asking what she'd like. Larisa watched him sip the wine, pucker his lips, and put on all the social graces of the educated wine drinker he was not. So many people failed to recognize the nakedness of hunger, how much could be revealed in the ritual of filling bellies. The well-worn edges of his performance made her want to talk quickly, using large words until he admitted he was nothing compared to her. The audacity of agreeing to this date as though he had something she might want was not the good kind of self-confidence.

"What do you like to do for fun?"

Larisa gave him her condescending you're-the-size-of-an-ant smile she'd used to dress down far too many first dates, her classmates, and sometimes even her supervisors. The only person it didn't make squirm was her father.

"I don't have fun, Greg. I'm a third-year resident in psychiatric emergency medicine. That means my life isn't my own because I'm being trained to save others, prescribe medications, develop treatment plans, and find funding for dying social safety-net programs because your blessed economy is too fragile to support the people who make it run. You're not one of them. You're a piranha profiting off the wealth of other wealthy people, who in turn are systematically demolishing the mental health of my patients in order to squeeze out a few more pennies before they are discarded for workers who are younger, cheaper, and less likely to argue."

Greg nodded along like her diatribe was the chorus of a song. When she paused for breath he said, "I think it's great that someone like you cares so much to really get into the grit with people. I would love to learn how to do that."

Someone like you. He was smart enough to remind her where she came from.

How dare he.

Deep breath, Larisa. When a man doesn't know enough to be insulted by you, he's not worth your rage. She pushed down her instincts, keeping her smile in place. They called it a night with a chaste kiss and no promises.

As she drove to the hospital, Larisa changed clothes. The plunging Valentino blouse became a striped button-up from Zara's, covered with a decades old Marni sweater. Her diamond studs became the fake emerald birthstones she'd received from her cousin one year for Christmas. She pulled her soft, first-date waves into a severe bun at the back of her head. As she parked at the hospital, she completed the transformation with her badge and sneakers. She cleaned off her evening-eye makeup but left her nude-toned lipstick.

Larisa jogged up three flights of stairs, scanned her badge at the back door for the psych ward, and entered what her cohort, Sophie, called the womb of chaos. A line of incoming patients with an assortment of nurses, orderlies, and police escorts stood waiting for admittance. Two members of the day staff were working intake. One was talking softly with a manic patient backed into a corner. The fourth was with Sophie at the desk trying to finish the shift transfer. Lucie, the bed finder, was on the phone asking the community clinic in West Hollywood if they had any open beds. Carl, the checks person, was jogging down the hall, trying not to look panicked. As soon as he saw Larisa he diverted, grabbed her sleeve, and whispered, "I lost one."

"Which one?"

"Boi George. Ten minutes ago, he was in the community room talking to himself."

"Talking to his friends," Larisa corrected. "Don't trivialize the voices someone hears. They're real to them. It doesn't cost anything for us to honor that."

Carl hung his head. "Is that why he's missing?"

"Let's divide and conquer. He's here somewhere. I'll do north side. You do south side. He's not a big man, so don't overlook crawl spaces under beds or any of the closets."

Larisa worked her way up the hall, murmuring apologies as she entered rooms where patients were sleeping. Her progress paused in room six where she found Lauren, one of the ward's regulars, ripping her pillow to shreds and eating the stuffing. Why? She needed something in her mouth. She was so hungry. There was no one available to supervise Lauren so Larisa took her along on the quest of finding Boi George with the bribe of a snack at the end.

They found him in the community room, not far from where Carl had spotted him on his last round but cloaked from easy finding. He'd tucked himself up under a table to hide from the Trucker, a voice who Larisa thought might have been a real person from his childhood, transmuted into a persona in Boi George's mind.

She brought three pudding cups from the kitchen. "Mind if we sit with you, Boi George?"

"It's not safe," he said. "You should run if you can."

Larisa looked around as though searching for danger. Lauren, eager for her treat, did not bother with pretending. She plopped down beside Boi George and cracked open her cup. "I don't see anyone."

"He's here. I hear him."

Larisa sat down on Boi George's other side, setting the extra pudding down in front of him even though she doubted he'd eat it. "What does he want this time?" she asked.

"It's too horrible to say."

"An entire roast turkey?" asked Lauren.

"My feet," said Boi George. "He won't stop until he gets them."

"Did he say anything about your pills?" asked Larisa. Her work phone was vibrating. A message from Carl. Then from Sophie. A bunch of exclamation points.

"He doesn't know about them. Remmy and I hid them."

Remmy was one of Boi George's more friendly voices, but also the least helpful.

"Hid them where?"

"In the bedpost."

"Good plan," said Larisa. "But you know what happens if you don't take your pills?"

"This."

Larisa nodded. She messaged Carl to please go to Boi George's room and retrieve his pills from the bedpost.

"You need to tell the Trucker he can't have your feet. Then we're going to crawl out of here."

"I don't think I can."

"Do you want to give him your feet?"

Boi George shook his head.

"Your feet are nice," said Lauren, as she eyed Boi George's untouched pudding cup.

"He's coming," said Boi George.

The footsteps they all heard belonged to Carl. They watched as the feet came into view, grew larger, then stopped at the edge of the table.

"Save me," whispered Boi George.

"Do it yourself," said Larisa.

"I can't."

"Sure you can. Lauren and I are right here. We'll back you up."

Boi George crawled out from under the table and faced off against Carl. "You can't have my feet, you murdering sonvuabitch."

"Okay," said Carl, sounding shaky. "But will you take these for me in exchange?"

Larisa listened to the exchange of pills and water, then Boi George gulping. She turned to Lauren. "Let's talk about what happened with your pillow."

Chapter 5

Not So Quiet on the Set

The alarms of Quinn's security system went off at two in the morning. He hadn't been fully asleep (it was the first day of shooting and his nerves wouldn't rest), but the sudden sound piercing the silence seemed a confirmation of the disaster his lizard brain had been anticipating the entire weekend.

There were no weapons in the house, so he crawled out of bed and crouched in the corner a few feet from the bed, his phone clutched in his hand. Over the weekend, he'd taken to barricading himself in the bedroom for the night by placing a chair against the bedroom door and a stack of books against the balcony doors. He had a clear view of the balcony, and he hoped he'd hear someone moving the chair if they came in through the bedroom door.

He tried to breathe. Precious minutes ticked by. The ringing alarms began to numb his eardrums, adrenaline seeping away to be replaced by cramping muscles. He didn't dare move. The moment he moved the intruder would find him.

The alarms stopped. His phone began to vibrate with an incoming call.

"Hello?" Quinn's whisper seemed too loud in the still room.

"Mr. VanderVeer, we've apprehended a woman attempting to climb your garden fence onto the property."

All Quinn could think to say was, "Alright."

"What action do you wish us to take?"

"If you could take her home." He paused. "Does this number receive SMS?"

"It does."

"I'll text you the address."

"We have the authority to submit her to the LAPD for—"

"That's not necessary."

Quinn uncoiled himself from the floor and crossed to the balcony doors. Down below, he saw the gate standing open with the security company's car just beyond it. Two men were hauling Parish up from the lawn at the edge of the driveway. She looked tiny between them, like a twisting, snarling, heinous animal.

What does she want so badly? he wondered. It seemed impossible it would be him, but the absence of another answer was also frightening. He tucked the question back into the forgetful part of his brain. In six hours, he would be shooting. He needed to focus. Sleep was out of the question, so he made coffee and sat with it on the front stoop where he would know right away if Parish returned and tried to invade again. He went through the shooting script in his mind, every shot, every beat, every lighting and lens change.

It will be fine, he thought. *I'm ready.*

The thing about making a movie is it involves other people. And each one of those other people bring with them an infinite number of behaviors, opinions, and limitations that might conflict with the director's vision. Most of them are too small to cause trouble. Most good directors know how to manage those variables. But Quinn began his day at a deficit of goodwill and confidence, the two most useful tools for managing human foibles. The deficit only grew as the day went on.

Quinn had scheduled the filming to start with location shots around LA because this was the style of filmmaking he knew best. He had thought it would be a nice way to ease into the work. He'd been wrong.

The grocer where they were shooting had small aisles and too many onlookers. The first three takes of Dansby moving to meet Lizette were wasted when he couldn't arrive at his mark. Then, when he started making it, he walked too fast. He came onto Lizette like a hurricane. After Quinn told him to slow it down and just have a conversation, Dansby lost his American accent. Quinn had never worked with someone so unaware of what he was doing. Every time he gave Dansby suggestions for adjustment, Dansby overcorrected, or seemed to forget some other key element of the scene.

"We're wasting time and money, and more time," Quinn hissed at Tish. He worked his fingers through his bracelet of Tibetan prayer beads as lighting set up for the next shot.

"The kid is new to this, give him a break."

A long silence followed, like Tish was debating if she'd say something else.

Quinn stared down at his beads; the Chinese characters had worn away years ago and, more recently, some of the black polish had begun to fade. The creeping shadows of Quinn's early morning still plagued his perception. During the last take, one of the onlookers had shifted their weight and Quinn had flinched as some part of his brain braced for Parish to come at him in a flying tackle.

Plus, Vince kept giving him looks of sympathy.

Plus, Tish trying to lighten up the tension by going around showing pictures of her new kittens.

Plus, Lane the doubting DP questioning everything Quinn wanted done. No one respected him. Even Dansby, the beautiful, gilded, inept, twenty-year-old Dutch giant, didn't respect him.

Plus Eddie. *What does he know?* Eddie insinuated himself between Tish and Quinn. "Just give him some good vibes," said Eddie.

Good vibes? Quinn wanted to scream. No one had ever bothered giving him good vibes when he'd struggled, or doubted, or flat out failed. No one was coming up to him now to reassure him he could do this.

He's sabotaging me because of Parish, thought Quinn. He texted Sid to look at his contract and review the list of fireable offenses.

"Alright people, let's look alive," called Tish as she clapped his hands together. "Any thoughts to set us up, Quinn?"

Quinn moved toward his actors on wooden legs. His skin crawled with the eyes of the crew on him, none of them his allies.

"Liz, you've got a good handle. Keep doing what you're doing. Play down any nervous ticks that'll make you look guilty. We want some doubt to be there for the audience. You could just be a nice woman living her life. You also feel safe here, a little naive, yeah?"

"I don't automatically think I'd be a target," said Lizette.

"Right. Let's try it that way." Quinn forced himself to turn to Dansby. "Let's get back into the scene. You're a failing college student looking for larger purpose. Your dad died last year. You really want to impress Walt even though you're not sure why yet. You won't let Natalia leave the store until you get something useful from her."

"I understand," said Dansby in his regular voice.

Quinn cringed.

"I understand," said Dansby in his American accent. He glanced at Lizette as he took his mark, then cracked a grin. "Break a leg, gal."

What the fuck is wrong with this kid? Quinn retreated outside the shot seething. There were two cameras, one focused on close shots of each actor as Dansby walked Lizette to the checkout line.

"Quiet on the set," called Tish.

Filipe, the Second AD, snapped the clapboard.

Cameras rolled.

"What about you? Who are you buying for?" asked Dansby, stiff, but passable as he glanced towards Lizette's packed grocery cart.

"I have a big family. All they do is eat."

"And all you do is cook?" Dansby, so very stiff, the words outside of himself, as though he'd never chatted up a woman at a grocery store. Quinn ground his teeth. Ahead of him, Lane shifted to tighten the shoulder shot to a low-angle close-up of Dansby's face.

I told him I didn't want that shot.

He watched Dansby's face fill the camera monitor, that impossible prettiness, a face entirely too memorable. Beauty couldn't make up for the lack of depth behind it.

Dansby's eyes widened. He'd forgotten his line. "Godverdomme!"

"Cut!" yelled Tish. She already had her phone out, ready to check in with her cat sitter for new pictures.

"Sorry all. I lost my line." Dansby looked at Lizette. "You were really good. I was almost losing track of you in there."

And that was the end of Quinn's patience.

Dansby didn't see him coming until the moment Quinn grabbed him by the collar and shoved him up against the magazine rack. "Do you think this is a game?" He slapped Dansby across the face. "Why are you smiling?"

Dansby tripped over his giant feet as he wrenched himself out of Quinn's grip. "I'm sorry. Sorry." Hands up, protecting his face like he had on Friday. That damn pretty face that had probably never taken a punch and didn't know anything about physical exertion or hard work or surviving day-to-day. Quinn was ready to pursue him across the grocery, but Eddie moved in with Filipe and the set designer. They made a wall with their bodies to protect Dansby who was now—what? Crying? Sobbing?

"For fuck's sake!" Quinn burst out. "Do you know anything about acting?"

"That's unnecessary," said Eddie.

Quinn glared at him.

"Let's take a break."

"No," said Quinn. *This is my movie, damn it.* "We finish the scene. You," he pointed at Dansby, "are Sam. This is Natalia. Walt is over there judging your performance. You close this deal before she reaches those doors. Got it?"

"Got it," sniffed Dansby.

Quinn, Eddie, Filipe, and the set designer moved back behind the cameras. Makeup rushed in. As he walked back, Quinn saw set security moving along the barricade asking onlookers to delete the recordings they'd made of the altercation. *Fuck. Fuck. Fuck.*

"Quiet on the set," called Tish.

A Meet Cute

Larisa thought of herself as a wise person. She rarely made mistakes and when she did, they were strategic and purposeful. As the daughter of famous people, the chances of her becoming a well-adjusted adult had been slim but she'd done it. She made rules for herself and stuck to them. Her secret life at Club D remained secret because she followed her rules. So, why was she breaking them by agreeing to meet Quinn VanderVeer?

The question lurked in the back of her head as she drove, switched cars, changed clothes, then continued driving. The answers came easily, sensibly. She was a mental health professional after all.

1. Larisa was tired of the way her life was going.
2. She'd overheard Sophie and Myhanh deciding to exclude her from their PRITE study group because they thought she didn't need to study. She'd pass by virtue of her name alone.
3. She wanted a challenge, or perhaps a touch of danger, to distract her from the days ticking by as Jaden's wedding crept closer, like some kind of doomsday countdown.
4. Tabloid coverage of her date with Greg had been more civilized than usual, but each failed date left her less desirable than before. Just like an aging actress, what

people were saying fed directly into what job offers came her way. Except in Larisa's case, the job offers were men who she might marry.

Did she think Quinn was one of those men? Not by her mother's standards. Maybe that was why she'd agreed to meet him. She'd never dated someone in the lifestyle. The idea was exciting, way more interesting than the next Greg her mother would find for her. This became even more true after she saw the fan video of him attacking his actor at the grocery store. Quinn was enough of a live wire that he was attacking people at work on his first day of shooting. She expected him to be tightly wound and easy to trigger, which would be a good counterpoint to her own needs.

He saw me in the Blue Room, she thought, as she settled herself at a table at the edge of Club D's bar space with Charity, one of her longtime submissive playmates. *What does he want from that?* She and Charity had walked through several plans for the night, which would give Larisa an extra layer of anonymity and test out what it was about the Queen that had prompted Quinn to reach out to her, but she worried she'd missed something. Deliberate contact with an industry person at Club D was a needless risk. Perhaps that's why she'd decided to do it.

He arrived in cheap jeans and a T-shirt, like Club D was just another dive bar. Larisa felt a flash of irritation at how casually he presented himself. He had no fear of being seen. In contrast, she wore a cape over her corset to disguise her figure.

"I'm Quinn."

Larisa didn't answer.

The silence lengthened. Quinn glanced at Charity, then back to Larisa. "Thank you for agreeing to meet."

More silence. Larisa waited for him to squirm. He didn't. In fact, Quinn nodded to himself as though he'd expected as much. The barest hint of a smile pulled at the corners of his mouth, an expression that appeared unnatural, as though he was unaccustomed to smiling.

The rest of his expression, Larisa couldn't really make out. The sharp angles of his face caught and held the shadows cast by the low light, making it impossible to truly see him. She'd found a handful of photos online, all of them more than two years old. In those photos she'd seen nothing remarkable except perhaps the absence of a smile, which now seemed significant.

Most people smiled when they first met someone. They also tended to smile in moments of great personal triumph. But when Quinn had won the Sundance Audience Award for his first feature film, he'd been almost expressionless. If Larisa the therapist had been asked to interpret his emotion, she'd have said Quinn was petrified.

And with terrible hair, then and now, thought Larisa. Black, close cut but uneven, like he'd done it himself, and rumpled from being stuffed under a beanie. Nothing substantial enough to hang onto in a moment of passion.

But hair could be changed. The nature of a man could not.

"I saw you in the Blue Room a few weeks ago," said Quinn. "Would you do the same with me?"

Larisa looked to Charity who extended her hand. "Charity. I've been the Queen's sub for a while. Not committed, just playmates. Your girlfriend going to be showing up?"

"Just me."

Larisa thought she saw the corners of Quinn's jaw tighten. *The girlfriend is gone.* Larisa took no pleasure in having predicted it the night she saw them together. Breakups always drove people half bonkers, their infantile selves marauding through what had been respectable lives without warning. Maybe that explained Quinn's outburst on set.

"On your knees or in the chair?" asked Charity, in reference to the two positions played by the men in the Blue Room.

Quinn looked to Larisa. "Whatever you prefer. Will there be three of us?"

"I'm your guide," said Charity. "The Queen does not speak to people who have not earned it."

"I'm fine with that. Anything is fine at this point."

Larisa nudged the toe of her boot against Charity's foot. "Why do you say 'at this point'?" asked Charity.

"Well, my life is . . . I just want someone else to be in charge for a little while, make me recognize how much I've fucked up."

"The Queen is not a priest," said Charity. "This dungeon is not a confessional."

Larisa suppressed a smile. Both she and Charity knew more cycles of confession and forgiveness crossed through Club D's doors than most churches. But Quinn was new, and Larisa didn't know what he thought he was signing up for.

"I've been strong my entire life," said Quinn. "And I've been my own worst critic for just as long. It seems I can't do both anymore." He held two clenched fists in front of him. "This is me. I've heard the greater the ability to surrender, the greater the release."

As motivations went, Larisa had to admit it was compelling. She hadn't expected so much honesty. Quinn sounded humbled, but not in the way he wanted to be.

I can work with that.

She nodded her agreement and watched relief ripple through Quinn's body. He'd barely moved through the entire exchange and now, as Charity stood and reached for his hand to take him upstairs, Larisa saw how tightly he'd been holding himself in the chair. His joints moved with the grinding resistance of a man twice his age. He walked like a statue come to life, arms lifeless at his sides.

Shrink Larisa thought, *He pulls awareness out of his body when he's stressed. He doesn't feel his arms. His feet go where he wants but if one of his toes was broken, he probably wouldn't even notice.* From this perspective, bondage, the systematic awakening of the body, seemed like a perfect decision. And he had chosen her to help, which demonstrated excellent taste.

At the top of the stairs, Charity led Quinn on, and Larisa stopped. She checked her phone for messages. The bridesmaids' group chat was busy with plans for the bachelorette party. Suzette had sent the link to a write up of the Saudi prince, Hasan bin Faisal Al Saud. Larisa's cohort chat was quieter. Larisa wondered if they'd left it to start a new one without her.

Larisa checked her watch. *A few more minutes.* A thrill of energy vibrated through her fingers. Finally, the prospect of a session excited her. She'd broken out of routine, found a new way to test herself, a new subject. She'd have preferred it to be someone outside of the industry, but Quinn's proximity to one of her other lives made what she was about to do more dangerous. The stakes were higher, and therefore, so was the possible reward.

Will I fuck him if it comes to that?

Not a great idea. He's on the rebound. He's already too interested in you.

Am I interested in him?

The question seemed irrelevant. They were on unequal sides of the scale. Quinn wasn't here for Dr. Larisa de France-Kahn. He was here for the Queen. This offered its own kind of release. Tonight, the Queen was all Larisa wanted to be. The rest she would keep for tomorrow.

She entered Room Three with her weight on her heels, her boots landing heavy on the floor. If they made it this far, she and Charity had planned for two scenarios, either a light beginner session or a medium limits session. What Quinn wanted would be indicated by his posture and degree of nakedness.

Quinn and Charity knelt side by side with their butts resting on their heels, their hands folded in their laps, heads bowed, backs to the door. Charity had stripped down to her usual latex leotard and fishnets. Quinn wore nothing. Larisa raised an eyebrow of surprise. *No half measures. Or he's more desperate than I thought.*

Besides being as pale as a slice of moonshine, Quinn was strikingly thin. The corners of his slight shoulder blades jutted out like sharpened knives. The two halves of his back came together in the carved gully of his spine. He looked more vulnerable than most men in this position but also more aware; he seemed to listen to the silence of her eyes on him. His body gave her pause. Larisa liked to whip men who looked like they deserved it, thick brawny men, or cocaine sniffing stockbrokers with secret tattoos, or all-star athletes. She wasn't aroused unless she could imagine her work as a kind of justice. What Quinn needed was his own therapist, not a beating.

And yet, he was here. He wanted this act of surrender. And she'd agreed to honor it. Caretaking was one of her favorite things to do as a domme. Normally, she was very good at it. But Quinn's lack of body fat would make anything she planned to do more painful, possibly even damaging. She would need to be extremely precise.

Larisa fetched the lightest riding crop from the wall of toys and walked up to her pair of submissives. She trailed the crop along the ravine of Quinn's spine, watched his skin stipple with attention. His shoulders began to shift up and down with the beat of his breath. She tapped the crop once against Charity's hip.

"Be careful what you confess," said Charity. "It will determine what she does to you."

The words burst out of Quinn in a flood. "I hurt my girlfriend. She frightened me and I lashed out."

"Is that all?" asked Charity.

"I have these thoughts. How I can get people to do what I want. Or how if I scare them everything would be easier."

Charity turned her head just enough to catch Larisa's eye, her mouth open in a *O* with a naughty raised eyebrow as though to ask, *What do you want to do with this?*

Larisa went back to the wall, selected a pair of metal handcuffs. Leather was gentler, but Quinn's wrists were too small for a secure hold, and something told her he needed his restraint to be real. Moving fast to shock him, Larisa crossed the room, pulled Quinn's arms behind his back, and cuffed his wrists. He rose to his feet as she pulled him, keeping his head down as she planted her hand against the base of his neck and walked him over to the whipping horse.

Charity turned to watch. "The Queen does not think you feel enough shame for what you have done."

Larisa pushed Quinn's legs apart and secured his ankles to each side of the horse. When she did this with Charity, it was a slow action with Larisa stroking the insides of Charity's thighs, sometimes kissing her, massaging her apart. But Quinn deserved no such consideration. This was not that kind of play.

"You're right." Quinn allowed himself to fall forward over the horse instead of holding his head up. When he spoke, his voice came to her muffled, his head hidden beneath the curve of his back. "I don't feel anything."

Larisa went still. It wasn't so much the confession that stopped her, but the familiarity of it. She also walked through life with all of it held at a distance. Nothing was allowed the chance to truly shock her, or scare her, or delight her. If she let one part in, the rest would come, and she couldn't manage her life feeling everything.

She blinked away unexpected tears and adjusted her grip on the crop. She teased him with it only for a moment before she began to beat him very, very lightly. The crop made no marks and began to redden Quinn's skin only after several minutes, but it seemed like enough. She felt the intensity in his concentration. Once he learned her rhythm, he arched into the blows, inviting the pain like an old friend.

After several minutes, Charity said, "Are you sorry now?"

"Yes," Quinn whispered.

"Will you do better?"

"Yes."

Larisa wasn't sure she believed him. She also wasn't sure what had really been accomplished. Quinn wasn't hard. She wasn't even close to arousal. But she felt uncertain about continuing. She released the restraints on his ankles.

"Kneel before your Queen and beg her forgiveness," said Charity.

Quinn slid off the horse and made himself a puddle of bones and skin at her feet. "Please forgive me."

"Forgive yourself," said Larisa. "And do better."

She had spoken.

Five words.

When Quinn lifted his face from her feet, she saw his engorged penis rising between his legs. *That's why he's here,* thought Larisa. *My voice.*

Not good.

"Take care of yourself," she said as she left the room. Charity would navigate whatever ending he wanted.

Outside Room Three, Larisa leaned her shoulders against the cold industrial-metal wall and caught her breath. This was new. Perhaps it shouldn't have been surprising; wordplay always came with bondage. But not like this. She'd withheld her voice from him to protect herself. And he'd waited, reduced himself to nothing through the whole session, on the hope that eventually she would speak to him.

She hid in the shadows at the end of the hallway until Charity showed Quinn out.

They met at the bar and shared a tonic water.

"Well?" asked Larisa.

"Might not be great to tell someone to forgive themselves when you don't actually know what he did to his girlfriend."

"Point." Larisa had already decided she would look up Parish's agent and see about getting a phone number for the actress. They'd seen each other at the fundraiser. A friendly hello wouldn't be entirely out of the blue.

Why do you need to know? Larisa asked herself.

She may not know how to help herself the way he does.
I need to know how bad he is.

"Did you have fun?" asked Charity.

Larisa considered the question, surprised that it did not have a simple answer. She'd been too tense to really have fun, but a first session sometimes went like that. "I don't feel like I gave him what he wanted."

"Would you do it again?"

"If I did, I'd need a way to disguise my voice."

"He did seem rather attached to it. You know each other in the world beyond?"

"Something like that."

"Kinky."

Rather than correct her, Larisa checked the time. "I need to go. Thanks for your help tonight. I know you'd rather have been playing a different role."

Charity shrugged. "I liked watching you work. Your hand is so precise." She stroked Larisa's gloved fingers. "Come back on Sunday? I'm taking an afternoon shift. Will be boring without you."

"Maybe." Larisa pressed a kiss into Charity's hair. "Ciao Bella."

Chapter 7

Collision Course

Quinn stood at the window of Eddie's office, rubbing his prayer beads through his fingers while he waited for Eddie to finish a phone call. The motion once again felt like meditation instead of desperation. The pain of the crop had burned away the toxic build-up of adrenaline and cortisol. The Queen's words, finally offered after he'd endured his punishment, had drained the weight from his shoulders.

Shooting that morning had gone well. Dansby was getting his feet under him. Tish and her incessant kitten photo sharing bothered Quinn less than it had every other day that week. And this morning, despite that skin crawling sensation of irritation, Quinn had managed to negotiate with Lane, the doubting DP. They'd both gotten the shots they thought were best. They'd hash out what to keep in the editing room.

But now, while the cast and crew were at lunch, Eddie had called this conclave. Just the two of them in Eddie's office. Quinn had arrived determined not to feel like a child brought in from recess. And yet, all his senses signaled wrongness. His tenuous grasp on peace was slipping as his body drew up preemptory defenses.

Compared to Quinn's, Eddie's office was a palace, with imported wood furniture, a granite countertop bar, and a private bedroom and bathroom. What would have been an elegant setting conveying gravitas and serious work, was marred by

Eddie's choice to hang vintage film posters featuring half-naked actresses on the walls.

Finally, the phone clicked into the receiver. The desk chair groaned as Eddie leaned back. "Alright, Quinn. What are we going to do with you?"

Quinn clenched his fist around the bracelet and shoved both beads and fist into his pocket as he turned to face Eddie.

"You could let me do my job."

"Dansby might quit."

"We could recover from that." Quinn thought of how much easier his life would be without Dansby. "I could call Matt."

Eddie waved a hand. "Matt's too meh. We need Dansby to sell this picture. If anyone's leaving, it's you."

"I'll sue."

"Sit." Eddie motioned to a chair on the opposite side of the desk. It was a chair built close to the floor so any visitor found themselves looking up at Eddie over the edge of his desk instead of at eye level.

Quinn sat on the armrest.

"What happened Friday seems to be becoming a pattern of behavior."

"I barely touched him. How is that—"

"I was at my brother's for dinner last night."

Quinn stilled.

"Perhaps you can explain to me why my niece is using makeup to cover a black eye."

What black eye? Quinn pushed down panic. "She stabbed herself with one of her heels?"

"She says you punched her."

"Well, I didn't."

"Then what happened?"

"Are you asking as her uncle or as my boss?"

"What God damned difference does it make? You strike a woman, it matters."

Quinn pressed his lips together. There was nothing to say.

Deny it and he looked more guilty than Eddie already assumed him to be. Argue and he might end up punching Eddie. If he tried to express sympathy for Parish and her situation, he'd sound like an insincere jackass.

"I will do better with Dansby." Quinn cringed. It sounded like he was conceding. But conceding what? That the first week had been hard? That he'd lost his temper? Directors across the industry did worse every day.

"You're right. You will do better. I'm requiring you to participate in an initial run of psychotherapy."

Quinn blanched. "What?"

"Or you're out. I will pay millions to get rid of you if you can't play ball, you understand? You will never work in this town again."

Therapy. Quinn couldn't imagine anything worse than sitting in a small room with a stranger trying to figure him out, then reporting their conclusions to Eddie.

"I didn't give her a black eye," said Quinn. "Maybe she fought with the security guard who removed her from my property in the middle of the night Sunday."

Eddie narrowed his eyes. "What are you saying?"

"I'm saying," he let out a pent-up breath, "love is hard."

For a moment, Eddie appeared to soften. He massaged the Botoxed wrinkles along his forehead. "You're scheduled for ten A.M. Monday. Get the details from my assistant on your way out. Tish will run the show until you get back. If you have any notes, give them to her."

Tish with the kittens was going to direct his film on Monday morning and Eddie hadn't even bothered to let Quinn be the one to tell her. The feeling that no one respected him had been more accurate than Quinn had realized. But he held himself together. With a salute to Eddie, he made his exit before he exploded.

Larisa had twelve minutes before grand rounds. Tucked back in a window alcove in the walkway between the hospital tower and the research center, she dialed the number she'd received from Parish's agent. It rang only once before Parish picked up.

"Hello?"

"Parish. This is Larisa de France-Kahn." (Larisa never said doctor when talking about herself in her parents' world.) "We met at New Years?"

"Hmm, pretty dress."

"You did like my dress." Larisa paused, then decided to go for it. "I enjoyed meeting you and your boyfriend. Maybe we could all go out sometime."

"He's not my boyfriend anymore."

Larisa strained her ears to interpret the subtext of Parish's inflection. Did she sound sad? Upset?

"I hope it wasn't one of those messy breakups."

"He called the cops on me."

"Why would he do that?" Larisa hoped she sounded incensed.

"I don't know. He won't talk to me."

"Did he hurt you?"

Silence.

Larisa regretted this question. Hurt could mean too many things. The silence could mean too many things. She knew nothing about Parish, had no cause to trust her more than Quinn other than the sisterhood of women, and that trust was easily misleading.

"Look. I love a girls' night out," said Larisa, moving towards the classroom door. "Text me a couple nights you're free. We'll do happy hour."

"Okay."

"Got to run."

Larisa tucked away her phone and slipped into the classroom just as Dr. Patel was walking to the podium. She sank into a seat on the aisle, her mind whirring to process, interpret, and fill in unknowns with probabilities.

It seemed likely Quinn had physically struck Parish but possibly in self-defense. (He'd said he was scared of her.) And she said he'd called the cops. Women were seventy-three percent more likely to call police during a domestic dispute than men. So, if Parish said Quinn had done so, he must have had good reason.

Very interesting, thought Larisa.

Chapter 8

Session One

L arisa's presession routine involved walking a circle around the room she'd been assigned for the day, familiarizing herself with the angles, the posters, and the play of light that would change as the sun made its way through the day. Then she heated water for tea on the electric kettle and powered up the room's scheduling tablet to preview her sessions.

"Nine o'clock: Kara. Ten o'clock—" Larisa froze, certain she was hallucinating. She'd only ever hallucinated once while high on mushrooms in college. That experience had been easier to understand than this. Larisa carried the tablet out to the scheduling desk and, doing a terrible job of moderating the anxiety in her voice, she said, "I have an error on my schedule."

Jez, the desk manager/insurance coder/all around fix the problem admin person cowered in his chair. (Sometimes Larisa had this effect on people.) "Uh yeah, that isn't a mistake. It came down from the chief."

The department chief was an entrenched old guard figure who thought the DSM, in its modern version, had become too large and watered down. A man who had gone on record multiple times saying patients were most comfortable with white doctors, and everyone else would be better served in administrative or research roles. He was the reason there were only two non-white people in Larisa's cohort—Myhnah and Fatima—and they were international students.

"How—" Larisa stopped herself. She knew all the answers to

the questions she wanted to demand from this poor hourly-wage employee who was guilty of nothing more than following orders. Deep breath. *This is not the end of the world.* "Does he have a file?" *It's very much the end of at least one world.*

"New patient. Never admitted. Just a supervisor email."

This also, Larisa could have guessed. She ignored Kara watching from across the waiting room, marched back into counseling room four, and very softly closed the door. As soon as she heard the latch click, she walked another circle around the room taking slow breaths. Then, because she still had five minutes before the hour, she called her mother.

"Good morning, dearest. This is such a pleasant surprise."

"How dare you?"

A pause. Larisa pictured the Matrix reshuffling its lines of heinous green code.

"I haven't the faintest—"

"Don't. This is low even for you. I do real work here, Mom."

"That's why I recommended you when Eddie said he needed help."

"Eddie?"

"Eddie Sacks. We saw him at brunch last week? Trouble with one of his directors? The problems intensified apparently. Production is practically stalled. So much money going out the door. So, I said to him, 'Eddie, my daughter knows about difficult people. She can make anyone do anything.'"

Larisa sank down to the couch. Her face burned even though there was no one to witness her horror. "It's unethical. That director he's sending? We've met. I can't treat someone I know."

"But Eddie would be so grateful. He's already pledged thirty thousand for my brush fire cleanup campaign. I'm sure you can help. You have all those fancy degrees. They must be good for something. Have to go, Sade is here for my dermo."

Larisa remained holding the silent phone to her ear, both eardrums ringing with something she recognized as false vibrations generated by shock. She stayed there, completely still for a full minute. Then, she stood, straightened her blouse, and prepared to meet Kara.

"What's happened?" asked Kara, eyes bright with interest.

"A scheduling conflict. How are you?"

"Do you want a real answer or are you just saying that?"

"I want whatever answer you're willing to give me."

"I told Mom my appointment was at eight-thirty so I could use the bathroom here to puke up breakfast."

"Thank you for trusting me with that. What did breakfast do to you?"

"It existed."

"When did you decide on this course of action?"

"Last night, when Mom announced she was making pancakes."

"Do you remember what you first thought when she told you?"

"It freaked me out."

Larisa nodded. Thank the fates Kara was in a good mood. Larisa doubted she was calm enough to concentrate and draw resistant Kara out, not with Quinn less than sixty minutes away from walking through her door.

"Can we role play a different version of the same event? You play you and I play your mom."

"I want to look at the social feeds again."

"We'll have time for both."

Kara flopped down on the couch. "What if I play my mom?"

"Let's do one of each. But both end up with you feeling safe, eating breakfast, and letting it stay inside you."

Kara cackled. "You live on Mars, Doc."

"We both live in Hollywood, the Land of Make Believe. But at some point, we'll have to talk about the fact that you're very sick."

"Not today," said Kara. "Let's pretend."

"Next time." Larisa held up her pinky finger. "Pinky promise."

Kara wrinkled her nose. "You're so old, Dr. de France-Kahn."

Kara left at 9:52. No sign of Quinn in the waiting room.

Eight minutes.

Larisa's best, most ethical, response would have been to report the situation to her supervisor, Dr. Bade, and have Quinn assigned to a different therapist. But doing this would draw attention to the fact that her mother had gone to the chief of psychiatry (three levels above Dr. Bade) to make this appointment happen, which meant it'd been approved beyond anyone Larisa could reach in the next eight minutes to do anything about it. Also, fighting the assignment could have unpredictable, likely unwelcome, consequences, such as the perception she didn't want to do her share of the work. (Already a problem.)

Thank God I wasn't turned on last week.

At two minutes after the hour, she opened her door and fell back in surprise when she found Quinn standing just on the other side. Beanie, jeans that firmly nestled his ass (*don't think about that*), T-shirt, and two layers of zipper hoodies.

"Quinn, come in. You're welcome to sit wherever you like."

He barely glanced at her as he entered. She retreated to her chair as he prowled the room, making the same circle of inspection she'd made earlier that morning, but with menace.

This was the first time she'd seen him in full light. He was at least as tall as she was, with all the height in his legs. Grey-blue eyes inventoried the room with fervid attention, accentuated by the sharp parallel lines of his cheeks, jaws, and prominent nose. He moved along a sharp rail of energy that wasn't quite confidence but could pass for it if no one looked closely. It hardly seemed possible this was the soft, gentle man she'd met (and flogged) Thursday night.

He scowled at the couch for a full five seconds before moving the pillows aside and sitting on the end farthest away from her.

"Your outfit is hideous," he said. "You can cover up those model legs, sure. But harder to hide the bone structure in a face, isn't it?"

When had he looked at her fully enough to see what she was wearing? Larisa blushed as she bristled. "I've never been a model."

"The camera would love you. Come in for a screen test. I'll give you a job as a Russian stripper."

Less than thirty seconds into the session and Larisa's grasp on professionality had already dissolved. "Is this how you pick up women?"

"Not usually." A pause. "Haven't had a lot of success with women."

She watched Quinn's hands reach out, grasping his jeans just above the knees, gathering and releasing the fabric. He wore a prayer-bead bracelet on his left hand. No recent manicure. Hands the size of an NBA player's, all bones. *Nervous or irritated?*

Another pause. "Not with women I might like."

Larisa felt her hostility dip. "I get that." She softened into her seat, trying to pull the session back to a professional tone. "Why don't you tell me what brings you in today."

"Don't play games. You already know Eddie has sent me here to 'improve on-set working conditions.'"

"Why?"

Quinn still hadn't given her a direct look. He stared at the wall opposite the couch. The corners of that strong jawline worked with some inner conflict. Her eyes snagged on the delicate hollow at the base of his throat, the only soft part of him he'd left exposed.

"My lead actor isn't cooperating," he said.

"But he's not here to see me. You are."

Quinn compressed his lips into a moue of irritation. Larisa stared at those ripe, abundant lips. They were the kind of sugar-pop lips that made the careers for popstars. How had she missed them before?

Fuck. Larisa discretely detached her gaze. Had he noticed her staring? As far as she could tell Quinn only saw the inspirational poster on the wall across from the couch. But she couldn't trust that assumption. It seemed clear, whatever else Quinn was, he was a man who noticed things.

Larisa redirected. "Why don't you tell me about your latest interaction with the actor? What's his name?"

"Dansby."

"What frustrates you the most about him?"

"He's inexperienced." Quinn paused, then added. "And nervous. It makes him sloppy."

"Did he tell you he's nervous?"

"He didn't have to."

"Did you ask why he was having trouble?"

Silence. More tightening of his jaw, like bolts twisting shut. Larisa used the silence to find her bearings. Eddie's email had described Quinn as aggressive, confrontational, and demanding. Not great traits in a person, but not unexpected in a director. Her father liked to say no one became a film director if they didn't have a giant ego and some kind of compulsion. Nice people didn't tend to make movies.

"You don't think you should be here, do you?"

"It doesn't matter what I think," he said.

"I care what you think."

His eyes slid toward her, looking for the lie in her expression. Those eyes. That scowl. The force of them felt like a heat lamp determined to sweat out her secrets. She began to itch with the overwhelming need to shift, adjust her hair, check to see if she'd managed to put on matching earrings.

"Has anything like this happened on your other films?" she managed to ask.

"My first two films were smaller. I worked with real people."

"Real people?"

"You know my work."

"Pretend I don't." Larisa wasn't about to admit she did not really know his work.

"My actors had life experience," said Quinn. "Miguel's story was part of his life; I just captured it. Kyle, Sam, and Roddie were all teenagers playing teenagers. They knew what it was like to be in that world."

"And Dansby doesn't?"

"Imagine the most beautiful man you've ever seen."

Larisa felt heat rising on her cheeks. In another time and place she might have batted her eyes and said, *I don't have to imagine. I'm looking at him.* Then she thought, *Quinn is not the kind of man who tolerates flirtation.*

"He's an untested spy captured by Russians when a mission goes wrong." A pause. "I called Langley. They didn't have any devastatingly handsome junior agents who had trained as actors." Those lips turned with the barest hint of a smile.

Larisa smiled in return as a reward for this crack in Quinn's severe demeanor. He'd made a joke. Progress.

"A lack of lived experience does not make Dansby a bad actor."

"Didn't say he was. But I find him as implausible in the role as he does. Maybe that's something we should psychoanalyze."

"He doesn't fit because he's beautiful?"

"Appearance is everything; I'm sure you know about that."

Larisa fought to keep her expression placid. She knew all too well, and yet also roiled against it. Her father believed anyone could play any role if they saw themselves in it. He'd guided actors to remaking themselves into the most unlikely characters hundreds of times.

"When will you see Dansby next?"

"As soon as we're done here."

"Let's say Dansby's behavior is unchanged. Either he struggles with his lines, or has locked himself out of his emotions, or something else. What do you want your response to be?"

"*My* response? He's the one who—" Quinn stopped himself, narrowed his eyes at the defenseless poster of a person throwing their arms up toward a forest of trees. "I would like to give him enough direction that he's able to complete his work up to expectation."

"You could give him notes."

"Obviously."

"And what else if that doesn't work?"

She felt Quinn internally rolling his eyes. Finally, he said, "I could ask him about blockage."

"Good. But what if he can't identify the blockage? What if he becomes paralyzed with anxiety? This is his first film, isn't it? How can you make him feel safe?"

"Safe," Quinn spat, "he's a spy in prison with a home country that isn't coming for him."

"He's an actor doing his job. And it's a hard job."

"You want me to coddle him with compliments?"

"Why not try and see what happens?"

He turned his head just enough that she again became the subject of his gaze. She could practically see the words forming in his mouth. *You don't know anything about this work. Don't tell me what to do.*

But he couldn't rightfully say that because Quinn knew she was the daughter of Gunter Kahn, big-budget czar of their parents' generation. She'd been visiting film sets her entire life. She wasn't as ignorant as he wanted her to be.

"When you give the cast their afternoon break, I'd like you to take one also," said Larisa. "Detach yourself from the set, take five or ten minutes, write down how you're feeling. Try and articulate the exact thought that triggered each emotion you write down."

"I'm not doing that."

"Just an idea."

He glared at some spot just behind her left ear. Larisa thought someone in his life had taught him to do this, to mute his reactions by avoiding eye contact during heightened moments. His lack of eye contact did not diminish the energy radiating off his body. Anyone else, she might have been afraid of violence. But she felt strangely safe with Quinn. His demons came from a place that felt familiar. She wasn't likely to be the subject of his rage unless she really pushed him.

"A standard initial treatment program is six sessions. Usually, the first two involve these kinds of get-to-know-you conversations. The last four focus on functional change."

She waited for a response. He was looking at the wall again, apparently detached from the conversation even though she knew he wasn't. She pulled out the scheduling tablet and saw that Quinn was already on her calendar for the next two Mondays. He was also scheduled for Thursday afternoons, with her name attached to the appointments even though she wasn't on the schedule.

"How does someone like you go into this work?"

"Someone like me?" asked Larisa, even though she knew exactly what he meant. The same thing Greg had meant when he'd said it.

"Neither of us should be in this dump."

"Our time is up," said Larisa. "Consider doing the emotion journal. You never know if it will help."

He snapped up to standing and strode from the room.

In the handful of minutes before her next appointment, Larisa emailed Dr. Bade and set up an emergency meeting for her lunch hour.

Dr. Sabita Bade did not ruffle easily. This was one of the things Larisa most liked about her; she could engage in the most difficult situations with empathy, but also not lose herself to them. However, the expression Dr. Bade wore when Larisa walked into her office looked like she was braced for an explosion.

"Close the door, Larisa."

Closed door meetings were never good. They were supposed to make people feel safe, but really the isolation emphasized how much trouble Larisa was in. "I've been assigned a patient I shouldn't be treating," she said.

"The chief looped me in on the request." Dr. Bade reached for her mug and took a calculated sip of whatever was inside. "How was it today?"

"It felt wrong."

"Besides that. What are the salient facts?"

"He doesn't want to be there. Resistant to personal questions. Defensive of suggestions. Personally insulting."

He planned his entrance to derail me. Knew exactly what to say that would hit home.

"Does he make you feel unsafe?"

"No."

"Can you work with him?"

"Yes, but—"

"This is less than ideal, I recognize that, but we might consider that you're in a position to be the most helpful to him."

Larisa had already considered that. She knew the industry. She wasn't interested in taming Quinn's foibles the way another therapist might by thinking of him as a regular person. But that didn't change what had happened Thursday at Club D. It didn't change the fact that she'd spent half their session with the back burner of her brain planning what she might do to him if given a second chance.

"Larisa?" Dr. Bade sounded like she was losing her patience.

Which seemed unfair. Because the answer she was looking for—

Oh, God. Do I have to say it?

"We've had a sexual encounter."

"In clinic?" Dr. Bade's hand went slack, her mug dropped onto the desk with a hard thud.

"In our personal lives. It's complicated. He didn't realize it was me . . . that the woman he was with and me . . . that we're the same. God, I can't believe this is happening."

"I'm going to say something that will horrify you."

Larisa already knew what it would be.

"If you're serious about pursuing medicine, don't see him in that environment again. Focus on the work. Satisfy his boss and get him off your schedule. Keep good session notes in case anyone asks questions."

"If I'm serious?" Larisa couldn't help but repeat.

"Well, obviously you are. But you have other options. Obviously, your mother—"

"What about my mother?" The heat on Larisa's face felt like the worse sunburn, painful, itchy, and slicked with embarrassing sweat all at the same time. "I'm a doctor."

"Yes, of course you are."

Larisa took a breath. *Just get out*, she thought. *End this conversation without burning bridges and work it out at the club.*

"Will the department support me if this gets leaked?"

"Of course."

Larisa considered asking for it in writing, then realized it would never happen. No matter what Dr. Bade said, if this went public, she was on her own.

Chapter 9

Session Two

Quinn sat in his office at Enterprise Studios waiting for Sid. Filming had finished for the day without incident, though he had an inventory of failures picking holes in his brain. There was Tish, more assertive since her stint as lead director Monday morning, questioning his decisions, and Dansby's sidelong looks at Quinn every time he messed something up.

But Quinn had managed to swallow irritation and say, "That was good. I liked that. How about a little more in the eyes for the next one?" Dansby had basked in the praise like a starving puppy, which had left Quinn exhausted. It was only Wednesday. He didn't care if Dr. de France-Kahn's strategy of unearned compliments had begun to generate semi-quality shots. He wasn't doing it again tomorrow.

A blank memo pad sat on the faux-wood desk, both cheap and repulsive, but they were what he had to work with. He'd decided he would give himself until Sid arrived to do the activity Larisa had assigned him. For the sake of the film.

- Dansby tapping his foot against the ground during filming = wanted to kick him.
- Dansby smiling like everything was fine = wanted to wipe that smile off his face. Doesn't he know his character's life is at stake?
- During break, he was flirting with a PA, so casual.

A knock sounded on the door. Quinn shoved the pad into his desk drawer.

"Come in." Quinn motioned to one of two chairs on the receiving side of his desk. Sid sauntered in with a grin. "This is the life, isn't it? You know the security guard gave me a special pass. I have an assigned parking stall. 'Director VanderVeer's Assistant.'"

Talking about their good luck at the studio felt like tempting fate, so Quinn didn't say anything about the dream world they'd fallen into. "What did you find?"

"Dr. Larisa de France-Kahn, daughter of—"

"Skip the basics."

"She's not related to Eddie. He and her father worked together back in the day."

Quinn nodded.

"High grades, commendations in school. But one research supervisor during medical school said she was easily distracted and underdeveloped. Not sure what that means. Rough first year of residency—that's the internship doctors do after medical school. She came out here due to family stuff, looks like. Lots of social appearances associated with various charities her first year. She struggled with PRITE, that's the Psychiatry Resident In Training annual Exam. Limited social appearances these past two years in contrast.

"Word is the family doesn't like her becoming a doctor. There's pressure for her to marry, switch to a part-time program. Infrequent dating. No long-term relationships of note. Hints of something serious in college, but I couldn't find anything definitive. I've compiled a list of romantic appearances she's made this year. All men, all presumed straight. Worst thing the press has said is about her lack of commitment."

Quinn frowned. He'd hoped for a secret, some vicarious life or shameful hobby, maybe an illegitimate child. "Are you sure this is everything?"

"What do you think is missing?"

"I need a way to even the scales. She was looking down on me like I'm something for her to drag out of the ocean and save."

Sid blinked. "Well, you could test out how sensitive she is to this marriage thing. I've heard it's hard to be a certain age and single."

Quinn's eyes shot up from the page of text Sid had handed him.

"I mean for women," Sid added quickly. "She's probably under a lot of pressure to either find someone or prove her career is a success."

"I'd certainly be a trophy."

"In a romantic way?" hedged Sid, confused.

"As a patient. If she solved me, people will be lining up at her door. It's an easier strategy than seduction; she'd see through that."

Sid opened his mouth to say something, then closed it.

"This is a good idea. I'll make her fail."

"I don't think therapy works like that," said Sid. "And if it did, this seems like a bad thing to do to someone who's trying to help you?"

"I don't need help from a shrink. Do you think I need help from a shrink?"

Sid wisely left enough space in the ensuing silence so he didn't have to answer. "Since Eddie expects you to finish therapy, it might be best to pretend to cooperate. Five sessions left. How bad can it be?"

"You have no idea how humiliating it is to walk into that dismal little office and pretend there's an answer for me. It's like I'm no one. Even worse, to her I'm a *patient*. Have you ever been a psych patient, Sid?"

"Yeah, actually. I got some pretty good help once."

"Well, that's great for you. But it won't help me."

"I suppose you could attend your required sessions but not participate."

"That's what I've been saying. Then, if she doesn't sign off to Eddie, I'll tell everyone she failed to fix me."

Sid frowned, now more concerned than confused. Quinn didn't bother asking why. This felt like a good plan. He'd go to his next appointment and stare at the wall. He would count the ceiling tiles. He would give Larisa nothing.

His phone vibrated on the far side of the desk. He glanced at it. Parish. She'd taken to calling him at night. Yesterday, she'd sent almost a hundred text messages about how he'd broken her heart.

When the phone fell silent, Quinn picked it up and typed a message to Club D. He was ready to meet the Queen again.

At five minutes to six Thursday night, as Quinn arrived at the clinic, he still had not received a response from the club. The silence nagged at the back of his mind, like it was the most important thing he'd forgotten. He sat on Larisa's dingy second-hand couch in her dingy little consultation room and told himself an answer was coming. He just had to be patient.

What if the Queen didn't like me?

He glanced at the clock. Eight minutes after the hour. He was sure it had been longer since she'd given him the same greeting from Monday and asked him about the emotion journal. Had she really expected him to do that?

Ten minutes of silence. He could see her at the edge of his peripheral vision. Expensive clothes purposefully oversized to hide her body, hair severely pulled back, no makeup. Did she think her patients wouldn't notice how far above them she was, or how much of a con she was running trying to offer them help, as though she knew anything about their lives?

"How was Dansby?" she asked.

Why is she asking about him? He doesn't matter.

Next time he was at Club D, he'd do better. Then the Queen would use her voice. Tell him what he was.

Twelve minutes of silence. Quinn moved his tongue around in his mouth like the thought of Dansby was there, the taste of a meal he regretted eating. He imagined telling Larisa Dansby was a child greedily accepting handouts in exchange for sex, just to see what she'd say. Sid hadn't been able to confirm it, but Quinn was certain that was how Dansby had gotten the part. He probably didn't even think there was anything wrong with what he'd done, skipping the line, robbing actors who had studied their craft for years.

"You can't change the casting decision," said Larisa. "So, why not adapt? What makes someone like Dansby a plausible spy?"

Quinn pressed his lips together. The answer was nothing. But he wasn't going to give her that and invite her to use mind tricks to argue with him. Instead, he said something sure to make her angry. "He's practically a woman. It only makes sense for him to be a spy if he's a femme fatale sent in to seduce the general."

"I'd watch that."

Not a hint of irritation in her voice, which made him irritated. "It doesn't matter what you'd watch," he snapped. "You're a single woman in her mid-thirties who probably goes to sleep with a vibrator and a romance novel." He couldn't help but turn just enough to watch her reaction.

All Larisa did was deepen that bland mayonnaise expression on her face. Her mouth was doing something, not quite a smile, but something like a smile or suppressed laughter. He glared at her, daring her to respond in kind. They would fight, which would make the time pass faster. Then he'd tell Eddie Larisa was unprofessional, and they couldn't work together anymore.

"I think you've landed on an important truth, Quinn. You know what many single women in their thirties have that not everyone else does?"

"Enlighten me."

"Time and disposable income. Which they could use to go see your movie."

He turned his face back towards the wall and recommitted to his silence.

Damn her. She's right. Against his will, Quinn's mind began to churn through the possibility.

We're not changing the movie two weeks into production.

How much would need to change?

A few lines in the script. Add one or two scenes. No reshoots for what's been done.

It could work.

But it's risky. A man seducing another man? Are they gay?

Don't introduce questions of sexuality. Most of it could be conveyed in Dansby's body language. His appearance would make it plausible.

Damn her.

"While we're on the subject of romance," said Larisa.

Despite himself, Quinn felt himself waiting for her to say more.

"I was sorry to hear about you and Parish. She's always been a sweet girl."

What the fuck do you mean, 'sweet girl'? You want to see the messages she sends? This was a trap, Quinn was certain. Eddie had asked Larisa to investigate the black eye situation. She was trying to tempt him into admitting violence.

"Are you still talking with her?"

Quinn clenched his jaw just the way he imagined Dansby's character, Sam, would clench it for the interrogation scene.

"Finding a true ending is hard," said Larisa. "But blocking her number could help make the decision feel real."

What did Eddie tell her?

The edge of the poster directly in front of him was peeling off the wall from the bottom left corner. Dust bunnies waved in the negligible breeze of the HVAC vent, most likely blowing asbestos into his lungs.

"In my professional experience, most relationships fail because people have different expectations of each other than when they started out. Or the relationship gets into its stable stage and one person, or the other, realizes they want something else."

How could she possibly know that's what happened?

"What are you thinking right now?" asked Larisa.

Twenty minutes left in the session. Quinn had failed to usurp her calm professionalism.

"Are your parents still together?" asked Larisa.

Where had that come from?

"It's one of the biographical questions," she said as though he'd actually asked. "Normally, we'd just have a friendly conversation about your family for this second session, but since that's not really your style, I thought this one might have relevance."

"Relevance because . . .?"

"Our parents usually serve as touchstones of evaluation. Are we doing things at the same age they did? Are we behind or ahead? Are we likely to succeed where they failed, or fall into the same traps?"

"My parents are celebrating their thirtieth this year."

"What do you think about that?"

"Fan-fucking-tastic for them."

"Are they having a party?"

The knowing satisfaction in her voice almost sounded like she knew he was lying, and this made her feel that she'd won.

Chapter 10

The First Time

The Golden Lily kept the dining lights on until nine o'clock, so it was easy to scan the room and pick out the people Larisa knew. Not that she was planning on needing help, but it never hurt to have an escape plan on a first date. Otherwise, Larisa had a tendency to do something too forceful, which ended up being recorded by someone and sold to a tabloid. Then her mother would call and complain about Larisa's atrocious behavior like she was a seven-year-old misbehaving at a White House gala, which Larisa had done once upon a time.

It was now February, Larisa's most reviled month, and officially less than two months until Jaden's wedding. This combination of terrible things was why she'd given into her mother's idea about a date with the Saudi prince. She needed to find a wedding date. And not just a date for the wedding, but a boyfriend who looked like a stable addition to her life, just like all her other sisters' husbands were a permanent addition to theirs.

She spotted a couple of starlets out for a girls' night with a pop star who was making a run on movies. A rapper's posse. A state senator who had once pulled her onto his lap. She'd punched him. But maybe now they were friends because her mother had supported his campaign.

And there, in the pink felt booth closest to the stage that would later host a throwback 1920s jazz band, was Quinn Vander-Veer. *Of all the gin joints,* thought Larisa. Her date was doomed to fail before it even began. There was no way she'd be able to concentrate on her Saudi prince with Quinn across the room.

He shared the booth with a young man so extremely beautiful he could only be Dansby Vaast. They were in the middle of a toast, apparently amicable.

A hand slid around her waist, followed by a body pressed up against her back. "Good evening," said a masculine voice with a thick accent.

Larisa smiled and pressed up against him instead of following her first instinct to push him away. "Do I call you Prince or—"

"I'm just Hasan tonight." He kissed her hand.

"Mutual, I'm sure." Larisa batted her eyes at him, doing a physical inventory. He was a little shorter than she was, nice skin, playful eyes with something a little naughty behind them, a fresh manicure, and Western-style clothing that presented as a confused cross between trust fund playboy (which he mostly was) and a drug kingpin who might have walked off the set of *Scarface* (which he hopefully was not).

Red satin shirt, thought Larisa so she wouldn't accidently say it aloud.

They were escorted to a booth by the bar, off to one side of the room and right beside the wall of art deco mirrors so that, even though there was a column in the middle of the room blocking her direct line of sight to Quinn's booth, Larisa could tilt her head just so and have a full view of Quinn and Dansby through the mirror.

She and Hasan started off talking about movies, a natural beginning given where she came from and where he was hoping to go. She liked that Hasan didn't seem desperate the way some aspiring actors could be. She disliked that he seemed to think people bought their way onto movie sets. He said it would be good for America to make more Middle East-positive films. She agreed and hinted that film financing could make him much more popular with the right kind of people than acting.

Across the room, Quinn and Dansby appeared to be having a

regular old conversation. Quinn had started off doing most of the talking, but now he'd fallen silent and was watching Dansby hesitantly offer his views on something. Larisa knew what it was like to sit under the spotlight of Quinn's gaze. Even his most neutral expression carried the intensity of an overzealous tanning bed.

Poor kid, thought Larisa.

After two drinks and not much of his dinner, Hasan was ready to talk about his ideal woman. She was as expected, plus some physical embellishments Larisa found interesting: round cheeks (both kinds of cheeks), hair down to her waist, hairless everywhere else, even on her arms. None of this screamed deal-breaker, though the idea of a man caring that much about little things made Larisa tired.

But if I could hang onto him for two months, just until after the wedding, he'd make the kind of impression I want to make.

She'd never done such a detailed inventory of her ideal man so, when it became clear Hasan expected an answer in kind, she decided to describe not Hasan, which would have been wiser, but Quinn. Because why not? He was sitting there, a ready source of inspiration. And he was, though not handsome, physically interesting.

"I like someone a little aloof, the quiet type who doesn't waste words, and when he speaks it's like gold dripping from his lips. A little vampish, dark hair, white skin, maybe he even bleaches it. Extremely strong jaw that extends his face so I can fit my whole hand on his cheek when I slap him. Neat hygiene, but a messy look that reflects his wild soul."

Across the room, Dansby was leaning in, finally getting comfortable, talking quite a lot while Quinn sat as still as a living statue taking him in. Larisa could practically feel his vibrating attention. *Was she jealous of Dansby?* She bit her lip and wondered if Doan had found a solution to her voice recognition problem. Then she remembered she'd promised Dr. Bade she wouldn't see Quinn again at the club.

"You have very interesting taste," said Hasan with an uncomfortable laugh.

"Ideals never really end up being useful in real life." Larisa smiled sweetly, but not enough that Hasan was fooled.

"Insults are part of American romance at a high level, I understand. This is why you have fundamentalists who are trying to make you better people."

Larisa blinked. She could feel her smile turning sour, but she suddenly didn't have the willpower to fix it. *Did he just compare me to—*

"If you're referring to those *terrorists* who kidnap good people and put them on *American Idol* show trials for their supposed 'sins,' I think you've misunderstood me. Unless you're trying to tell me you like 'sinful' women." She said it like a flirtatious joke, but she couldn't quite pull it off, she was so irritated that he'd already revealed himself to be so basic.

"I suppose this culture will take some getting used to." Hasan pushed away his frown. "But I find you delightful. Really," he reached for her hand, "I can't think of anyone else I'd like to spend my evening with."

Larisa allowed him this touch even though she'd already decided he wasn't a candidate for a wedding date. When enough time had passed, she offered to get him a fresh drink and made a strategic retreat to the bar.

"Girl, you're smokin' tonight," said Giselle the long-time Golden Lily bartender, who didn't look so bad themselves, wearing a sparkly flapper dress and feather boa.

"I think I might be too much," said Larisa, as she watched Hasan check in with his phone. His bodyguards sat at a table by the door, also on their phones. Another senator had arrived and joined the first. Both were looking at her in that way that made her skin crawl. *Fucking politicians.* She checked the time. Three hours until her shift at the hospital started. If she got out soon, she would have enough time to visit Club D before work.

Across the room, Dansby had moved over to Quinn's side of

the booth and was leaning into the table, his head propped on his fist, looking up at Quinn. Was his other hand busy under the table? She couldn't tell from Quinn's face. Probably half of him was turned on and half of him resented Larisa for being right about Dansby as a femme fatale. She grinned.

"I love it when people take my advice."

"What's that?" asked Giselle.

"Nothing." Larisa gathered the drinks and returned to her booth. It was so very tempting to go over and introduce herself. She wanted to squeeze in beside Quinn and be a secondary target of Dansby's seduction. She didn't really like pretty young things, but for Dansby she might make an exception, just for play, not for keeps. *Wonder how he feels about bondage?*

"The bartender likes me, so be careful, your drink might be a little stronger than the others," she told Hasan.

"Likes you how?"

Larisa tensed. That possessive note in Hasan's voice was such a turn off. Seriously. They barely knew each other. It was a first date.

So of course, the obvious answer was, "We were seeing each other for a while, but a long time ago." A strategic pause. Larisa stirred her drink. "My current boyfriend is over there," she motioned toward the column, "being seduced by one of his actors."

Hasan frowned. Then, before she knew what was happening, he'd seized her wrist and was dragging her across the room right up to Quinn's booth.

"Is this your girlfriend?"

Dansby lurched back like a startled colt, wide eyed, nostrils flared, still absurdly beautiful. Quinn didn't even blink. He just raised those hard eyes up from the level of the table to Hasan's face. His gaze flicked from Hasan to Larisa. His right eyebrow gave the smallest arch of an unspoken question, but he said nothing.

"I demand you release your claim on her. She's been

unfaithful and I will not associate with a woman who is claimed by another."

"Good luck finding a wife, asshole." Larisa wrenched out of his grip and stormed down the side aisle. One of Hasan's bodyguards rose as though to stop her, but she waved him back. "Don't even. I'm out of here."

She did not look back to see what Quinn was doing. She told herself it didn't matter what he thought, he already resented her.

She texted Doan:

The Queen: Arriving in thirty minutes. Find
someone who wants it rough.

Less than two hours later, Larisa had pulled a muscle in her shoulder straining to control her swing so she didn't damage either of her partners. The exertion hadn't been enough. She didn't want to be a caretaker tonight. She wanted to be a destroyer, and other people didn't deserve that. The lack of true release meant she couldn't come down from the date, from the mess of thoughts half-articulated, buried and unburied, running haywire in her mind. Sex might have helped, but she didn't have sex with strangers, and she especially didn't have angry sex with strangers.

She met Doan at the bar for a Pellegrino. "Do you ever wonder what you're doing with your life?"

"No."

I could have done better with Hasan.

"If I ask again, could you lie to me?"

"We have people you can pay for that service," said Doan.

Larisa pulled her phone from her holster, ready to text an apology to Hasan. Maybe if she groveled, she could still use him. "What the fuck?" She had over a dozen missed texts. Her first thought was the paparazzi had sunk their fangs into her date with Hasan, but if that had been the case her mother would have called.

The first two texts were from Hasan, which she'd missed while driving to Club D. Several more Hasan texts were mixed into the sisters' group chat and made for surreal reading. Larisa wished she and Doan were the kind of friends who shared things like this.

Hasan: Where did you go?

Hasan: We're not done.

Jaden: I had my dress fitting today!!!!

Krissy: 🤍🤍🤍. I'm still in charge of your bachelorette outfit, right?

Jaden: Just promise me not one of those T-shirts and veil. They're so gauche.

Hasan: You can't walk out on me.

Hasan: No one walks out on me.

Rosa: Which limo service? I had a bad experience with City Lights, remember?

Kahleah: Big fail, gals. I can't get those toast glasses like I promised. There's a hurricane in Poland of all places.

Parish: Happy Hour on Tuesday or Wednesday?

Jaden: I know we talked about firemen, but I'm not sure now. Couldn't it just be us?

Krissy: The plans are set. BTB. You'll love it. @Kahleah, no biggie on the glasses. We'll drink from the bottle!

Krissy: @Rosa, transpo is set.

Hasan: You're teasing me. I don't like it.

Hasan: I want you.

"What part of your life are you questioning?" asked Doan.

Larisa blinked up from her phone with Hasan's words ringing through her mind. The beginning of an idea. It wasn't a good one, but . . .

"Pretty much all of it."

"Maybe this will help?" Doan passed Larisa a necklace-shaped jewelry box that was twice as high as usual. "Charity told me about your voice problem."

Larisa opened it and lifted out a velvet collar three inches high. "What am I feeling inside?"

"Those are metal rods. The idea is that you line them up along your vocal cords, then you latch it as tight as possible while still being able to breathe. The pressure and lack of airflow will alter your voice."

"So, I'll be completely anonymous but I might pass out?"

"Basically."

If only Quinn walked through the door right now.

But Quinn was probably still at The Golden Lily with Dansby, reworking their movie. And she needed someone tonight or she was going to burst into a million partitions of her various selves: Daughter of ________, Doctor of ________, Lover of________, Friend of ________. As Larisa walked out to her Murano, she texted Hasan the GPS location of her usual corner of Sacred Heart's parking lot.

She drove to her rental lot with the Sex Pistols vibrating the doors of her car. She changed back into her cocktail dress and heels, leaving off her G-string, then drove to the hospital to the almost constant vibrating of her phone with new messages coming in from the chat.

Ten minutes until her shift. Hasan and his two bodyguards stood waiting in the parking lot. When Larisa pulled up, the bodyguards melted away. She came at Hasan with her fiercest stare down.

"No one owns me," she growled.

He grabbed her wrist, pulling her arm behind her to bend her back against the car. He held her in place while he fucked her like the sinful American slut he believed her to be.

When he finished, Larisa didn't have enough time to change into work clothes. She grabbed her white coat and her badge and walked away.

"When will I see you again?" called Hasan.

"Never."

She climbed the back steps up to the third floor and let herself in, thinking she could sneak into the bathroom without anyone seeing. But there was Dr. Bade, just down the hall coming out of a patient's room. She looked at Larisa's disheveled hair and jeweled manicure. Larisa pinched her legs together so the semen sliding down the inside of her thigh wouldn't be visible.

Dr. Bade shook her head and walked the other way. Face burning, Larisa's heels clicked against the cold tile floor as she ran to the bathroom.

It would be a long night. She would end up breaking one of her heels while running to respond to a suicide attempt. She would rip the skirt of her dress wrestling two fighting patients apart. She would weather not one, but two, cops bringing in patients who then stuck around to stare at her chest and ask for her number. Sophie would often be silent in that gentle, troubled way of hers.

But in the last moments before the night began, Larisa stood at the bathroom mirror, sponging her sex with paper towels and straightening her hair. The woman she saw wasn't quite a stranger, but more an inverted reflection. She'd surrendered to Hasan because she needed him to replace the satisfaction she couldn't conjure on her own. It had been a mistake. (How many times had she done the same thing with Lucas?) But perhaps it was also a good step toward imagining she could be that woman, that kind of wife. She'd played the role in college with the wrong man, but that didn't mean she couldn't make it work.

Larisa squeezed back tears. Hasan had hurt her wrist. He hadn't even looked at her when he'd been inside her. *Deep breath, Larisa.* She checked messages one last time before putting her personal phone in her locker. Skimming, then typing.

> Larisa: I'll take care of the toast glasses.
> There's twelve of us, right?
>
> Jaden: Larisa to the rescue!
>
> Krissy: Buy a couple to spare in case we're
> clumsy.
>
> Larisa (to Parish): Let's meet at Sizemore's
> Wednesday at 5.

As she walked to the charge desk, Larisa texted Ulrike at Tiffany's, who she'd worked with on the fundraising dinner party for the sleezy senator. She sent the color swatches for Jaden's wedding, the bachelorette party details, and the number of items needed. Then she blocked Hasan's number. He would never appreciate what she could do for him. If she was going to fit herself into the box of a submissive wife, at the very least she was going to find a man who recognized all she could do.

Session Three

Around six A.M. Monday morning the messages began to come in. Larisa had been awake for four hours trying to catch up on client reports and make progress on the grant she, Myhanh, and Sophie were supposed to have finished by the end of the month.

The first came from Lucas, who never failed to notice when she was in the press.

Lucas: Naughty Girl.

Two words. But they were enough to set her mind spiraling. Seeing his name bloomed a warm feeling in her stomach that couldn't be sorted into pleasure or panic. He'd been so good at pushing her into this unknown space where boundaries became permeable, and violation masqueraded as pleasure.

Respond? Don't respond?
Don't you dare respond, Larisa.
One text won't hurt.

Krissy: OMG Larisa what were you doing this weekend?

Rey (Suzette's private assistant): Do you want me to try and keep this from her?

Rosa: Are you okay?

Every so often, this happened. Larisa went to bed in one world and woke up in another, its familiar characteristics subtly marred with an unknown intrusion. At sixteen, she'd gone on a date (her first real date) to the Hard Rock Café for dinner and a concert. Her date had left her for another girl and the paparazzi had photographed Larisa tackling him to the ground and beating him. The next morning she'd become the girl with a temper and "beautifully ineffectual little fists."

In such world-shifting moments, Larisa had learned it was useful to stop and consider the worst-case scenario before investigating what had changed. This allowed for a diminished shock value and gave whatever was coming a grounding metric.

Larisa followed this technique even as she also argued with it. Whose worst-case scenario? And in what context?

Someone knows I like bondage.

Someone recorded me and Hasan in the hospital parking garage and now its online.

Both seemed unlikely. She'd been careful even in her recklessness.

Would such a video make me more or less appealing to the next guy?

Larisa thought it would depend on the guy. At least it would make her seem younger, more up for adventure.

When she walked into the clinic, Jez stood up and greeted Larisa with a beaming smile. "Look what my mom found at the grocery store!" They held out the grey paper and bleeding ink of a tabloid with Larisa's face printed on the front, an action shot of her exiting The Golden Lily with Hasan running after her in the background. She hadn't realized Hasan chased her out. The head-line screamed: ICE QUEEN LARISA LEAVES SAUDI

PRINCE HEARTBROKEN. HAS SHE USED UP HER NINE LIVES?

Not her worst-case, just another sharp needle stabbing where hundreds had already stabbed before. But placing this in the realm of the banal did not make it feel better. Realizing she'd had yet another failure and was no closer to a wedding date made worst-case imaginings irrelevant. This was just more of the same. Failure to adapt was the true worst-case for Larisa's life.

Jez held out a Sharpie. Larisa signed her autograph.

"Thanks so much. Oh, I already let your nine o'clock into the room."

"Why would you do that?" Larisa pointed at the clock on the wall. "It's eight-forty."

"He asked for privacy. I didn't—"

"He? Where's Kara?"

"Canceled."

"Why?"

Jez held up their hands in surrender. From their terrified expression, Larisa realized she was coming on too strong. She backed up, trying to think. The scheduling tablet was locked in the desk drawer inside the room, but it only took Larisa a moment to realize Jez was not so green or inept that they would break the rules for just anyone. Quinn was her nine o'clock. He would see her flustered, still reeling from the tabloid. *Which is probably his plan. The fucker.*

"Don't do that again," Larisa said to Jez, as she yanked the doorknob and entered counseling room one. "Good morning, Quinn. I'm sorry, but there's been a misunderstanding. I need you to sit in the waiting room until the top of the hour."

He was sitting in her chair, feet planted on the floor, arms on the armrests, an aggressive stance all around. "I decided to do my homework."

"That's great. We can discuss it at nine."

He didn't move. A slight smile played across his lips, waiting, those hard eyes so very interested in what she was going to do.

Larisa thought of her mother and the thirty thousand dollars Eddie had pledged to her wildfire cleanup project. She thought, *Eddie needs you to crack this guy.*

Hadn't she already done enough? Quinn and Dansby were getting along. He had a new vision for the film which would probably solve most of the conflict Quinn had created between his aesthetic ideals and his work constraints. If she called Eddie and wrote off the remaining sessions, he would accept her judgement. She would be able to schedule a session with Quinn at the club without digging herself into an even deeper conflict of interest.

And yet she knew there was much more work to be done.

And he was sitting in her chair like it was a throne, a challenge that made her want to punish him even more than she did already.

In demonstrations of power, the human animal only has a few options. Answer back with a similar demonstration and hope it's enough. (It wouldn't be.) Flee and live to fight another day (Larisa couldn't indefinitely cede her counseling room to Quinn.) Or submit and work to undermine from within.

This week has a theme. Larisa relaxed her posture, closed the door, and performed a stiff flop onto the sofa. "Alright. How did the homework go?"

"You seem upset."

"I'm doing twenty minutes of unpaid work."

"Before you came in, you were upset." His eyes glinted.

Larisa thought that if she lied, he would be even more determined to act out against her. They'd waste the session in a battle of wills.

"Well Quinn, it was a shitty weekend. And it's been a shitty first month of the new year. And I don't feel like you're here in good faith."

"Your date accused me of a crime I haven't committed yet."

Larisa considered his use of the word yet, how there had been a slight pause before he'd added it onto the end of the sentence, twisting it through his mouth so it felt like an insult. As though he would never consider dating her. Somehow, his voice, so matter of fact, brought tears to her eyes. *Fuck.* She pushed them down.

"You were a convenient target," she said, too sharp, openly aggressive now. "I thought you could hold your own. Was I wrong?"

"You're the one with a code of ethics."

"We left ethics behind the day Eddie made your first appointment." She was almost yelling. Her bitterness far too obvious. *Deep breath.* "How did it go with Dansby?"

"You saw."

"And Eddie?"

"Didn't even argue about the proposed change. The screenwriter will have new pages by the time I arrive today."

That's the Larisa magic. No one appreciates how amazing I am at everything.

"So, we can finally get to that bio work."

"Where to start?" Quinn steepled his fingers together under his chin. Larisa tried hard not to stare at the hollow in his neck, how it beckoned to her tongue. How it seemed like an entrance to the rest of him concealed beneath his clothes.

Why would he cooperate now?

He feels like he's in control.

Because of my scene at The Golden Lily?

"You said your parents are celebrating their anniversary. Let's start with them."

Without further challenge, Quinn described an ordinary childhood. One younger brother, parents who liked theater and never allowed their boys to play sports. Acting classes and auditions at the community playhouse, a memorable family vacation to Italy and Spain when Quinn had been a teenager. How his parents had both come from unstable homes, so they worked hard to make their family different. They had been an island of four, with only a handful of holidays spent visiting cousins, aunts, and uncles who were strangers. He'd never met any of his grand-parents, but there had been plenty of other people who played a similar role in his life. Quinn spent a full ten minutes describing a woman named Nora who mentored him in high school and encouraged him to try for film school.

He spoke without embellishment. Short sentences, almost perfunctory thoughts, but still somehow vivid, as though he'd collected all the most salient details from the whole of his life's experience and compiled them into a movie trailer.

His willingness to talk allowed Larisa the space to compose herself. What the tabloids said didn't matter. This was who she was. The guide and caretaker helping her patients build meaning and order into their lives, giving them a safe space on their own terms. Despite his efforts to sabotage the process, Quinn had settled in. Maybe now they'd make some real progress.

The story flowed so seamlessly Larisa didn't ask any questions until it was almost time to wrap up. "What was your first sexual experience?"

"A boy in my drama class in eighth grade," said Quinn without missing a beat. "What was yours?"

Larisa smiled. "We're almost out of time. What are some things you want to build on with Dansby this week?"

"He's off. This week we're filming Walt, the senior operative, and his stateside machinations to bring Sam—Dansby—home from Russia. Next week we'll start Walt's recruitment of Dansby at college." Quinn shifted in his seat. "We should discuss an arrangement."

"For what?"

"Being your fake boyfriend."

Larisa's mouth dropped open. *The nerve of him.*

"It seems like something that might be valuable to you."

"Because the tabloids say I'm a lost cause?" A sudden sob left-over from earlier rose up Larisa's throat. She swallowed it down. *Get him out of here before you lose it, Larisa.*

"I believe you have given me something of value," he said.

"I'm willing to return the favor." That voice, so cold, like speaking the words was an extra step to clarify something she should have already recognized.

Favor? This is my job, you fucking asshole.

In five minutes, she would need to start her next session. She wanted Quinn out the door so she would have time to look at emails and see why Kara had canceled. And yet she sat on the couch blinking at him. Because she did need a boyfriend. In fact, she was looking for almost exactly what he'd just offered.

"I don't think people would find me dating you plausible."

"Why not?"

Her eyes drifted from his clothes up to the beanie.

"I suppose you'd have to give me a makeover."

Larisa pressed her lips together, then let them fall open again when she found it too difficult to breathe.

I would love to give him a makeover.

What about Club D? He can't find out.

He's a better option than Hasan.

Before she knew it, Larisa found herself saying, "I need a low-maintenance date to a wedding in April. I'm in the bridal party, but there's a dinner the night before and the reception, both very high profile." She managed to catch herself just before she said, *I promised my mother I'd have someone.*

Quinn was standing, heading toward the door. "Text me the dates." A superior smile toyed with the corners of his mouth. "I promise to be charming."

The door clicked shut behind him. Larisa studied the poster across from the couch, her mind empty. *What just happened?*

Then the pieces snapped into place, her mind functional again. A hiccup of laughter bubbled up. Perfect. It was perfect. She immediately shifted into planning mode. What would she need to pull this off? What were the known unknowns and the possible unknown unknowns? Could she be fired for this? Not without bringing the department chief down with her. *Fuck him. He'd already fucked her.*

Texting her lawyer, who was also her father's lawyer.

> Larisa: I need an NDA drawn up to include all
> the general. Then associate it with a contract
> for services: Date for one weekend of
> wedding-related events, plus five to ten hours
> preparation for role. Surrender all decisions
> about clothes and appearance to me.
> Minimum four public appearances in weeks
> leading up to wedding.

A knock sounded on the door. Larisa put away her phone, calling "Come in" as she went to the desk and unlocked the client records tablet from the desk drawer.

Chapter 12

Gal's Vals

There had been a hand-shaped bruise on Larisa's forearm. Maybe that was what had prompted Quinn to make the offer. He passed it off as something condescending, in the mode of his previous resistance to her presence in his life. Something that would offend her enough that she'd break out of her professional role and lash out at him. But it was more than that.

Some form of the idea had been circulating in his head since Sid had suggested Larisa's weak point might be her singleness. Quinn hadn't believed it until he'd seen her with that prince at The Golden Lily. The look on her face when he'd accused her of being unfaithful, her horror when he'd yanked her around like some prize animal to be traded among men. It had all become clear. She needed someone. Maybe she liked being single, but from a PR perspective, her situation was a problem, and she couldn't solve it herself.

"How's Larisa?" asked Eddie on Wednesday morning, as he and Quinn watched the crew change the lighting for the close-ups.

"Fine." Quinn tracked a particular lighting technician across the stage. Yesterday, the guy had broken a rod. Today, he seemed just as careless. Quinn made fists at the sides of his pants and released them.

"You seem better."

I'm sure she's keeping you updated.

"You know its Valentine's Day," said Eddie.

Tish had invoked Love's national holiday at least five times that morning while showing updated pictures of her kittens, which were about to be old enough for adoption.

"Parish says you've been ignoring her."

"I'm making a movie, Eddie."

"There's space for you to be human, you know."

Quinn decided not to argue the semantics of being human equating taking an ex-girlfriend out on a date because it was the worst day to be single in America.

"I have plans," he said.

"Yeah?"

Quinn flinched as the clumsy lighting technician waved a spotting lamp through the air. *Ignore it. He's just doing his job.* But no. Even as he told himself it was fine, Quinn charged across the set and started yelling, "What the fuck do you think you're doing?" so that the guy startled and, of course, dropped the spotting lamp.

Other people began shouting. Some were running away from Quinn when they should have been running toward him to clean up the mess. It felt oddly satisfying to be frightening again. He was tired of being nice to inept people.

"Quinn."

Quinn whirled, almost smacking into Tish coming up behind him with a big, fake grin on her face. "Hey, buddy, you okay?"

"No, I'm not fucking okay. How hard is it for people to fucking do their jobs?"

An eerie stillness descended across the set. Every direction Quinn turned, eyes stared back at him, judging, judging, judging.

"We're making a movie! Can't you all appreciate that? One weak link and the whole thing fails." Was he shouting? Maybe. The set had a high ceiling that swallowed sound. "Cameras roll in ten. Call Vince to the set."

Larisa was in bed. For ten minutes she'd been staring at the message, trying to decide what to do with it. Tonight, she was going out with Parish (a dubious, but strangely interesting decision), then working at the hospital. Would it be terrible to invite Jaden along to meet Parish? No. So, why was Larisa hesitating? They'd been single together since college graduation. Every Valentine's they'd celebrated together, even when Larisa had been in Minneapolis for medical school and celebrating meant each of them sitting alone in bars with half a country between them while talking on the phone.

But Jaden wasn't single anymore. If therapist Larisa asked patient Larisa how she felt, there would have been only one word needed to answer. *Betrayed.* But that wasn't fair to Jaden. *Everyone is happy except for me.*

Sizemore's was a beach club that served breakfast all day and most of the night. Larisa liked it because she could wear cutoff shorts and no one cared. To meet Parish, she wore sparkle pants and a matching crop top, both pink. She pulled her hair up into a top pony, which made her feel a little like Barbie, but maybe that was okay for tonight. She certainly didn't want to feel like herself. Larisa plowed into the club in her platform sandals and three karat earrings. Without a second thought, she greeted Parish with smoochie side kisses as though they knew each other.

"So glad we could make this work."

"Me too." Parish still wore purple highlights in her hair, which was ironed and shimmeringly soft. She wore a mini dress that was more a torso shrink wrap than dress. It barely covered the lip of her ass and her nipples. Once upon a time, Larisa had worn such things and had spent blood, sweat, and tears trying to keep them in place. She wanted to tell Parish there were other ways to be noticed, but at that moment Jaden breezed up the walk with a fresh manicure in green and blue (her wedding colors), twirling her keyring of a bedazzled Chinese character for love—a tepid connection to her mother's heritage—and the fuzzy head of her toy poodle sticking out of her Coach purse.

"Happy Vals, Gals!" she cried, while flashing that giant diamond on her finger. "I'm Jaden. You must be Parish. Larisa has told me so much about you."

"And so much about you," said Parish with matching enthusiasm that made Larisa slightly nauseous. Jaden had not always been like this, the breezy, confident leader in a social setting. Larisa had taught her, made her. And now, it didn't quite feel fair watching her take control, as though she thought Larisa needed her help even though she hadn't asked for it.

"I'm getting the first round for my two favorite single ladies," said Jaden, as she linked arms with Parish then Larisa (Larisa got the purse with pooch arm), leading them into the club.

Two margaritas and a blueberry pancake later, Larisa lounged on the beach deck, the roll of ocean waves blending with the club's muted dance beat. She resolved to schedule more drinking into her life. The only time she ever drank was on dates, when she'd sip on one drink for hours, never able to truly relax.

Was she relaxed at this moment? Mostly. One part of her that wasn't intoxicated yet was thinking, *Jaden is getting married. This is the end and I'm not even enjoying it.* While the other part was watching Parish, trying to put together a profile of the woman Quinn had dumped.

You want to see if she's like you.

You want to know what he's hiding.

They'd been lounging, dancing, and drinking for almost an hour. Parish seemed remarkably average, an aspiring actress who wanted to be loved.

"So, what went wrong?" asked Jaden, playing the role of love expert, also something Larisa had done back when she'd been taking her intro to psychology classes. Back when it seemed everyone she knew walked around with five or more mental health disorders that needed solving.

When did this happen? wondered Larisa. *Jaden has become what I used to be.*

"He just stopped wanting me." Parish lowered her voice. "He couldn't get it up, no matter what I did. He hit me."

"Like a spank or—"

"Both."

Larisa stared up at the sky bisected by the grid of the deck awning.

She's lying. Quinn is a submissive.

Why lie?

Why does any woman lie? She's ashamed she couldn't give him what he wanted.

"I was okay with it, but then he kept accusing me of not liking it the way he wanted. And it just got so hard." Parish drew a shuddering breath that prompted Jaden to reach over and pat Parish's thigh.

Who wants a boyfriend who likes to be beaten?

Parish was probably traumatized. Everything she'd been taught to expect about men had been subverted, her trust betrayed, along with whatever love she and Quinn had shared. Quinn treated the sharing of personal information like a special kind of torture, and Parish's views of the world were so vapid, she could probably fall in and out of love every week. She needed a nice guy who was also simple in his own way.

Maybe Greg, thought Larisa with a smile. Greg had been nice, was probably one of those guys who could make a simple woman happy.

"I think he still loves me, though," said Parish. "I'm going to be in his movie."

Really.

Larisa thought she'd do almost anything to be on set to watch that go down.

Too soon, her alarm started sounding.

Jaden moaned dramatically. "Already?"

"Time for Dr. Larisa to switch to water," said Larisa with false cheerfulness. "Got to get to work."

"Don't you miss those days when we'd sit here for hours and talk?" asked Jaden.

Here we go.

"Maybe once you're married, we'll do it again. Rosa and Krissy do happy hour every Friday. We'll be the breakfast club loungers."

"Are you getting married, Larisa?" asked Parish.

"No. And even if I was, I'd still be working. Some people do that."

Dansby had arrived on set somewhere during hour ten of tense, teeth-clenching shooting. His presence, when he didn't need to be there, made everything worse. He was like a pebble in the proverbial shoe of Quinn's mind. Between every take, Quinn felt Dansby bouncing around, making a joke with someone, flirting with someone else, pulling attention away from the work. Since his outburst at the lighting technician, Quinn had been so taut his calves had started cramping, and he couldn't move his right thumb from its folded position in his fist without using his other hand.

When Tish called the day a wrap, Quinn made his exit. He managed an uneven, painful gait that was almost running (but not fleeing) through the backlot to the offices. He didn't realize Dansby had followed him until he was opening his office door and saw the shadow of a person behind him.

"It wasn't a very good day, was it?"

Quinn's eyes sank closed. *Not this. Not now.*

Dansby followed Quinn into the office, pausing in the middle to look around, then, without invitation, went over and sprawled across the longest of the couches. "Do you hate me?"

"No."

"Do you think I'm a bad actor?"

"You're not an actor, Dansby. You're a lifeguard from a resort town in the Netherlands." Quinn pushed the door closed and rolled his forehead against it.

"I'd like to be an actor."

"What do you think an actor does?"

"Takes a character, plays that person to the camera."

"And how is that different than what you're doing?"

Silence. As Quinn knew there would be. With dread, he thought of the next week, the beginning of the Russian prison sequences, scenes that required more emotional range and gravitas than Dansby could wrap his fuzzy little brain around.

"You could help me."

"There's no way to help you," said Quinn to the door.

"I watched your other movies. They were rough, gritty, kind of like this one."

"They're not anything like this one."

"Well, I like them. It seems like you know what you're doing."

The lifeguard has decided I know what I'm doing, great.

"Those actors had life experience," said Quinn. "They knew not only how to act, but also what it was like to be in those situations."

"Well, not many people know what it's like to be a thief turned spy seducing a Russian general. Does that even happen in real life?"

"I bet you couldn't even seduce me," muttered Quinn. As he said it, an idea flickered in one side of his mind and out the other. "Don't you have somewhere to go?"

"Not really."

Quinn drew his head up and stared at the door. Another stray thought, clearer this time, one of the few not pockmarked with fissioning tension and a looming tipping point into despair.

"Why don't you come over to my place?"

"Yeah?"

"We'll pick up dinner, drink a little."

"Great."

Quinn checked his phone. Still no message from Club D. Alright then, if he could not invite productive self-immolation into his life safely, he would do it unsafely.

Chapter 13

Self-Immolation Scene Take One

By the time Larisa found herself at the end of her Thursday, she'd left three messages on Kara's and each of her parents' phones. No one had called her back. In the course of an afternoon with Sophie in the library, then in the weekly reflection class where her cohort reported on what they felt about their experiences that week, Larisa had tried not to worry. But in the back of her mind, a little voice whispered that this was her punishment. She'd shared too much of herself, a boundary had been crossed and now both Kara and Larisa were paying for it.

As she walked from University Tower to Hospital Tower Two, Larisa typed an email to Greg asking if he would be willing to let her set him up on a blind date. Then she answered the two-days-late email from Dr. Patel requesting Larisa's preferences for her next rotation. When she made it to the outpatient clinic, Quinn stood in the far corner of the waiting room looking out the narrow slit of a window. He wore his usual beanie and a London Fog trench coat, the first thing she'd seen him wear that suited him.

"Hey Quinn. Come on in." She unlocked consultation room one and turned on the lights. *One hour of this, then I'll speed over to the ward and have Lucie check the other hospitals to see if Kara has been admitted.*

Larisa waited by the wall until Quinn came in and sat on the

"

couch. She sat in her chair, calm, outwardly in control. *Should I bring up his proposal now or later?*

"Last time, we started talking about your family. I thought we might continue with that."

He removed the bracelet of prayer beads from his wrist and began to move them between his fingers. They were the only part of him that moved. For what felt like several minutes, he didn't even blink. There were just these stutters of his eyelids, as though he was fighting off sleep, or flinching away from an imagined fist about to strike him.

Finally, he said, "Do you think you're a good person?"

"I do."

"How do you know?"

Larisa opened her mouth to answer, then closed it. *It isn't your job to share yourself. This is only about him.*

"Has something happened?"

"I'm not a violent person."

"I believe that."

"My whole life, I've seen what it should be. I've tried to create that." His tongue came out and licked his lips, lingered over them without any apparent awareness of the movement's sensuousness.

Don't go there right now, you horny idiot.

"It never ends up being what I've envisioned. There's always some flaw."

"Are you talking about people?"

"Eddie shouldn't have made me do this. He doesn't know what I am, but I think you do. You're going to report me. I'll be locked up, only allowed to create scenes in my head." Again, that stuttered blinking. Larisa thought he was holding back tears. "Maybe that's the way it should be."

"If you'd be willing to tell me what happened, maybe we can work something else out. I'm on your side."

"He's still at my house," said Quinn. "I thought, I can't let him leave, he'll go straight to Eddie. I guess you both will. Such a neat trap set. I should have been able to stop myself."

"Can we go to your house?"

He looked at the clock. "You don't have enough time. Shift starts at seven and doesn't end until after seven tomorrow, then maybe you sleep. Or maybe you don't."

Why does he know my schedule?

Think about that later Larisa. Your patient is in crisis.

She stood, walked over to him, waiting there until he arched his neck and looked up at her. For a moment, he reminded her of a baby bird, a too large head at a wrong angle to a small body, starving for answers.

"Let's go."

"I don't need your help."

"Do you really believe that?"

"I wanted him to feel what it would be like in prison."

"Walk with me."

He unfolded himself from the couch, the movement so stiff she wondered if he was in pain. He followed her out of the room, down the staircase to the parking garage. As they walked, she typed an email to Dr. Bade saying she would be late for her shift.

"Are you telling them where to find me?"

Larisa turned her phone screen so he could see the email.

At her Bentley, she opened the passenger side door and closed it after he climbed in.

Deep breath. Your patient has admitted to harming another person.

You don't have enough information.

You should call for help.

Wait.

In the car, Quinn sat as still as he had in the clinic, hands on knees, eyes ahead, a live wire trapped in a coil.

"What do you feel right now?" she asked.

"Too many things."

"Pick one."

"If I were a better director, this would not have happened."

Larisa put the Bentley in gear. "Shall we listen to music? What do you like?"

"I don't listen to music."

Larisa adjusted her grip on the steering wheel, carefully trying not to react with horror imagining a life without music. "Alright, then tell me your scene."

"Which scene?"

"The one you shouldn't have made."

"The scene," said Quinn softly. "It's called, 'Dansby Learns to be Afraid.' Two short exchanges and a montage pulled from ten shots." He glanced at her.

"I'm listening."

"We see him first, our beautiful hero, invincible in his innocence. He trusts easily because he has never learned not to trust. He accepts a dinner invitation. The dinner is pleasant. Warm lighting, a single candle in the center of a worn-out table, chemistry between two people. Drinking towards a flirtation that remains unresolved. He falls asleep."

Quinn's voice gained volume and confidence as he continued through a description that would have been alarming if it had not seemed so unreal. The process of dragging an unconscious Dansby to the basement, removing his clothes, handcuffing him to a support pole, blindfolding, then abandoning him. A portable speaker set to play a looped track of footsteps, men shouting, then silence. Quinn's assistant, Sid, had been instructed to occasionally walk up and down the stairs and pound on the door.

On one level, the extent of it impressed Larisa. On another, she could hardly believe what she was hearing. The fact of the act itself. The realization that Quinn had gone to the studio that day as though nothing was wrong, then went straight from the studio to the clinic. Dansby had been alone in the basement without water for almost twenty-four hours.

"How does the scene end?" asked Larisa.

"I don't know. If I free him, he might lose what he's gained."

"Fear," said Larisa, trying to keep her voice even. *You fucking bastard.*

"Connection to his body, his character."

They arrived at Quinn's house. Once inside, Larisa was careful not to look around; she knew Quinn would notice and assume she was judging him. She saw enough to help her remember Quinn was still early in his career. The house was modest, unadorned, and presented the feeling of an empty shell. It was the place Quinn came when he wasn't working, but it wasn't a home.

Sid met them at the door, a formidable wrestler type with a shaved head and imprecise goatee. "He was calling for help in the morning," said Sid. "Quiet since four or so."

Quinn led her further into the house. He waved at a closed door and said, "Down there," before walking on into the kitchen. He sat down at the table he'd described, well used with a burned down candle on a plate at its center. Larisa sat down at an adjacent chair, feeling that being across from him would be too confrontational.

"What do I do?" he asked.

"What have you considered doing?"

"I'd like to free him. But I don't want him to lose what he's experienced. I think, we could drug him, take him home. The isolation might—"

"May I say something?"

Quinn took a breath, then nodded.

"You've gone through extraordinary lengths to help your actor realize his character. It's possible you may not be able to recognize what is enough."

"It will be enough when it works."

"When are you shooting the scene you've helped him prepare for?"

"Monday."

"So, even if this wasn't enough, there's some time. You could make the choice to trust Dansby tonight. Give him the opportunity to absorb what you've given him."

Quinn pulled his head into his shoulders, hunched, thinking. Finally, he nodded.

"Alright. You go down and release him. Ask him not to speak. You come back up here and I'll walk you both through some reflection exercises."

"Why me? Sid could—"

"Because you violated the safety of another person, Quinn. And what's good for the movie is not always good for people."

"What was I supposed to do?" he said softly, more to himself than her.

"We'll talk about that." She wanted to touch him, if only to set a reassuring hand on his shoulder. He looked so lost. But, as his therapist, that was one boundary she absolutely would not cross. Once she knew what it felt like to touch him, Larisa knew she would want more. Already, she found herself drifting into problematic thoughts. Her shock at what he'd done was being overwhelmed by the desire to take him into her arms and protect him. From other people. From himself.

Only when Quinn went down to the basement was she free to absorb what had happened. She felt Sid's eyes on her, wary.

"What do you think about this?" she asked.

"I believe in him."

Interesting answer, thought Larisa.

"Does he have paper and pens around here?"

"Sure thing."

Sid went off jogging up the stairs.

Larisa checked the time. *No one at the hospital will understand this.* But she understood. Even as part of her scrambled mind worried over Quinn's lack of obvious regret or of the wrongness of his actions, she understood. In some twisted way, it felt like genius. What does one do to save a film from an unqualified actor? Sit by and watch him fail? Of course not. And when all other options have been exhausted? You force him to live his character.

Footsteps on the basement stairs. Quinn returned to the kitchen with Dansby behind him. When Quinn stopped, Dansby leaned into him, resting his head on Quinn's shoulder.

Interesting.

"Hi Dansby, I'm Dr. Larisa de France-Kahn. We met briefly at The Golden Lily."

He nodded a hello.

"With your permission, I'd like to walk you through a written meditation to help sift through some of your experiences over the past few days." She motioned to one of the kitchen chairs. He wordlessly eased into it. Quinn returned to his seat.

Sid arrived with a legal pad, a composition book, and a handful of assorted pens.

"Can we all have some water, please, Sid?" Larisa squared herself to the table. *Okay, here we go.* A small thrill rose through her chest at what she was about to do. The shock at what Quinn had done was gone. In its place, a warm ember of understanding, of seeing his half-polished plan and knowing without a doubt how she could now come alongside it and make it whole.

"Sensations of body are the fastest type of memories to fade. So, for the next ten minutes, I'd like you to write down everything you feel physically right now, and what you've felt since yesterday."

"It was only yesterday?" Dansby's eyes widened. "I thought I'd missed work." He looked to Quinn, eyes welling. "I thought you'd gotten rid of me."

Quinn studied the table, hands pressed tight in his lap, shoulders drawn in as though braced against Dansby's presence.

"And Quinn, you're going to do the same. How did this process affect you physically? If either of you struggle with beginning, just start at the top and work your way down. Your head, eyes, mouth, throat, neck and so on. I'll set a timer on my phone." Larisa tore a page from the legal pad for herself before pushing it in front of Quinn. She took a pen and began to write, not full sentences, but fragments of thoughts, impressions. Then she wrote down what she could remember of what Quinn had said at the clinic.

"I'm not a violent person."

"Are you going to report me?"

He knows what he did is wrong. But does he feel it?

What does guilt look like for Quinn?

She held her hand up at the top of the page to shield it even though this felt unnecessary. Both men were writing steadily. Dansby had already covered half a page with a list of words. Quinn wrote lines across the page in one long paragraph.

After ten minutes, they moved on to the thoughts that had come to their minds. Then, for the last ten minutes, they wrote about the feelings that had come with those thoughts. Though Larisa had written comparatively little, she felt centered. She knew what she was doing. From the outside, it might not look correct, but then working with humans rarely followed ideals.

"In a few minutes, I'm going to drive Dansby home. So, we're going to close with this. I want you to write down what is something you want to take away from this experience? Two, what is something you want the other person to know?"

She gave them five minutes.

"Dansby, if you're comfortable, please share a few thoughts for Quinn."

Dansby leaned back in his chair, raking a giant hand through his hair. "Jah, so there's a lot to take away. I've been really worried about next week and I think now I have some material to work with. I'm kind of excited." He looked at Quinn, a big grin spreading across his face. "I think I'll do better."

"Stop smiling," said Quinn.

"Why? I'm happy."

Quinn sent Larisa a desperate look as though to say, *See? He can't be reached.*

Dansby diluted his smile. "Well, I appreciate you trying so hard for me."

Larisa suppressed her own smile. Dansby was lovely, charming, and yes, perhaps just dense enough to be Quinn's worst nightmare. But she'd glimpsed some of the things he wrote down. He wasn't as untouched as he seemed.

"Quinn? What would you like to share?"

Quinn's tongue came out and licked his lips. "I express regret for my actions. They went too far. I hope we can still work together."

"Of course we can. I'm so honored you would do this for me."

They said their goodbyes. Larisa worried Quinn didn't seem any more at ease than when he'd arrived at the clinic, but he had Sid. She needed to focus on making sure Dansby was stable enough to be alone, and she needed to get to work.

As soon as they got in the car, Dansby turned on the radio, fiddled with the tuner until he found the oldies station, then turned it down to an ambient hum, bopping his head along as he said, "You work for the studio?"

"Not exactly."

"Too bad. You'd be a great acting coach."

"I'm a psychiatrist."

"For Quinn?"

"For anyone who needs me. I'm going to give you my number. You're free to call at any time for whatever you need."

"On Monday?"

"Yes."

"That's great, because I'm really worried about it."

They'd arrived at the parking lot of the studio's temporary actors' housing.

"Are you alright?" asked Larisa, as she realized just how inadequate this question sounded.

"Jah, I think. I mean, it was a little scary waking up like that. And the banging on the door was scary, and not being able to move around. But I knew Quinn wouldn't let anyone really hurt me. I think that's what I learned the most. You have instinct fear that shoots off right away, but then, as time goes on, you start pulling it apart, you realize there's different layers. You can teach yourself to adjust and you focus on what you know. He was going to come for me. My job was to hang on until then."

There were so many things Larisa wanted to say in that moment, many of them she felt obligated to say as a clinician. But they also felt irrelevant. Instead, she said, "I think you could be a great actor, Dansby. I'm excited for you."

"Me too."

"But call me, okay? You're not alone. And if anything that happened starts to bother you, we can talk about it."

"That's great, thanks."

Larisa sat in her car and watched Dansby saunter down the sidewalk and into his building. He reached up and massaged his shoulders as he went, bending and stretching like a football player just after a hard workout. *Is it possible he's really okay?*

What would it be like to trust Quinn like he did?

Maybe it was more than that? Sid had used the word believe. Both he and Dansby believed in Quinn. Maybe the problem at the heart of Quinn's trouble was he didn't believe in himself? Maybe what she needed to do was help him feel worthy?

Such things could be done in the clinic. But Quinn didn't feel safe in the clinic. To him, she was Eddie's tool. Where did Quinn feel safe? Who would he trust to tell him his worth?

Larisa smiled to herself as she pulled out her phone and began typing a message to Doan.

Dr. Bade caught up with Larisa on her way out of grand rounds and asked her to come along to the chief's office for a short meeting. Larisa had been awake for all but three hours since the previous afternoon. She'd lost count of the coffees she'd ordered. This made her distant from her environment, as though she was watching herself agreeing and walking with Dr. Bade, while some other part of her scrambled to anticipate what the meeting would be about. Hopefully, it was about Kara, who was still absent from her court-mandated therapy.

In the dim hours of that morning, as her shift ended, Larisa had started checking police reports to see if the entire family had died in a car accident. She couldn't think what else would cause this sudden silence.

The chief had grown older since the last time Larisa had seen him. It couldn't have been more than a few weeks, but his usually tan skin had gone a little grey. The age jowls along his jaw were more pronounced. She looked at him and thought, *I hate you.* And was surprised to feel no regret.

"So, Larisa . . . we need to talk."

"Yes, sir?"

"I've begun to feel you're unhappy here."

"Of course not," said Larisa too quickly. "Why do you think that?"

"Perhaps you think our patients are below your talents."

Larisa's cheeks flamed. "No." She sucked in a breath to pause before she said something wrong. She looked to Dr. Bade. "What's this about? I'm making all my commitments. Last night was the first time I've ever been late. It was an emergency."

Dr. Bade looked to the chief and gave a subtle shake of her head. "I told you she didn't know. Larisa is one of our best."

"I don't know what?"

"We've had a request to move you to a special assignment for the rest of your rotation."

"What? Why? Who?"

"Enterprise Studios would like you on set as their mental health consultant."

Oh no. No. No.

"I didn't ask for that."

"Still, it presents a problem," said Dr. Bade. "The studio representative doesn't want anyone but you. And refusing could expose us to public inquiry."

Larisa read between the lines. "You want me to do this because I'm already compromised by Quinn VanderVeer being my patient." She drew a breath. *Calm. Calm.* "I assume resident interns don't usually have special assignments like this?"

The fatigue lines on the chief's face deepened. "No. But you'll make what you can of it, won't you?"

Larisa's stomach churned with coffee acid and fraying nerves. "I will."

"Good. You're still expected to serve weekend shifts on the third floor. Sunday nights will be added to compensate for the weekends you are missing for . . . personal reasons in April—"

Tears burned her eyes. "My best friend's wedding," said Larisa, as though this could possibly be a reasonable excuse to a Chief of Psychiatry.

"You'll have no further contact with your outpatient clients, and you'll explain to Sophie and Myhanh why they are now writing an NIH grant alone. Send daily activity reports to Dr. Bade. That is all."

Larisa fled the room. The faculty bathroom was too close to be a safe refuge. Someone who knew her would overhear, so she ran down two escalators, down a flight of fire exit stairs, and out to the parking lot. The sobs came before she reached her Bentley. The tears that came with them refused to be suppressed. She cried and cried, her thoughts piling on top of one another, each freeing a fresh surge.

It's over. They'll never respect me now. I'm being banished because they don't trust me.

Her phone began ringing. Larisa forced herself to answer.

"Hi, Mom. What's up?"

"Why are you ignoring me?"

"I didn't know I was."

"Your father wants a movie night. Come Saturday?"

"I can't Saturday." Larisa's tears melted away as she remembered her weekend plans. "Can we wait until next week? I have a date."

"Try not to make the front page this time."

Chapter 14

Make Me Worthy

Quinn couldn't remember the last time he'd felt settled in his own skin. Every waking moment, if people weren't coming to attack him, his mind did it alone, the doubts building as he failed over and over to maintain control.

To achieve.

To be the person he wanted. (Was that even possible?)

The movie would fail.

Eddie hated him.

Dansby hated him.

Parish calling and crying on the phone. Parish yelling at him. Parish and her unending text messages, like a thousand cuts slicing away his skin.

But as he knelt on the floor of Club D's Purple Room, he felt the first inkling of peace. The Queen wore her usual costume, plus a tall velvet collar around her neck. During their first session, he'd spent most of the time with his eyes down, afraid of angering her. Now, he took in her solid body, so compressed within the corset that her breasts rose up and rested at the top. Wide shoulders. An even wider stance as she stood looking down at him with the most thrilling derision.

"You're so beautiful," he whispered.

She slapped him across the face with a riding crop. "You haven't earned that yet."

That voice thrilled him. Energy surged through his body so he could barely keep his pose. He lowered his eyes and waited, his breath stammering in excited puffs of damp air.

"Get on your feet. You can't earn anything worth having hunched up and hiding yourself. Or are you a coward?"

Quinn got to his feet, unable to stop from sneaking a glance. She saw him looking. Another strike at his face. Fire licked across his cheek.

"It's clear you can't be trusted."

She stalked to the side wall where the toys were kept. He covertly soaked up all the details he hadn't been able to see at their last meeting. Athletic legs. As tall as he was. Hips that moved like they owned the world.

"Eyes down!" She came back to him with a blindfold and leather cuffs that attached to the suspension chain hanging from the ceiling. She didn't ask permission before shuttering his eyes, locking his wrists in the cuffs, then attaching them to the chain so his hands hung above his head with just enough tension that when she struck his stomach, he could only lurch forward a few inches before the chains stopped him.

"So, tell me." She trailed the crop down to his groin. "How bad have you been this week?"

"Worse than bad," he whispered.

"I can't hear you."

"Worse than bad."

"You failed?"

"More often than I can count."

"You're a worthless waste of your mother's precious life."

Quinn shuddered as she struck the fronts of his thighs. "Yes."

"This little crop isn't going to be enough to wipe that out."

He listened to her boots knock against the floor as she again went to the wall, then returned. She seemed to stop in front of him just looking, waiting. His groin tightened as blood rushed between his legs.

"I see you," she said. "I'm not impressed. I might leave you here and find someone better."

"No!" He surged against the chains. "Don't leave. I'll do better. I'm sorry."

"You expect me to fuck you."

"I don't. I'm sorry."

Silence. He brought his left leg up, turning to the side to try and hide his growing erection.

"Stop that." Some object whistled through the air and slammed into his right hip nearly knocking him over.

He gasped as tears of pain burned his eyes. The fire flamed through his side, all-consuming, sweet, and pure. Deserved.

A second and third blow, in quick succession, sent delicious panicky signals through his nerves all along his waist. She was hitting him as though the rules of civility, the fear of hurting a stranger, were little rules that constrained little people.

"If you survive this," she said, "I will fuck you. But you have to earn it. I don't give sympathy fucks to pathetic failures who can't manage their own lives."

"What counts as survival?" he asked.

"You outlast my arm. If you tell me to stop before I'm done, you fail yet again."

He swallowed. "Make me worthy."

The words barely left his mouth before the beating began in earnest. The blows she'd initially given him were nothing compared to the force that rained down on his defenseless body. She started with his back, his shoulders, ass, and thighs. When she'd covered him in fire, she returned to places she'd already struck. It felt like the skin was being scoured from his back. He cried out. And when she paused, the stillness brought tears of relief to his eyes.

"Give up."

It was a question as much as a command.

"Make me worthy," he gasped.

And it began again, his chest this time. The Queen worked her way down until her tool pounded against his thighs, bare inches away from striking his groin. She never did. Each blow fell precisely where she intended. He knew she was tiring when the blows began to slide sideways rather than land directly.

She stood still. Their mutually labored breathing filled the room. Quinn's body throbbed like a strobing light, flaring back and forth with his pulse. His mind was empty of everything else, blissfully free. So very alive.

"I admit I'm impressed," she said. "Very few people can withstand that beating."

Her boots tapped forward. He felt the shift of cool air against his burning skin that told him she was right in front of him. Her finger stroked the line of his lips.

"These are nice."

"Let me please you with them."

She removed the blindfold. He blinked in the sudden rush of light. His eyes were level with her mouth and just below her blacked-out eyes.

Who are you?

She released his wrists with surprising tenderness. For a moment she held his hands in hers and examined his wrists and fingers. "You're trembling."

"I haven't eaten today."

She clucked her tongue. "I expect you to come better prepared next time." She led him over to a padded bench in the far corner of the room. "Lie down."

The pain, as his burning skin met the latex surface, made him moan in agony. As he settled himself into position on his back, he realized how much more exposed he was lying down spread before her than he'd ever been kneeling or standing. He tried to relax. The pain became a pleasant ambient heat at his back, secondary to his heightened awareness of the movement of his chest and the way her eyes on him felt like a caress.

The Queen did not waste time asking if he was okay. She slid out of her hot pants, tore open a condom, and mounted him. He gasped as her thighs enclosed his hips.

"You have earned the right to touch me," she said.

He looked up at her. Were her eyes blue or grey? He held her gaze as he grasped his erection, rolled the condom down, and massaged his head around her clit.

"Hmm," she purred. "Good choice. You might not be as pathetic as I thought."

He set his free hand on her waist expecting any moment she would brush him away. They began to move together. When he felt her softening with pleasure, he entered her.

"Tell me what to do," he said as she rocked against him.

"You don't need instructions."

His first instinct was to challenge her. No woman he'd been with ever seemed satisfied. But as he felt her tightening around him and the wet rush of her pleasure, he stopped worrying. She didn't owe him anything; she'd take what she wanted. And so she did.

"When can I see you again?" he asked later.

"You'll be contacted by the club if I'm interested, same as before."

If. The word rang in his ears.

"Do better by yourself," she said. "You're worth it." Then she walked out the door.

Boi George had returned to the ward after a two-week absence.

When she'd first started this rotation, Larisa had thought returnees were a sign of treatment failure. Now she knew better. The possibilities for failure were much wider than what she, as a doctor, had failed to do when a patient came under her care. In the case of Boi George, a fellow resident of the cardboard and plastic village downtown had stolen his meds and Boi George's otherwise controlled schizophrenia had taken charge of his mind.

It was easier for Larisa to sit with Boi George, who was zoned out on a high dose of Olanzapine, than to try and talk to Sophie about her reassignment to the studio. The TV in the patient lounge played a rerun of *The Late Show,* where an actor she'd met at a party once was teaching David Letterman the two-step shimmy he'd used in his upcoming film.

"You smell like seeeeeezzzzzz," said Boi George.

"Does it bother you?"

"Hmmm. Details."

"Can't tell you that. I'm your doctor."

"You're glowing. *Love* and Sezzz?"

"What is love?"

"Hmmm."

"I just feel full," Larisa said, patting her stomach. "Satisfied. I did something good."

"Hmmm. Like him?" Boi George pointed to the TV.

Larisa considered the actor, his gregarious grin, smooth moves, warm charm that even came with a secret twinkle in his eye. She'd met so many men like that, who were able to turn it on for the cameras. She thought of Quinn shuddering below her as he came, the relief of spent energy, of peace finally descending. Even then, he remained distant, locked within himself like a cold moon.

"Not like him," said Larisa. "A gas giant with a secret world hidden beneath his clouds. A man who withholds his smile like a precious gem."

On Set

After Club D, Quinn went home thinking he would watch a movie until he fell asleep. But somewhere between his car and the front door, the thought of his usual routine became a burden. Instead, he laid down in the driveway and stared up at the sky. He marveled at the passage of his breath through his lungs, of his still throbbing skin burning even hotter against the sun-warmed pavement.

His mind wandered from stars to silhouetted trees to insects around the lamppost, and, for the first time in months, he encountered no triggering thoughts. As though the Queen's tool was a magic wand; they had been whisked away and all that remained was delicious, tantalizing possibility. He felt safe and whole. The tension he'd carried in his efforts to control his temper was gone. Suddenly, he had hands and feet and a beating heart swelling within his chest.

When Parish began sending her messages, he read them without fear. He even felt able to respond.

Quinn: I'm sorry I couldn't do better. You deserve to be happy.

Parish: I can't live without you. I think you've ruined me.

Quinn: That's not true. It'll get easier. You're beautiful. You'll find your way.

Quinn: I'm glad you're going to be in the
movie.

Parish: Are you really?

At some point he fell asleep there, splayed out in the middle ground between his car and front walk. In the twilight of sleep's descent, he imagined the Queen finding him there and not thinking it strange. He would unzip her boots with his teeth and trace the lines of her muscles with his tongue.

He woke to a morning chorus of birds and the first ribbon of rising light, cement damp with dew, and a wondrous ache from his shoulders to his knees.

He messaged Doan at The club.

Quinn: Please tell the Queen, 'Thank you for
last night. When will you allow me to soil your
presence once again?'

The word soil became disgrace, then switched back to soil. Neither quite fit how he felt—honored, satiated. He'd crossed a line between needing and wanting he hadn't realized existed. To see her again, if only to lie in her arms, would be enough. He'd surrendered fully to her will and she'd taken him in, held him in safety so that now he could stand alone without shame.

On Monday morning, Quinn arrived on set early. He visited Vince in his trailer, thanking him for doing the film and saying all the things he knew Vince probably already knew about his personal brand of greatness. Then Quinn walked on set and worked his way through the crew as they were setting up for the first shot.

He knew he didn't have the ease with people other directors did, but he considered himself well-spoken, and today, bolstered by the ache in his body and the Queen's voice in his head telling him to do better with himself, it didn't feel like it cost him anything to make eye contact and exchange a few words with the people who had previously felt like a demonic army set to ruin him.

When Quinn approached Lane, the man started back as though expecting to be struck.

"I have an idea in my head," said Quinn, "but I'm not sure how to shoot it."

"Really?" Lane still looked wary. Quinn had not once been unsure how he wanted a scene shot.

"You did something similar in *The Red Scarf*, when the girl climbs into the taxi."

Lane's eyes narrowed. "You're thinking about the scene when Sam leaves the general's for the first time."

"Maybe we could talk it through tonight?"

"I'll think about it."

Which was all Quinn could hope for. He combed through his actions over the past few weeks to find something he should apologize for. But, in this case at least, Lane had always been the instigator. Quinn didn't feel he'd done anything unworthy.

Dansby arrived on set in the phase one version of the costume that would gradually deteriorate over the course of the week's shooting. When he saw Quinn, he stilled. For once, the winning smile was absent from his handsome face.

Quinn pressed two fingers into the top of his right thigh, exacerbating the pain of his bruised muscle. "How was your weekend?"

"I watched some of the old movies you recommended."

"What did you think?"

"I think they're all better actors than I am."

"I think you can do it."

"That's nice of you to say." His eyes shifted to the set, a series of carefully lit dingy hallways and a larger room, where he'd spend the day being dragged by Russian soldiers, fighting back, then escaping to run back through those hallways before being recaptured.

"We'll do it together," said Quinn.

"I'm just a little scared, you know?"

"Good," said Quinn gently. "Use it."

The choreographer and stunt coordinator had finished their meeting with lighting and were ready for rehearsal. Dansby moved to his mark. Quinn watched him go, feeling he should have said more, or perhaps apologized again for Thursday. *But if it works . .* .

Tish sidled up to him. "You're in a good mood today."

"Thanks."

"Eddie is stranded at the gate having a fight with some woman, FYI. He'll most likely be late."

"Wife?"

"Leggy redhead. Too young for him if you ask me. But then, you men never do ask." She blinked accusing eyes at him, then moved on. "Half the litter adopted this weekend. My house feels so empty." Tish held up her phone and scrolled through images of three fluffy Persian kittens.

"They're cute."

Tish beamed. "I like this version of you. Is he going to stick around for the rest of production?"

"No promises. Can I give you a special project today?"

"I'd be honored," she laughed, partly mocking him, but not in a mean way.

"Keep everyone away from Dansby between takes. If he tries to do his usual thing, pull him aside, give him notes."

"You want *me* to give him notes?"

"I trust you."

"You *trust* me."

"Am I being unclear?"

"You want him to sit with his discomfort. I can do that." She paused. "At the risk of ruining this miraculously good mood, I feel the need to point out you should've given him a minder on day one."

"Thank you."

She gave him a long look, like she couldn't quite believe what she was seeing. Then she crossed the stage to take Dansby's chair and drag it over to a corner. She pulled her chair up next to it.

Quinn began his pre-shoot inventory while watching rehearsal out the corner of his eye. Normally, he'd have been at the edge of the stage overseeing the process, but there'd been a lengthy meeting with the team on Friday. Everyone knew what he wanted. And if there was some deviation from what he saw in his head, it might be okay.

A daring thought. Something he couldn't have entertained the week before. Now, it felt safe to relax his grip and let some things come naturally. Instead of one straight line, he saw a richness of possibilities growing from the diverse perspectives of his cast and crew.

I'm doing it, he thought. *We're doing it.*

Then Eddie arrived, and with him, "the leggy redhead," who was in fact Dr Larisa de France-Kahn. Quinn had never noticed her hair was more red than brown. *What the fuck is she doing here?* He felt something solid dropping through him, a bullet with pieces of shrapnel breaking off, stabbing his throat, his chest, his gut. Heat burned his face. The feeling of peace and possibility that had felt so secure moments before, dissolved into that old skin, crawling with the awareness of dozens of eyes seeing too much.

She told Eddie what happened.

I'm going to be supervised on my own fucking set.

He couldn't look at her, so he looked at Eddie. "What's going on, Eddie?"

"I've hired Larisa as our mental health consultant."

"Have you?"

"He's *suggesting* it," said Larisa, a sharp correction in her voice. "I told him this is your set. Ultimately, it's your decision."

"It's the right one," said Eddie. "We're doing heavy lifting this week."

Quinn struggled to unclench his jaw enough so he could speak naturally. "Eddie always has good ideas."

"See? He's fine with it." Eddie directed Larisa away from Quinn. "So, you know how this goes. We'll get you a chair. I'll introduce you to everyone and say you're available for short check-ins, and they can also schedule formal sessions during breaks. Have you met Dansby yet? He's got a lot going on today."

Quinn watched Eddie walk her over to meet Tish.

That woman in his space, talking to the crew.

That woman who knew too much.

Shooting went well, but Quinn barely noticed. Even when the camera was rolling, he found himself glancing her direction, convinced she was watching him. When one of his people approached her to introduce themselves, his stomach clenched with dread. *What would they say about him?* he worried, even though it seemed like most of the interactions were less about her work and more about her life. He saw her sign a few autographs. And more than once, he heard that strained, bright pitch in her voice as she found something to say in response to an over-wrought compliment.

By lunch, Quinn had regressed into the half-numb throbbing ball of tension he'd been before Saturday night. As soon as Tish called the break, he fled the soundstage, crossed the lot, and hurried past reception in the administrative building to hide in his office.

Larisa followed him.

"Quinn. Hold up."

She said his name like they knew each other. How many people had heard her, and were now coming to the obvious conclusion he was her patient? He tried to close his office door before she caught him.

"Can I eat with you?"

"I don't eat with other people." Even this felt like too much, like he'd just given her another weapon to use against him. Now she was wondering what he was hiding. Why didn't he eat with other people? Did he have an eating disorder?

Fuck.

"Then I won't stay long. I just wanted to apologize for showing up like this. It appears Dansby was impressed with my impromptu session Thursday. He asked Eddie to bring me on board." She paused. "He seemed pretty good today."

All Quinn could do was nod. She was standing in his office talking about Thursday like it had been nothing.

"I'd like to finish out our two remaining sessions even though I'm not in clinic anymore." Again, she paused. There'd been a tremor in her voice, something bitter.

She doesn't want to be here, he thought.

"My schedule is pretty flexible, since I'm here all day now. We can do before or after shooting. Or lunches."

"I'm not comfortable continuing," he said.

"What could we change that might make you comfortable?"

Quinn shook his head. As he did, he felt the twinge of tender muscle left over from the Queen's paddle. He closed his eyes. *Do better by yourself. You're worth it.*

Armed with these words, he squared his shoulders and made eye contact.

"Your presence here undermines my authority over my crew. Eddie is using you to control me."

"I recognize that."

"So, why the fuck would I want to continue private sessions when I know you'll be carrying everything I say back to the set?"

"That's a legitimate concern."

"I don't need you to tell me it's a fucking legitimate concern," he hissed. "Stop with the mind games. I can't trust you. Do you see that?"

"Quinn, I'm not going to have you committed."

"Not yet."

"Not until you commit an actual crime."

"But I—"

"You were trying to help him. You took great care not to hurt him and I know you wouldn't have done it if you'd seen any other option."

Quinn wasn't so sure that was true, but he kept his mouth shut.

"May I offer an observation?"

Please just leave.

"The expectation of betrayal is a learned response."

"I told you I had a great childhood."

"Maybe we don't need to go back that far. Eddie often makes choices that reflect a lack of respect, doesn't he? He's tried to intervene with your actors behind your back. He forced you to come see me or lose your job. And now he's brought me onto set without even telling you ahead of time. It's entirely reasonable for you to feel unsafe here.

"But unlike your crew, I'm not beholden to Eddie for references or future work. I can't talk to anyone about you. And I can't talk to you about anyone else who comes to me for help."

But you'll see, he thought. *You'll know what a fucking disaster I am.*

"If we were going to finish our sessions, we might think about how to manage Eddie," she said.

"What do you mean?"

"Has he always treated you like this?"

"Just since the filming started." Quinn stopped. "Since Parish."

"Maybe he's projecting some personal animosity into the professional arena? So, the first thing we could do is realize Eddie's behavior isn't entirely tied to your qualities as a director. Then we might think about what could be done to help him feel better about the personal situation."

"Don't you think if I knew what to do, I'd have tried it already?"

"Then let's come back to that on Thursday. What are you feeling right now?"

"Trapped," he answered without thinking.

"Why?"

"Because the shrink I never wanted is spying on my work." He glanced at her. She was smiling a white-tooth, slice-of-Julia-Roberts smile that seemed wholly detached from the conversation. "What?"

"I don't think you've ever given me an honest answer until now."

"I'm not a liar."

Her smile deepened. "You're in movies, Quinn. It's your job to weave deceptions that somehow reveal the truth we hide within ourselves."

"That's a romantic way to think about it." He finally managed to pull his gaze away from her mouth. "You're also in the business of revealing hidden truths."

"I was. But, for the moment, it seems I'll be busy buffering the fragile egos of your cast and crew. Present company excluded of course." Her eyes narrowed, toying with him. "You don't need me."

He should have felt the barb of her too keen knowing. Instead, his mind had snagged on her use of the past tense, the line she drew between what she considered her true work and what she'd be doing on set. Maybe she felt as trapped as he did.

"It's not fair Eddie stole you from your patients," Quinn paused. "But even though we're less in need, it doesn't make your work less valuable. Just because I hate the fact of your existence doesn't mean I can't see that you're helping. You'd have helped more if I'd let you."

"Maybe we can call a truce." She held out her hand to shake.

A shiver went through him as he took it. Their first physical contact, a threshold crossed. Larisa did not touch her patients. Did this mean she no longer thought of him as one?

"Don't think I haven't noticed you tricked me into a session."

She smiled a smaller version of the smile from before. "Guilty. But it needed to be done. Sometimes I work for my patients even when they won't work for themselves. We could just meet casually at the end of the day Thursday and see what happens. If you want to talk, we can. If not, maybe we'll talk about that offer you made to be my date."

"You're considering it?"

"Was it a real offer?"

"I'll do it if you'll have me. I'm not the most socially adept—"

She moved towards the door, taking her smile with her. "I'll have my lawyer send a contract to Sid. We'll negotiate on Thursday, unless you decide you're going to remain my patient."

After the door closed behind her, Quinn waited to see if it would open again. If it had, he might have apologized for his cruelty in their earlier sessions. But then he thought, she'd seen through all that. She'd been so gentle with him. She always had been. All he'd done was attack her.

But we're starting over. I can do better.

I will do better.

Chapter 16

Strategic Deceptions

"I'm going to send Eddie Sacks a gift," declared Suzette, as she served dinner at the small patio table on the veranda of the estate's family wing.

"You will not send Eddie a gift," said Larisa. "Eddie is a selfish, self-important, ass-covering prick. No offence, Dad."

Gunter waved a dismissive hand through the air. "He hasn't been the same since Kim left him."

"The best spouses do so well at smoothing each other's rough edges," hinted Suzette.

"Not tonight, Mom. We're having a nice dinner. Dad and I are going to watch a movie while you fall asleep pretending to be interested. I'm happy single." Larisa made the mistake of looking toward her father as she said this. He gave her a knowing look.

"I think Prince Hasan would give you a second try," said Suzette. "I hear he's been talking about what a great find you are."

"I'm sure he's not. Anyway, I'm thinking about someone else."

"Really!" Suzette leaned in like one of Larisa's sorority sisters, eyes as wide as her ears.

"I'll tell you if anything comes of it." Larisa tried to laugh. Really, she wished her mother was capable of being as happy for her on her own than she was at the prospect of a partner. But it also felt good to be able to finally offer this. To know her mother's concern came from her own fears of being an aging woman alone in the world, and what it meant not just socially, but for her heart. Larisa wished the game of social acceptance and the game of hearts were more compatible.

Later, as her mother dozed in a recliner in the home theater, which was in the family wing and much cozier than the entertaining theater in the main part of the house, Gunter turned down the volume on a film they'd both seen over a dozen times and cleared his throat.

Unlike most people who cleared their throat as a prelude to speaking their mind, Gunter cleared his throat as a way of clearing space in the air, the way an emcee clears the way for a featured speaker, then cedes the microphone to them.

Larisa was nestled under a blanket, an assortment of finger toys on her lap, which she fidgeted with during the film so her mind would be less likely to wander. Despite her father's best efforts, watching movies remained a hobbyist's activity for Larisa. The process of viewing, especially a film she'd seen often, didn't fully engage her when she had so many other things to think about.

"It feels like everyone resents me at the hospital. They think I asked to work on the movie." She twisted a plastic, jointed snake around her pointer finger, unwound it, wound it again. "I was already on the outside and now these people who I've been trying so hard to be friends with have shunned me like a pariah."

"Hmm."

"Did you mean it when you said you didn't want me to end up with someone in the industry?"

"When did I say that?"

"At brunch last month."

"This new prospect is on your movie?"

Larisa exchanged the plastic snake for a rubber pufferfish that had come from a project Gunter had done in Japan when she'd been in elementary school. When she squeezed the head, the body inflated and the spines puffed out.

"Do you know what you don't have that many other people have in abundance?" he asked.

"I don't think I'll like where this is going?"

"Bad decisions."

"Ha."

"It's true. Tell me one thing you've done that you regret."

"Everything." Larisa cupped her right palm over the pufferfish body and stabbed herself with the spines over and over. "Okay, maybe nothing big, the fact of my existence. Trusting Lucas not to sell our life to EW for fifty grand? Trust is always a beggar's bargain between villains. Is that my problem? I'm not human enough to be normal. Even when I'm reckless, things mostly work out."

"Whatever you see in this person, I would trust that. And maybe remind yourself they don't need to be a husband. They can just be a tasty treat."

Larisa smacked the fish against her father's shoulder. "Don't ever say that again."

He chuckled from deep in his throat.

"Can I ask you a professional question?"

"Hmhmm."

"If your director broke up with a producer's niece after a possibly abusive relationship, what would you do to keep production going?"

"Keep the producer off the set."

"What if that isn't an option?"

"Make the girl happy. If she's happy, the producer will be happy."

"I'm trying to set her up with Greg, the hedge fund manager."

"Strange world you live in."

"You have no idea. Mind if I take this?" She inflated the fish spines into his face.

"It's yours, isn't it?"

"Don't tell Mom I might be serious about my person. It's not going to lead anywhere."

"You never know."

Larisa thought of Quinn glaring at her Monday afternoon. That jaw working, those shoulders practically trembling with the strain of keeping his turmoil internal. He'd been insulting and strangely beautiful. It had been a challenge not to reach out and wrap her arms around him. That's really what he'd needed. Whatever idyllic childhood he'd had, it hadn't involved comforting touch. It hadn't involved gentleness, or consideration, or patience. He walked through the world in a default defensive mode, braced for any attack. He trusted himself in that world even less than he trusted others.

What kind of boyfriend would he be?

Certainly not mother approved. Her friends would probably find him off-putting and rude. And, of course, there was the problem of her alter ego banging him at Club D. But maybe that wouldn't end up mattering. He might not need the Queen if Dr. Larisa could teach him how to be comfortable with himself.

That would never happen if Eddie kept attacking him and inciting other people to attack him. Larisa had been on set for three days. It was no longer a mystery why Quinn tended to scream at people who made small mistakes. Tuesday, the continuity manager had missed Dansby's prop wristwatch. Today, an assistant had brought Quinn caffeinated black tea instead of herbal. When Quinn exploded, shockwaves of bad energy rippled through the set. Crew members traded knowing looks. She'd seen more than one eye roll and disparaging shaking of heads. She'd seen Eddie, going around exchanging covert whispers with those same people. The DP challenged everything Quinn said, and sometimes he outright did something else and forced Quinn to either accept the shot, or waste time doing it again.

Quinn's not a monster, she thought. *But he thinks he is.*

Larisa came early to the set Thursday morning and met with Frances, a key grip struggling with anxiety, a condition the tension on set had exacerbated. After Frances, Larisa made herself available as people began populating the set. Some conversations were casual, as though she was just another coworker. Others were more serious. A best boy who'd made a mistake the day before came to her in near tears; he was afraid of being fired if something happened again. Mostly, she listened. She told people their best work came from themselves; everyone made mistakes.

The scene of the day involved Dansby being stripped down to his boxers and restrained in a chair by the Russian hitmen who worked for the general. She'd noticed that even though the footage had been good enough on Monday, the actors playing the hitmen, with a few exceptions, lacked conviction. Which was fair, as it could be difficult to get into the mind space of hitmen, mass murderers, and sadists. (Well, not necessarily the last one for some people.)

But what could be easily overlooked in the fast-paced hallway shots of Monday would be more obvious today. She watched Quinn arrive, a stiff column of skin and bone, in his ever-present beanie. Tish had confided in Larisa that Quinn had been outright cheerful on Monday morning before her arrival. Now that she'd seen that side of him, she kept wanting to see it again. Larisa had caught herself before apologizing for being the ruinous catalyst. Too much honesty opened up liability. She had to be a professional even if it meant being alone, absorbing all the competing conflicts, and prioritizing them over her own comfort.

Now, as Quinn went through his morning routine, she debated how to approach him about the hitmen so he wouldn't feel attacked. When Quinn left his conversation with the lighting tech to watch rehearsals with the stunt coordinator, she made her move.

"Morning."

He nodded acknowledgement.

"I thought you might say a few words to the hitmen before we start today."

"What words?"

"Mind games."

He slanted his eyes at her.

"For instance: What do they most fear happening that they might kill to prevent? What do they believe about themselves and their country that might lead them to do things they couldn't usually do? To be a hitman is to be above questions of good and evil. It's about loyalty, and patriotism, and money. I think they're trying to imagine themselves as Russian hitmen and they feel alien from that. So, if you could give them something to channel from something they know . . ."

"I'll think about it."

"Great."

"What about Dansby?" he asked.

"What about him?"

Quinn lasered his eyes at the poor innocent dolly track and gritted his teeth as he said, "Do you have thoughts on guiding him?"

Larisa resisted the temptation to tease him. *Was the great Quinn VanderVeer asking for her advice on his work?* She looked over at Dansby, who was listening closely to the stunt coordinator describe the sequence of moves the hitmen would follow.

"Acting is reacting, isn't it? What would he do if the hitmen go off script?"

They both watched Dansby joke punch one of the hitmen and derail the choreography. She felt Quinn studying her. *There's no way he recognizes you as the Queen. Relax.*

"Take Dansby outside for five minutes," said Quinn.

"Not six?" she asked. Serious people were so easy to tease.

Quinn pointed to his watch. "Four minutes and fifty seconds. Go."

"Hey, Dansby." Larisa motioned for him to follow her as she jogged toward the stage door.

"We're starting in six," said Tish.

Larisa gave her a thumbs up, then pushed open the door so Dansby could follow her outside. The air was cool and damp with the promise of rain. Spring had come, and with it the magnolias, wisteria, and orange blossoms.

"Hey, Doc. What's going on?"

"Just thought we should check in with each other before the day starts. How are you feeling?"

"Good, I think. I mean, I always feel good until it starts." He laughed. "I'm more worried about tomorrow. My big breakdown scene starts."

"I bet you'll be fine."

"I'd like to be better than fine. When I signed on for this, I thought it'd be fun. I didn't realize there was so much . . ."

"Acting?" asked Larisa with a smile.

"Yeah."

"Well, today comes first. How does Sam feel about these guys?"

"He's scared of them."

"Scared is kind of obvious, though, isn't it? What else can you use from Thursday?"

"The layers I told you about before?"

"Yes, definitely. We go through stages of fear, and they all look different. What else?"

Dansby raked his hand through his hair.

"Maybe it isn't about the guys," said Larisa. "Maybe it's about the general. You want to explain yourself to him. Or maybe you've been thinking about changing sides? On Thursday, didn't you spend a lot of time thinking about what you would say to Quinn if you could just see him for a few minutes?"

"But that's not in the script."

"Doesn't have to be. You just need to have a good reason to fight against those men. Once they get you in that chair, game over."

"It's already game over."

"Maybe Sam knows that in the back of his head, but he doesn't know it here." She tapped his heart. "In real life, we're lost-cause fighters." She checked the time. "And do yourself a favor today, stop joking with the guys who are your enemies, okay? It makes everything harder."

They went back inside. She came to a stop beside Quinn, where he stood near the camera and watched Dansby walk to his mark. No winning smile. No jokes. He didn't look at Quinn. He didn't look at the hitmen.

"Take it a little wider than we planned," said Quinn to the camera operator. "And when they move to the chair, drop down so you're looking up from the floor when he's sitting."

The camera operator glanced to his right to check in with the Lane the DP, who shrugged. Not a great sign of support, but not an overt challenge. Quinn walked over to camera two, which was tasked with following Dansby.

"Even if you can't see him, keep rolling," said Quinn to the second camera operator. He signaled Tish.

"Ready on set!" called Tish.

The clapper sounded. The hitmen descended on Dansby like a pack of starving wolves. His panicked scream was cut off by what Larisa was sure was a real blow to his solar plexus from an actor who had played college football. With Dansby's struggle weakened by pain, a hitman took Dansby's feet, another his hands. In tandem, they pulled off his clothes, including the boxers he was supposed to keep on, shoved him into the waiting chair, and bound him.

Panting breaths filled the set, interrupted only by Dansby's raspy squeaking, and then the heavy footfalls of the Russian general's boots. Ominous. Meditative.

Perfect, thought Larisa.

The hitmen fell away as the Aussie actor, Sal Peffer, strode up to the chair, leaned down, and stroked a gloved finger along Dansby's jaw. In the corner of her eye, Larisa saw Camera Two change angles to center Dansby's face in frame. Camera one was wide enough to catch the way Dansby quivered at the touch in a way that could be seen as either desire or fear, or perhaps both.

"Such a shame to waste a pretty thing like you." Sal leaned in further, inhaled the scent of Dansby's hair as though for the last time, then he stepped back. "But I cannot share you with another lover. You will stay here, and we will see who comes for you."

Dansby didn't move. He was supposed to look up and deliver his line, instead his legs pulled against the restraints trying to cover his penis, which was thickening.

You should call cut, Quinn, thought Larisa.

Long moments of Dansby's shaking shoulders. Sal looking down at Dansby, holding character. Finally, Dansby tilted his head up, met Sal's gaze, then slanted his expression into one he'd probably shown Quinn at The Golden Lily, seduction tinged with desperation. Because Sam wanted to do his job no matter how unqualified he was, no matter that his country planned to use him, then disown him without a thought.

"I could have loved you," said Dansby as Sam.

Quinn let the cameras continue to linger. Dansby looked like he was going to cry. If that happened, Quinn wanted to get it on film. But no. Dansby only held on for a few more moments before he popped the prop restraints free and yanked his discarded shirt up onto his lap.

"Cut!" called Quinn.

In a moment, Eddie was at his side. "What the fuck happened to the choreography?"

Quinn stepped around him to intercept Tish on her way to comfort Dansby. "He's fine."

"We don't have full nudity in his contract," said Eddie, hounding him.

Larisa inserted herself between them. "Hey Eddie. Come sit with me."

"Reset for second take!" called Quinn.

"He needs a break," said Tish.

"He doesn't."

Both Eddie and Tish looked at Larisa as though she was the higher authority. When she refused to say anything, Quinn turned to Lane. "Any blocking problems?"

"Not that I saw."

"Be ready this time. Places!"

They ran the scene again. Not as vibrant as the first time. The hitmen were amped up, starting to get antsy in their heads about what had happened and how they felt about it. But now they also had a taste for it. They weren't as sloppy. They pulled in some of the stunt choreography, left Danby's boxers on. Dansby's diction gained clarity, a little more seduction than fear.

When Quinn called the end of the day, he waved off Eddie wanting a meeting and escaped to his office. Larisa hung around set chatting. In Quinn's absence, the cast and crew relaxed enough to throw jokes back and forth, to chat about sports, the hot actress filming on lot nine, and a band coming to town on their world tour. Tish circulated with her kitten pictures, and no one, not even the burly teamsters could resist a few minutes of cooing over them.

Dansby invited Larisa to walk with him to his trailer.

"That was a day," he said, relief mixed into his laugh.

"It was," agreed Larisa.

"Do you think I did okay?"

"You did great."

"Quinn doesn't think so. I got stiff there at the end. I was tired."

"You're off the clock. Let's not worry about Quinn. How do you feel?"

"Besides tired? Good, I think. I mean, I felt things. That's good, right? Get into the character's head?"

Larisa nodded, careful with her words as she said, "Do you feel safe?"

"Of course."

"And how do you feel about coming to work tomorrow?"

His eyes widened. "Terrified."

"What can we do to help you be more comfortable?"

"Quinn thinks I shouldn't be comfortable."

Larisa gave him a look. He laughed, and an easy grin creased his face. "Will you walk me through it in the morning? And stay with me?"

"Of course."

Chapter 17

Session Six

Larisa was still thinking about Dansby when she walked through the studio offices and knocked on Quinn's door. Part of her worried he was hiding his true feelings from her. It was impossible to be a newcomer on a film set and feel empowered enough to express true feelings about the working environment or the process. But every time she spoke with him, she sensed nothing more complicated beneath Dansby's surface expressions. Besides completely normal anxiety about his performance, he seemed fine. This preoccupation was perhaps why Larisa thought she heard Quinn telling her to come in.

She opened the door and found him kneeling with his back to the door, his hands folded on his lap in the submissive position Charity had taught him at Club D. Another person might have thought he was meditating. In the end, Larisa supposed there wasn't much difference except the occupation of the mind. *Is he thinking about me?* she wondered. *Not me, the Queen.*

Larisa rapped on the doorframe. Quinn started as though from a trance, then unfolded himself upward until he was standing and turned to face her. For a moment, his face was marked with horror at being discovered, then he smoothed it into his usual cool distance.

"Do you want me to come back?" she asked.

"It's fine." He moved over to the couches where two documents and two pens sat on the coffee table. "I was just processing the day."

"Chopra calls meditation a metabolizing of our painful emotions so that our bodies can regulate."

"Metabolizing," he repeated. "Interesting."

She looked closer at the documents on the table. "You printed off our contract?"

"I like killing trees."

Larisa picked up one stack and flipped through it. "I sent you an eight-page document. This is almost twenty."

"You left some things out. But we can discuss that after the session."

Larisa looked up in surprise. His expression was unreadable. If anything, a little smug, as though he lived to surprise her. This was a power dynamic strategy, entirely reasonable given he'd been forced into therapy and seemed to live his life at a power deficit.

"Alright." She sat on one of the couches. He sat on a single chair directly opposite with the length of the coffee table between them. "I was impressed this morning with how you managed the first scene," she said. "I didn't expect you'd be open to my suggestions."

"They were good suggestions. I also told them Dansby planned to prank them by wearing multiple layers of clothing so it would be hard for them to undress him. They took it as a challenge." The smallest quirk of a self-satisfied smile.

"It doesn't bother you Dansby was terrified?"

"He didn't break character."

"He might not have felt he had a choice."

"What's that disease for someone who doesn't worry about other people's feelings?"

"I think you expect people to be as tough as you," she said. "Able to deal with whatever comes and adapt." She watched Quinn's expression still, his posture stiffening.

Instinctual defense, she thought. *Against what?*

"I don't usually diagnose people who've failed at therapy. It wouldn't be fair to you. I have an incomplete picture."

"You've seen more than enough," he said.

"But you've given me nothing willingly. My job isn't to judge you. It's to guide you. Which means the direction comes from you or nothing happens."

"What do you see?" His voice rose, so it sounded almost like a command instead of a question.

This isn't a good idea, Larisa. He'll lash out no matter what you say.

"When you're alone are you comfortable?"

"Alone in what way?"

"In your house when no other people are around. Do you feel peaceful?"

"Mostly. But sometimes it makes me restless. I'm more aware of how far I have to go."

"How so?"

"Materially. Career. Establishment."

She waited to see if he'd say more.

"I've answered your questions. You answer mine." He centered his eyes on her, unflinching, dark, dark blue. His lips drew together, making them seem larger than usual.

God help me, thought Larisa.

"Alright. But when I'm done, you have to promise not to say anything for two full minutes afterward."

"Fine."

Larisa hesitated. It would've been natural to take a breath, but she didn't want Quinn to feel she had to make some deep plunge into her mind to understand him. He wasn't as complicated as he thought.

"You've been the only one believing in yourself for a long time.," she said. "It's been so long you aren't able to believe other people when they see how capable you are. You expect them to pass judgement, so you sabotage yourself and it becomes a self-fulfilling prophecy. Nothing lives up to what you prescribe in your head. There's so much beauty in the world, but you've trained yourself to see it only in the scenes you've created. The people who should have loved you have failed you so completely that the only way you'll ever let another person in is when they tie you down and leave you no other choice but to trust them to treat your heart with care."

Her voice broke at the end as she pictured him at Club D, gazing up at the Queen with such hope in his eyes, so different than how he was with Dr. Larisa.

Quinn's gaze hadn't wavered. As though he'd been determined to stand up under the weight of her judgement, his expression remained glazed with chiseled determination until the very end. When her voice broke, his eyelids flickered against the force of her breath, tears welling, but not falling.

True to his promise, after she'd finished, he didn't speak. Quinn noted the time on his phone and then he sat, jaw working. The beautiful, fragile flickering in his eyelids holding back a tide. Nothing else moved. Even with the coffee table between them, she felt the battle within him. He wanted to flee. He wanted to come back at her with some cutting observation of his own that would diminish her power over him. But he remained, sitting silently with her words because he knew they were true.

The two minutes passed.

His posture shifted ever so slightly, a softening. Something like a sigh escaped from his chest. "If this was a movie, you would've said I crave enchantment but am trapped in a world of sloppy wizards."

"That's a much better line." Larisa smiled. It was pure agony staying on her side of the coffee table with him so desperately alone on the other side. "I believe we're about out of time. Any last thoughts?"

"I regret taking you away from people who want your help. Deep down under all your shrink professionalism, I think you must hate me."

"I don't hate you." Larisa felt she was very likely about to say something too close to how she really felt, so she broke eye contact, reaching for her bag. "In fact, I brought you a gift."

"Really."

Larisa leaned forward and set her Japanese pufferfish toy in the middle of the coffee table. "It's you in fish form."

Amusement lit Quinn's expression as he picked up the fish and examined it.

"Squeeze the body."

Quinn squeezed, then dropped the fish in surprise as the spines puffed out of the expanded torso.

"Ha." He laughed. "Very clever."

"I have my moments." Warmth stirred in her chest as the smile of his pleasure turned from the fish to her. It was not so much an expression in his mouth but in his eyes, the dark intensity surrendering to pure joy. It stole the breath from her lungs.

As though Quinn also felt it, he cleared his throat and said, "We should go through this contract before it gets too late. I assume you have better places to be."

Larisa thought of her empty apartment, the place that had been more storage container than residence since she'd moved in. She couldn't remember the last evening she passed at home.

"All I do at home is sleep."

The smile deepened.

"What?"

"You wouldn't have said that as my shrink."

"True."

"Now we can both be real people to each other."

Something fluttered through Larisa's chest, like the flicker of a match setting the air on fire inside her. *He doesn't mean what you think he means.* "Except of course, we're about to be actors in the romance of the year," she said quickly. "What did I leave out that warrants all these extra pages?"

"Details. And I've adjusted the fee structure. I don't want your money."

Larisa found the fees outline on page ten. It had previously been one paragraph of legalese with three figures reflecting payments Quinn would receive at the beginning, middle, and completion of the contract's obligations. In its place were two new paragraphs of entirely different legalese and no fee structure.

"You want me to buy you clothes instead?"

"And whatever else you think I need. I'm not doing this as a favor. Being associated with you will give me access to new people, new places. I want to learn how to look the part."

"So, when I find a real boyfriend, you'll be able to make your own way. I hadn't thought of that. You realize the first thing I'd tell you is the beanie has to go, right?"

"I like this beanie."

"Well, it looks like you hate your hair."

"Maybe I do." That smug smirk.

Toying with me. Larisa tried to breathe. *Can I really do this? I'm halfway in love with him already.* She focused on the contract. "We're going to a premiere?"

"Eddie wants me to go talk about the film at other films."

"Have you done a red carpet before?"

"Nope. But you have."

The rest of the changes included an impressive amount of detail, outlining physical contact expectations, gestures, and even a safe word (Penelope) either person could use to exit a situation. He wanted some kind of rehearsal/plan before every public appearance. Kissing would be restricted to hands and cheeks. Her heels could never be more than three inches. *Because then I'd be taller than him.*

"You thought of everything." She laughed, impressed and a little disturbed. *Did he manage his relationship with Parish like this?* The answer was probably yes. And she'd probably judged him for it, not understanding how much he needed to eliminate variables when he was out in public.

"Are you willing to meet my parents?" asked Larisa. "They'll expect it. I'm happy to meet yours also."

"That's not necessary."

Larisa thought of the parents he'd described, hardworking, purposeful, involved with their sons' lives. It surprised her Quinn wasn't the kind to bring girlfriends home. But then, if he was as ambitious as he seemed, maybe he didn't want fancy girlfriends like Parish seeing where he'd come from.

"Anyone going to be upset or try and interfere with this?" asked Larisa.

"Not on my end," said Quinn. "I'm not much of a catch."

"In that way, we're even." But Larisa couldn't help but wonder about Parish. Maybe what they'd shared hadn't been true love. But there were so many other ways people attached to each other. And if ever Larisa had seen an attached ex-girlfriend, it was Parish.

The next day she shifted back to life at the hospital. She felt set apart, her mind divided between the routine of the set (Dansby sent regular text updates), and her life as a resident, which suddenly felt irrelevant and overburdened with regulations and rules. No one here would appreciate what she'd manage to accomplish with Quinn.

On Monday, she had resented her reassignment. But now, it felt like she was part of the crew, supporting the film and their ability to do their jobs. Being away from them meant missing out on something vital. She couldn't help but notice Quinn at the center of this feeling. How was he managing his people? This was the day to shoot Dansby's big prison scene. What guidance would Quinn provide? Would Dansby rise to the occasion?

At five, as Larisa was on her way to crash Rosa and Krissy's regular happy hour at Cloud Nine, Dansby messaged the scene had been changed at the last minute. He'd spent the day doing pick-up shots. Monday, he'd be on location outside. Maybe the prison scene would be reslated for Tuesday, but there was no guarantee.

Larisa: This happens all the time. Don't take it personally.

Dansby: He doesn't think I'm ready.

Larisa: Find a way to prove it to him.

And then, because Larisa could imagine too many reasons Quinn had pushed back the prison scene, she messaged Doan, telling them she'd be at Club D on Saturday at four if Quinn wanted to meet her. Next, she messaged Quinn directly, asking if he had a spare hour on Sunday afternoon for their first official date as a fake couple.

It's not a big deal. Larisa pushed back a pang of guilt. *People lead double lives all the time. I'm at least doing it with the same man.*

"I can't believe you really came!" gushed Krissy.

"Cheers to the new job!" said Rosa.

Larisa held her smile in place. Yes, she wanted to be here. Yes, she was glad she now had more time for a social life. But no one seemed to realize she liked what she did at the hospital. Even as she settled in for her one-drink-then-water routine, she felt her mind already moving toward work, anticipating how the night would go. Would Kara make an appearance? Would Sophie speak to her or continue passing all work communication through Lucie as she had on Sunday night?

This time was normally reserved for the grant work she'd been doing with Sophie and Myhnah, but that was over now. It hadn't been worth the drive to her apartment where Larisa had nothing to do but think and drive herself into panic mode, so she'd come to crash happy hour.

In a group, it's natural for some to be closer than others.

Larisa and Jaden, the long-standing single women trying to find true love, had been an established pair since graduation. Rosa and Krissy had been the two sisters waiting for their boyfriends to propose after Kahleah and Cade, high school sweethearts, tied the knot their junior year of college. They'd held onto each other as they waited for their turn to answer the question they felt would define the next chapter of their lives. Rosa had been asked first. Larisa thought this had something to do with her refusal to have penetrating sex before marriage. She wasn't the best Catholic, but on that at least she'd stood firm. Then, after what had felt like an eternity, but was really only six months, Dev worked up the courage to ask Krissy.

Their first children had been born in the same hospital, two days apart.

Now, their bond persisted even though the importance of those initial milestones had faded because both their husbands worked demanding jobs where they made good money, but not the kind of money Rosa and Krissy had grown up with. This situation required a standing weekly happy hour for the privacy of conversation with someone who really knew.

Larisa was not one of those people. Even as Rosa's round cheeks dimpled with her welcoming smile and Krissy's elfin chin jutted up in the greeting she'd been using since freshman year, when she'd thought she'd be a rap star, Larisa knew she was an invader. She realized the conversation would be about her, not them, and there was nothing she could really do about that.

"How's the movie? Are we getting tickets to the premiere?" asked Krissy. "Something like that would be great for Cade even if it's just the afterparty. Did Kahleah tell you he's been tapped to run for mayor?"

"Wow."

"She's hosted like three strategy dinners in two months," said Rosa. "So glad that's not me. Bor-ring!" But the look in her eyes said something different.

"Drink your drink, Rosa, and let Risa talk or she's going to remember why she never hangs out with us."

"Right. Talk. Talk. Talk and I'll drink. God, it's like you're a total stranger. What's new?"

"I guess you should know before it's in the papers," Larisa teased.

Krissy's eyes flew open. "That Saudi prince?"

"The director on this film," said Larisa.

Rosa gasped.

"No way. You just started on Monday. What's today?"

"Friday."

"We met in January," said Larisa.

"So wait, did you get this job because of him or—"

"The producer brought me on. He knows my parents."

"Ah okay. So, that's better." Rosa wrinkled her nose and looked at Krissy. "Isn't it better?" They both knew Larisa had been trying to distance herself from her parents.

"Way better," said Krissy. "Who is he?"

"Quinn VanderVeer. He grew up here. Did a couple indie films that showcased the city. He's pretty good."

"Seriously, Larisa. You treat dating like a chore." Krissy punched Quinn's name into her phone. Rosa leaned in to look. "Kind of harsh looking."

"But look at that jawline."

Heat rushed up Larisa's face.

"Hair needs help."

"Very intense eyes," said Rosa. "What's he like in bed?"

"Nice," said Larisa with a smile.

"Nice," chorused Krissy and Rosa.

"You're embarrassing."

"Well excuse us," said Krissy. "We have to make up for 'I'm banging the director and its *nice*.'"

"Hey wait," said Rosa. "I think I went to high school with him."

"He went to public school," said Larisa.

"So did I. For a year while my parents were fighting over custody. I lived with my aunt, and I survived one full year. I do remember him. Quiet, part of the shift-class schedule, only took core classes so he could go to work in the afternoons."

Larisa stilled. She knew about the shift-class option, a way to encourage low-income kids to stay in high school through graduation, but also allow them to work full time. Kids on that plan didn't take drama classes. Their families didn't travel to Europe.

Chapter 18

The Statue

Quinn responded to Parish's latest message while sitting in Club D's parking lot.

Parish: I don't think I can go on without you.

Quinn: I'm not coming over.

Parish: What are you doing instead?

Quinn: I'm at work.

This had been true until an hour ago. He hadn't gone home last night because his alarm had been tripped at three A.M. the night before. Today, still avoiding the house even in daylight, he'd made his office a cave where only he and the movie existed. He'd watched all the footage shot so far and made notes, and lists, and sent the production team a dozen emails in preparation for Monday. None of it had solved the core problem: Sometime in the next four weeks Dansby would need to act or the movie would be ruined.

Absurdly, somewhere in the back of his head, he kept thinking this next session with the Queen would magically solve his problem. In her presence, some secret knowledge would unlock from some unknown place, and he'd realize what could be done to make Dansby into the actor he needed to be.

Parish: Can I come visit?

Quinn: I'll see you on set next week.

Parish: It isn't enough.

Quinn locked his phone in his glove compartment, then entered Club D. Parish did not exist in this world. No one did except the Queen.

On the stage in the central room, a dominatrix led a class for other dommes on whipping techniques. The club itself was mostly empty. Of the clients there, all seemed the same variety of tourist, or couples waiting for the happy hour role-playing scene: Miss Petty Gets a Spanking.

"You look preoccupied," said the Queen.

She'd come up from behind him and now stood to his left. *How long had she been watching?* The idea of her eyes secretly on him made his groin tighten. *Does she like what she sees?*

He shook his head. Not a useful question. She'd agreed to see him again. She'd come. That was enough.

"Long week." He noticed she carried a small purse she hadn't had before.

"I can solve that." She circled him. "Interlace your hands behind your back." After he did so, she adjusted his posture, pulling his shoulders back, moving his hands to rest on the top of his ass. "Follow me with your eyes down. You're not allowed to watch me walk."

"Yes, ma'am."

He lowered his eyes and concentrated on following her boots. Once or twice, he allowed his gaze to travel higher, but each time his fear of being caught made him lower them again.

Club D boasted eight themed rooms, one for every color of the rainbow, including a Victorian bedroom and a medieval torture chamber. As sets, these two historical rooms irritated Quinn for their lack of authenticity. The presence of rubber and plastic in either room was wrong; he had avoided those during his few visits with Parish. Now, he worried what he'd do if one of them was their destination.

Submit.

Surrender.

Allow possibilities.

He clung to his resolve to please the Queen no matter what. When they came to a door painted with the yawning, human-sized vagina of a mythical goddess, he relaxed. Of course, the Queen wouldn't take him to the wrong room.

Parish had never wanted to visit the pagan room, which was also the Green Room. But Quinn had hesitated several times on the threshold of this doorway, which always stood open like an invitation. Grey curls of smoke from a fog machine drifted around the Queen's boots.

Standalone lighting, on both the floor and suspended from the ceiling, spotlighted bowers and alcoves of satin greenery. Quinn followed the Queen along a stone path projected on the floor through intimate stations, offering various enticements. The satin plants and low light hid restraints embedded along the edges of a bed covered in painted leaves, and along the branches of a saint Andrews cross disguised as a tree. He passed plaster statues that looked like French gargoyles, Celtic talismans, and the ruined fractures of ancient Hindu temples.

In the far back corner of the room, ensconced with the sound of chirping insects, sat a life-size statue of dull bronze, a hermaphrodite figure sitting on a bench. Their mouth curved in a perfect circle. Two of their four arms lifted before them with open palms, ready to hold up a body approaching that mouth. Their lower arms extended out, above their waist to buffer a body positioned over the substantial phallus rising between their legs.

A couple women emerged from a curtain of willow branches with chapped red lips and flushed cheeks. They were young. Maybe even as young as Dansby. One woman climbed up onto the statue's bench and began to massage herself on the fingers of an upper hand. The second woman mounted the statue's waist and ran her hand over the phallus.

"So big." She giggled. "Should I?"

"If you do me at the same time." The first woman turned sideways to pump a dollop of lube from the thoughtfully-placed adjacent bottle, prepped herself, then shifted the statue's long fingers into her anus, tilting her hips forward. The second woman turned to face her, kneeling on the statue's lap in a way that would have damaged a living person. She lowered her hips over the phallus as she leaned her mouth into her partner's folds.

"She's so hard," said the second woman, her voice muffled by her partner's legs.

"Deeper. No. Stop, right there," gasped the first.

Feeling like an intruder, Quinn tried and failed to shift his gaze away. He'd never seen anything like it. The statue was lifeless, yet it felt like part of the women. They caressed it, checked in with it with their bodies as their passion grew. It felt like a promise that would never fail.

The Queen set a possessive hand on the back of Quinn's neck and directed him further down the path to a greenery-wrapped massage bed. "Remove your clothes and lay down on the bed."

Watching the women on the statue had made him hard. He saw her notice. His face burned with embarrassment, but also excitement. Her silence felt like more than words. As he lay on his back, fully exposed to her, he couldn't help but say, "I'm sorry for my . . . the statue . . ." He didn't know what to say. *It interested me.*

Terrified me
Was so beautiful.

"Arms above your head. Apologies come when I know you're truly sorry." She used leather cuffs to fasten his wrists to the top of the bed. "You think you can speak freely now?"

"No, ma'am."

"You think I want to hear your little thoughts?"

"No, ma'am."

"Turn onto your side."

He hesitated. She'd not said which side. Before he could ask, she stepped away into the leaves. He heard the gears of a box opening and closing. She returned holding a split-end flogger. A shiver of anticipation ran through him. He twisted himself over so his left hip pushed into the air, his left arm twisted behind his head. Not terribly uncomfortable, but certainly not easy, which he supposed was the point.

"You will not move. If you fall, we start over. Do you want permission to make noise?"

"No, ma'am."

"Good."

The first strike of the flogger made him jump with shock, and he did very nearly fall onto his back. But then, after the jolt to his nerves, the burn began to creep over his side, enlivening his skin and everything beneath. He steadied himself, letting his body stretch taut in anticipation. When the second strike came, he didn't move. He barely breathed. And when it came time to turn to his other side, he did so without a whimper even though the pain of his weight on that side of his body banished all other thoughts from his mind.

All other thoughts, except of course, for the Queen. Every part of him not straining to hear the summoning whirr of the flogger disturbing the air, listened for her movement, for her breath, her voice.

"You're still distracted," she scoffed. "Do you expect to fuck me tonight?"

"No."

A harder than usual strike.

"Why would I defile myself for your pleasure?"

"You wouldn't."

Her voice rose as she asked again, "Why would I defile myself for your pleasure?"

Quinn's mind raced. What was the right answer?

Another strike. Hot fire surged across his ribs and back. For a moment, all words left him, then a thought, shining bright with perfect clarity.

"My pleasure is nothing. All I want is to please you."

"Infamous words," she barked.

"Test me. There's nothing you want I wouldn't give."

The flogger broke its rhythm. For a moment, he could hear her breathing. He thought he could smell her growing wet behind the shield of her latex shorts. She released the cuffs.

"Up."

He obeyed.

"Eyes closed." He didn't hesitate. In any other place, he would have balked in panic. A small part of him was panicking with a flurry kind of anxiety that came from choosing to ride a roller coaster. The Queen's hand on the back of his neck was the safety restraint promising he would be alright.

She pushed him out of their alcove, down the path, then abruptly turned him around, pressing his back up against cold metal.

The statue.

"Eyes closed," she snapped, as she fastened his wrists to restraints on the statue's own wrists. And then her hands were on his ass, pulling him apart, wet fingers rimming, then lowering him onto the—

Quinn thrashed against her, eyes flying open.

The Queen stepped back from him. "Tell me no, we stop." The usual imperious tone was gone from her voice. In its place, a tenderness he wasn't sure he deserved.

"Forgive me," he whispered. "I wasn't ready." He moved himself back, letting the pressure of the phallus rest against his entrance. The size of it felt immense. The tremor that rippled through him was unlike anything he'd ever felt. Delicious fear. Not the kind that ate away at him day in, day out, but its cathartic double. The plunging, bottoming out that came from leaping from the edge of something. Of trusting.

The Queen still stood apart from him. He steadied himself under her watchful gaze. Could he do this? She believed he could. She wanted it for him. Quinn gripped the statue's wrists and pulled himself up, then lowered himself onto the statue's phallus.

His feet found small indentations along the statue's ankles where he could rest his heels and control how far down he went. The pressure was immense, but not uncomfortable once he found the right position. In these few moments of negotiating with the statue, his erection had thickened so quickly his balls ached.

"Please," he said.

She dropped her pants as she came to him, pulling herself up onto the statue and straddling him on her knees, so he was breathing into the line of buckles along the front of her corset. With one hand in the statue's hand, she held herself against him. With the other hand, she grasped a fistful of his hair and pulled him back until he was looking up at her and she down at him.

In one fluid glide, she drove down on him, taking his entire length within her. His mouth parted in a silent, breathless *O*. They remained like that, a moment suspended in time, gazing at each other. Then, the Queen began to move her hips, guiding him into oblivion.

Later, when he'd finished, and she'd finished more times than he'd counted, she took him back to the massage table in the leaves and laid him out, loose limbed and spent. From her little purse she brought out massage oil and Tylenol. He lay like a deboned fish as she tended him, his body taken in and soothed as her strong hands massaged away the last remnants of tension.

"How many times have you done this?"

"A few," she said.

"Ever with a partner? I mean, someone who knows you?"

"Too complicated."

"But with the right person—"

"Be quiet."

For a few minutes Quinn was quiet. But his mind had snagged on an idea, a wish for more. It didn't sit easily to feel so much for someone who kept her identity a secret and was now touching him with more gentle knowing than any woman ever had. He couldn't imagine dating someone else or fucking someone else when he could have the Queen.

"What do you do when you aren't here? Are you seeing someone?"

"Yes."

"But he doesn't know you come here?"

The Queen's boots clicked angrily against the floor as she came up the length of the table and pressed her hand over his mouth, filling his nostrils with a rush of lavender. "Stop. We're not friends. We're not even lovers. If that's not enough for you, find someone else."

He kissed her hand. His tongue licked the oil from her palm. When she removed it, he said, "We don't have to hide from each other."

Which was exactly the wrong thing to say apparently. Something unreadable flashed across her expression. She turned on her heel and began to gather her belongings.

"I'm sorry. Please. My Queen—"

She brushed past the table and out to the walkway, gone before he could even think of where his clothes were.

Quinn drove home preoccupied with apologies, sometimes eloquent, sometimes outright begging forgiveness. He didn't understand why the Queen didn't see they were perfect for each other. Didn't she feel how easily they came together, without shame or even the clumsy fumbling of early relationships? She'd been startled tonight because he hadn't said the right things. But he could. He would.

On the verge of dictating his third message to Doan to forward to the Queen, Quinn pulled up to his gate and found a note stabbed through one of the posts. Parish had been there.

Dear Quinn, I know what you did. I'm going to make you regret it. If you want to negotiate, set a time and place. I'll be there. Yours forever.

It probably wasn't a great sign that Quinn had done enough questionable things that month that he wasn't sure which one she knew about. The obvious answer was she'd found him at the club and spied on him with the Queen. Or perhaps it was as simple as Parish had gone to the studio and discovered he'd lied about working that evening.

He found no evidence she'd broken through the fence or entered the house. Drawing on the peace of both body and mind his session with the Queen had granted him, Quinn entered his house and went to bed. Despite Parish's note, he slept well and woke with enough time to drive to the studio to spend a couple hours doing some initial edits of the footage before he met Larisa on Rodeo Drive for their first date.

Any time he'd gone out with Parish, he'd been nervous. She'd expected him to lead even though he was an interloper in her world of expensive restaurants and exclusive clubs. When he'd floundered, she'd laughed at him. When he'd managed to sit her down and plan out how an evening would go, she'd reveled in flaunting the plan, sometimes throwing it back in his face just to watch him unravel.

But this was different. After he'd agreed to this date, Larisa had sent him what essentially amounted to a one-page scene treatment. She'd bought him an outfit to wear and told him the beanie would be left behind or else. Embedded in the document was a link to a video of a hair stylist slicking gel through hair that looked similar to his own. She'd sent him the gel by courier, along with his new clothes. With all variables accounted for and a solid plan, the worst part would be surviving the actual eating of his half of the ice cream sundae she planned to order.

Chapter 19

The First Fake Date

They met at a parking lot in West Hollywood, two blocks from the throwback 1950s soda fountain where they planned to stage their date.

She eyed his Subaru like it was a specimen.

"What's wrong with my car?"

"Nothing." Her gaze shifted to him. He did a turn for her approval. "Good. So, as I outlined, I thought we'd hold hands while we walk down the street. Get some ice cream, sit in the window seat, close contact."

Quinn nodded.

"You're sure you can do this? You seem distracted."

He reached for her hand and was surprised by how large it was, almost the same as his own.

"You don't like my hands?" she asked.

"In real life, I only date small women," he said, which was not a great thing to say, but there was something about Larisa that made him want to say things. As though delivering these small wounds to her impenetrable confidence was an act of honor instead of just his own insecurity.

"Your shrink could probably give you some insights on that," she said.

They walked together out of the parking lot and turned the corner onto a street lined with jasmine bushes, interrupted here and there with gates into tiny courtyards which led to houses smaller than his that cost twice as much. Despite the fact that there were plenty of regular-looking people around, Quinn felt underdressed in his new designer hoodie and jeans. Larisa wore low-rise cargo pants and a shirt so small her stomach showed. He would never have allowed a real girlfriend to wear clothes that made her look like a teenager. Parish had tried that. She liked to dress down for her age. They'd argued about it.

With her free hand, Larisa pulled out her phone. "Are you on socials? You should follow me. I'm trying out this new one called Instagram. Have you heard about it? All photos like polaroids." She leaned into him and snapped what was certainly a terrible selfie.

They turned onto the street with the soda fountain. Behind them, Quinn heard the rapid rat-a-tat-tat of a professional camera.

"Don't turn to look," said Larisa. "I sent anonymous tips to a couple of places so this wouldn't be a waste of time."

Quinn held the door open as they entered the soda fountain, but once inside Larisa did the ordering. A double sundae, two spoons, as planned. His stomach turned at the sticky sweet smell inside the shop. *You can do this.* He sat on the inside of the window seat. She pressed in beside him, a smile on her face so obviously not for him he was tempted to give her notes on her performance.

The sundae was a perfectly proportioned, picture-perfect sculpture of sugar and dairy. Quinn stared down at it as Larisa took a picture.

"You should smile more. Or at least lean into me when you talk. People are happy together at the beginning of their relationship." She filled her spoon with sundae and held it up to his mouth.

Are you kidding me? he asked her with his eyes.

Her smile deepened.

He leaned over and closed his mouth over the spoon. Sweet cold flooded his mouth. He almost gagged before he managed to swallow. And in the midst of that, another feeling, a heat between his legs and deep within his belly, beyond the place that felt sick. He liked her feeding him.

Quinn banished that thought as quickly as it came.

"What's wrong?"

"I don't usually eat ice cream."

"Why didn't you tell me that when I suggested this?"

"It's fine."

"You look like you're going to be sick."

Quinn looked around for the bathroom. He did feel sick. *Focus on something else.* "You were missed on set Friday."

"Do you avoid dairy?"

"How was the hospital?"

"Are you lactose intolerant?" She was still smiling, but her tone was serious. "Are you poisoning yourself doing this with me?"

Quinn pointedly picked up his spoon, scooped up a bite of ice cream and fudge, and shoved it into his mouth.

"Why won't you just answer me?"

"Because it's not important."

Larisa hid her face from him by looking down at the table, momentarily focused only on navigating her spoon to capture equal portions ice cream, hot fudge, and one half of the cherry, which proved difficult. Her hair fell forward like a curtain across her face. Quinn reached to catch it and tuck it behind her ear before it landed in the ice cream. The gesture drew her attention. She nodded acceptance. A truce.

"If this were really a date, what would we talk about?" she asked. "We should know some things about each other so we're more natural at the wedding."

"What's your favorite color?" he asked.

"Black."

"That isn't a color. What music do you like?"

"All music. Look at me like you love me. Why don't you listen to music?"

Quinn set his eyes at the level of Larisa's temple, knowing a camera wouldn't be able to tell he wasn't gazing into her eyes.

"The ice cream is melting."

Larisa stabbed at the sundae. "You're terrible at dating," she said.

"Fire me."

Larisa lifted her spoon to her lips, slowly moved ice cream around with her tongue. "What are you going to do about Dansby?"

"What do you mean?"

"I heard you moved the scene."

"Scenes move."

"Yes, but what's your plan? The whole movie hinges on him being able to pull it off."

"I fucking know that."

Silence. Larisa holding onto her smile for dear life, the sundae slowly diminishing.

Finally, she said, "I saw something happen on one of my dad's movies. This actor was supposed to fall off the side of a building. They did like fifteen takes; it wasn't working. And by that point, the actor had gotten used to falling, the process had developed a rhythm.

"So, my dad pulls the stunt coordinator aside and tells him to release the belt the actor holds two counts earlier than usual. And then my dad goes down to the mat operator and has him lower the mat a foot, so the actor will be falling further than before.

"The actor gets into place, unaware anything has changed. Stage left, the AD is doing his countdown to tell the actor when to get his startled face on for the fall. It's supposed to happen at the count of five. The belt snaps at two. The actor actually cries out, he's so scared. And then he becomes even more scared when the mat isn't where he expects."

"What's your point?" asked Quinn.

"My point is, there are some choices that deserve to be questioned and some you just need to own as the best possible thing to be done." She shoveled the rest of the sundae into her mouth.

"Come on, let's go."

They held hands walking back the same way they'd come. Quinn snuck a few glances at her, not quite sure he could trust what she'd just said. A story that sounded like permission. He could've kissed her for it. But since that wasn't in their plan and he wasn't sure how she'd react, he merely brought her hand to his lips and softly brushed her knuckles.

"Nothing shocks you, does it?" he asked.

"Being shocked requires boundaries and some sense of duty to convention."

"No wonder you turn men into scared mice."

They arrived at their cars. She huffed out a breath. "I thought you'd be less of an insulting prick now that I wasn't your therapist."

"Why don't we write it off as a coping mechanism?"

"Goodbye, Quinn. Whatever you're going to do with Dansby, remember you're responsible to him. Don't break what you can't fix. And if anyone calls you for an interview after this date hits the tabloids, call me first so we can coordinate."

Long after Larisa had driven away, Quinn sat in his car thinking. What could he do with Dansby that would give him access to the tools he needed? It seemed an insurmountable task. As he sat, Quinn massaged his side, which was still sore from the Queen's beating the previous night. He thought of her towering over him on the statue, him entirely at her mercy, knowing she wouldn't give him more than he could handle. But, as Larisa had astutely pointed out, he could handle quite a lot. And he expected others to do the same. He wondered what the previous night would've looked like with different people. A less experienced version of him, a more demanding, less caretaking version of her.

Chapter 20

Primordial Scream

On Monday, production moved out of the studio and into greater Los Angeles. For the first time, Larisa saw true collaboration between Quinn and Lane, as they constructed a dynamic shot where the camera followed Dansby out of the general's apartment, down a short flight of stairs, then swiveled around him for a side view as he flagged down a cab, then turned again to the window to get the first look at his face as he realized what he'd just done.

For this to work, the camera operator wore rollerblades and followed Dansby down the stairs on a ramp, pivoted to stand beside him, and then held onto the side of the cab to keep the camera peering in through the open window as the cab drove away. Watching the video village with Tish, Larisa loved how intimate the shot felt, how the rattle of the rollerblades down the steps foreshadowed the tense conflict on Dansby's face as he sat in the cab. The movement felt like running, it felt like dread, even though Dansby remained outwardly composed.

"I wouldn't have ever thought of shooting it like that," said Tish.

"He's adapting," said Larisa. "Dansby doesn't manage his face well, so Quinn changed the angles. That way, we're less likely to notice."

"It's beautiful."

"You should tell him. Them," Larisa corrected herself. Lane deserved some credit.

On Tuesday, they moved to the beach to film the scene where Dansby and Walt conduct surveillance on the general's operations, and the scene where Dansby and the general have their meet cute.

On both days, the disruption in established studio routine meant the cast and crew were less likely to seek Larisa out for a conversation. Quinn also didn't seek her out, which was probably wise since she was still processing the weekend.

Lied about his childhood.

Quinn suspended on the statue, looking up at her like she was his universe.

Won't talk about ice cream.

Quinn's long, pale body quivering under her lash as the self-loathing drained out of him.

Her hunger for the lips she refused to kiss because she wanted him to know they were hers. Wanted him to want her, not the Queen.

Larisa attempted to keep herself occupied, which wasn't easy to do on a film set. On Monday, she had caught up on emails (still nothing about Kara), read the apologies Quinn had sent her through Doan, told herself they changed nothing, and then hung out with Dansby in his trailer while waiting to be called to set. They'd discovered a mutual love of punk rock. His easy interest was a nice distraction from the clutter of her mind. She'd been with Dansby when the pictures of her ice cream date went live online and began to circulate through the gossip feeds.

"It was just a date," said Larisa. "Nothing between us needs to change. I won't tell him anything you tell me."

"Maybe it would be good if he knew?" asked Dansby.

"Whatever you want him to know, you should tell him yourself."

"I don't know what I'd say." Dansby turned up the music. End of conversation. She'd focused on her phone rather than pressure him to engage with her.

Krissy: Your boyfriend is so cute.

Jaden: Why am I the last to know about this?

Rosa: @Jaden, you should've come to happy hour.

Lucas: Sexy new toy.

On Tuesday at the beach, Larisa started her day with a strange email from Dr. Bade asking if she was planning to come to the hospital that day. *I was banished to the film set, remember?* thought Larisa. The beauty of email was it allowed for a degree of self-editing, if one could manage to not impulsively hit send. Her next day at the hospital was Friday, she wrote. But she could adjust her schedule if needed.

Then she waited, trying not to worry as the hours dragged on with lighting placements, rehearsals with extras, and setting up the screens to block out the Santa Monica boardwalk so digital French Riviera could be pasted in. Dr. Bade was not a forgetful person, no matter how overworked. And even if she had somehow managed to forget Larisa's reassignment, she could've checked the schedule.

I should call her. If I'm in trouble, better to know now than wait and worry.

Larisa was just making up her mind to look up Dr. Bade's number when a licking beat invaded her ears, breaking through her thoughts. Dansby had flagged down some beach dude with a portable stereo. They were both walking toward her. Dansby wore the come-hither face he'd been practicing in preparation for his scene. She laughed at how good it was, a perfect blend of daring flirtation and implied knowledge. That look said, *I'll take you places you've never been.*

If she'd been at a different stage in her life, or if they'd met under different circumstances, she would have taken him up on the offer. Today, playing at flirtation while knowing they weren't going to follow through, seemed even better. She allowed him to grab her hand and pull her up out of her chair. She let her sandals fall off as he dragged her from the staging street down the boardwalk onto the beach to the water's edge, where the Dead Kennedys growled the opening lyrics of "California Über Alles" over the oncoming waves.

Larisa pounded her feet in the wet sand, splashing, kicking water at Dansby, who kicked right back. Their arms beat the air. Larisa's hair blew free of her braid. More people convened around her, swelling their little display to an impromptu mosh pit. Her body knocked into people. Sand flew all the way up into her mouth. She lost her footing and crashed down into the surf. Dansby tried to pull her up, but he lost his balance and they both fell together into the surf.

"Oh God," gasped Larisa. "I haven't danced that hard in years."

"It's not enough though," said Dansby. "We didn't scream."

"We can now."

"You sure?"

"I'll do it if you do it. One long, no-holding-back scream, to the pier and back. Ready? Set? Go!"

They took off running, away from the beach dude and the strangers they'd attracted, past families with children, past the set security barricade and the crew doing their jobs. They ran and ran. And as they ran, they screamed. Dansby's sound was a deep-throated roar, like one might do at a punk concert. Larisa's sound was higher, desperation ripping from her throat like a character in a horror film.

It felt amazing.

Free! Free! Free! Her bursting chest called to the sky. And for once, the pain, the burning lack of air in her lungs, made it uncomplicated. She did not ask, what is freedom? She did not question how her life had become a trap. She flew with the gulls.

Dansby won the race, but Larisa could have won if she'd tried harder. When they turned, they caught the eyes of several startled people, on the pier above them and on the beach. And there, running after them, a PA holding her headset on her head calling, "Dansby, are you okay?"

"*Are* you okay?" asked Larisa, half-teasing.

"I am now." He grinned. "You have stuff in your hair." Then he jogged forward to meet the PA, leaving Larisa to walk back to the set at her own pace.

The stares followed her. Usually, the blank interest of rubber-necking made Larisa feel judged, but today, she supposed the notice was warranted and did not have as much to do with her celebrity as usual. Yes, there would probably be some hideous picture of her online with a terrible headline questioning her sanity, wondering if she was on drugs, but it felt like the staring had a tinge of something else.

People stared because they couldn't imagine true release. These people were the same ones who said bondage was violence and should be criminalized to protect all the vulnerable people sucked into fetishized sex slavery. They were the ones who thought women who could not keep a man were somehow flawed.

Eddie met her at the security barricade. "There you are! I was afraid we'd lost you for the day."

"You nearly did. I was planning to abscond across the ocean with Dansby."

Eddie chuckled, then turned serious. "I'd like to schedule you for lunch tomorrow. Are you free?"

"What kind of lunch is this?"

"It's a . . . uh, let's call it a mediation of sorts. I believe you know my niece, Parish."

"I do." Larisa couldn't help shifting her gaze beyond Eddie, looking for Quinn.

"She'll be on set with us tomorrow for a small part."

"You want me to stay with her while she's on set?"

"Yes, wonderful. But I had something more strategic in mind."

She saw Quinn start to approach them, then stop short. She couldn't tell if it was because she was with Eddie or because he was shocked by her wind-tossed braid and sand all over her wet clothes. Probably both. Quinn, who had lied to her about his family, she remembered. In an instant, she assembled a new history. *Single mother, only child, food scarcity, utilitarian education, survivalist, imposter, pretender.* He's not just hiding from me. Tears burned her eyes. He looked so vulnerable standing there, trying to decide to come forward or turn away.

Parish is coming tomorrow. If she'd known this, Larisa would have delayed their first date until the following week. Maybe Eddie didn't keep track of fresh gossip, but Parish had certainly seen the feeds and knew Larisa and Quinn were a thing. It would add more volatility to what was already going to be a difficult day.

"Can we talk for a minute?" asked Larisa.

Quinn was making his usual fast exit, but to his car this time instead of his office.

"I'm late," he said.

"For what?"

"Package delivery." He reached his car, turning to face her. "Have fun today?"

"In fact, I did. How about you?"

"The lighting wasn't right. I don't think the sand looked—"

"You can fix that in the editing room."

"Maybe."

They both knew lighting was the worst thing to try to correct in post-production, but neither wanted to say it.

"You hear we're officially an item?" she asked.

"Sid's mother called and screamed in my ear." Quinn cringed. "And there have been messages on my phone. My old crew. People I haven't spoken to in years. They're all very impressed." He paused as though he wanted to say something about how he'd never be with someone like her in real life, but instead he said, "I've heard from more people about my new girlfriend than when I won Sundance."

"That's how it always goes."

"You'll be here tomorrow?" he asked.

"Eddie is conspiring."

"I noticed."

"What's your plan?"

"I'm going to treat Parish like everyone else."

"Good. What if that doesn't work?"

He stared at her.

"Always have a plan B, Quinn. Especially with ex-girlfriends. Ex-girlfriends who are related to your producer probably require plans C and D."

A faint smile pulled at the corner of his mouth. "I'll think about it."

"And I'll be there to back you up. Or I'll back her up if necessary."

The smile faded. "What did Eddie say about us?"

"What should he have said?"

For a moment, she thought he would tell her, but then he shook his head. "Have a good night, Larisa. I'll see you tomorrow."

Larisa watched his taillights blend into the stream of other taillights, her chest swelling with warmth at the promise of the next day. It wouldn't be easy, but at least he wouldn't go through it alone.

He shouldn't ever have to be alone.

An impossible thought. But that didn't prevent her from wanting it.

As she walked to her car, Larisa checked her phone. One message stood out from the others.

Sophie: Kara is in the ER. Organ failure.

Larisa's first thought was, *HIPPA violation.* Her second thought was, *Oh God.*

Chapter 21

Parish The Russian Stripper

Quinn's on-set assistant was waiting for him as soon as he arrived the next morning. "One of the actors has an urgent need to speak with you. Parish? She says you know her." The PA's face was carefully bland, but beneath it, Quinn could see judgement churning like a cesspool.

"I'll see her during rehearsal."

"She's been insisting—"

"I have work to do. Is Lane here yet?"

"He just stepped out. Otherwise, we're on schedule for an eight o'clock call."

Quinn looked around the Russian nightclub set, which the crew was lighting with stand-ins for the first shot.

Nothing is wrong, he told himself. And yet Quinn couldn't stop feeling like he was walking in the footsteps doom had marked for him. His gaze probed the set for a problem lurking in the shadows.

"Where is Larisa?"

"Not here yet."

Quinn checked the time and frowned. The stage door opened. His head swiveled toward it, expecting her to walk through it. Instead, it was Lane and his first camera operator.

She'll be here. Quinn waved at Lane. "Morning. Ready for the walk through?"

And so, the day began. They shot the scene in the bathroom

where Dansby calls Walt to tell him he thinks he's been made, and Walt promises help is on the way. They shot Dansby alone in the hallway, off the central room of the club, as the general's second in command approaches ominously.

Larisa did not arrive.

Lighting began resetting for the crowd scenes and the table scene where Parish would play friendly with Dansby, facilitating his escape by way of romantic liaison. Yuri, the Russian language consultant, stepped out from the bubble of void space around craft services to introduce himself, but before Quinn could give him directions, Parish arrived.

Quinn knew the exact moment Parish arrived on set because she screamed his name with the horrifying ecstasy of every clingy-girlfriend stereotype ever seen on film. Before he could even turn to greet her, she was barreling into him, arms clutching his neck, pulling him down to kiss him.

While everyone watched.

He couldn't push her off without risking an explosion, so he simply endured it, stiff, unyielding, feeling like every second that ticked by was a betrayal of the Queen. He filled his mind with her, a woman who would never be hysterical over any man, let alone Quinn.

When Parish finally calmed down, he attempted to start rehearsals, but his nerves were vibrating and scattered, and he kept giving the wrong instructions. When one actress did what he'd said but it was the wrong thing, he barked at her to do the thing he'd meant to say, and she shuddered away from him in fear.

He didn't have the time or energy to apologize. *Larisa should be here. Why isn't she here?*

Finally, Tish stepped in. She was a little uncertain, perhaps as frightened of him as the girls were, but determined to salvage the operation. She did just fine until Parish said, "I don't think that's my part. I'm the one with the speaking line. I should be over here."

"You'll block the camera over there, darling," said Tish. "Trust me on this. You come in beside Dansby from behind the couch. Make eye contact. He'll be looking at you, right here. Then you move over there and sit beside him."

Parish looked to Quinn, stuck out her lower lip in a pout. "Is that what you want, baby?"

Quinn couldn't even answer her. Just standing in the same room with her made him feel overexposed, pinned up for secret knives to come flying toward him at any moment. She was acting out and it was working. People were watching. *Everyone* was watching.

How did he get a girl like that?

We know how. She's Eddie's niece.

Explains everything.

Didn't you hear he was abusive?

Poor thing.

She needs a real man.

A hand on his arm. He jerked away, nearly slapping Tish in the face.

"I'm calling main cast to set for full rehearsal," she said. "Then we'll do final lighting?"

He nodded, thankful for the help he didn't know how to ask for.

They broke for lunch at three. Quinn was headed to the privacy of his office when Eddie called out for everyone to hear, "Quinn, join me and Parish down the street, will you?"

What was he going to say? No? Perhaps if he'd been clearer headed, calmer, or a better person, he would have summoned an excuse that felt plausible enough. But it didn't matter. He wasn't any of those people.

The three of them walked to the bistro just around the corner from the studio gates and settled in at a corner booth with stuffing coming out the torn corners of the bench. A fry-oil-scented haze tinted the air of the small, noisy dining room. Eddie ordered a round of tap beers, even though he knew Quinn didn't drink beer, especially not on-tap domestics.

"To our new partnership," said Eddie, as they raised glasses.

"To the future!" said Parish. Out in the real world, her stripper costume seemed garish and overwrought. People kept glancing toward the booth. The waiter had nearly tripped over a chair leg when he brought the beers.

"You did great today," said Eddie. "Didn't she, Quinn?"

She's better than Dansby, he thought. But really, that wasn't even a fair thing to think. He was asking Parish to seduce a stranger in a club. She'd done that dozens of times. She'd even done that to him. *Find a way to make your exit. Nothing good is going to come of this.* "I might just take something to go. I'd like to—"

"You can take a real break this once," said Eddie. "You and Parish haven't seen each other in weeks."

Quinn clenched his jaw. He was about to say something pointed about filming schedule demands when Larisa squeezed herself past the adjacent table and sat down in the open bench space beside Parish.

"I'm sorry," she said breathlessly. "There was an emergency at the hospital."

"No problem," said Eddie. "Now we're all here, we can begin."

Begin what? wondered Quinn. *Why did she apologize to him instead of me?*

"What emergency?" he asked before he could stop himself.

Larisa glanced at him, then away. "Just a work thing." She seemed flustered. Beneath the padding of more than her usual thin veneer of makeup, her eyes appeared swollen. She'd rimmed them with black eyeliner and shadow. And for a moment, she looked like the Queen. Quinn blinked away the mirage.

"Parish, this is Dr. Larisa de France-Kahn. She's a psychiatrist."

"Obviously." Parish dangled her hand over to Larisa to shake. "Nice to see you again."

"Why can't you talk about it?" Quinn's voice pitched high enough, he sensed heads turn his direction.

Larisa said nothing.

"Until recently," continued Eddie, "Parish and Quinn were romantically involved, as I think everyone's aware. Quinn became violent shortly after production started and I encouraged Parish to leave him."

"But I didn't want to," said Parish as she slanted her eyes toward Quinn.

He clenched his fists together and sat on them so he wouldn't do something stupid like lunge at her across the table.

"It's clear they belong together," said Eddie.

Quinn snorted.

Eddie ignored him. "But I don't want Parish in an unsafe environment."

"That's understandable." Larisa had yet to look directly at Quinn. It felt like he wasn't even there, that this was a stage play being performed by the three of them and all he could do was watch.

"I'd like us to all come together and understand why Quinn would strike my niece and how to make sure it doesn't happen again. Larisa will be an impartial mediator."

Parish giggled, now her eyes slanted back and forth between Quinn and Larisa.

She thinks we're dating.

Their food arrived.

But she's not going to say anything because she wants to see what I do.

"Doctor, please guide us," said Eddie.

Larisa cleared her throat. Quinn thought for a moment she seemed unsteady. When was Larisa ever nervous? There was something wrong. *Everything about this is wrong.* The brain fog coating his mind made her feel further away than the other side of the booth; he couldn't see her clearly. *She never wears makeup like that.*

"I think it's always good to start with active listening," said Larisa. "Each person takes a turn talking about how they see the relationship and identifying the main problem."

"Ooh, fun. I'll go first," said Parish. "I love Quinn. He's like the best thing that's ever happened to me and these past weeks without him have been horrible. I totally understand he gets off on violence. It was shocking when I found out about it, but now I think I can be a better partner to him if he'll take me back. I just want to have normal sex sometimes."

"He gave her a black eye," said Eddie.

Quinn looked down at his burger, his shoulders hiked up almost to his ears and his back slouched down in the wayward hope that the bench would open up and swallow him. Parish had a voice that carried. It was entirely possible all the people at the tables around them had heard her call Quinn a sexual deviant.

"Quinn's turn!" Parish loudly slurped her milkshake.

"I'm not doing this."

"Quinn, this is important," said Eddie. "You're going to throw away love because of some dark impulse?"

"I haven't thrown away anything I wanted to keep."

Eddie's face turned purple. His lips worked, spittle flying, as he struggled to voice a response. Parish got there first.

"He's already moved on." She heaved a dramatic sigh.

"Moved on to who?" Eddie looked ready to explode. "This person should be warned that—"

Quinn's eyes flashed up from his plate. "I'll be interested to see how that plays out for our movie, Eddie. You want everyone to know you hired a known abuser?"

Larisa held up her hand. "Let's pause here for a moment. Everyone take a deep breath with me." Eddie and Parish followed her example. Quinn was practically hyperventilating. "Alright, now let it out. Good. I don't think we're at the point of making public accusations. If Parish wants to sue for damages, that's within her right."

"I just want him back." Parish puckered her lips in a pout. "Please, Quinn. I'm sorry. I promise I'll do better. I'll do whatever you ask."

"No."

Parish's pout turned into a glare. "Well *Doctor* Larisa, at least now when he asks you to play his dirty sex games you won't be as shocked as I was."

Even with the makeup masking her full expression, Quinn was sure he saw disgust in Larisa's face. For all her medical training and the exposure she'd certainly had with sexuality, she wasn't open minded enough for this. *She won't want anything to do with me now.*

The table shuddered as Quinn launched himself out of the booth and began to navigate the tables to reach the door. He heard Eddie loudly ask, "Larisa, why would you be—" And Parish's answer, "She's the next girl. Kind of a downgrade, isn't she?"

Someone was coming into the bistro as Quinn made his exit, a collision he barely felt. His body had once again stepped beyond his awareness, driving forward to a destination he didn't know. Back to the set? The office? Nothing felt safe. There was no place Parish could not follow.

She'll be gone tomorrow. Just get through the day.

The promise of only one day with Parish ended up being a false hope. They worked up to the limit of daily union hours and still didn't finish the nightclub scene. Parish, and everyone else, would be called back the next day.

Larisa had been on set for the second part of the day, but they hadn't spoken. She mostly sat in her chair, far back from the action, only speaking to people who approached her. The exception to this rule was Parish. More than a few times during breaks, Larisa left her chair and made a point of talking with Parish and the other actresses playing strippers. They looked like friends during these conversations. Sometimes, their heads bent together like they were sharing secrets. Seeing them together made Quinn's skin crawl. He kept looping his forearms around his neck, unconsciously protecting against attack.

The only good thing to come from Larisa talking with Parish was that there were no more extravagant displays of affection or whining. Parish did her job. She even gave him ten good takes of her falling down, looking startled as she realized she'd been shot.

He expected Larisa would come to him at the end of the day wanting to hash out what had happened at lunch, or at least follow up on the email she'd sent with the plan for Saturday's dinner with her parents. She didn't.

She's on Parish's side, he thought. *She thinks I'm one of those guys.*

The next day, not having slept much and still wound up from the day before, Quinn found it all too easy to play the part everyone expected him to play. He snapped at his assistant about his afternoon sparkling water for no good reason. He grabbed one of the actresses and bodily pulled her into position after she failed to do what he wanted. And then, when he heard one of the extras complaining about lunch being late, he fired her on the spot. From her seat in the back, Larisa saw it all. She said nothing.

At the end of the day, he was on his way to his office when he saw Larisa with Dansby at his trailer. The actor had his arms around her, a prolonged hug, his head bent down, speaking into her ear. They looked like lovers.

I don't care, thought Quinn.

Friday, Larisa didn't come to the set. This was the arranged schedule, but it still felt like avoidance. In the middle of the night, Quinn woke feeling panicky from a dream he couldn't remember. The club scene with the strippers was over, but Parish haunted his steps. He stalked his phone, watching for messages from Larisa, anything to distract him, to help him refocus his ire.

On Saturday afternoon, with the parental dinner looming, Quinn decided he had no choice but to break the silent standoff.

> Quinn: Do you still want me for dinner tonight?

> Larisa: Cocktails at 5. Dinner at 5:45. No need to impress. Be your usual.

> Quinn: Maybe you should take Dansby instead.

> Larisa: If you're not up for it, just say so.

She didn't give him directions on what to wear or what they'd be eating.

I can salvage this, he thought. *I can explain it to her. I'm not the monster she thinks I am.*

Chapter 22

Meet the Parents

The Kahn estate was tucked back in the hills overlooking the city. With its circular drive and columned façade, it looked like it had been lifted out of a film set from the gilded forties. It looked even larger than it had the night he'd come as Parish's plus-one for Suzette's New Year's gala.

Then, he'd been an anonymous guest among hundreds. Now, he was alone, meeting Gunter Kahn and Suzette de France under false pretenses, which would have bothered him less if he'd been confident Larisa was in control of the scene. He had no idea how the event would go, but he was here. He was going to save his fake relationship and convince Larisa he was worth keeping.

Quinn lingered in his Subaru, which he'd parked off to the side of the front drive where some long willow branches partially concealed it. He finished a round of texts finalizing his plans with Dansby for the evening. Originally, he'd planned for Dansby to visit his house Sunday night, but the actor had wanted Saturday, which was probably better. If meeting Larisa's parents went terribly, at least Quinn had work with his actor waiting for him. It would be different than the last time, better.

A staff member in a Lakers hoodie escorted Quinn across a foyer of marble inlaid with stones and metals, depicting a swirling galaxy. From the foyer, they entered a receiving room, then turned left into a room full of windows, finally ending at a patio shaded by trees.

Larisa sat alone on a daybed swing, one foot on the ground to push her back and forth as she stared up at the leafy canopy. She turned and looked at him with a surprised expression that could just as easily be read as irritation.

"Quite a house," he said. Not the best opening line, especially since she knew he'd already been there. But really, what was there to say? He wasn't going to bring up the bistro, or Parish, or any of the other things he'd done that she'd certainly written down in her mental ledger of judgements.

She needs you as much as you need her. Get through it, go to the club tonight after Dansby, fix yourself. Do better next week.

Next week they were shooting Dansby's prison scene.

Exhaustion descended like a weighted blanket, pulling Quinn toward the ground. He took a seat in a chair near the swing. "I don't want to fight with you."

"Are we fighting?"

"It feels like we are."

"Hmm."

"Is there anything you'd like to say? Or ask me about Wednesday?"

"Nope."

Quinn peered at her out the corner of his eye. She looked like the same Larisa, but she felt like someone completely different. "Have you given up on me then?"

"Let's just drop it."

Drop what?

The patio door opened and Suzette de France strode out, all legs, cheekbones, and huge hair. "Larisa, honey. Are you okay? Your father told me—" She stopped when she saw Quinn. "Hello. You're Quinn." She extended her hand. "Suzette. Can I get you a drink?"

"Uh, no. I'm fine."

"He drinks sparkling water, chilled, no ice," said Larisa, as she sent the swing into a hard swoop by kicking at the ground. "I'm having vodka straight."

Suzette frowned. "You look a little puffy. Why not a—"

"Vodka. Now please? I have to be sober in two hours."

"I'm sorry," said Suzette to Quinn. "She can be difficult. Would you like to walk with me?"

"I'm okay here," said Quinn. The chair felt safe even with its proximity to Larisa. The last thing Quinn needed to do was go off alone with her mother and expose himself as a novice.

"You didn't come to the set Wednesday morning," he said.

"That's correct." Larisa again kicked at the ground. The swing groaned under the movement.

"Why not?"

"I had other things to do."

"You could've called."

This was exactly the wrong thing to say. Larisa bolted upright, eyes bright with fire as she glared at him. "Is this the part where we start being honest with each other? Or are you just upset because I wasn't there to make things more comfortable for you with the girl you used to get your job? You deserve everything she gives you."

"Then what am I doing here?"

"Moving onto your next target apparently."

Quinn jumped to his feet and moved toward the house. Blood pounded in his ears. His hands reached for something, anything, to grasp, destroy, throw.

"That's it, run away, you social climbing whore," Larisa called after him.

He only made it a few steps across the atrium before he encountered Suzette returning with a tray of drinks.

"Oh. I see you're leaving." She didn't appear surprised.

"I think its best."

"Dinner's almost ready. I'll pack your food to go?"

Quinn hesitated. Larisa was clearly done with him. It felt wrong to stay. But Suzette de France was motioning for him to follow her into the kitchen. He might never have a chance like this again.

The kitchen was the size of the ground floor of his house with a dining area, a prep counter as long as a banquet table, and three different types of ovens. Gunter Kahn, four-time Oscar winner, president of the PGA, producer of an entire generation of dearly-beloved films, was pulling a pizza out of the woodfire brick oven.

Quinn tried not to stare.

"He lasted seven minutes," announced Suzette.

What the fuck was I thinking coming here?

What has she told them about me?

"I'm just going to pack some up for him."

"Pizza has to be eaten fresh." Gunter slid one handmade pie onto the counter, then turned to extract a second from the oven. He glanced at Quinn. "You look tough. You can survive dinner."

"I feel unwelcome." Quinn cringed. He sounded like he was whining.

"She does this when something goes wrong. You just have to remember what she says right now comes from a place of hurt."

The only thing to do when receiving dating advice from a film legend was to nod. Quinn planted his feet and tamped down the urge to run.

"She lost a patient," said Gunter, as he surveyed the pizzas. "I don't know if you two are at the stage where she tells you things—"

"She didn't tell *me*," added Suzette.

"It hit pretty hard."

"But we're so glad you're here," said Suzette, as she handed Quinn a stack of the most expensive looking plastic plates he'd ever seen, picked up her drink tray, and walked him back to the patio.

Larisa was gliding back and forth on the swing as before, but now everything felt different. *She lost a patient.* He must have sounded like such an asshat going on about his movie and her absence, like his work was more important than hers.

Apologize.

But Suzette was chattering about the spring weather, and

Larisa was glaring at the sky like she was going to murder it. And it was easier to stay silent. Always, his silence like a shield.

Gunter came out with the pizzas and the three of them sat at the patio table adjacent the swing. Quinn took the smallest slice of pizza and told himself he could eat it and be okay afterward.

"So, Quinn, how's the film going? I hear you're almost wrapping."

"Please, no work talk at the table," said Suzette. "You grew up here, didn't you, Quinn? Not one of those star-struck transplants, I mean."

"I did."

The swing stilled. Quinn felt his ears burning. *She knows you're lying.*

If she knew the truth, she'd understand.

You do it again, she'll call you out and embarrass you.

The truth about where he came from was impossible. So, he stepped past it and mustered something he hoped sounded like a tease. "Weren't you once a star-struck transplant?" Quinn held his breath, but Suzette only laughed.

"Transplanted, yes, but only after the bloom had worn off. Three years modeling all over the world, terrible hours, starving myself, almost no money. Then I nabbed Victoria's Secret."

"And me," said Gunter.

"We met at the Super Bowl, of all places."

Quinn stilled. Was this a trap? He fought back the instinct to rush to self-defense and checked in with his other senses. Two very famous people eating pizza, nothing malicious. Larisa, still on the swing staring up at the trees. Not a trap.

So, it felt okay to say, "My parents also met at the Super Bowl."

"You're joking! Were they fans of opposing teams? We were."

"They were working." Knowing what the next question would be, Quinn rushed forward. "My dad's an investment banker. My mom died when I was eighteen."

"Oh, so young," gasped Suzette.

Larisa chose that moment to peel herself up off the swing and join them at the table. "Don't get weepy, Mom. If you cry, I'll cry."

"Oh, honey."

"Pizza looks good." Larisa's eyes briefly flashed up to meet Quinn's. He found the gentle understanding that still frightened him with its prescience. Even in her grief, she was saving him. Even though she knew he'd lied about his family, she was willing to help ease his way.

Somehow, they made it through dinner. At a quarter to seven, Larisa began to make her exit, which meant it was time for Quinn to leave as well.

"I didn't expect them to be so charming," said Quinn when they were alone in the driveway.

"You thought they'd be more like me, judgement and knowing looks?"

"People who run screaming down a beach?"

"Why did you stay?" she asked.

"I thought maybe you needed the distraction. A fake boyfriend, no matter how repugnant, is always interesting."

"Or an easy target." She sounded rueful, almost apologetic. "You're not repugnant."

"If you'd made me your target, I'd have managed."

"As you do."

"Sometimes better than others." He walked her to her car. "Maybe I have a talent for rising to the occasion when someone else is behaving badly."

"Thanks."

"Are you going to be okay tonight?"

"It's better to work than sit around and think," she said. "What about you?"

"I'm beginning to think I need a shrink."

"Ha!"

"I need to figure out how to stop thinking people are out to get me." He paused. "I'm sorry about your patient."

She shrugged. "It's part of the job. And maybe you won't assume people are out to get you when you're not dealing with the ones who actually are. What Eddie did at the bistro wasn't fair, you know that, right? There was no way your side of the story was going to look legitimate after what Parish said."

Quinn did know that, somewhere in the back of his head, but it helped to hear her say it.

"You're going to need to do something about her, you know. She's not just going to go away."

"Do you have a suggestion?"

"What's going to make the relationship feel over for her? Even though she thinks you're dating me, she's acting like you're still interested in her and it's just a matter of time before you're back together."

"I'll work on it."

"My mother is watching us from the window. How do you want to end this?"

"You're in charge," he said.

"Well, then." She leaned in and kissed the side of his temple. "Have a good weekend, Quinn."

The scent of her hair filled his nose as her cheek brushed his. He wanted to put his hands on her, draw her in and keep her against him, hold her the way Dansby had because it was just dawning on him how much she gave and how little she received. *She told him about her patient, but not me.*

Because they weren't actually dating.

They weren't even really friends.

He retreated to his car as Larisa turned on her engine and a rock band screamed out of her speakers at a decibel level that seemed illegal. Worried he might get trapped at the stoplight beside her, Quinn waited a few minutes before leaving.

When he arrived home, he checked the gate for notes and the shrubbery around the gate for broken branches or fallen leaves. He told himself it was possible to feel safe, if not in his life, then at least within his skin. He'd eaten pizza with Gunter Kahn and

Suzette de France. They'd treated him like he was worth knowing. Now, he was going to save his movie and prove them right.

Chapter 23

Climax

It had meant more than she wanted to admit when Quinn had stood in her parents' driveway and asked if she was going to be okay. Obviously, she wasn't delusional enough to think he really cared. But he'd asked her a personal question, the first not cloaked in insult or defensive malice. The thought of it, that maybe he was warming to her—not the Queen, but Larisa herself—carried her through the weekend. She used it as a protective barrier to hold herself together in the thin hours of Sunday morning at the ward as she pretended to listen to a police officer complaining about the homeless camp he'd just raided. At the same time, she was listening to Carl and Lucie discussing who would be working the ward in the next rotation.

"I heard they're going to keep Larisa here because she missed so much time," said Carl in his regular voice, as though Larisa wasn't standing four feet away.

"Especially with what happened with Kara," whispered Lucie. "Can you imagine her with peds?"

Meanwhile the officer went on. "I don't know what you're going to do with all of them. Lockup is a better solution. Gets them off the streets longer, costs less." The officer cast his gaze around the intake station as though seeing it for the first time. "It looks like you could put the money to better use."

"We're here to serve people," said Larisa, handing him a form to sign. As she turned to the desk to file it, Lucie accidentally met her eye, guilty.

At five o'clock, more tired from the feeling of eyes on her back than her actual work, Larisa wandered into the office cubicle they used for transcription and startled Sophie just as she was settling in for a brief nap. It would have been more awkward for her to get up and leave when she'd obviously been planning to stay, so she sat, swishing her eyes around, not sure where to look.

Finally, Sophie said, "I'm sorry about Kara. I know you were handling her outpatient care before you were reassigned."

The words held a touch of reproach, so Larisa couldn't help but say, "She had left treatment before I was reassigned. There wasn't anything that could be done."

Sophie narrowed her eyes like she didn't believe there were patients who couldn't be saved, then shrugged the thought away. "It's weird hearing about your new boyfriend from the internet instead of you."

"It happened fast," said Larisa.

"Well, I'm happy for you," said Sophie. "You look happy."

Larisa's hand went to her face as though she expected to feel whatever Sophie was seeing. She wished this was easier, that it didn't feel like an ending. Her cohort was supposed to be her normal friends, the people she would build her professional life around once they graduated. "Would you believe me if I said film work isn't as glamorous as it sounds? The people there are almost as messy as what we get here."

"I don't believe you," said Sophie.

"As an example, yesterday—" Larisa's phone vibrated, followed shortly by Sophie's. A moment later, alarms sounded from room four. "You have code alarms on movie sets?" asked Sophie, as they moved to respond. She said it as a joke, but Larisa felt her resentment. Larisa couldn't help but wonder if Sophie would like her better knowing the relationship was fake.

She wouldn't understand why I'd need a relationship I can control.

Thoughts of Quinn in the driveway were even stronger on Sunday afternoon, as Larisa fled her empty apartment to meet Charity at Club D for a session in the Victorian room, which included corsets, dressing gowns, scarf bondage, and feather tickling. Larisa usually enjoyed tickling because it asked for more precision and attention to her partner than straightforward flogging.

"You're somewhere else," said Charity with a sigh. "I'm not enough for you anymore, am I?"

Larisa didn't say her time with Charity had almost always left her wanting, even before Quinn. Charity was too nice to be interesting. She accepted whatever Larisa wanted as though it was her own desire and never thought about what she might want for herself.

But her distraction was more than that. More even than Quinn and the enthusiastic messages Larisa had received from both her parents after Saturday's dinner. She hadn't expected them to like him. On the surface, he wasn't a likeable person, which was probably why she couldn't stop thinking about him. It felt like cheating that her brain could still carry him around in her head like some unrequited fantasy, all the while tearing itself to shreds thinking how she could have done better with Kara.

"Someone I knew died last week," said Larisa.

"Oh." Charity blinked. "So, why are you here?"

"The funeral is today, and I needed somewhere to go. I'm sorry," said Larisa.

"It's fine. I just . . . I mean . . . would you like to do something else?"

I want you to need something from me that I can do, thought Larisa. But that again would require Charity to have a desire drive of her own. So, Larisa went home. She tried to masturbate in the shower and found it a lifeless exercise. At ten o'clock, even though she'd only been awake since noon, Larisa went to bed. There was nothing else to do. The emptiness of her apartment amplified her loss. Only sleep gave her shelter from the rotten feeling inside.

Quinn was with her in the twilight of half-awake dreams as she waited for the start of Monday morning, that dark sarcastic half smile, his jaw working in his long silences. She lay in bed with her phone catching up on everything she hadn't seen over the weekend. There had been an interview printed with Hasan and his experiences in America. Her name had been dropped. She didn't need to read the article to know how it looked.

The messages began as the sun began to rise.

> Lucas: You made a mistake with him.
>
> Rey: Your mother is reading it right now. I tried to hide it from her. He used the word slut four times.
>
> Lucas: Admit you made a mistake leaving me. I'm the only one who can keep up with you.

The temptation to respond was stronger than usual, she wanted to tell Lucas that Quinn was more a man than he'd ever be, but Larisa knew a single message would be enough to unravel her boundaries.

Today I see Quinn, she thought. Again, her mind returned to him in the driveway and that inkling of consideration. She imagined today might be the day he asked how the rest of her weekend had gone, or perhaps complimented her outfit.

When Larisa arrived on set, the PA who signed her in presented Larisa with a covered picnic basket.

"What's this?"

"A gift?"

Larisa carried the basket onto the soundstage and over to the actors' holding area, where her chair now lived. Whatever was inside, the weight was unevenly distributed to one end; she had to carry it in both hands to keep it from tipping.

There wasn't a note. She untied the satin ribbon holding one side of the double lid closed and peeked inside. Nestled in the cloud of a fleece blanket was a completely white Persian kitten. For a moment, Larisa stared at it, then she closed the lid and retied the ribbon. She looked over at Tish who was directing Dansby's stand-in through blocking so the lighting crew could place their spots. It was obviously one of her kittens. But Tish had no obvious reason to give Larisa a gift.

"Morning."

Larisa jumped as Quinn materialized at her elbow. He glanced at the basket, then shifted his gaze toward the set as he took an overly casual sip of his tea. *Did he see the interview with Hasan?*

"Did you arrange this?" she asked.

"What if I did?"

Larisa opened her mouth to answer, then stopped. She didn't know what to say. After trying on and discarding several possible responses, she finally said, "Why?"

"Because everyone loves kittens."

She stared at him. "I'm not sure I love kittens."

"Not possible." He set his tea aside, leaned down, opened the basket, scooped the kitten up, and cuddled her against his chest. Larisa was vaguely aware of her jaw falling open, of feeling the need to blink compulsively until this illusion of Quinn cradling a kitten fell from her eyes. "You've never held a cat before?" He gifted her with one of his rare smiles. Coherent thoughts, awareness of the stage and the people around them, and everything else in her head scattered like startled mice. In the emptiness, radiant joy. *Oh God.*

"Get the blanket from the basket and make a puddle on your lap," said Quinn, apparently unaware he'd come to work that morning as an entirely different version of himself.

A puddle, thought Larisa, as she followed his directions, still dazed. It felt painful to turn away from him to reach for the basket. All she wanted to do was watch him, to soak up every nuance of this other, freer Quinn, who smiled and loved kittens.

Quinn leaned over and transferred the kitten into the middle of the well of blanket she'd created. "There. Now, most people would pet the kitten." His smile deepened. If she hadn't been so afraid of the kitten running off, she might have reached out and touched his mouth. She wanted to feel that smile in her hand, to brand its miraculous existence on her skin.

"Larisa, it's just a kitten."

"What if she runs away?"

"You'll chase her. The PAs will help."

"Why are you doing this?" Tears began to well in Larisa's eyes.

Quinn removed his bracelet of prayer beads and slipped it onto her wrist, a deft movement, apparently nonsexual, though his touch left her skin sizzling. He took the pencil from behind his ear and stabbed it into the base of her ponytail. "You'll be fine," said Quinn. "When Dansby comes on set, it would be great if you could coach him to cry."

Larisa blinked to clear her vision. "Are you serious?"

"Today's the money scene. Hold nothing back." He took up his tea and walked over to the set.

"What the fuck just happened?" muttered Larisa. For a moment, she watched Quinn, waiting for the telltale shift in his posture that foreshadowed stress. It didn't come. Somehow, despite this being the day of the scene he'd been dreading, Quinn was relaxed, even cheerful.

He brought me a kitten.

Tish dispatched a PA to call Dansby to the set for the final rehearsal and saw Larisa sitting with the kitten. "Isn't she just the sweetest thing? I hated giving her up, but I couldn't keep two, and Sebastian loves me so much. When Quinn told me you were looking, I knew it was the perfect home for her."

Bullshit, thought Larisa. "Did he say anything else?"

"Just that you're going through a hard time and might want something comforting. Sorry about that article. Prince What's-His-Face seems like a prick."

Comforting, thought Larisa, *it's a baby with claws.* Then, she thought about all the things people usually said that Tish hadn't, innuendos of judgement, how Larisa should have known better, how Hasan's prick-ness should have been obvious before she'd decided to fuck him over the side of a car.

"Thank you," said Larisa.

"She likes to eat first thing in the morning, wet food preferred, dry food tolerated. She scratches sisal posts not cardboard. Lactose intolerant. Balls are more fun than wands. And she loves attention as much as she loves her beauty sleep."

Larisa nodded like she knew what any of that meant.

"Tish, do you have the notes on the transition?" called Lane.

As Tish left, Larisa realized she'd been holding her breath, braced like she expected to be caught in a trap. She gazed down at the kitten and flinched as it shifted into a tighter ball, bringing her paws up in an *X* to pull her head down.

Quinn . . .

She refused to let her mind go any further.

This doesn't mean anything.

"What's its name?" asked Dansby, as he came up and deposited his phone, script, and water bottle in his chair beside her.

"She doesn't have a name yet."

"Lille skat." Dansby leaned over and stroked his thumb along the kitten's head. Larisa watched closely so she could imitate his movement later. As she watched, she also noticed Dansby appeared to struggle with the motion. He looked exhausted and pale, as though he'd lost a lot of blood.

"Long weekend?"

He struggled to summon a smile, which was a dim reflection of his usual buoyant grin. "Big day today." He looked toward the set where movement was starting to pause. People were waiting on him.

"Step one," said Larisa, "Get through rehearsal."

Dansby took a shallow, almost painful breath and walked toward the set. Even his walking seemed affected, like he'd slammed his hips into a moving car, or a car into him. Her gaze shifted to Quinn standing at the camera. No eye contact between them. No greeting.

Not unusual, but . . .

The kitten stirred in her lap, and Larisa clutched the edges of the blanket to keep the kitten from rolling off.

Normally, a camera rehearsal was a full performance of the scene with the actors doing everything they would if the camera was rolling. But with Dansby the only actor in the scene, and no one to play off of, the rehearsal ended up being Dansby doing a poor imitation of an actor playing an imprisoned spy. He moved from one side of his cell to the other, looked up toward the distant ceiling, lay down, examined the walls, all of it with more than his usual deer-in-the-headlights stiffness.

At the end, Quinn held a brief conference with Dansby. If he was frustrated, Larisa couldn't tell. He set his hand on Dansby's shoulder, something Larisa had never seen him do with anyone, let alone the man he believed was ruining his movie.

When Dansby came back to his chair, he asked Larisa how she thought he'd done.

"I thought it was a good rehearsal," she said carefully. "What did Quinn say?"

"He said I don't believe I'm in prison. I mean, what does he think? I wouldn't be able to do any acting if I was in prison. I'd be all hyperventilating and yelling to be let out whenever someone walked by."

"Could you try that for your scene?"

"Five minutes to last looks," called Tish.

The kitten was fully awake now and squirming. Dansby reached over and rubbed her tummy. When her little claws sank into his thumb, he didn't even flinch. Under the tattered sleeve of Dansby's distressed costume, Larisa thought she saw a mark on his wrist that didn't look like it had come from Makeup.

"Did you see Quinn this weekend?" she asked, as neutrally as possible.

"We went over some things at his house like before. But I still don't feel ready."

What did he do to you this time? But now wasn't the time or place for an interrogation. "Read me the scene description."

Dansby grimaced with pain as he reached for his script. "Prison scene four: The truth sinks in about my situation. As the time stretches, the harder it is."

"Not much to go on." Larisa pulled the pencil from her hair and drew circles in the air. The kitten's furry little head zoomed around to follow it. "But that's good for you. It gives you options."

"I just want it to be good. And I'm not sure I know how to do that."

"You can break it down by shaping the scene into a beginning, middle, and end. Where are you after the clapper sounds?"

"I've been worked over by the guards and thrown into this pit." Dansby motioned to the stage.

"And then what?"

"And then I . . . lay there for a while because it hurts so much."

"But only for a moment because you're high on adrenaline. That door locks behind you and you panic. Even the company of those guards who beat you is better than being alone."

Dansby nodded. "So, you think I could do something like I said, with the yelling and waving around?"

"If it feels real."

"Dansby, we're ready for you," called Tish.

Larisa snapped her fingers in front of Dansby's face. "Quick, finish the story. You're panicking, you yell for help even if you're only going to summon the guards. What's the climax?"

"I realize I'm trapped there."

"Quinn wants you to cry."

"He didn't tell me that. I can't just—"

"I bet you can. What makes you cry?"

He stared at her.

"I'll tell you mine. It's super embarrassing. At the end of *You've Got Mail*, you know that movie? At the end, he goes to meet her at the park. There's this perfect music cue that starts just when she sees him coming, and she's so happy. Then she tells us, 'I wanted it to be you.' Never fails, I bawl my eyes out. Don't know why. It's a textbook example of an innocent woman being deceived and manipulated by a powerful man, but it doesn't matter. I always cry."

"I'll try to remember that."

Larisa gave him a thumbs up as he began to walk away, but it didn't feel like enough so she called out, "You can do it, Dansby."

She knew Quinn would hate her for this positive note, but he was too far away to overhear. And she knew better than he did how important positive words could be.

The kitten had rolled herself onto her back and was pulling on her paws. Tish appeared from nowhere and swooped her hand in to tickle the kitten's belly. When she zoomed her hand out, the kitten extended all four paws like a starfish.

"Did he tell you what happened?" she asked.

"We just talked about the scene."

"He's really struggling this morning. And Quinn's not . . ." Tish chewed her lip, as though afraid of revealing a secret. "He's not the most nurturing."

It's a spy thriller, Tish, thought Larisa, but she smiled as though she understood. The word nurturing gave her a vague, panicky feeling that felt like something old and forgotten. She knew what she felt wasn't old, that it had to do with her last best friend getting married, the rituals of women who didn't work, Hasan saying she was a slut, and her terror of killing this helpless little cat.

"Last looks!" called Tish.

Makeup, Wardrobe, and Props rushed in to give Dansby a final inspection. He closed his eyes as people buzzed around him, breathing, and hopefully visualizing, or doing whatever process he'd created for himself. At the primary camera, Quinn stood ready, still relaxed, unnaturally confident.

What did he do?

"Quiet on the set."

As the clapper fell, Quinn lunged at Dansby, not far enough he broke the edge of the camera frame, but enough for Dansby to start back, stumbling into frame as though he'd been thrown by guards and landing hard on the padded floor. His groan of agony sounded real. Tense moments ticked by as he lay unmoving. Then, he slowly dragged himself to his feet with agonizing slowness, straightening a body that did not want to stand straight. He felt his way around the boundaries of his cell. He picked up speed as he went, fists testing for weaknesses, limping. Then, even though there was no scripted dialogue, he called to the guards. The sound tore out of his throat, until it gradually died away and he dropped to his knees, sobbing.

It was perfect. Or perhaps not perfect, but compared to what Dansby usually produced, it felt flawless.

"Cut!" called Tish, as Dansby's sobs rose up to the light fixtures.

The crew burst into a round of applause. Still, Larisa held her breath. She watched Quinn walk over and squat down beside Dansby. His hand rested on Dansby's knee as he spoke. Dansby was nodding, serious, not smiling, like a real actor would be in his situation.

Quinn gave him a hand up and called for a reset to start take two.

Larisa focused on stroking the kitten with her thumb the way Dansby had so she wouldn't watch him too intently as he returned to his seat.

"You were brilliant," she said.

"Thanks."

Larisa waited for Dansby's usual smile. It didn't come. He looked equal parts shaken and content. "Tell me about the crying thing again," he said. "I didn't get it this time around." He didn't look at her or even at the kitten. His eyes remained on the stage, on his cell, like it was a challenge he had set out to conquer.

Three takes later, Lane and Quinn agreed they had enough and moved onto close-ups. By then, Dansby had nearly mastered the art of crying. He was so wrung out, he had trouble controlling himself for the close-ups, but eventually these too were deemed enough and lunch was called. Larisa wanted to follow Dansby and eat with him, if only to watch for warning signs, but the kitten on her lap held her prisoner. She didn't know how to move her.

The set cleared. Larisa gingerly set her hands around the kitten's sides, testing out a possible lift, then immediately abandoning it. The kitten was so small, and soft, and fragile. It seemed any pressure Larisa applied would crush her.

"I didn't think you'd be this bad," said Quinn. "Didn't you have to take a class on alternative therapies or something? The value of animal companions?"

"Can you just move her for me? I want to go talk to Dansby."

Something uncertain flickered across Quinn's expression. *Guilt?* she wondered. *Is it even possible for Quinn to feel guilt?*

"I'd rather you talk with him at the end of the day, when we've got what we need from him. He's in the right place."

Not necessarily a good place, thought Larisa. But then, that was part of the work actors took on. Maybe the idea of it made her uncomfortable because Dansby wasn't a trained actor. She felt he'd been manipulated.

"You're judging me," he said.

"I'd have to know what you did in order to judge you."

"You know enough."

She lifted her gaze to meet his. Those murky blue (sometimes gray) eyes were equal parts determination and an open question, vulnerable, waiting.

"Did you do it to satisfy your own needs?" she asked.

"No."

"Did you respect him as a person with agency?"

"I was careful."

"I believe you."

"This is the first day on this set I feel like I know what I'm doing."

When he believes in himself he's beautiful. Not just beautiful. He could convince anyone of anything.

"You're the director," she said. "You made a decision for the good of your film. You own that, no matter what people think. Even me."

He gave her a sidelong glance as though he still didn't quite trust her.

She changed the subject. "We should plan some kind of outing this week. Something simple. Maybe groceries. And maybe dinner next week or something."

"Yeah, sure. I'm waiting to hear from someone on a possible thing this weekend, but I can be flexible."

"Parish?"

"I've met someone." Quinn hesitated. "But it's complicated. I mean, it won't be a problem for our project."

Something twisted in Larisa's gut. The nausea deepened. The Queen had almost made up her mind never to meet Quinn again. Being with him was a better high than cocaine and just as much of a dangerous dead end, especially in the wake of Kara's death. Her lizard brain was desperate for escape from the gnawing, rotten feeling in the back of her head. She'd never felt more alone, never wanted to be touched more. Not just touched, but held, nourished. It frightened her that Quinn seemed more able to do that than anyone else she'd ever met. If only they'd met under different circumstances; if only they'd been different people, they would already be true lovers.

"I promise," said Quinn, mistaking whatever he read on her face. "It won't be a problem."

"I believe you. I was just thinking, I don't think I can accept this cat."

"Sure you can."

"But I—"

"One day at a time," said Quinn, as he stood and walked away.

Bastard. Larisa again set her hands gently around the kitten's sides, squeezed in, and lifted. The kitten squirmed. Larisa dropped her back onto the blanket. *For fuck's sake, Larisa.* She bundled the blanket together over the kitten, pushed it back into the basket, then tapped the blanket back down so the kitten wouldn't suffocate. The disturbed kitten scrambled to jump out. With a startled screech, Larisa slammed the basket lid down and tied the ribbon.

Chapter 24

Performing for the Internet

Quinn had dreamed of this moment. In those dreams, he was more muscular and a little more handsome in a distinguished, artistic way. In the spotlight of a perfect California day, he confidently entered the boutique. The inventory specialist with the earpiece smiled at him and even gave a little bow of respect.

"Welcome Mr. VanderVeer," he would say.

Quinn had also had a few nightmares, including the one from the previous night, when he'd dreamed the inventory specialist had found him restrained by thousands of dollars' worth of neckties while the Queen rode him in the dressing room.

In the waking world, the day was cloudy and cold. He wore the outfit Larisa had bought him. Despite his best efforts to be late, he arrived at the towering, white stone façade of Tom Ford on Rodeo Drive before Larisa. Loitering on the otherwise empty sidewalk, trying to avoid eye contact with the inventory specialist standing on the other side of the glass door, he debated going down the block to the park. Before he could decide, the inventory specialist opened the door and stepped out.

"Are you lost?"

"No, I—"

"He's with me." Larisa breezed in beside him. "How are you, Hans?"

"Well enough. Come in. Come in. I pulled all the items you requested."

Larisa linked her arm through Quinn's and directed him farther inside the store. "We'll do measurements first if that's alright. Hi, Dash!" She twisted herself around to wave at someone coming up from the back. "This is Quinn VanderVeer. The director? In the middle of a big project for Enterprise."

"A pleasure, sir." Hans gave a short bow, no handshake. Which was fine. *Not an insult, Quinn.* Both Hans and Dash wore nicer suits than what Quinn had managed to rent for Sundance. He shrank in his shoes. This was a mistake.

But Larisa had a hold of his arm now, as though she could feel him wanting to retreat to the front door. She pinched his elbow against her ribs, steering him forward.

"We need a formal serious, a formal artist, and a couple statement looks. There's a bit of a rush. Last minute wedding in a few weeks and then a red carpet."

Dash clicked his tongue. "Shame on you, Larisa. Making us rush." He eyed Quinn. "But I think we can manage. Are you drinking Cristal today?"

"Yes. Quinn?"

Quinn nodded, certain he'd give himself away if he used words.

"Excellent. Make yourselves comfortable in the fitting room. Everything is laid out."

Quinn tried not to gawk at the displays as Larisa led the way deeper into the store, then around a corner into a leather-appointed sitting room set up around a fitting platform and a half circle of mirrors. On a rack along one side of the room, various shirts, trousers, and suitcoats hung waiting.

For him.

"You okay?" she asked.

"Yeah. I mean, it's nice. But it's not Valentino."

She smiled a smile that didn't reach her eyes. "Look at you, making a joke. This doesn't have to be hard. If you see something you want just interrupt. Otherwise, I'm in charge."

Her words warmed his chest. It felt good to be taken care of, even if he'd signed a contract with her to have it done. There was no way he would have survived something like this himself. He watched the movements of her impatient hands as she explored the clothes, eyes narrowed with a critical gaze. On the surface, she looked wholly occupied with the task at hand, as invested in it as though she was his assistant or an actual girlfriend. He wondered what was going on beneath the surface. Once or twice, he caught a kind of hard edge in her expression that he recognized as the byproduct of an extremely high functioning person holding herself together because the alternative was simply not something they did.

He wanted to say, "Thank you for doing this," but then Dash returned with two flutes of champagne and a measuring tape draped around his neck. Hans entered on his heels with a pair of shoe boxes in his arms.

Quinn sipped his champagne and pulled off the hoodie Larisa had bought him. *Here it goes.*

An hour later, they left the store. The champagne had left Quinn buzzed, the experience had left him giddy. He felt slightly sick as he always did with alcohol in his stomach, but it also felt good.

He'd successfully withstood Dash measuring and evaluating his body. Fabrics he couldn't name had brushed his skin. He'd stared at himself in the mirror and seen a man transformed into a version of the man he'd always wanted to be. He'd seen that same man reflected in Larisa's eyes as she pulled at sleeve cuffs and evaluated his ass in various pants. She knew exactly what she was doing, what worked, and what fit for Quinn's newly curated public persona.

This is what the muses of the old masters felt like, he thought. *Held so well in knowing hands.* When the contract ran out on their dating scheme, he wondered if Larisa would be willing to continue consulting with him.

They drove to Whole Foods in her Bentley for the second part of their errand even though it was faster to walk. The champagne buzz vanished when Larisa started the Bentley's engine and screaming rushed out of the speakers at full volume.

"Sorry." Larisa turned the music down but not off. "You can change it to something you like. Oh wait, you don't—never mind."

The dismissive tone in her voice as she remembered he didn't listen to music momentarily raised his hackles. But he remembered Gunter Kahn's wise advice the previous weekend about words spoken from a place of pain.

Larisa's fingers tapped the steering wheel. Her shoulders jiggled to the music as she took a turn so sharp her wheels squealed.

"Do you think we should start talking about your friends?" he asked.

"What about them?"

"The usual stuff a boyfriend would know?"

"They're not super observant."

The Bentley swerved into the Whole Foods parking lot and screeched to a stop.

"You up for carrying things out?" she asked. "People like to see that kind of thing."

Quinn had to hurry to stay at Larisa's side as she speed-walked across the parking lot and into the store. There, she trolled down one aisle after another, pulling apparently random items from the shelves.

"Do you ever buy your own groceries?" he asked.

"My parents' chef, Estelle, manages all my food. But the people watching us don't know that."

Quinn had been so preoccupied keeping up he hadn't noticed anyone watching. Now, he saw a store clerk at the end of the aisle giving them an interested side-eye. As they turned down the next aisle, a too casual, beefy dude stood on the sidewalk peering into the store.

"Are you on socials? Oh, cat food! I feel like I asked you that already." Larisa whipped out her phone and navigated to her new app. "You should follow me and our pretty baby." She leaned into him as she showed him three posts with several thousand likes. Each picture showcased the white kitten in a frame that looked like a polaroid complete with lighting flares.

The first post was captioned: Look at this adorable gift from my honey.

"You call your boyfriends honey?"

"What's wrong with that?"

"It doesn't seem like you."

Larisa emitted a harsh laugh. "What do you know?"

She wants to fight, thought Quinn. *Don't fall for it.*

"This is my favorite." Larisa shoved her phone toward him with the screen displaying the kitten bundled in a faux fur blanket just as white and fluffy as she was. Caption: What should I name this cute little bundle?

"You're going to let the internet name your kitten?"

"Why not?" said Larisa, in the same aggressive tone. She began pulling cans of cat food off the shelf.

"Seems strange." He brought out an arm to stop her. She jerked away from him.

"Lay off!"

"Those are adult cans. You need kitten cans."

She was panting like they'd just had a physical fight. For a moment, he thought she would punch him. But then, she turned the can in her hand, looking at the label, then comparing it to the others still on the shelf.

"I don't know why you gave me a fucking kitten," she muttered.

It didn't seem like he'd get anywhere asking her outright what was wrong. Instead he repeated the thing that had lodged itself in the side of his brain. "Why have you given strangers permission to name your cat?"

"I'm inviting them into my life. It buys me goodwill. You should try it."

Quinn couldn't imagine anything he wanted to do less than invite a world full of strangers into his life. "No amount of goodwill will bribe them into respecting you," he said before he could stop himself.

"I think we're done here. You need anything?" She didn't wait for him to answer. He found himself once again rushing to keep up as she plowed down the aisle to the checkout.

"Run for your life, man," called a fellow shopper as they rushed past. "She's no Queen of Hearts."

Larisa's face turned bright red. Quinn expected her to shout back an equally cutting insult. Instead, she pressed her lips together, ignoring the cashier until the end of the checkout process, when the girl asked for an autograph and gushed about Larisa's high school reality show. Quinn grabbed the bag of groceries and followed Larisa out the door, rushing now because he wasn't entirely sure she wouldn't leave him behind. They passed the beefy guy who had been loitering at the window. The rat-a-tat-tat of his camera shutter followed them all the way to the car.

"I guess today we're fighting," said Quinn once they were inside.

Larisa's fingers seized the steering wheel with a white-knuckled grip. "What would we have to fight about?" she whispered, more to herself than to him.

"Maybe one of us isn't happy having our *baby* on the internet." Quinn paused, hoping for at least a smile. She didn't move. "You're upset about my spending habits, but really you just wish my ass filled out a suit better, and you're thinking about that hunky guy over there and how your secret fantasy is being with a guy who can toss you around like an ice skater."

Larisa glared at the windshield, then, still in her fighting voice,

"Big men are never comfortable with their bodies. It's exhausting."

"I wouldn't know."

"I'm not sure I can do this."

"This what? Dating?" A thrum of panic vibrated up Quinn's spine. "We just started."

Larisa put the Bentley in drive and pulled out of the parking lot.

"What's the problem?"

"Everything."

"Okay, well. That doesn't make any sense, but fine. What will you do?"

"Move back to Minnesota."

Quinn frowned. "What?"

The Bentley took a turn so sharp Quinn felt the weight of the body shift, his passenger side wheels momentarily airborne.

"Why don't you just let me out here? I'll walk back to my car."

"People will see."

"Yeah, well. Your driving is scaring me. So please, let me out."

She slammed on the brakes. "Get out!"

For a moment, he thought about fighting back. But the exit had been his idea, and he really didn't like the way she was driving. So he got out and stood there as she peeled out and tore down the road.

WTF?

Chapter 25

Bachelorette Party

nother Friday on set without Larisa. *Which is fine,* thought Quinn. *I'm not dependent on her.* And yet. When she was away from set it felt like half the crew had also disappeared. The soundstage became cavernous and ordinary. In that emptiness, he found himself waiting for her to make an appearance he knew she wouldn't make. He even checked to see if she had posted new kitten photos online. She hadn't.

During the dailies screening, his mind wandered. She'd been so upset the previous day. Should he have called her later to ask if she'd made it home? He could call before she started work. But then, he was sure there were people in her life who worried over these things. She didn't need him.

I'll just send a text.

What would the text say?

Please don't break up with me.

Quinn shook his head. Instead of texting Larisa, he texted Doan, asking if any messages had come for him.

"Are you happy or sad?" asked Sid when they met in his office. "I can't ever tell."

Both, always, thought Quinn, but he didn't want to lay that on Sid, who preferred people to be happy.

"Movie's almost in the can," said Quinn. "We're celebrating tonight. Name the place."

"Somewhere I don't have to dress up?"

"You look better than I do. Did you do the thing?"

"I did. She's at work. Seems fine."

"How close did you get?"

"She didn't see me."

"Well, she's good at hiding, so she could be upset but unless you were up close watching for a while you wouldn't know it."

"Spying on your fake girlfriend is not a thing I should be doing as Director VanderVeer's assistant, especially since we're moving up in the world now."

"She was upset yesterday."

"I know." Sid pulled a rolled-up tabloid from his pocket. "Congratulations. You've launched."

On the right side of the front cover, in all its grainy glory, was a photo of Quinn running after Larisa as she came out of Whole Foods. ICE PRINCESS ALREADY IN TROUBLE WITH NEW HONEY. Quinn flipped to the interior coverage, reading the paragraph that accompanied several more photos taken from the parking lot:

"Larisa de France-Kahn spotted having a tiff with presumed new beau, film director Quinn VanderVeer. Did a certain Saudi Prince have something to do with it? The couple was seen at Tom Ford before driving over to Whole Foods to stock up on cat food and snacks."

How do they know what she bought?

"I'll get you a frame," said Sid. "We'll put it up at the house."

Quinn finished reading.

"How does it feel?"

"Surreal." Quinn laughed. "But it's horrible to Larisa. They have a whole laundry list of guys here. No significant relationships ever."

"Well, that's what you're helping her out with, right?"

"Hard to imagine what kind of guy is going to sign up for her." As soon as the words left his mouth, Quinn felt guilty. But then Sid was nodding, and it was too late to take it back or explain.

"I wouldn't date a shrink. Can't believe you're doing it, fake or not."

"Well, tonight my fake girlfriend is going to get us into a club with a waitlist out to July."

They went to Ysabel, a lounge so high up on the list of places to be it didn't even count as a place to be seen because the only people who got in were already known.

"What's the name, sir?" asked the concierge.

"de France-Kahn," said Quinn.

The concierge's eyes rose from her tablet, looked him over, then looked at Sid. "I wasn't aware she was coming tonight."

"Last minute thing. Bad week."

The concierge clicked her tongue sympathetically. "We can get her in. But maybe she wants to go somewhere else?"

"Why?"

The concierge leaned forward conspiratorially. Quinn also leaned forward, one eyebrow arched like he was curious, but he really didn't want to be bothered. "Prince Hasan is here."

"That Saudi guy?"

"Boasting about having her over the hood of his car."

An image of Larisa's bruised wrist flashed through Quinn's mind. With it came a wave washing out all other thoughts. It was a wave fed by a thousand other things—Parish, Eddie, the film, Dansby, Larisa keeping her distance, doubts, doubts, doubts, how close he felt to losing everything—but mostly he saw that bruise, a mark given without respect. He brushed past the concierge and into the club, up the staircase to the entrance on the second floor. He scanned the deck, then plowed straight through a clump of people and into the first central room.

Sid hovered at his elbow, out of breath. "What are we doing here, boss?"

Quinn moved into the second, larger room. There, in the far corner on a sectional sofa, the Saudi prince held court with a group of admirers.

"The papers had it wrong," he was saying. "She ran out because she was so hot for me, she couldn't stay decent in public. We barely made it to the parking lot before she—"

That was the last word Hasan would say clearly for the next three weeks. Quinn broke his jaw, knocked out two teeth, and disconnected a retina before the prince's admirers dragged him away.

Jaden's bachelorette party started with karaoke, sushi, and sake flights in a private alcove at Morimoto's. These were all things Larisa loved. They were, in fact, hallmarks of the sisters' college years, skipping classes for manicures and surviving dead week by clubbing until the thin hours of the morning.

But this call back to those days, when they'd all walked the same path toward mirrored futures, now felt like an insult, which Larisa took personally. She'd gotten dressed for this special event in a third of her usual time, with even less of her usual effort. Since she'd arrived, she'd been waiting for the moment someone dared mention she'd left her hair natural, so she could tell them exactly what she thought of all of it. Of this.

The twelve revelers included the sorority sisters, Larisa, Krissy, Kahleah, and Rosa, and Jaden's two actual sisters, her future sister-in-law, her neighbor Chung, and three coworkers from her ToeBeans for Good foundation (Feral Cat Rescue). All ten were married (or divorced) with children. They spent the first part of the evening passing around school pictures.

"What about you, Larisa?" asked Jaden's future sister-in-law, who either didn't follow celebrity news or was being intentionally snotty. "Any kids?"

"This is my fur baby," said Larisa, showing her phone and the ten thousand likes on her latest socials posts.

"I totally support fur babies," said one of the ToeBeans employees.

"Larisa has a cool new boyfriend," said Krissy. "She'll be pregnant by this time next year."

Like fuck I will, thought Larisa.

"Work fast," said Jaden's older sister. "It gets harder to pop them out every year you get older."

"We've started trying again," said Rosa, as she held up crossed fingers.

"Didn't I just hear about you?" the snotty sister-in-law continued. "In trouble with a prince or something?"

"I skipped out on dinner," said Larisa.

"But with a prince?" The woman's eyes went exaggeratedly wide as she swayed into the shoulder of one of the ToeBeans women. "I'd love a prince."

"Why?" asked Larisa, too sober, too angry. Larisa, always too *something*. Her social acceptability was melting faster than the ice in her drink.

The woman laughed. "Who doesn't?"

"That's not really an answer."

The group had gone quiet. Somewhere in the back of her head, Larisa knew she was spoiling the mood, but she couldn't summon enough feeling to care.

"I hope your new guy is better," said Jaden finally. "I don't want you all sad and alone on my big day."

Larisa swallowed down something sharp that might have come out as *I'm not sad and I don't mind being alone.* Instead, she pulled Jaden's head down into her lap and stroked her hair like they'd done as girls when they'd drunk too much or cried too much, and the room was spinning. *And that one time when we—*

So, so tired.

All of it.

"I just think it would be exciting to be that important," said the woman. "Everyone looking to you, how you dress, what your opinions are on everything. My husband doesn't even know I'm allergic to shellfish."

"Are you really?" Krissy surveyed the remnants of the first round of sushi.

"A prince is not going to remember your allergies," said Larisa. "Or your birthday, or probably even your mother's name. All he wants to do is prop you up on his arm and make sure he's well ornamented."

"So why did *you* go out with him?"

"I'm an ornamental slut."

"'Risa!" cried Jaden and Krissy at the same time.

"There's no shame in it. I mean, you all have gotten there first, so tits to you. I sleep around. No one respects me. I really should try holding out for some lawyer who's losing his hair." She glanced at Kahleah sitting in the corner keeping to herself. "Or maybe a scientist just looking to sell out and play golf." She glanced at Rosa. "But for sure, chastity until I do. That's the fast track to happiness. If I can make it through a six-month engagement without pointing out all his flaws," she glanced at Krissy, "or embarrassing him in front of some hot waitress," eyes back to Kahleah, "and promise him three kids and twelve dinner parties a year, what more could I ask for? I certainly would never be sad or lonely then."

Larisa finished breathless and almost yelling. The sequined clutch in her right hand had started and stopped vibrating several times. In the shocked echo chamber that the room had become, Larisa decided this was a good time to answer it. She used her full title instead of her first name like she usually did. She wanted whoever was on the other end to be scared. "This is Doctor Larisa de France-Kahn, you better have something important to say or I'm hanging up."

"This is Officer Valdez with the LAPD at Wilshire Station. We have a Quinn A. VanderVeer here in custody. You can remand him on bail for two thousand dollars. The address is—"

Larisa hung up her phone. Laughter burst out of her cramping chest. "See? This is what ya'll miss in your settled little lives, phone calls from the police saying your boyfriend's been arrested."

"What happened?" Rosa's face puckered with concern.

"My first weekend off in three months." Larisa shook her head. *Un-Fucking-Believable.*

"He can rot until morning."

Quinn will be a mess in jail.

Someone like him probably isn't safe overnight.

The sisters-in-law and foundation employees wore almost mirror expressions of horror, not even aware they were staring at her. Her friends were less shocked. Jaden was sipping her drink, probably wishing she could start the night over. Krissy and Kahleah were exchanging knowing looks, comforting each other in the wake of Larisa's barbs. Rosa looked torn between coming to give Larisa a hug and drawing back into the couch to play wallflower with Kahleah. She never did well with other people's embarrassing moments, especially if they didn't have the good sense to be embarrassed for themselves.

If I don't go bail him out, I'll be thinking about him all night.

"You know what? I'm going to take a break. I'll meet you at the resort." Larisa gave a bow of apology to Jaden and made her exit before anyone could protest.

Chapter 26

Big Feelings

By the time Larisa arrived at the station, she had worked up a second storm of rage, and had organized exactly how she would release it when she saw Quinn. The storm seethed as she identified herself to the desk officer and discovered the bail was one thousand dollars for Quinn and another thousand for Sid, his apparent accomplice in a club fight.

While she waited, she ignored the sidelong glances of cops passing through and the outright leers of arrestees being processed. A picture arrived on her phone of her sisters, all with sad faces, then another picture of them blowing kisses while they rode in the limo. What Larisa most noticed was all the wedding rings. How did the old poem go? Two roads diverged in a wood? She barely remembered the series of decisions that led her down a path where she'd be passing time at a police station on a Friday night instead of a luxury resort. She'd never planned to be the one left behind.

Sid emerged from the Personnel Only door with a fat lip and a tear in his pleather jacket.

"Thanks for doing this."

"I would think it's your job to keep him out of these situations."

"In theory." Sid grinned. "It happened pretty fast."

The door opened and Quinn walked out, maddingly intact, not even sweaty.

"It was that prince," said Sid. "We were going out to celebrate and he was there talking about you and . . . things happened."

God damn the day I fucked around with Hasan.

Quinn shoved his hands in his pockets and walked past Larisa without making eye contact. "Call us a car, Sid."

Growing more incensed, Larisa followed them to the door and out onto the street. Sid got on his phone, then decided to wisely step some distance away.

"Who the fuck do you think you are?"

"It won't happen again," said Quinn, still not looking at her.

"You're right. It won't because next time I'm not coming. You call someone else. Maybe one of those great parents you told me about."

Quinn stared straight ahead, the only sign her barb had landed was a tightening at the corner of his jaw. "I take it your event is not going well."

"It was just perfect until the police called to say my *boyfriend* was in jail. Do you think I owe you for defending my honor? Let me tell you something. You take that bullshit chivalry and stick it up your coward's ass. Only cowards need to lie to people trying to help them and beat up men who are just doing the same things other men have done since the beginning of time. Including you, I'm sure."

Another jaw tightening. No eye contact. Lips clamped so tightly together they were almost the same bloodless color as his skin.

"Car's coming," said Sid, as he hesitantly inserted himself in front of Larisa. "Do you want to handle the money transfer for bail now, or . . ."

"Forget it. I'm late for my life."

A black Escalade pulled up as Larisa turned to walk away. Sid opened the passenger door and the back side door of the Escalade.

"We'll drive you back." Quinn reached out and took her elbow hard enough she lost her balance when she wrenched away.

"Hands off."

"Get in," said Quinn.

The underlining command rattled down her spine like a land-slide. She went still, allowed him to take her elbow, steer her into the backseat.

"Where are we going?" asked Sid.

"Palisades Resort," said Quinn.

Larisa glared at him. "How do you know that?"

"Your friends are posting pictures on socials with location tags." He drew his mouth together as he considered her. "Sid keeps track of these things."

"Stalker," muttered Larisa. "Take me to Morimoto's. I'll figure it out from there."

"What's there?" asked Sid.

"My car."

"You can't drive right now."

"Watch me."

"Are you drunk?"

"Like you care. Just—you know what—fuck this." The Escalade was at a stoplight. Larisa reached for the door handle and yanked on it. Quinn's arm flew out and stopped her as the door opened.

"Let's not kill ourselves tonight."

"You got to try. Why not me?" She looked down at his arm blocking her way and saw the row of scabbing knuckles on his right hand. "Of all the people you could attack." She paused as something uncomfortable churned through her rage. "And you did it for the worst reason. I'm not worth defending."

"I did it for selfish reasons," said Quinn. "My honor is also at stake now, *honey*." His eyes glittered. She reached out to slap him, but he caught her hand, pressed it down against the other and held them between his own.

Larisa opened her mouth to yell at him and found no words at the ready. His skin was cool and soft, his hands surprisingly strong. In that moment, she realized he was probably a much better man than she'd given him credit for. He wasn't doing this to get in her pants. He was doing this because she was clearly in need of help.

She would have preferred him trying to sleep with her. Then, at least, she'd have known how to fight him. But this, kindness without ulterior motive, the fact that every other man she'd ever met would have run from her or lashed out, was so much worse.

The rage drained out of her. Tears came, but not strong enough she couldn't hold them back.

"I'm really good at my job."

Quinn nodded.

"I'm not dating you because I need someone to hold my hand and tell me I look nice and remember I'm allergic to shellfish." She paused. "I'm not allergic to shellfish. Just, as an example."

"Now we know." Quinn released her hands and sat back into his side of the bench.

"What are you staring at?" She swiped at her eyes.

"You're human." A slight smile pulled up the side of his mouth, triumphant.

"Surprise."

"We should celebrate."

"Celebrate you knowing I'm human?" she croaked. "Haven't you had enough for one night?"

"We didn't even get to drink," said Sid from the front seat.

"I prefer ice cream when I'm this miserable," said Larisa.

Sid pulled out his phone and began a conference with the driver. Ten minutes later, the three of them sat in a row on a bench outside Paradis Ice Cream. Larisa devoured three scoops of three flavors mashed into a waffle cone. To her right, Sid slurped a milkshake. To her left, Quinn made slow work of his kid size, single scoop orange sherbet.

"What's with Quinn and food?" she asked Sid.

"I'm sitting right here," said Quinn.

"I don't feel like weeding through your bullshit answer when I know Sid will tell me straight." She gave Sid a dazzling smile.

"Small stomach," said Sid without hesitation. "Gets sick if he eats too much."

"Traitor," muttered Quinn.

"She's a shrink. She can probably help."

"She's not my shrink anymore."

Sid shrugged. "We could tell her other things."

"Not right now."

"You might have more fun with this dating thing if you stop being afraid of her."

"I'm not afraid of her."

Sid gave Larisa a knowing look. "I bet she knows already and is just waiting to see if you hang yourself."

"I can't talk while I'm eating." Quinn shoved his little plastic spoon with its equally small portion of sherbet into his mouth.

"How long have you two known each other?" asked Larisa.

"Sophomore year of high school."

"Classmates?"

"Coworkers."

"Seriously Sid, shut up."

Larisa glanced at Quinn and judged that despite what he was saying, he did not seem particularly tense or uncomfortable. *It probably felt really good to punch Hasan,* she thought. It seemed safe to proceed.

"Single mother," she said. "She struggled to keep a job, former prostitute, maybe trafficked, found herself a Prince Charming at the Super Bowl. Dad started out in the picture then left. No extended family around to help. No siblings. Started working at fifteen."

Sid gave an impressed whistle. "Sixteen."

"Sixteen is young to be in charge of survival," said Larisa.

"How did you know she was from overseas?"

"Quinn was chatting with Yuri, the language consultant, in Russian."

"Keep your psychoanalysis to yourself," muttered Quinn.

"I'd like to hear it," said Sid. "He's a verifiable mess."

"She already knows that," hissed Quinn.

"And your mom's gone now?" asked Larisa.

"Went back to Ukraine when he started college. His dad is—"

"We're both very impressed by Larisa's powers of deduction," said Quinn.

"How did you know his dad left?" asked Sid.

"Trade secrets."

"Aw, come on."

"Honestly, I'm more interested in the cat." Larisa looked at Quinn, checking in to see if he was still alright. "You have had an important cat in your life."

Sid laughed. "Quinn stole a stray tabby that lived in our warehouse, right? I barely remember that. Junior year? When did it give me rabies?"

"It didn't."

"Did you know he gave me one of Tish's kittens?" Larisa held out her arm to show Sid the scratches she'd acquired.

"No one should be alone," said Quinn softly. "Especially not when everything's going wrong."

Tears burned Larisa's eyes. She wanted to argue she wasn't alone and not everything was going wrong. But then she would've had to find the energy to lie. And it didn't feel right to lie with Quinn sitting beside her so vulnerable, probably waiting for her to pass some sort of judgement.

The truth was, she did want to pass judgement. *I knew your mom was alive but gone because men whose mothers die young need to prove themselves to her. Men whose mothers abandon them need to prove something to themselves.* Larisa wanted to say it, to show Quinn she saw even more than he knew, and she accepted him. But it seemed too personal to come out and speak that kind of truth, especially since she thought it was probably something Sid didn't even know.

Do not let yourself fall for someone who is using you to solve his issues.

Too late for that.

She'd seen the oncoming edge of the abyss since the beginning, yet she had not diverted. What was beyond that edge? Couldn't there be some unseen bridge waiting to slip invisibly beneath her feet? So many years spent depriving herself, now her self-restraint had dissolved. Every day, she longed for the galloping heat to rise on her face when she thought of his dark scowl, relished her gut swooping when she pictured the line of his back and the pert curve of his ass pressed over his feet as he knelt and waited for her at Club D.

Not me, the Queen.

Larisa covertly pulled out her phone and messaged Doan. At some point tonight she would have to face her friends, apologize, then wind herself up for the rest of the party, but she could at least give herself a reward when it was over.

Chapter 27

On His Toes

As soon as the Queen arrived, Quinn sensed this session would be something different than before. She circled him as he knelt, eyes lowered, hands in his lap but not covering his penis. *Because I offer everything.* The thought gave him chills. Every moment that passed, he itched to stand up and assert himself, to touch her. She was so close. Her nails scraped along the ridge of his shoulders. He could have reached out, grabbed her arm, and pulled off the mask.

Surrender.

The toe of her boot nudged his knees apart. He swallowed back giddy anticipation and tried to hold still.

They were in the Victorian room because all the others were full. He'd made up his mind not to think about the problems in sublimated experience, to focus on the only thing that mattered— being worthy of her. Thankfully, the Queen didn't seem interested in playing a pseudohistorical scene. So far, she'd ignored everything in the room except the gilded, Louis XIV imitation armchair. She'd sat down twice to watch him, only to jump up a few moments later and resume pacing.

"Do you have a confession for me?" Her voice had lost its hard edge of derision. Or was he just imagining its absence because he no longer felt driven to be derided? This was the first time he'd come to her feeling at peace. He wanted her, but he wasn't consumed with his need for her. The peace mingled with short bursts of energy that felt like light exploding inside him.

What had she planned? How would he feel? What would happen after? All of it he fought down so she wouldn't see how difficult it was to keep his pose.

"Forgive me," he said. "I forgot my place last time. It won't happen again."

She circled.

He tried not to hold his breath. It felt like something was coming, but he couldn't tell what. Punishment, but also a ruling on his indiscretion at their previous meeting. He listened to her boots clip over to the wall of instruments. He raised his eyes just enough to see her select a chain several feet long and a cane.

She returned and knocked the cane against his thigh. "Stand. Hold your hands out, palms up." She brought the cane down on his open palms. His arms wavered under the shock of the blow, the burst of pain, but then he raised them again to the level of his shoulders. She draped the chain across his palms, easy enough to hold in that moment, but in five minutes, he knew it would feel like an anvil. He wasn't likely to last longer than ten.

"On your toes," she said. "Your heels will not drop. Your arms will not drop."

"Yes, Mistress." Quinn worked to conceal his disappointment, and the flurry of fear buried inside it, as the Queen retreated to her chair and settled in to watch him from a cool distance, the cane inert on her lap.

"I deserve worse," he said, if only to entice her to speak to him.

"I decide what you deserve. Heels up." She leaned forward and tapped the cane against his ankles.

"But you don't know everything. I've thought of you every day. I can't stop thinking about you."

The cane struck his ass, causing him to lose his balance. His arms dropped. He scrambled to resume position.

"Beat it out of me then. Punish me for loving you."

"You know nothing of love!" Another blow, this time across

the small of his back, which hurt so much it sparked tears in his eyes as he gasped.

"I'll do anything."

The Queen jumped up from her chair and began to circle him. The cane stirred the air, restless with malice. "Who am I to you?"

"Goddess."

"Liar." The cane struck his left leg.

"My queen."

"Liar." The cane struck him again in the back. Pain radiated down his legs and up his spine. He held his position, tried to breathe. His penis was thickening, a vulnerable new target. The cane trailed down the inside of one thigh and up the other. He closed his eyes, savoring the rise of his nerves, everything within pulled tight, posed on the brink. And how desperately he wanted to plunge.

"Give up," she said. "It's too hard."

"I can do it."

Were they talking about holding his position or something else? It seemed they were playing a game, but they were also negotiating. The cane moved as she circled, struck his shoulders three times in rapid succession, leaving him breathless and dizzy. The arches of his feet had begun to spasm. His left calf cramped. Another blow, hard against his back. He pitched forward onto his knees. She caught him before he hit the floor and lowered him down. But then, just as he dared hope this was the moment he'd been waiting for, she retreated to her chair where she watched him gasp and shake.

"You failed," she said with finality that seized his chest with cold dread.

"Let me try again." He started to push himself up.

The cane came down and rested on the back of his neck. "Stay there."

His arms burned. The fire in his lower back burned with

sharp edges like she might have broken him open. His groin ached for release, but he dared not touch himself.

The silence lengthened. Gradually, he was able to pull himself into a kneeling position. He kept his gaze at the level of her boots and waited.

And waited.

The feel of her eyes on him heightened the insistence of his erection. He remembered what it had been like to be inside her, that infinite, luscious space that had so well wrapped him up and carried him away to a place he'd never been. *It won't happen tonight,* he thought. *I've ruined it.*

"What you love does not exist outside this room," said the Queen.

It could.

The cane came down on his left shoulder with a sharp thwack. "Don't argue with me."

He bowed his head further so she wouldn't be able to see his face and read his thoughts.

"Find your love in what you already have outside."

What do I have? Does she mean Parish?

Quinn felt his erection withering. The Queen left her chair and stood before him. "Stand up."

When he struggled to obey, she reached down and supported him. It took all his control not to collapse into her arms and hang on until she saw what he saw. No person out in the real world was ever going to be to him what she could be, if only she crossed the threshold and revealed herself.

"You're better than you know," she said. "Let people in."

"I've tried—"

"Stop trying to control the scene." With that, she withdrew, leaving him as wobbly as a baby deer against a backdrop of gaudy Victorian pastels and lace. And too many unspoken arguments curdling in his head.

Chapter 28

The Calm Before

Eleven days to Jaden's Wedding

On Monday, Larisa wore black leather pants and did her makeup with dark, dramatic eyes and lips, but Quinn barely looked at her the entire day. She'd thought, after he'd done so well on Friday night, keeping her from driving, seeing her as a regular person, allowing her to confirm some of the secret parts of his life, that things would be different between them.

Instead, it seemed the unveiling, or perhaps his embarrassment, or who knew what, had pushed them apart. He clearly wasn't at a place where the Queen's advice, to find the love he already had, was going to lead him to Larisa.

That night, she went to her parents' house for dinner and a movie. It was the week of her cousin's Tuscan destination wedding. So, her mother, rather than waste time sleeping through a movie, decided to skip it and focus on packing.

"Italy in March," she muttered, as she picked over Estelle's plating of their dinner. "It's cold, isn't it?"

Gunter already sat at the kitchen table with Larisa. They were scrolling through IMDB, trying to decide what to watch. Larisa was listless. Nothing sounded interesting. Her father was trying to be considerate, recognize her fragile state, and let her choose something she was comfortable with, but really, she just wanted him to pick something, and she would sit with him until it was over. This was how she'd decided to manage her life, one hour at a time. She would get through tomorrow, and the next day the same way, until something changed.

What would change?

The wedding day would arrive.

And then it would pass.

"I hope it's warm enough for an outside reception," said Suzette. "The stars will be visible in the mountains. A dance under the stars. That's the only true romance at a wedding reception. Larisa, we should remember that for when your time comes. We'll take a side trip after Milan next February, look at some villas. Or wait, that would be too late. You'll want to be married in May or June. A two-year engagement is not fashionable anymore, is it?"

There's no fucking way I'm going to Italy, thought Larisa. Lucas lived there. The whole of the Atlantic and all of North America between them barely felt like enough distance. She wasn't going to dare fate by coming that close.

"Really, Mom, I think you'll be happier in the long run if you just assume I'm never getting married."

"Quinn was lovely the other night. He handled you so well."

"I don't need to be handled," muttered Larisa.

"We could watch one of Quinn's films," said Gunter.

Larisa shrugged. "I suppose I should, shouldn't I?"

"You did put Milan on your calendar, didn't you Larisa? It's just five days. The hospital can spare you for five days if you give them ten months' notice?"

"Why would I go to fashion week, Mom?"

"Because I'm being honored by the Milano Fashion Institute for my contributions to the industry? Because you're my daughter and I want to see you?"

"Be seen with you."

Gunter raised his eyes from his tablet and gave Larisa a warning look.

"Ask me again in October."

After dinner, the family separated. Suzette went up to her rooms to share a bottle of wine with Estelle and pack, and Larisa and Gunter went to the theater. Larisa tucked herself under a blanket, then dumped her basket of finger toys onto her lap.

"Where'd my Japanese fish go?" asked Gunter.

"It's at my apartment waiting for its mate."

"I hope that's not a metaphor."

Larisa's eyes drifted to the screen ahead of them. They'd decided to watch Quinn's second film, a high school drama about two friends trying to avoid gang violence and unstable home environments. It was more atmospheric than she'd expected, with minimal dialogue and long scenes of the boys out in LA, where the setting seemed to dwarf them with its cruel, impersonal vastness.

"Is he any good?" she asked.

"What do you think?"

"I think there's no music. The story's been done."

"All stories have been done," said Gunter. "But see how he makes you feel like these boys are trapped? Have you noticed all the fences? All the closed doors?"

"Wouldn't we call that obvious?"

Gunter shook his head. "I wonder about you sometimes."

"Me too."

Larisa took the long way back to her apartment. As she drove, she listened to her favorite playlist of movie scores as a secret revenge against Quinn for having to sit through an entire movie of traffic sounds, police sirens, and no music. While she drove, she tried to think of nothing but music, the throbbing pulse of it, its infinite variety and possibility. And she composed an argument in her head for a conversation with Quinn in a future where they were friends, if not lovers. When she got home, she thought she might send him an email with her thoughts but discovered he'd already sent her a message.

To: You
From: VanderVeer, Quinn

We should start planning for the wedding. What do I need to bring? And we need to decide how we're going to do it. And I should at least know about your friends. The obvious things.

Larisa wanted to start writing immediately. But her nameless kitten was curling around her legs mewing.

"You have food," said Larisa. "What do you want?"

The kitten followed Larisa to her bedroom for her laptop, then back out to the living room where she plopped down in the floof of her beanbag chair. She set the laptop on her thighs. The first line of her response was already in her head. But then,

"Oh my God! What the fuck?"

The kitten had dug her claws into Larisa's leg and was climbing her jeans.

"Why would you do that? See the beanbag? Right here? You can climb this. Destroy it for all I care, but I can't walk around with holes in my legs."

The kitten, remarkably undeterred, rounded the horn of Larisa's knees and hopped onto the beanbag, tottered past the laptop, then clawed her way up Larisa's left side. She came to rest on Larisa's collarbone, where she curled up under her chin and began to purr.

"Okay, fine. Just stay there and don't bother me."

Larisa took a selfie with the cat. Then, she turned her attention to the email.

"Dear Quinn, The next time you want to buy me a gift, please consult with me first. I like the usual things: jewelry, handbags, concert tickets. The thing these all have in common is they aren't living."

She took a breath, then deleted everything and started over.

First, she typed a list of what she thought he might need for Jaden's wedding weekend, including everything from toiletries to the number of socks, to business cards, and a charming personality.

Then, she began a treatise on The Friends of Larisa, which was easier than diving into his second question about how they were going to act at the event. They couldn't even manage to make eye contact at work.

She wrote about how the sisters had met their freshman year of college, during sorority recruitment week. They came together because Rosa's dress had been ruined when a guy on a bicycle had almost run her down in a crosswalk. They'd gone to a restaurant bathroom to offer something to help fix her. Kahleah had had a huge belt to cover the tear in her skirt. Jaden had had half a makeup counter in her clutch. Krissy had had a scarf she used to wrap around the gash in Rosa's knee. And Larisa had been the emotional support, talking Rosa back into a place of poise and self-confidence.

"It was a bit *Legally Blonde*, but hey, we're people too," joked Larisa.

The kitten didn't laugh. It had fallen asleep and become a miniature heater against Larisa's neck.

This story didn't seem like enough of the basic information Quinn was looking for, so Larisa made a list.

Krissy: The second tallest, wanted to be a rapper when she was a child and it still shows in the way she talks, often yells. She doesn't take shit from anyone, including her children. Unfortunately, she married a man who can give it right back.

Dev thinks arguing is a sign of a healthy relationship. They argue about everything, then they have sex to make up for it. Most recently, they've been arguing about staying in Brentwood. Part of this has to do with her parents not doing great financially, so she's trying to cut ten grand a year out of her living expenses.

Kahleah: Once played Malibu Barbie in a commercial even though she's Black and from Pittsburgh. This idea stuck in her head, so she got some work done to fit her body into those measurements. When she goes home for holidays people stop her on the street for her picture. No joke, she has like two hundred pictures of her with these salt-of-the-earth, red-faced Pittsburgh people. She likes to collect things. Spoons, stuffed animals, and diamonds are her top three. She followed her high school boyfriend, Cade, out here for college and they got married. She didn't graduate, but I think she's okay with it.

This was about the point Larisa felt she'd been typing a long time about things Quinn probably wouldn't find very interesting, so she made sure to do shorter versions for the last two.

Rosa: Catholic, will always look like she's twelve, even when she's trying to be sexy. Always remembers birthdays and anniversaries.

Jaden: Thought she was never going to get her chance at trophy wifedom, so she founded a non-profit rescue for feral cats. Tish would love her. Her fiancé came to the annual fundraiser last year and they hit it off while doing a silent adoption auction. I think she loves him. Idk. At this point, even the most reasonable woman wouldn't be able to tell the difference between her ticking biological clock and Romeo-and-Juliet passion.

"Enough of this."

Larisa hit send without rereading, snapped the laptop shut, and shoved it aside.

The kitten groaned in her sleep.

"Why does anyone get married anyway?" She pulled out her phone and began to scroll. She'd already posted a picture of the kitten that day, so she couldn't post another. That would be one lonely cat lady vibe too many for her brand.

"I'm going to play music. If you wake up, that's my sign to clean the house. If you stay asleep, I guess I'll just sit here."

Larisa dug her iPod out of her bag. She needed something, the right kind of something, but she didn't know what. Her phone vibrated with an incoming email.

To: You
From: VanderVeer, Quinn

What should the business cards look like?

Ten days until Jaden's Wedding

To: You
From: VanderVeer, Quinn

Who do you think I'll meet at the wedding? Should I have a pitch ready for my next project? I've identified four goals for the weekend. Please let me know if they're okay.

1. Begin a conversation with potential investors about a production company.
2. Establish my brand. VanderVeer belongs with artistic, culturally relevant, zeitgeist.
3. Secure three follow-up lunches.
4. No self-sabotage

What do you think?

To: VanderVeer, Quinn
From: You

Do you even know what zeitgeist means in this town? Enterprise Studios doesn't do that kind of work. They make money. You only say zeitgeist after you have a cult hit or you make a hundred million at the box office.

Nine Days Until Jaden's Wedding

On set, one of the teamsters asked for Larisa's phone number, apparently on a dare from the rest of the teamsters, just to see what she'd do.

A woman working craft services confided in Larisa about a surprise pregnancy.

Lane asked if Quinn was the same kind of boyfriend as he was director.

And Quinn continued to ignore her. A behavior Tish finally commented on. "I suppose it's good he's so focused on professional distance."

Eight Days Until Jaden's Wedding

To: You
From: VanderVeer, Quinn

You realize none of what you wrote about your friends tells me why you like them? But thanks, now I know how to typecast them in a movie. Do you have a model relationship you want to follow? I thought something between *Driving Miss Daisy* and *The Princess and the Pauper*.

To: VanderVeer, Quinn
From: You

I love my friends and I don't have to explain our relationships to you.

They will have low expectations for our relationship. Body language is the most important thing. We need to remember to lean toward each other. Perhaps some light touching. They will want to know your views on marriage and children.

To: You
From: VanderVeer, Quinn

Are we kissing?
I imagine my views on marriage and children should be flexible and vague.

To: VanderVeer, Quinn
From: You

No mouth kissing.

Larisa and Dansby passed the time waiting for his call to set by tossing a hacky sack back and forth in front of his trailer. She hadn't gone to Club D for fear Quinn might try and find the Queen. As a result, she'd built up a store of excess energy, which she now put into the hacky sack as she flung it at Dansby like a projectile weapon, all while singing Kiki Dee's side of "Don't Go Breaking My Heart" and Dansby responding with Elton John's side.

Quinn walked by them once, then came back a few minutes later. He stood awkwardly off to the side until Dansby said, "You ready for me?" even though it was always a PA who came for him.

"You're fine." Quinn came up to Larisa, leaned in like he might kiss her cheek and slipped something into the back pocket of her jeans. As he did, his palm lightly cupped her butt cheek.

She arched a surprised eyebrow. "Yes?"

"Just practicing."

It was a line men had used on her before. Not in the least original, but she thought Quinn really meant it. She was the one who felt something in it, whose face was bright red with heat.

How can he not feel something?

After Quinn returned to the set, Dansby tossed the hacky sack to her with a question in his eyes. "You two are weird. You know that, right?"

Larisa waved away his comment with a roll of her eyes as she reached into her back pocket to find Quinn had slipped a business card into her pocket. It was a cream matte with a gray embossed watermark. Veer Straight Productions by Quinn VanderVeer. On the other side, there was a phone number and email address.

Seven Days Until Jaden's Wedding

Larisa marked time hour by hour through her weekly ethics lecture, through a grand round lecture by an expert on neurodivergence, and the cohort check-in. Afterward, she followed Dr. Bade to her office.

"How is the studio work going?"

"Good. The film wraps next week."

"And I've heard you solved your problems with the director."

Larisa couldn't tell from Dr. Bade's carefully impassive face if this was meant as a joke, a critique, or something else. "He never should have been assigned as my patient."

"Well, it's over now. How do you feel about being back in the clinic full-time for your next rotation?"

"Fine."

"Tell me more about that."

Larisa shrugged. "I honestly haven't had time to think about the next rotation."

"Why?"

"I have a lot going on."

"Would you say you're distracted?"

"I'd say I'm working hard to distract myself. And I'm good at doing that when necessary."

"You think about Kara?"

Larisa didn't know how to answer. The simple answer was yes, she did. But the more truthful answer was she thought about everything else so she didn't have to think about Kara. She was just a pressure on the sides of Larisa's head, like palms pressing against her temples, slowly crushing her skull.

"I'm a good therapist," said Larisa. She wasn't sure if she wanted Dr. Bade to argue or agree. "More than one in four psychiatric residents lose a patient to suicide."

"It's higher than that," said Dr. Bade. "But that's not what I asked, is it?"

After her meeting, Larisa wasn't in the mood for happy hour, but she'd already committed. And the new-Larisa with more free time didn't want to revert to the old-Larisa who was overcommitted and always canceling. So, she played ska in her car on the drive over. And she drove with the windows down, even though it was a little too cold. And she gave the finger to anyone who honked at her, complaining the music was too loud or her driving too sloppy. And she rolled into the Cloud Nine windblown and breathless, her throat aching from trying to imitate the sound of a trumpet.

She was surprised to find Jaden alone at Krissy and Rosa's usual table.

"You look stressed."

Jaden's hand went from petting her puppy to stroking a hand through her long black hair with its soft beach waves. "My mother's parents have decided to come from China."

"Is that bad?"

"They were under the impression I'm having a traditional wedding."

"Oh."

"So now I'm planning one, or part of one, just for them."

Larisa didn't know what to say to that so she flagged down the waiter. "Where are our girls?"

"I don't know. I think I'm early. They said I could come. I missed out last time." She gave Larisa an uncertain smile. "You've never had a boyfriend I didn't meet first."

"Yeah, well . . ."

"What do you like about him?"

"Jaden, look. I don't really . . ." Larisa couldn't think of a way to end the sentence. She couldn't remember the last time they'd been alone together without the buffer of other people smoothing out what had become very rough edges. *For how long?*

Since the engagement.

"What? I'm not cool enough for you now that I'm getting married? Are you replacing me with that actress I met on Valentines?"

"I'm sorry I didn't tell you. Or have you approve. I mean, it's not like our system has been working."

"The last boyfriend you hid from me was Lucas."

Larisa watched Jaden's poodle rearrange itself in her purse, settling in for a nap almost the same way her kitten did. Except she would never carry her kitten around in a purse.

"Do you ever hear from him? Lucas?" asked Jaden.

"He sends me messages sometimes. Let's me know he's watching."

"Promise me this director isn't another Lucas."

"There was a lot to like about Lucas," said Larisa, half-heartedly picking a fight. "He was never boring. I never had to manage our plans. I could just exist. Being with him was like floating down a lazy river in an inner tube."

Larisa's drink arrived. She sucked down half of it in one swallow.

"According to Kahleah, he's a violent megalomaniac."

"Some girls like strong men."

"Risa."

"Why don't we talk about you, beautiful bride-to-be. How's everyone holding up? Aside from the obvious."

"We're fine," said Jaden, pointedly using the same word Larisa had used.

"Well, I'm excited for the weekend. I think it'll be great. You can examine Quinn all you like. Or have the girls do it since you'll be distracted."

"Getting married isn't the end of the world, you know. I'm still the same person. I still need my friends."

What do I need? thought Larisa. The answer to that question had never been her friends, even though she felt it should. Even the idea of needing people struck her as challenging. They were so unreliable and always, always, a disappointment.

"We're not going anywhere." Larisa glanced out the window and saw Rosa and Krissy coming up the block together, as though they'd been somewhere else together, perhaps waiting so their absence could facilitate this private conversation.

Larisa rolled her eyes. "Did you tell them to come late?"

"Of course not. You think I have space in my head for that? The grandparents I haven't seen in a decade are arriving from Harbin tomorrow."

"It's going to be great," said Larisa. "They'll love you."

Jaden looked close to tears. "We're doing the tea ceremony Thursday morning. I'm wearing a traditional red dress. If I make it through all the kneeling, and my grandfather's disappointment that my Mandarin isn't any better than when I last saw him, everything else will be easy, right?"

"If he gets rough, just remind him you're a good ole American girl. Proudly monolingual with thirty pairs of shoes and cultural traditions appropriated from everywhere else."

"Do you think Google can translate that for me?" Jaden smiled. For a moment, it felt like old times. But then, in the rush of energy as Rosa and Kahleah arrived and Krissy called an embarrassingly loud greeting from across the bar, Larisa wasn't even sure what she meant when she thought of old times. It felt like she'd spent most of her life trying to hold onto relationships that didn't otherwise make sense just because they were what she had. And she was supposed to have people. She'd never chosen anyone. She'd always taken what had fallen into her orbit.

What do I need?

The words of Quinn's email complaining that she'd given him character profiles instead of what she liked about her friends had apparently sunk in. But really, who was he to judge?

The following week passed the same way as the one before. Quinn avoided her on set but sent her emails at night or very early in the morning. She began to wonder when he slept. By the wrap party on Thursday, they'd determined they wouldn't dance together at the reception because Quinn didn't dance. They would limit themselves to two drinks per event (rehearsal dinner, after party, and reception). One public kiss per day, never on the lips. And always holding hands when walking together.

The Enterprise Studios' watering hole was crowded with over a hundred people, half of whom had confided in her at least once over the past several weeks. The business of secret keeping often breeds extreme emotions. In Quinn, fear and terror, in others—as seemed true for most of the cast and crew—a bewitched kind of adoration, which was even stronger because she wasn't just any shrink, she was Larisa de France-Kahn, a somebody who had spent her time listening to their problems.

When Eddie stood on a chair and led the room in a round of cheers for Larisa "saving" the production, the rise of voices around her felt like triumph. She *had* saved the film. And she'd given these people more access to their emotions, given them tools to sift through their experiences and organize the nonsense of life into meaning. She was being seen exactly as she wanted by everyone except Quinn.

Which is fine, she told herself. *I'm fine.*

She stayed at the party until the last of the revelers began to disperse. Even then, she lingered, knowing nothing waited for her at home but a sleepless night and a kitten who couldn't decide if Larisa was friend or foe. When the cleaning crew nudged her out of the bar, she wandered over to the offices and found Quinn watching footage, already starting a rough edit of the film.

"If Eddie were a better producer, he'd have dragged you out of here four hours ago."

"He'd have failed," said Quinn. "I have it in my head. It'll bother me if I don't get it laid out."

"Don't let me keep you." Larisa laid down on one of his couches.

For several minutes the clicking of his mouse and snippets of dialogue filled the room. Vince, as Walt, said, "The job and the life are one in the same," five times before Quinn's computer went silent. Quinn sighed.

"Do you need something?"

"Nope."

"You're worried about tomorrow?"

"It's today. Eighteen hours and counting. Did you try on your new clothes?"

"Yes."

"And you know where you're going at the resort for—"

"Yes."

"I've been thinking we could act like we're fighting. You know, allow some physical distance? No PDA."

"You want to change the plan now?"

"You're right, sorry."

The clicking resumed. Quinn's phone vibrated with a new message. He ignored it until two more came in.

"Why haven't you blocked her?"

"How do you know who I'm talking to?"

"It's three in the morning, Quinn. I don't think Sid is that dedicated to you."

"Do you think we should exchange numbers?" he asked.

"So you can send me a lame excuse last minute and back out?"

The desk chair wheels squeaked as Quinn rolled back, left his seat, and came to perch gingerly on the edge of the opposite sofa. "That woman I told you I was seeing?"

Larisa's breath caught in her throat.

"She cut me off. Said I have what I need already."

"She meant Parish?"

"Who else?"

Larisa stared at the ceiling and wished she had a pillow to

hang onto. It took several moments before she managed to say, "So, you're going to get back with her?"

"When the contract is up, maybe. It would make Eddie happy. And it would be nice to . . ."

"To what?" asked Larisa.

"To not be alone." He passed her a Post-it note and a pen. Because of course Quinn wouldn't do the thing everyone did now, which was hand her his phone so she could put her number in. She couldn't imagine being allowed to touch his phone. It felt so intimate, a safeguard of his secrets, all the things that passed between him and Parish.

Light spots grew and dissolved across Larisa's vision as she strained her eyes not to blink. Here was her moment. She could tell him. She could suggest the idea that he apparently could not find on his own and give him the chance to join her two disparate halves into one woman.

"You're in love with her."

Quinn laughed. "Have *you* ever been in love?" He paused, as though realizing how terrible that had sounded.

Say yes. Tell him.

"I mean, I just can't imagine you mushy over someone. Or losing your mind waiting for them to touch you."

"I *am* human, as you pointed out last week." She turned onto her side and looked at him. "But you're right. I don't tend to let myself go. Every time I've held a rose, what I end up feeling are the thorns."

"Poetic."

"It's a song."

"Of course it is."

"A good one for you too, I think. It's about a man who sees silence as self-defense and has been rejected as often for protecting himself as for being vulnerable. Here, I'll play it for you then I'll go away."

Quinn laid down on his couch facing her. In this position, he looked ten years younger, like one of those coltish adolescents disproportionately composed of limbs and raw emotions. He pillowed his head on his arm and looked at her. "I'm ready."

It could have been so easy to go to him, bundle that long sapling body in her arms, smother him with her mouth until he was hard, then fuck him until he screamed her name. But that was absolutely not the answer to what she was feeling. Instead, she set her iPod on the coffee table between them and passed him one side of her headphones. She watched him hesitate, debate the possibility of shared ear germs.

He nested the pod in his ear. She watched his face compose itself for deep focus (half-mocking), as it began to play Billy Joel's "And So It Goes."

"This is a fucking depressing song," said Quinn. "I like it."

"My anthem," muttered Larisa. *Do not cry.* "Can I give you unsolicited shrink advice?"

"Stay away from Parish?"

"She's not going to be what you need."

"It might be good for me to be less demanding." He gave her one of his barely-there knowing smiles.

"Can't argue with that. But there are lots of girls like her in this town, if that's what you really want. I'll introduce you on Saturday."

The last notes of the song died away. Quinn tossed his side of her headphones at the table. Larisa scooped up her iPod and sat up. *Just go over there and kiss him. Give him the chance to choose.*

But Larisa knew how that would go. She didn't have the strength to watch his illusion crumble. If he was going back to Parish, he would need his secret Queen to sustain him even if he never saw her again.

Chapter 29

Day One

Larisa eased herself into the frenzied excitement of the bridal suite the same way she'd entered swimming pools as a child, certain something was a moment away from chewing off her toes. But with caffeine and enough determined focus, she forced herself into the bright, chatty valley-girl-lite that had always been her forte, bouncing off other people's comments, and diminishing uncomfortable silences with quips and jokes (always at her own expense). Everything breezy and fine, not even visible puffs of sleeplessness under her eyes.

"Isn't this just a dream come true, Jadie?" said Rosa.

"Just think, after me we'll only have one more wedding until our children grow up."

Krissy reached over and gave Larisa a squeeze. "We're so excited to meet Quinn."

"Where *is* Quinn?" asked Kahleah, as they walked to the hallway to line up for the rehearsal processional. She nodded to a far table where their three spouses sat looking bored. Larisa glanced around the ballroom. Miscellaneous people sat at round tables that would soon be covered in tablecloths and decorated with flowers, candles, and wood cut figurines of the Chinese symbol for double happiness.

No Quinn.

"He'll be here."

She pictured Quinn, lying on his couch that morning—peaceful but as intense as ever—outwardly still, but inwardly busy. He'd forced himself to give her attention even while his mind had been on work.

You should have fucked him last night, Larisa.

Sex would not have solved our problems.

"Ow!"

"Sorry." Larisa had stepped on the back of Kahleah's shoe as she walked down the aisle.

"We want a gently curving line, out from the center," said the event coordinator. "Miss with the red hair, could you move this way? There are those small white dots on the floor."

"Larisa!" hissed Kahleah.

Larisa looked down and found she was the (not really) redhead out of place.

A videographer glided by on her left. She tried to smile and found her capacity to perform happiness was beginning to feel strained.

"That's good. Now, we'll just have the Father walk through an abbreviated outline, then dinner!" The event coordinator was altogether too enthusiastic.

Larisa watched Jaden standing with her hunky baseball player fiancé and tried to picture herself in Jaden's place. She'd done the same thing at each of her sisters' weddings. It had always seemed surreal, but perfect to see them fall into their role for this rite. It was the climax of hundreds of movies, the promise of a happily ever after, with lifelong dreams suddenly fulfilled in such a natural way that wasn't at all natural. They'd all stood at the altar, earnestly listening to instructions, gazing up into their beloved's eyes with such solid trust and no hint of all the complexity and heartbreak that goes with marriage.

"What if I'm too smart to get married?"

Larisa hadn't realized she'd spoken aloud until Kahleah turned and jabbed her with her elbow. "What's with you tonight?"

"Jaden's getting married."

Kahleah smiled like she was going to cry. "I'm so happy for her."

Larisa heard Krissy and Rosa whispering behind her. Then Krissy stepped off her magical white dot to wrap her arms around Larisa's waist, gently rocking back and forth. "Risa, you didn't tell me he was such a Heathcliff."

Larisa followed Krissy's gaze to the door at the head of the aisle. Quinn stood in the doorway, his weight slightly back on one foot as he paused to take in the scene before he committed to entering.

He wore a dark gray, mid-length suit jacket with a high collar and a T-shirt underneath. His hair had been liberated from his beanie and was an artfully stylized mess on his head. The long pieces drifted down to cover part of his broad forehead and hung in his face just like the video she'd sent him weeks ago, when his hair had been shorter and almost a lost cause. He was scowling as she knew he would be. All his foundational expressions came from this scowl, like he resented being dragged out into the world. But his clothes made it more acceptable. They said he was an artist who was allowed his cultured disdain. Now that he looked the part, people would be more likely to forgive him his dark scowl.

A flutter of pride brushed across her chest along with something else, a flurry of added pleasure that increased her pulse. He'd actually come. He was hers for the entire weekend.

"Hey, new guy. Seat for you!"

Quinn followed the call to a table with three men camped around it like they expected to be there a while. Adrenaline still roared in his ears from the moment with the concierge when he'd been so sure they would refuse to let him in. The resort staff had all looked at his Subaru like it was diseased. But his name had been on the list and now he was in, and there was Larisa, and here he was, somehow at the rehearsal dinner of a baseball player and the daughter of an oil executive.

"I'm Dev." The guy who had invited Quinn to the table was scrawny but well-kept, with polished nails and a Ralph Lauren sweater. "I go with Krissy." He pointed to the bridesmaid behind, then he pointed across the table to the guy leaning back with his feet on the adjacent chair, watching a sports talk show on his phone. "That's Tate, he goes with Rosa." (Bridesmaid two behind Larisa.) "And that's Cade the very important one." Dev pointed to the man on his right, busy on a laptop. "He's prepping a run for mayor next year. Goes with Kahleah." (Bridesmaid in front of Larisa.)

"You got all that?"

"Sure."

"It gets easier. By the third kid's birthday, you'll have all the names down."

"Lay off Dev," said Cade from behind the laptop. "He might not be around that long."

"Larisa doesn't even know all the kids' names." Tate looked up from his phone. "What's it like with her anyway?"

"She calls and you come, right?" said Cade with a smirk.

"By showing up today, you've broken the record for being her longest relationship."

Under the table, Quinn made fists against the very nice fabric of whatever his pants were made out of. His tailored *Tom Ford* pants. Over the past two weeks, Larisa had sent him several pages of instructions for what he should expect. But now, burning under the expectation of these men, who were looking at him for an answer to what seemed a question they'd long been asking, he wished she'd given him more.

"Our assistants do wonders with the shared calendar," said Quinn.

This brought a knowing smile from Dev and a huff of appreciation from Tate.

"And what's she like in bed?" asked Cade.

Quinn hesitated. Whatever he said would get back to Larisa. She didn't need that; the environment was obviously hostile. It seemed like something she should have warned him about. *Maybe she doesn't know.*

"No comment."

"We have a pool," said Cade, eyes on his laptop. "You can join if you want."

"Naw, he can't join," said Tate. "He'll skew it."

"He can try."

Quinn looked to the front of the room where the bridal party was receiving instructions for the recessional. Everything was so beautiful, it almost hurt his eyes to look at it for too long. His eyes shifted from one woman to the next, trying to take them in and make them real when they looked like something out of a dream. All of them were more confident and elegant versions of what he'd liked about Parish.

He couldn't help but feel a twinge of disappointment that they were already taken, even though he knew none of them would ever consider marrying him. They'd demand honesty, and if he managed to find a way to that honesty, they would run for the hills. Or worse, they'd tell all their friends about how a warehouse worker, who had made some amateur films in his spare time, was now posing as a major studio director. This new version of himself, director of a big budget project for Enterprise Studios, who had a mortgage in Los Feliz, and a girlfriend with soft hair, wasn't even skin deep.

What does Larisa's hair feel like?

Larisa looked like she belonged with the other women. But underneath the surface, he felt she was an outsider. He'd thought he'd been hired to fill the empty space at her side. But he saw now it was more than that. She needed him to make her seem like everyone else because that was the role she played among her friends. The irony of Quinn filling this role was laughable, the task so large it made him want to jump up and run. *You're sitting in the ballroom of the Palisades Hotel.* This was the world he wanted to join. These were the people he wanted to know. It didn't matter that they drew him in and repulsed him in equal parts.

"I always bet on love," he said.

Dev clapped him on the back. "Look here, a romantic."

"He's in film," said Cade, as though this was an obvious connotation.

"How did you get into that?" asked Dev. "Family business?"

Quinn felt the familiar defensive responses rising in him, which he now recognized as fear. For a moment, he allowed it to fill him, then he tucked it away. These men were not out to unmask him. Their target was Larisa. He was, so far at least, seen as a sympathetic peer. *No self-sabotage this weekend.*

"Film chose me," said Quinn. "It's the largest canvas for creation." He paused. When no one laughed, he added, "It's life writ large, revealing all the nuances and meanings lost in the chaos of the every day."

Dev gave a golf clap.

Quinn worked his face into something that looked embarrassed. "I guess I'm a bit of an egotist."

"Nothing wrong with that," said Tate.

"Do you do political ads?" asked Cade.

"If the price is right."

Cade smiled. "You have a card?"

Quinn prayed his hand wasn't shaking as he reached into the interior pocket of his jacket and pulled out one of his new business cards.

Sure, he thought, *I'll help the next mayor get elected.*

The two sides of the bridal party began drawing together, pairing into couples like a zipper closing, as they followed the bride and groom up the aisle. Krissy blew a kiss that seemed aimed at Quinn rather than her husband.

"Don't eat all the caviar before we get there!" called Rosa.

"Is dinner a buffet?" Cade wrinkled his nose.

"Looks like the parents are going in." Tate nodded toward the people who had been sitting at another table and were now moving toward the side door of the ballroom. "Should we go or wait?"

"If we eat without them, we'll be stuck sitting there," said Dev.

"We better be done by the time the game starts," muttered Tate.

"So, Quinn. What's new in Hollywood?" asked Dev.

Here was a question Quinn could answer without having to worry about what he was saying. He provided a few tidbits from the studio gossip churn Sid had kept him updated on, then he punted back to the husbands. Quinn learned Cade was a lawyer taking some heat at his law firm for his political aspirations. Tate worked for big pharma where he'd once done science but was now in executive management. Dev was a neurosurgeon. They'd all gone to UCLA together. They'd all married 'the sisters' in the year following graduation.

"A long year," said Dev. "Because I didn't manage to pop the question until Diwali."

There were eight kids between the three couples. The birthday parties, as Dev had alluded to, were required social events that had been one hundred precent attended over the years by everyone except Larisa.

"Med school is demanding," said Quinn, already a little tired of trying to keep track of all the slides and insider messages embedded in their conversation.

"True," said Dev. "I did a five-year residency. Most of it's a blur."

"But she didn't *have* to do it," said Tate. "Counseling only takes a masters. Larisa always has to make a statement."

"A new reality show would've been better," said Dev.

"Because you would've been in it," said Cade.

"What's the point of knowing a celebrity if she doesn't work it for us? I mean, have you ever seen a psychiatrist in real life who looks like Larisa?"

Before anyone else could dig themselves into a hole of misogyny, complaining about Larisa's career ambitions, high-pitched laughter rippled in from the hallway. Quinn turned and watched the bridal party return. First came the groom's two brothers with their wives. Then the groom's two baseball teammates, Krissy, then Larisa, strangely bouncy and smiling just like the women following her, all of them throwing their bodies around like they were still in college making their grand entrance at a frat party.

He stood as Larisa sidled up to him. *Just follow the plan.* He put his arm around her shoulder, leaned in as if to kiss her and instead whispered, "We should've gone through blocking on some of this."

She laughed, a forced little sound that felt like glass cracking.

As a group, they walked into the dining room and worked their way through the buffet line. This room was smaller than the ballroom but still grander than any place Quinn had been. A wall of windows looked out on one of three pool decks. Beyond the sparkling cerulean water, the ocean stretched to the horizon, the sunset just beginning to paint the sky.

He took a picture and sent it to Sid.

"Oh, Risa," said Krissy. "He's a sunset guy."

"We should eat fast and take pictures out on the deck," said Jaden, making eye contact with the photographer who began capturing candids, mostly of people with food in their mouths. *There will be pictures of me eating with these people*, thought Quinn.

Thanks to Larisa, Quinn looked like he belonged. Someone's mother complimented his jacket. The flower girl, Tate and Rosa's oldest, asked to touch his hair, then told him she wanted to be a rock star when she grew up.

Though Quinn ate more than he usually allowed himself, the food left him with a pleasant fullness instead of cramping and low-grade nausea. The new-guy attention diluted into casual questions, mostly fielded by Larisa. All he had to do was follow her lead and throw in occasional gestures of affection, which he copied from the couples around the table. He leaned into her, put his arm around her back. During dessert, he placed his hand on her lap under the table.

The fact that he knew he hadn't earned these gestures made them strangely invigorating, almost distracting in their hyperreality. His mind's eye marked out new territory on a body, that before that evening, hadn't existed. He'd never allowed himself to look. And now, he felt it. *This is Larisa's back. This is the top of her thigh. I am touching her.*

In a real relationship, he would have never felt the need to mark his territory over a woman the way the other husbands did with these cloaked gestures of dominance. He and Larisa were duping these people using their own tricks. In a movie, he imagined placing the camera behind their shoulders as a spy who would capture the moment he whispered in her ear, "See the way Kahleah stiffens when Cade touches her?"

And Larisa would maintain her smile, take a bite of her dessert before giving him an answering whisper, "Nothing compared to Krissy and Dev. He's already drunk. They'll be fighting tonight."

The three of them—Quinn, Larisa, and the camera—would be a world unto themselves, looking out on this pageantry of love and picking at its loose threads for the pleasure of a knowing audience.

After dinner, they moved outside. Taking pictures on the pool deck added complexity to Quinn's boyfriend performance. He didn't do well with social pictures. Smiling he looked boyish, but not smiling made him look like a serial killer. Jacket buttoned or open? Where should he put his hands? And how was he going to do any of it while looking like he was in love?

Larisa saved him by insisting she wanted silhouette pictures.

They stood side by side with their backs to the photographer, their heads bent together, looking out at the water.

"Good so far?" he whispered.

"Perfect," she said without confidence.

He searched for a clue to where he'd gone wrong, then remembered his promise not to self-sabotage. She wasn't being critical. She was just unhappy. "You're doing good too."

He saw a quiver ripple up her throat.

"Oooh, you guys are so cute!" said Krissy. "Turn and face each other."

They turned. Quinn set his hands on Larisa's hips. An automatic gesture, but it felt—

"Kiss her!" cried Rosa.

Kahleah took up the call. "Kiss her!"

Quinn thought Larisa would break away with a joke, allowing them to escape. It felt like a trespass, touching her, the surprising gravitas of her hips in his hands. Instead, she just stood there looking at him. The camera shutter kept clicking, capturing whatever confusion was on his face. She'd never failed to take the lead. But now she didn't even seem aware of people staring at them. She was looking at him like he was about to break her heart. He couldn't think of anything else to do except follow orders. He leaned in and brushed his lips over hers.

Cheers erupted from the rest of the party. He felt a shiver travel through Larisa's body. She didn't pull back. In fact, she leaned into him, turning what he'd thought would be a ghost of a gesture into a true kiss. The heat of her mouth flooded his. Her hands gripped the lapels of his jacket, holding him in place.

And then, just as quickly as it started, it ended. Larisa released him, turned, and strutted back to the gaggle of bridesmaids with her arms raised like she'd just won something. They cheered.

Quinn remained in place. He knew if he tried to move, his legs would collapse beneath him. Energy sparked and fizzled through his body, a thousand signals going haywire, his mind fragmenting.

She . . .

That was . . .

Jaden clapped her hands. "Okay, everyone! We're moving to the lounge for Who Knows You Best and tequila shots!"

Cade groaned. "Can't we skip that?"

"I vote with Cade," said Tate. "It's just your way of making us look bad."

Rosa made a pouty face as she pulled Tate down the deck toward the stairs leading up to the bar patio where umbrella tables, trellises of blooming gardenias, and glowing string lights set the perfect ambiance for the transition from day to night.

"It's not fair to Quinn," said Cade. "Play it girls only."

At the sound of his name, Quinn felt some part of him lift out of his daze. Someone was pulling on his arm. Not Larisa, Kahleah. He allowed himself to be led to the bar. The sisters crunched together on a padded banquette as their partners reluctantly took chairs on the opposite side of a long table.

"Take a picture for us." Larisa handed him her phone as she dove onto the banquette, throwing herself across Jaden's chest. No eye contact. No apparent awareness of what had just happened. *Nothing happened,* he tried to tell himself.

"I can't breathe," called Kahleah. "Picture now!"

Quinn considered the light and shifted to the left. He tilted the phone various angles, taking several shots that would all be terrible. His hands weren't steady enough to be worthy of any photography at that moment, especially not using a phone. He handed it back. She still didn't look at him.

"Send it to all of us," said Rosa, as Larisa flipped through the shots. She shared the pictures to their group chat, then busied herself with composing a post for her socials.

"Alright!" said Krissy, "I kept it to ten questions," she slanted her eyes at Dev, "so our men can go watch sports before they get drunk."

Dev gave her a salute of thanks.

"Movie themed, in honor of Quinn." She winked at him.

"He's the only one exempt. You've only been dating a few weeks after all. But obviously, answer if you know."

Quinn realized he was the only one still standing. There weren't any chairs left, so he sat on the end of the banquette beside Larisa's feet. For a moment he looked down at them. He'd never seen her bare feet before. They seemed remarkably large, but what did he know about women's feet? He rested his hand on her ankle, stroking the line of her bone with his thumb.

It didn't seem possible he was allowed to touch such an ankle. To be kissed by such a woman.

We're pretending.

The energy in the group had shifted into something less frenetic. He struggled to turn his attention to the table. Krissy had passed around half sheets of paper embossed with *Jade and Adrian Forever*, which had ten questions and spaces for the answers. The pens that followed were custom-made gel rollers also commemorating the wedding.

"This is a drinking game of high skill," said Larisa, sitting up and knocking her shoulder against his like nothing had happened. "You write your answers to the questions and don't show anyone. Then we go around and guess each person's answer. Partners go first and if they don't know an answer, they have to drink."

Quinn nodded to Cade with dawning appreciation. "Is it too late to vote for girls only?"

"See?" said Tate. "It's torture."

"Don't ruin my wedding, Tate."

"Ten minutes starts now," said Krissy. "Write."

Quinn looked down at the questions as he turned the pen around in his hand. It was as fat as a cigar with a polished wood shell and silver tip. The most expensive writing utensil he'd ever touched. It seemed criminal to use it for something as ordinary as writing, especially writing answers for this inane game. He answered a few of the questions that felt easiest, folded the paper in half, then sat back to wait.

She wasn't pretending with that kiss.

"Alright, number one," said Krissy. "If your life was a movie? Bride first. You may provide three clues."

Jaden batted her eyes across the table at her almost-husband. "Second date. 'Thriller.' Thirty."

"Second date from the first time you dated or the second?" asked Rosa.

Jaden pursed her lips. She couldn't give any more clues.

"First time," said Larisa with a secretive smile.

"Risa knows it!" said Krissy. "You're on the hot seat, Groom."

"*Thirteen Going on Thirty*," said Adrian.

"Right," said Jaden.

Adrian wiped fake sweat from his brow.

They worked their way around the circle to Jaden's right, which meant it was Quinn's turn before Larisa, who would be last.

"Alright Quinn, three clues."

He absolutely hated games like this. As though knowing facts about someone meant you *knew* them. As though the answers were concrete facts instead of interpretations that could change with someone's mood.

"Silent film star looking for a comeback. A kept writer. A swimming pool," he said.

A beat of silence. Then Kahleah said, "So dying to know how this fits with your life."

"*Sunset Boulevard*," said Larisa.

"*Is* that his life?" Tate asked, looking at Larisa like this confirmed his worst suspicions.

She laughed. "Spoiler alert. She kills him out of jealousy, so I hope not. My turn? Okay," she glanced at Quinn, mischievous, a sly smile on her lips. She'd worn that look before, but he'd never seen it quite like this. Heat thrilled through his chest so he almost didn't hear her. "Solarium. Champagne glasses. Paris."

"I know!" said Krissy, Rosa, and Kahleah at the same time."

"I have no idea." At that moment, he couldn't have told any

of them the name of his own movies, let alone the answer to the clues.

Larisa.

"Aw, come on, guess."

"Really, no clue."

Larisa.

"It's *Sabrina*," said Cade sourly. "Let's get going. It took half an hour to do number one."

"Which *Sabrina*?" asked Quinn.

"The remake," said Jaden. "Obviously, she hasn't let you in on her Harrison Ford obsession yet."

Larisa flushed bright red with embarrassment.

"No one lives up to him, so you only need to try for second place," said Kahleah.

The game continued. Quinn disengaged to scroll through his phone, which gave him something he could at least pretend to be doing while his mind scrambled through an avalanche. He hadn't seen either of the *Sabrina* movies. Leave it to Larisa to pick a movie he'd never seen.

They were interrupted at question five when a little girl in a nightgown came tearing through the bar, a frantic nanny running after her, to come kiss her parents goodnight. She turned out to be Dev and Krissy's only child. Dev used the interruption as an excuse to make his exit and went to put her to bed.

Most of the rest of Larisa's answers Quinn could guess. He learned she had a thing for music cues in movies. Krissy had written question seven in Larisa's honor because she was always waxing poetic about the way music made a scene.

"What does our resident expert think about movie music?" asked Jaden, drawing Quinn back into the game.

"Quinn doesn't do music," said Larisa. "In his first film, there is less than five minutes of music total, and it comes from a radio. There's nothing in his second."

She watched my films.

"Terrible," said Jaden with mock horror.

Quinn moved his tongue over his teeth, pushing back the instinctual defensiveness that would make his words too sharp. This was a game. She wasn't insulting him. He hadn't done anything wrong yet.

"I like the camera to shape the scenes. Music can sometimes be a filler, unconsciously manipulating the audience to feel something."

"So, Quinn doesn't know the answer to this one. What's the best music cue for Larisa?" asked Krissy, trying to move the game along.

All around the table people shook their heads.

Quinn saw something like resignation flicker across Larisa's face. She'd expected this. Her friends had all given predictable answers to the question, favorite pop songs, bestselling soundtracks, none of the answers truly responded to the question. All her years with them, they'd failed to learn how to see movies as she did. Not at all surprising, but still, he was strangely moved by how isolated she suddenly looked, alone in a circle of her friends. Before he knew what he was doing, Quinn reached over and wove his fingers through hers, drew her hand onto his lap and held it there even when she tried to pull away.

The game only made it through question eight before the awaited basketball game started. The grumbling husbands killed the mood enough that the group disbanded. Sensing this next part of the evening would be less structured, and thus more full of possible pitfalls and even more hours of Larisa avoiding eye contact, Quinn excused himself and went to find his room.

Their room.

Larisa had already claimed the queen bed closest to the bathroom by spreading an abundance of belongings around it like she'd come for a week instead of two days. His new Tom Ford overnight bag sat on the chair by the balcony door where the concierge must have left it. Quinn had said no to the resort's unpack service. Because of course the resort had an unpack service.

The bathroom was a wonder unto itself, with a jacuzzi tub, towel warmer, and dressing alcove where Larisa had hung her bridesmaid dress, which Quinn decided wouldn't suit her. It was strange to think of Larisa and what she would wear, to think of her body as something more than just an abstract shell attached to her professional self.

She kissed me.

Quinn ordered room service and set it up on the side of the tub while he soaked in a bubble bath and watched Sydney Pollack's *Sabrina* on his laptop. He took a picture of himself for Sid.

Sid: Tempted to make this into a real thing?

Quinn didn't even begin to know how to answer that question. He wanted to tell Sid about the kiss. But everything he imagined saying didn't convey the shock of it. His certainty that she hadn't just done it for show.

Quinn: Doomed to fail. Her friends' husbands already betting how long we'll last.

After he'd pruned himself in the bath, Quinn transitioned to a bed that felt like sinking into clouds and moved the movie from his laptop to the television because it was a fancy television that could steal what was on his laptop for itself. He'd barely settled in when he heard the buzz of the door lock just before Larisa entered the room. She looked at him, then at the second half of *Sabrina* on the TV, then disappeared into the bathroom. He heard her turn on the water for a shower. More avoidance.

What are you going to say, Quinn?

The timer said he had almost an hour of movie left, which meant this would become a shared viewing experience. He threw the shirt he'd worn that day over his ratty sleep shirt and prowled the gilded hallway until he found a self-serve snack kiosk (because such a resort wouldn't have something as ordinary as a vending machine). He returned to the room with a bag of freshly popped popcorn and a bag of M&M's.

Larisa was clearing her belongings off her bed when he walked in. For a moment he froze, not even his natural stoicism could hide his shock at Larisa wearing a lacy camisole with matching panties, covered by a sheer pink robe trimmed in feathers.

"This isn't for you," she said. "The mayor of Las Vegas gave me this robe. It's my away robe."

Quinn averted his eyes as he took two glasses from the shelf above the mini bar and walked carefully around her to his side of the room. He poured popcorn into both glasses, setting one on her side of the end table like a peace offering. They weren't at war, but it felt like the ground had shifted and now he was walking on what appeared to be Earth but felt like Mars.

"Thanks." She flopped down on the bed. He felt her eyes on him as he opened the M&M's and poured some into his popcorn. He held his hand over the glass and shook it to coat the candy in salt and grease.

"Are those just for you?" She held out her glass, looking shy. He stood up, poured some M&M's into her glass as he stared at the wall above her head.

"This is what it takes for you to find me attractive?" she asked in a voice that seemed like it could murder him. "How do I compare to Parish? Larger, I suppose."

"You don't," he said, which was possibly the only thing he could say. It could as easily be a compliment as an insult.

He returned to his bed. She settled into hers. They watched the movie for several minutes without speaking. He considered what he might be able to say without it being a big deal.

How did you expect me to react to you wearing that? he wondered.

That was quite a kiss.

Do you usually fall in love with your clients?

But every time the words rose to the tip of his tongue, they felt ludicrous. *You imagined it. She wouldn't. You're not even friends.*

"So, what is it with this movie?" he asked.

"That's above your paygrade."

See? She just has you here as a stopgap until a real man comes along.

He watched Julia Ormond make coy eyes at the camera, secretive, like she has no idea how beautiful she is, as she tells Harrison Ford about the origins of her name. Sabrina, the water sprite rescuer. Quinn found it implausible that Harrison Ford's character was really in need of rescue, but he supposed it made sense within the equally implausible rules of the movie. He listened to Larisa eating her popcorn. Or rather he listened to the silence of it, one kernel passing through her lips at a time, her mouth barely moving. Didn't she know the whole point was to eat the M&M's with the popcorn so they melted together?

The Queen would understand. She wouldn't be shy about chomping popcorn as it was meant to be chomped.

Thinking of the Queen stirred him. He tried to picture her luscious body released from its corset and tall boots. Did she look like Julia Ormond? Short, curly hair? Overlarge, bright ingénue eyes? No. She carried more weight than that. For a moment, Larisa in her negligee and transparent robe flashed across his mind. He banished the thought before it could take hold. The Queen didn't waste time with bright, glowing smiles and bashful glances. She took what she wanted when she wanted it. Just as she had taken him. Remembering stole his breath from his chest. He was getting hard.

Not a good time.

The movie ended. Larisa turned off her light, dropped her robe on the floor, and crawled into her bedding. Quinn folded himself under the covers with his phone on the pillow beside him so the vibrations of Parish's late-night texts wouldn't bother Larisa. He wanted to forget her and think only of the hard line of the Queen's voice, stripping his soul down to the bones, then slowly pulling him back together, a complete person, free of doubt and the impulse to lash out at anyone who marred his enchantment.

The bed was almost too soft to sleep. He drifted, thinking of Larisa avoiding him on set the week before, Larisa so beautifully furious at the police station, and in the car after. It was the first moment she'd ever seemed like a real person. Larisa feeding him ice cream on their terrible fake first date.

She wants me.

What did it even mean to be wanted by such a woman? For the night? The weekend? For forever? It wasn't possible.

Beside him, a blue square of light marked out the borders of his phone coming to life with Parish's first message of the night. He buried the phone under the pillow without looking at it. He listened to Larisa shift in her bed. He considered the possibility that she wanted him to come to her. He entertained the idea for about thirty seconds before dismissing it as one of his worst ideas ever. Maybe he drifted into sleep, but his mind never quieted enough that he wasn't aware of her. She didn't sleep.

Around five o'clock, he sensed her movement. She got out of bed and pulled on her robe, then began to feel around in the dark for something.

"Leaving me?" he asked.

"I'm going to walk the beach." The thing she'd been looking for was her iPod.

Quinn pulled out his phone. Thirty-seven unread messages. "Dressed like that?"

"I've done it before."

"While listening to music?"

Larisa heaved a dramatic sigh.

"I'll come with you."

"I don't need a minder."

"But think if someone sees you alone, they'll wonder why I'd let you out of the room unsupervised."

He saw the dark shadow of her mouth opening to argue. But

they both knew it was true. In Larisa's world, they weren't just selling their relationship, they were selling a traditional power dynamic and all that came with it.

Their balcony opened onto a patio that led around the south pool deck and down to the beach. The moon was a full orb sending glittering silver over the water. Quinn dismissed Parish's messages and took a picture. He paused to breathe, to appreciate. It had been so long since he'd felt this alive. This was what the Queen had given him. He wished he had a way to tell her. Instead, he stretched muscles that ached with the memory of her cane and began to follow Larisa as she marched down the beach.

Her robe flared out behind her she moved so fast, as though reaching the end of the shoreline was a competition she was holding against the dawn. Quinn struggled to keep up and then decided he didn't need to. She had her music. The beach was empty. They didn't need to be attached at the hip to keep up appearances. Besides, there were too many things he might step on in the sand to not watch where he put his feet. He turned and took some shots of the resort buildings basking in their soft, nighttime lights. He scooped up a handful of sand and seashells that had been masticated by the ocean and filmed them as they fell through his fingers.

When he caught up to Larisa, she had her hands on her knees and was breathing hard. He waved at her to signal he wanted to be heard even though her music wasn't blaring out of the buds so she might have heard him anyway. She paused her music.

"You know I'm a captive audience. If there's anything you'd like to voice and have it swallowed by the infinite void of my NDA." He shrugged. It felt like an inadequate offer. Why would she talk to him?

He knelt in the sand, filming the foamy, white line of the edge of the surf creep up the beach and retreat. Then, without thinking about it, he twisted sideways and took a picture of Larisa, now standing upright, towering over him like an imperious sea goddess trapped on land. The wind whipped her hair behind her, the edges of the robe rippled. She looked ready to devour the world and yet, he suspected, she felt it was somehow devouring her.

Larisa pulled her headphones from her ears and clenched them in her hand. She shook her head as though words were impossible. "I don't know what to say," she said. "It's all such a mess. I can't think. And I can't *not* think."

"Maybe I can distract you. Give my outsider's view on all your friends. Or I could provide you with a psychological puzzle only an excellent therapist could solve."

"The second option, but only if it's really about you and not a story you made up."

"This one is real, and I do need your advice."

She laughed. "When have you ever wanted my advice?"

"This might be a first." He stood, brushed the sand from his hand. "Walk with me."

He turned to start walking back the way they'd come. She turned with him.

"Is it possible to be in love with someone without really knowing them?"

"Of course," she said. "Love is a chemical reaction to a variety of stimuli. Knowing is rarely something that's part of initial attraction or first love. I hope we're not talking about Parish."

"We're talking hypothetical and abstract."

She slanted her gaze like she didn't believe him. "I don't counsel people about hypothetical love. Real love is hard enough."

"Your friends' husbands seem to think I'm your longest relationship."

"From their perspective, that'd be true."

"You've had secret boyfriends they don't know about?"

She shrugged. (Which wasn't a no.) "They don't know you're not a real boyfriend."

Ah yes. She wasn't about to let either of them forget.

"So, what's wrong with you?"

She gave a bitter laugh. "You're not going to ask what's wrong with the old boyfriends?"

"Probably too many things to list. But I'm something of a student of self-loathing and I think you might have the same problem."

"Maybe that's why you can't leave Parish. It scares you to think there could be someone else who will treat you better."

"I think I've found her. Not Parish, someone else. But you're changing the subject."

"If we're so alike, I imagine you asked this mystery person to save you because you think it will somehow be easier than years of therapy."

"What's so wrong with that?"

Larisa shrugged. "Sometimes nothing. It's a romantic idea."

"Yeah, well. I'm a fucking romantic." He took a deep breath. "She refused. So it doesn't matter."

They were coming back to the resort. Larisa reached for his hand as they approached a pair of early morning runners. He noticed her hand fit well with his. Their hands hung at the same level from their shoulders. Her skin was soft and warm.

What do you see, Larisa?

What do you want from me?

Day Two

Larisa found it remarkably hard not to think about Quinn while she sat in the suite-turned-hair salon with one stylist working her hair and another doing her makeup. Conversation swirled around her, but Larisa couldn't track with it enough to add anything. Behind the shelter of her closed eyes, she saw his pale face glowing in the moonlight. How enchanting his vulnerability had been when he'd talked about the Queen, his voice going soft.

I shouldn't have kissed him on the pool deck.

Wearing a pale green dress that would have sent the fashion police reeling, Larisa drifted down the hallway from the dressing room and leaned against the corner that opened into the main resort atrium, and waited for her mother to arrive. Her father did not do weddings now that he had reached an age and status where he could be forgiven almost anything, so Quinn would also be her mother's date.

She adjusted her posture, careful not to crush her hair. *By this time tomorrow, it will be over.*

As the thought flitted through her brain, Larisa felt something clench inside her. She didn't want to return to the hospital, to the cohorts who didn't like her, or to Dr. Bade who thought Larisa thought she was doing medicine a favor. She was so tired of trying to prove herself worthy.

Then her mother was there, making a grand entrance at the far end of the atrium in a crepe caftan and her trademark statement jewelry. Larisa watched as she expertly greeted the bellhops and the concierge, then dispatched Rey to oversee her bags up to her room.

If I give up school, I'll be like her, but without the good husband and sparkling reputation.

What value did that kind of life give the world? Larisa felt both the pull of its familiarity and the revulsion of distaste. She would be bored to tears in a year. And then she'd start misbehaving. *Maybe if I'm able to continue going to Club D, I'd balance things enough. If I find the right husband.*

Whenever she was outside the privacy of her own home, Suzette de France remained every inch the model. From the top of her gently waving hair down to her toe cleavage, she carried a single long line of angular perfection, a blank canvas of a body that today had been written on by Armani, with Dolce & Gabbana embelishments. She tossed her hair back from her face as she made her way toward Larisa, stopping every ten feet to smile and greet the resort staff. Going anywhere with her mother took twice as long as it should because she insisted on this "touching the people" method of public relations.

Because you never know who will talk about you. And you never know when you'll need them to say the right thing.

"Hello, Mother. How was Italy?"

"Paradiso infinite." Suzette kissed her fingers as one does when pretending to be Italian. Then her gaze narrowed as she inspected Larisa's appearance. "Have you gained weight?"

"The dress still fits."

"Jaden's decorator should've been fired. Blue and green wedding colors. The ballroom probably looks like warmed over Easter."

"Our opinion hardly matters."

"You'll do better when your time comes."

Larisa nodded. She would do better *if* her time ever came, which seemed even less likely than before. Now, every man she met would be measured against Quinn.

It's infatuation, she told herself. *It'll pass.*

"So, where's Quinn?"

Larisa nodded her head past her mother. Quinn had just stepped out of the elevator into the lobby. He wore a navy suit with a white ruffled opera shirt and Chelsea boots. Her friends at Tom Ford had done good work fulfilling her vision, but . . .

"He's wearing a hat," said Suzette. "What is that? A Cuban style short brim? To a wedding?"

"Appears to be." *And makeup,* thought Larisa. She watched him pause to take a picture of the lobby before turning toward them. He walked heavy in his hips, a slow saunter so casual Larisa could've believed he dressed like that all the time. *He's proud of himself.*

A slight blush deepened the natural color of his lips, making them stand out like two pouty invitations. A rim of thin eyeliner framed his eyes, making their cloudy-blue even starker against his pale skin.

She saw him see her notice the hat. The corner of his mouth pulled up in the delicious half-smile that haunted her dreams.

"Like it?"

"I'm not sure."

"Americans don't wear hats to weddings," said Suzette.

"I'll pretend to be something else then." Without warning, Quinn slipped into a perfect posh-British accent. "My Lady de France, charmed to see you again. Have you come to help me survive the wolves?"

A delighted smile lit up Suzette's face. "I knew I liked you."

Inside the dressing room down the hall, Krissy called out for Larisa; they were doing spontaneous photos for their socials.

"I love you, Mom. Make sure he meets Karl. And Paula if she doesn't arrive late. They'd be perfect for each other. I'll see you after."

Larisa ducked into the dressing room, smiling to herself. *Of course, he'd break the rules for a hat.*

The bridesmaids took picture after picture, documenting

Jaden's last moments as a single woman. Larisa floated through them on autopilot, smile on her face and ears blocked. This was just another party. These were her friends doing what they'd always done. It wasn't an ending. She thought of Quinn and his hat, his surprising accent skills, even his more surprising ability to rise to the occasion, that sly little smile that somehow contained more than all the careless, teeth-filled, slice-of-watermelon grins people flashed to the world.

The ballroom did look a little like Easter. As Larisa walked the processional down the middle aisle, she inventoried the round dining tables passing in her peripheral vision. She felt two or three different choices (white tablecloths instead of alternating blue and green for starters) would've made a difference.

She also inventoried all the wedding guests' faces to prepare herself for the reception ahead. Jaden's parents' friends—oil executives in stuffy, unimaginative suits with big bellies and gaudy watches—took up one corner of the ballroom. Baseball players with their huge bodies in more interesting suits—hardly any ties and lots of diamond chain jewelry—took up another corner. There was a corner for Adrian's parents' friends. And finally, there was a corner of Jaden's personal network, most of which was filled with her foundation employees, its board, and the singer-actress Awkwafina, who knew Jaden from spin class.

In this last corner, Larisa found Quinn seated beside her mother, his expression shaded by the brim of his hat. Cade, Dev, and Tate sat at the same table with chairs left open for their wives.

By the time I sit down again, Jaden will be married.

Think about something else, Larisa. What will you do when this is over?

Go work at the hospital for twelve hours.

And then?

And then, meet Dansby for lunch and do an informal check-in.
And then?
Learn how to be a cat mom.
Alone. I'm alone.

Larisa found her little white dot on the floor, settled her right foot over it, then took a deep breath. The ceremony would last forty minutes from this point. The processional music ended. The priest cleared his throat. Larisa fixed her gaze on the back of Kahleah's head, even though she could easily see over her, and began to count. When she got to sixty, she started over. Two minutes passed. Three minutes.

What if the Queen dated Quinn? Would I really be worse off than I am now? He's going to hate me whenever he finds out. Might as well get something out of it while I can.
Irresponsible.
He's already dangerously attached.
More exposure might help his fantasy dissolve naturally.

At thirty minutes, Larisa detected movement beyond her narrowed field of vision. She shifted her gaze, carefully avoiding Jaden, in her big white dress, and Adrian, gazing at her with open adoration. She saw Quinn get up from his seat and walk (almost run) down the side aisle and out of the ballroom.

Weird.

She glanced at her mother, who appeared equally bewildered.

Larisa passed the next ten minutes debating likely explanations.

Adverse reaction to wedding ceremonies?
Ate something bad for breakfast?
Crohn's Disease?
Family emergency?
Work emergency?
Leaked video of him attacking Hasan?
Side thought: Why hadn't there been any coverage of that fight?

Her last thought, that it was something to do with Parish, was cut short as applause erupted from the audience.

"Let me introduce, for the first time, Mr. and Mrs. Adrian Marino!" the priest announced.

Recessional music. Larisa continued staring straight ahead as everyone else turned to watch Jaden and Adrian walk down the aisle.

You're not hopeless.
You're not hopeless.
You're not hopeless.

She matched up with her equivalent groomsman (one of the baseball players) and walked up the aisle. A left turn, then another left turn and they were in the adjacent hall where the dance floor had been set up. There was a bar on one end and the dessert station with a towering blue and green cake in the middle of the table. Jaden was laugh-crying in Adrian's arms as the rest of the party whooped and cheered, all while being liberally sprayed by a bottle of champagne the other baseball player groomsman had popped open.

More pictures for socials. To hide her lack of enthusiasm, Larisa focused on picking the best one to post to her feed. Her pre-ceremony post had collected over a thousand likes and fifty-some comments. The first one caught Larisa's eye.

CherishedParish: Aren't you just the prettiest eva?

Larisa tapped the avatar image and swallowed down a surprising flood of unease as Parish stared back at her, those glossy candy lips, that daring gaze out from beneath her false eyelashes.

Does Quinn love her?

The resort staff pushed back the walls separating the two ballrooms. The DJ tested her mic, then began giving guests instructions. The bar was now open. Dinner would begin in thirty minutes. And the bride and groom would be coming around to every table.

Larisa put her phone away and allowed Rosa to pull her toward their table where Quinn's seat remained empty.

"His phone rang, and he ran off," said Suzette in a tone of judgmental exasperation Larisa knew all too well. She resisted the impulse to make up an excuse to soothe her mother at Quinn's expense.

"Wish I'd thought of that," said Cade. "Weddings, seriously. I'm glad this is the last one."

Kahleah smacked him. "We'll have Larisa's, silly. Then your daughter's."

Cade made a horrified face. "Our daughter is never getting married. She's not dating. She's never going anywhere."

Larisa was just leaning back in her seat, reaching for her napkin so she could wipe the champagne off her face when Quinn slid into his seat beside her.

"Did I miss anything?" he said, still with his British accent.

"The kiss, the announcement, Larisa on the arm of another man. Basically everything," said Kahleah on his other side. "What's with your voice?"

"Americans don't wear hats to weddings," said Suzette.

"Well, damn." Quinn glanced at Larisa, his expression unreadable. "I hope it wasn't too spicy."

When do you ever say spicy?

"Everything okay?" asked Larisa.

"Great. Are drinks self-serve? Shall the men fetch the first round?"

"Drinks!" Dev launched himself up from his seat.

Quinn was gone again before Larisa could press him for a real answer. Maybe she didn't need one. But she still felt uneasy. She knew Quinn was uncomfortable in the spotlight; he wouldn't have left at a time when everyone could see him leaving unless it had been an emergency.

Quinn returned with two white wines and a club soda, which he pretended to offer Suzette then stole back for himself.

"No drinking?" asked Suzette; she was always suspicious of people who didn't drink socially.

"Not tonight," said Quinn. "It's the only way to reliably stay off the dance floor. You don't want to see that."

They wove their way through small talk, then dinner. People

came to say hello, first to Suzette, then to Larisa. Larisa made a point to introduce everyone worth knowing to Quinn to facilitate the professional goals he'd had for the weekend.

His manners weren't as terrible as they'd been on set. Certainly, he lacked the warm charisma ideal in this kind of setting. There were no smiles, no effort at compliments or personal questions conveying intentional interest. At first, this made her want to fill in the gaps for him, so people would feel he was interested in knowing them better, but by the time the Emcee announced people should gather for the cake cutting, no one had seemed particularly turned off, so Larisa stopped worrying.

She couldn't imagine Quinn as one of those people who leaned into a double handshake and doled out compliments like pennies. It was a nice thing about him; he knew his limits and didn't try to be someone else. She didn't know many people like that.

Stop it, Larisa.

Their table emptied as everyone else went to watch the cake cutting. Quinn took out his phone, tilted the screen away from her, then glared at it while typing furiously.

"It's okay if you need to leave."

"I'm fine," said Quinn. "Just a thing."

What thing? she wanted to ask.

A cheer rose from the guests gathered around the dessert station. Larisa dug her nails into the tablecloth and thought about how unfortunate it was that the cake wasn't white, or even a nice cream, which was so much classier than this blue color usually reserved for babies' clothes.

"Why are weddings only romantic in movies?" she asked.

"Curated narrative," said Quinn without missing a beat. "And the music cues."

She turned and found the barest smirk toying with the corner of his mouth. "I can't believe you think music exists to cover failures in technique."

"Would you like to fight about it? We'll start with *Love*

Actually."

Her eyes flew open. "Don't you dare." She smacked the side of his chest so hard her hand caught on his jacket. Something in the pocket rattled like a pill bottle. "What's that?"

"Nothing."

"Are you playing games?" She lunged toward his lap, digging her hands into both pockets. The pills were Viagra. Larisa stared at them for just a moment before putting them back where she'd found them.

"What the fuck, Larisa?" Quinn was out of breath and flushed with something that might have been embarrassment but felt like more.

"Sorry. I just—" She stopped. What could she say? The sinking feeling in her gut was so awful it made her nauseous. Those weren't for her. They weren't for the Queen. She tried to cover it with a joke. "You know how many psychological disorders are associated with ED?"

"All of them?"

"Close."

"I'd prefer you don't assume something about this. Is that possible?"

"I'm not here to judge you, Quinn."

"You'd be the first."

Their tablemates were returning with cake. Larisa swallowed back something hard in her throat as she pulled her smile back onto her face. She held it there until the bride and groom's dance. She'd known she wouldn't be able to tune out that moment; the moment the music would make it real.

They'd chosen the perfect song. The lighting was turned down, the spotlight not too harsh. Jaden and Adrian had taken dancing lessons and worked with a choreographer, so it really did look like a movie as they swept across the floor.

This is the end, thought Larisa.

A sob was rising up her throat. She swallowed it down. On the other side of Suzette, Krissy had tears in her eyes as she tried to hold her phone steady enough to record. Probably Rosa and Kahleah were also teary. But they were happy, beautiful even, with that shimmer of moisture in their eyes.

When the song ended, Rosa's hands slapped the table so hard Larisa jumped. "Round number two. Ladies get the drinks! Except for Suzette. What do you want, Larisa's Mom?"

The DJ started up the first song. The dance floor flooded. Larisa numbly followed Rosa through the people to the bar. She waited, holding herself so still she wasn't sure she was breathing, until the drinks appeared before her, and she again followed Rosa back to the table. She didn't sit down. It was too hard. Anything she said, even a stray look, she was going to lose control, and no one would know what to do with her, and there she'd be, sitting at the table with her only friends, who didn't know any of the most important things about her, ugly crying loud enough for people to hear her over the music. Then someone would take a picture and post it online with some horrible caption about Larisa being jealous it wasn't her wedding.

Larisa, last sister standing.

"Larisa, you look constipated," said Suzette. "Do you need something?" She reached for her clutch.

All Larisa could do was shake her head.

"I think that's my cue," said Quinn, rising. "We're going to dance."

"Didn't you say you don't dance?" Krissy's voice dissolved into the crowd noise as Quinn slid his arm around Larisa's waist, guiding her away from the table. He led her into the thickest part of the crowd on the dance floor, farthest from the table. They stood there, surrounded by the press of strangers. If Larisa had been able to look around, they probably wouldn't all have turned out to be strangers, but she couldn't look. She just stood. Everything inside her bunched up and braced. Her mind so forcefully blank she wasn't even sure how she'd gotten there.

She felt movement at the back of her head and realized it was Quinn's hand releasing the pins that held her hair up. With a stuttering attempt at a deep breath, she focused on the light pressure of his fingers on her scalp, on the clumsiness of his inexperienced movement as he fished for the hard-to-find pins. She focused her gaze on him. They were almost eye to eye, a new experience for Larisa with a date. Even more surprising, he was looking at her like he knew exactly what she was trying not to think about.

As her hair fell down around her shoulders, he took his hat and moved it to her head.

She might have asked, *What are you doing?* But what came out was, "I'm really happy for her."

"I know."

"It's just that I hate weddings."

He stepped forward so his hips touched hers, then took her hands and guided them inside his jacket to rest around his waist. "You know what I like about this shirt? The ruffles are huge." His arms enclosed her. One hand pressed her head down to rest against his chest with her face turned into the ruffles. He kept his hand there, holding the hat in place so that between the ruffles and hat she was completely hidden.

"No one can see you now," he said. The softness in his voice, the kindness she wasn't sure she deserved, pushed her over the edge. Larisa sobbed into Quinn's ruffles, her body shaking so hard with the expulsion that she clung to his waist to keep herself upright.

The song playing blended into the opening chords of the Tony Bennett classic Larisa loved so much. The crowd around them thinned into swaying couples. Larisa managed to quiet her sobs, though tears continued to fall. Quinn swayed his hips, nudging her body to follow along. She felt his chin rest on the top of the hat.

"There's a jacuzzi tub in our room," he whispered. "You're probably fine, but my feet are killing me. Squeeze my ass if yours are too."

She cupped his left cheek and gave it a good squeeze.

"I know bridesmaids have things to do to send off the happy

couple. But don't you think our relationship would be more convincing if you were mysteriously absent? I'm feeling particularly hot and bothered seeing you in that terrible dress. It needs to come off."

She squeezed his cheek a second time.

"Alright then. Dance with me." He took one of her hands in his. Assuming a traditional ballroom dance stance, he led her in a slow sashay across the floor to the side doors. Out in the hallway, they walked side by side, the hat low over Larisa's eyes so she couldn't see where she was going. Quinn held her hand to guide her. Someone called after them. It didn't matter. What mattered was the elevator, the dinging of the doors closing, and their whoosh of safety.

In their room, she buried herself under the duvet so he wouldn't see her face splotched and her makeup ruined. From beyond the cocoon of bedding, she heard him order room service, then go into the bathroom and start running water in the tub.

To him nothing has happened, she thought, which made the tears flood anew.

Room service came. Larisa listened to Quinn tip the attendant then move back and forth, carrying his order into the bathroom.

Champagne and chocolate covered strawberries, she thought. *He's celebrating and I'm in bed crying.*

When Larisa heard the bathroom door close, she bolted out of bed to the mirror on the side wall to wipe her face clean. It was a sloppy rush job, but it was enough. Then, without knocking, she entered the bathroom.

He'd removed his shirt and was sitting on the side of the tub, pulling off his socks. She couldn't tell if he was surprised to see her. He didn't freeze or start or scowl as she'd expected.

"What's that smell?" she asked.

He motioned to the tub, which was only a third full. "Epsom salts. Eucalyptus. Scented, I think. My mother used to do this on her day off."

"Champagne and strawberries in the bathroom?" asked Larisa, which coaxed his ghost smile onto his face.

"Soaking her feet. She was a waitress."

It seemed like a good sign he'd added this extra thought, information that hadn't been required.

"If you're joining me, you have to go get your own glass."

Larisa went out and came back with the extra glass from the room service tray. When she returned, he'd rolled up his pant legs and dangled his feet in the water. She joined him.

"What are we celebrating?" she asked.

"My last night in this fancy hotel."

"I'm sorry I made you leave the reception. You could've met more people. I think Georgie Han was even there. He's a big—"

"You didn't make me do anything." Quinn poured the champagne and held up his glass to toast. "What should we toast to?"

"You call it. This is your celebration. I'm basically in funeral mode."

"To hope," said Quinn without missing a beat. "The dream that doesn't come with a price tag."

"To hope," echoed Larisa, almost breathless.

"Why funeral mode? You really hate weddings that much?"

"I guess I thought Jaden and I would go on forever. Grow old and laugh at all the people who said women needed a man and kids to be happy."

"Like in a romantic way, or . . ."

"Just as friends. Or I mean, I'm open to that, but I don't think she is. Jaden has always been . . . straightforward. But she was what I had. It's hard for me to have friends. Real friends."

"But she's not really like you. None of them seem to be at your level."

"Like you are?" she teased, as she reached for the bottle and poured herself more champagne.

"I mean, aside from your shared history and that you all come from money and maybe get your nails done at the same place... Dansby seems to know more about your life than they do."

Her expression hardened, so he backtracked. "It's nice of you to say I'm on your level."

"Well, it's true," she said. "We're both hawks. We watch. We keep track of things. We think relationships are things that come with planning and hard work, not just something that happens when we have time or feel like it." She swished her foot over and tagged his pinkie toe with her big toe. "We're a good team."

He stared down at their feet like she'd bitten him, and he was looking for blood. "So, what will you do now?"

"Obviously, I'll still be friends with her. I am with all of them. We won't ever not be friends. It's just more work to fit in. Their lives are so different than mine."

"They'll find you someone to marry."

"They would if they could ever agree on what I'm looking for."

"You don't know?"

Larisa laughed. "Well, I've eliminated a lot of possibilities. So, I feel like I'll know when I see him, and it'll happen fast. On the outside, it'll look like I've lost my mind, but actuality, it's just that I've been waiting. If you weren't so attached to women with small hands, I think I might fall for you."

For a long moment Quinn swished his feet through the water. When he finally looked at her, there was nothing in his expression showing any interest, just a quiet kind of regret, of him holding himself back from the full truth of what she was saying. As one did when they believed themselves in love with someone else.

"Well, you won't think I'm such a prize when I tell you how I feel about all the music in *Love Actually*." He picked up a strawberry, but she snatched it from him and shoved it in her mouth.

"Fine then, Mr. Cinema Réaliste, ruin it for me. I dare you."

Day Three

Larisa woke up tucked into bed with Quinn sitting beside her on top of the duvet, his back against the headboard like he'd been awake for hours or perhaps had never gone to sleep. His phone was balanced on his knee. The screen lit up with a new message, but he didn't look at it. He was scowling at the far wall, where the TV was playing the local news on mute, but with a distant look in his eye that told her the news was the last thing on his mind.

"Good morning," he said, not looking at her. "We went viral. I think I deserve a raise."

"If you ask nicely." She found her phone on the bedside table and scrolled through her notifications. There were lots of messages asking where she'd gone, some hinting at how jealous they were of what she was off doing. There were shared pictures of her sisters sending Jaden and Adrian off with sparklers and rose pedals, which she quickly skipped through until she found the video Rosa had taken of Larisa and Quinn dancing their way to their exit.

"We look like we're in love."

"The line would've been better if you'd taken off your shoes," said Quinn.

Larisa nodded in agreement. "Next time I'll do that." She set aside her phone and gazed up at him, willing him to look at her so she could see if there was some glimmer of interest. He kept staring at the TV. When his phone went off, his eyes diverted for a moment, then slid back as though there was only one safe place for him to look.

It's fine, she thought. *He doesn't see me like that.*

Tell him who you are.

"Thank you," she said. "Best date ever."

"Best date where you sobbed through a great song and ruined my nice shirt? Low bar."

"Not everyone can make that be okay."

"If we were actually dating, you'd have such high expectations after last night I'd be doomed to fail."

"Probably."

He sucked in a breath and let it out. "Is the plan still brunch and then departure?"

"Yeah, why? You need to leave early?"

"It can wait."

"Viagra?"

His expression darkened.

"Sorry. I don't need to know."

"Parish came here during the wedding yesterday."

"*Here* here?" Larisa glanced around their room as though Parish might suddenly pop out of the closet.

"She said she was tired of being kept on hold and if I didn't agree to meet her, she'd make a scene. She put the pills in my pocket. I imagine she hoped you'd find them."

"You're meeting her." Larisa felt her chest constrict, her breathing becoming painful. "What will you say?"

"I don't know yet."

"Well, you'll be a free man soon." She hated saying it. Her hands itched with the impulse to reach out and pull him down against her, to keep him with her forever. "Are you still okay with one or two more public appearances before we call it off?"

He looked relieved she'd given him a way to change topics. "There's that premiere next week. I'd appreciate your expertise as a semi-sane woman with years of red-carpet experience."

Semi-sane is an interesting choice of adjectives. Is he comparing me to Parish?

Couldn't he just say he wants to spend time with me?

He probably doesn't.

"Does that offend you?" he asked.

"It tells me you're a very wise man."

"Then I'll have my people call your people."

"I bet you love saying that."

"In fact, I do."

"Maybe if psychiatry doesn't work out, I can go into consulting. I'll teach newbie celebrities how to present themselves."

"Not a terrible idea. But I doubt you'll need a plan B." The words slipped so easily from his mouth she almost thought they were rehearsed. But why would he bother? Of course, it was her fate that the only man on the planet who acted like her medical practice was a foregone conclusion had fallen in love with her alter ego.

She studied his expression, the way his jaw worked as though he was chewing through an invisible problem. The banter coming too easily, like lines of dialogue in a scene he composed. *The Morning After.* Except all they'd done between the fade to black and the return to camera was sit side by side eating chocolate dipped strawberries from room service, soaking their feet, and arguing about music in film.

Which wasn't nothing.

In fact, it had been wonderful.

She'd tried to push him in the tub and they'd both ended up soaked. And maybe she'd fallen asleep with her head in his lap. But he'd only allowed it because he felt sorry for her.

They went down to brunch with the bridal party, family members, and Suzette, who responded to Krissy shamelessly teasing Larisa about their dance floor escape with the sardonic one-liner, "She's done much worse." By which, of course, her mother had meant Lucas, and everyone within hearing distance knew what she meant except Quinn.

If he were a real boyfriend, I'd have to explain Lucas, thought Larisa, suddenly exhausted. *Being single is good, simple.*

Then came the goodbyes and the overburdened when-will-we-see-you-agains. Larisa told them her next event would probably be her mother's autumn masquerade, which made her friends pouty in a way that made her feel guilty even though she knew they were all busy, and October wasn't that far away.

It felt like an eternity before she and Quinn returned to their room to pack.

"I have a close-out session with Eddie tomorrow afternoon at the studio," said Larisa. "We could do an early dinner or drinks for the cameras?"

"Yeah, sure."

She watched him zip his jacket with the pills into his bag, almost like he wasn't planning to use them. *It's not your business, Larisa.* But she couldn't resist saying, with a touch of bitterness, "Your silence really is your best defense."

For a moment he gazed at her like he wanted to voice the truth they both knew. Last night had meant nothing to him. He was in love with a woman he couldn't have. He was going to try to make it work with Parish. There was no space for Larisa among those twin pillars of his heart.

They walked out of the resort holding hands. He kissed her cheek before she climbed into her Bentley and drove away.

Her cheek burned all the way home.

She had six hours of empty space before work. Walking through the living room, she stepped on a cat toy and realized she'd forgotten to stop by Tish's house to pick up her still unnamed kitten. She decided to text her to see if it was a good time to swing by. As soon as Tish's response came back in the affirmative, Larisa escaped her apartment. She took the long way with the Foo Fighters, Green Day, and Jimmy Eat World. A playlist to rip her heart out and watch it bleed.

Larisa parked under the shelter of an orange tree overhanging Tish's driveway and sat holding on to her steering wheel until her hands cramped.

Tish isn't scary. If you cry for no obvious reason, she'll make it okay. She won't sell you out.

A few minutes later, she was coiled up on a kitchen island stool receiving coffee and waffles. The white kitten sat on the adjacent stool, tail swishing with interest. A second kitten sat in the curve of a cat tree by the window, watching from a distance.

"How was it?" asked Tish.

"Good."

Tish gave her a measuring look so severe and unlike her it made Larisa laugh. "What are you really asking?"

"I wouldn't take Quinn to a wedding if he paid me," said Tish.

"He ended up being the best part."

Larisa's phone vibrated in her pocket. She ignored it. The only person she really wanted to talk to was Quinn, and he was busy.

"I never liked weddings much myself," said Tish. "If you ask me, spend the money on the honeymoon. But then, I suppose people have expectations."

"If I eloped, my mother would never speak to me again." Larisa tentatively reached out and stroked her kitten's head.

"She needs a name."

"You could name her. Keep her for me."

Larisa's phone vibrated again.

"The human lap to cat ratio is already one-to-three in this house."

Another vibration. Larisa set down her coffee and pulled her phone out of her pocket. "I'm sorry. I don't know who's . . ."

Three messages from Quinn.

The first was a picture of him on one of Club D's massage

tables, shirtless, apparently asleep, with his arm folded under his head, like it'd been last week when they'd laid on the couches in his office and listened to Billy Joel.

Quinn: Isn't he beautiful?

Quinn: Come play, my Queen.

Larisa's free hand lurched out and grabbed the edge of the island.

"What's wrong?"

For a moment, Larisa couldn't speak. She couldn't even think. Then bits of clarity sifted through her rush of panic. Parish had Quinn at Club D. He didn't know about the Queen yet. But he would know soon if she couldn't talk Parish out of it.

How does she know?

It doesn't matter.

"Larisa?"

It's a trap.

What if she hurts him?

"I need to go handle something. Can the kitten stay here one more night?"

"Yes, but—"

"I can't talk about it."

"Sure you can," said Tish. "You've just trained yourself not to."

Larisa stared down at her waffles, only half listening. She could call Doan. She could call the police. *And what? Accuse Parish of kidnapping at a sex club?*

"I've seen you four days a week for the past month," said Tish. "Do you know what I know about you?"

Larisa's phone vibrated again, but this time it was only Krissy on the group chat asking about happy hour on Friday.

"Nothing I couldn't read about online."

"There's a lot about me online," said Larisa.

"It's good to trust people."

"When I trust people, they make fifty grand repeating it to the papers. I'll see you tomorrow."

Larisa drove to the long-term parking lot with her stereo off. At her Nissan, she got dressed and drove to Club D. In the silence, her mind churned. *Find Parish, do whatever you need to do to keep her quiet.*

Club D had just opened. Two minivans and a pickup were parked in the lot. Quinn's Subaru sat in the stall closest to the back door. Larisa checked in with the daytime version of Doan and was told her partner had reserved the Blue Room. Larisa passed the stage where new employees were watching a flogging technique demonstration. She brushed her hand along each doorknob as she walked down the hallway. *Please don't tell him. Please don't tell him. Please don't tell him.*

She came to the last knob and turned it. The Blue Room's massage table was empty. The upright chair with the restraints sat at the far side as before. Someone had left a pair of cuffs and chains attached to the ring in the center of the floor. The room smelled as it always did, of soapy lavender and an undertone of sweat.

Larisa inhaled and tried to center herself. This was her safe place. It wouldn't betray her. Parish was just a woman, upset, possibly psychotic, but manageable. Larisa would work with her. They would find a way through this together.

The scuffle of a footstep sounded behind her. Larisa turned too late to block the blow to the side of her head. Everything went black.

Quinn woke up in the Red Room with only a vague impression of how he'd gotten there. He'd met Parish for lunch. He'd been surprised by how calm she'd seemed after the scene she'd made during the wedding. When they'd finished lunch, she'd suggested they go to Club D. She wanted to prove she could be the woman he wanted.

Why had he said yes?

He didn't even remember doubting his decision. It had seemed like the right one.

She drugged me, thought Quinn, as he struggled upright and reached for his shirt. *Did we . . .?* He looked around the room for artifacts of activity, but nothing seemed out of place. He was still wearing his pants. He had his wallet but not his phone. His head remained foggy as he took the elevator down to the first floor.

Club D's bar was mostly empty. Quinn didn't see Parish or the Queen. *Would she be here without me?* His stomach spasmed with what might have been irritation from lunch. Or it might have been the thought of the Queen with another submissive. Or his stomach-brain connection trying to make sense of what was happening.

"There you are, Mr. Grumpy Sunshine," said Anapurr from behind the bar. "You sure know how to keep a girl waiting."

"The Queen is waiting?"

"You're in the Blue Room today. But hang on, you need an escort."

Anapurr sauntered around the bar and presented Quinn with a satin blindfold.

"I'm not allowed to see her?"

"I'm sure that's down the line." Anapurr slipped it over his eyes, tied it behind his head, then led him into the quiet stillness of the main floor hallway. He heard a door click open and Anapurr's husky voice living up to her name as she purred, "Your treat has arrived, Madam. Have fun."

The door swished shut behind him. Silence rushed in to fill the space in Anapurr's absence. *What is this?* He wanted to believe somehow the Queen had surprised him, but he knew that was too much to hope for. The absence of his phone, the covert manipulation, was all Parish.

Quinn reached for the blindfold. A riding crop reached out of the silence and slapped his hands down. No spine-tingling reprimand followed.

"Parish?"

The crop came around to his back, nudging him forward. He walked, certain at any moment he'd crash into something. But then the crop fell away and hands reached out to turn him and pressed him into a high-back chair. They secured his wrists to the armrests with cuffs.

Despite his worry, Quinn felt a prickle of interest. His entire body stood on alert with that pulsing, anxious anticipation he loved so much. The promise of surrender, the rest of the world dissolving as he allowed himself to be taken in, his worst tendencies beaten out of him, all the failures, and wounds, and doubts released.

Let it be her.

The blindfold lifted away. Parish stood before him. She wore a leopard print latex bodysuit complete with a headband of fuzzy ears and a tail.

"Hello, Quinn. Have a good nap?"

His eyes swiveled around the room, the toys on the far wall, the door, the one-way window. This was the room at the end of the hall where people could watch.

And on the floor, kneeling with cuffs around her wrists, was the Queen, with none of her usual makeup. Tears in her eyes.

"Parish, what the fuck are you doing?"

He knew why. It just didn't seem possible.

"Do you recognize the room? We were on the outside looking in last time. Now, we're part of the action." Parish gave a gleeful little screech. "So exciting! When I heard you two like to play here, I knew I had to be part of it. I tried really hard to make it perfect. I know how much you like things to be just so."

Quinn's eyes scanned the Queen's body. She didn't appear hurt. Seeing her on her knees brought blank spots of rage scattering across his vision. He jerked against the cuffs.

"See if I got your fantasy right," said Parish. "The two lovers, separated. The interloper—that's me—coming in to save their love by bringing them pain. Is that how it goes?"

He had no idea what she was talking about. "You'll never fucking understand."

"I just need to beat her with one of these toys, right? That's what you like?"

Quinn surged against the restraints. "Don't you dare touch her!"

"I think we're off to a good start." Parish pranced over to the wall, browsed through the toys before picking up a flogger with knots tied into the strings. "This looks fun."

His rage turned to panic. She was really going to play out the scene she'd described. "Parish, stop. Please. Let's talk."

"Talk about what?" Parish tried out a few flicks of her wrist with the flogger, sloppy, unpracticed movements. She approached the Queen from behind. "Talk about how I rode you in the resort bathroom while you were supposed to be at a wedding? Talk about our romantic lunch? Is this woman even capable of a relationship like that?"

Parish bent over and hung her head in the Queen's face. "Are you capable of real romance?" Parish flicked the flogger toward the Queen's shoulder.

"Why do you think she's so quiet?" Parish asked Quinn. "I think we should make her talk." Parish planted her feet.

Quinn screamed, "No!" as the flogger connected with the Queen's bare shoulder above the back of her corset. She grunted with pain.

"I'll try again."

"Parish, enough!"

"If she doesn't like it, she can say so, right?"

Another blow. The Queen's lips pressed together.

"Maybe she likes the pain and doesn't want to admit it."

Quinn's wrists twisted desperately against the restraints. This wasn't happening. It couldn't be happening. The Queen, *his* queen, desecrated while he stood by helpless.

The flogger whistled through the air once, twice. The third

time, the Queen cried out. Parish's inexperience with flogging had split the skin on the Queen's shoulder.

"Is she wet?" Parish crouched down and put her hand between the Queen's legs.

"Get your fucking hands off her!"

"Harsh, Quinn. I'm surprised. You're not the least bit curious why she's so quiet? Maybe she has a secret in her voice."

Quinn stilled. Something in Parish's tone warned him this was the money shot, the linchpin around which the scene hinged. *What's worse than this?* Quinn's gaze shifted to the window. An unyielding plane on this side. A transparent glass on the other.

"Who's watching?"

"Everyone." Parish smiled. "Are you ready for the unveiling? No wait, I want you to guess. Who's your mysterious woman?"

Quinn was still looking at the window, straining to see beyond it. Shivers rippled across his skin under the imagined attention of dozens of invisible eyes. Any hope of a future with the Queen lay in tatters at his feet. With it, possibly his career, and a chance at a scandal-free upward trajectory.

Maybe that was how the story was always going to go. He'd reached too far. Someone like him didn't deserve to craft moments of perfect humanity that lifted audiences out of their ordinary lives, giving them a taste of magic if only for a few hours. Someone like him didn't deserve designer clothes, and celebrity weddings, and chocolate strawberries while playing footsie in a jacuzzi tub with a woman who knew where he came from and didn't seem to care. It had all been just a beautiful dream. And now it was over.

Quinn sagged back against the chair. "Alright Parish, you win."

"What do I win?" she pouted. "I haven't asked for anything."

"Whatever you want. Just let me out of these cuffs and we'll never come back here again. I'll be what you want."

"That's not possible," said Parish. "You were never what I wanted. We're not here for that. We're here for her. This woman is living a lie. It makes me sick she can't be as honest with you as I was."

Parish hooked her fingers under the edge of the Queen's hood and pulled it up over the side of her face. A cascade of auburn hair broke free from it.

"No," said Quinn.

"Shocking, isn't it?" Parish brushed the hair back from the Queen's face, turning it toward the window. "All you little people out there in the dark watching, I give you Dr. Larisa de France-Kahn. She's a psychiatry resident who's been using torture on her patients instead of therapy."

Larisa wrenched out of Parish's grasp and looked up at Quinn. He was vaguely aware that what she must see in his face at that moment was horror. But he was frozen, unable to shift his expression. Words formed a line in his head, it wasn't what he wanted but it was what came out anyway. "All this time?"

"Since that first night we saw her," said Parish. "Disturbing, isn't it, that she could lie to you for so long? And you had no idea, poor thing." Parish knelt down and released Larisa's wrists from the cuffs. "Would you like to say anything for our audience?" Parish motioned toward Quinn with one hand and the window with the other.

Larisa got to her feet. For a moment her eyes held his, the eyes he should have recognized. *Her* eyes, the eyes of his—

"I'm sorry," she whispered. With a shudder, she turned and said to the window. "I'm not sorry." Then she fled the room.

Quinn strained against his cuffs. "Larisa, come back! Larisa!"

CHILD STAR CAUGHT RED-HANDED AT BONDAGE CLUB

PSYCHIATRIST-IN-TRAINING ABUSES PATIENTS

IT USED TO BE SEX, DRUGS, AND ROCK AND ROLL, NOW ITS SEX, VIOLENCE, AND EXPLOITATION

WHAT IS THE TRUE STATE OF PSYCHIATRIC CARE IN THIS COUNTRY?

HOW MANY PEOPLE KNEW WHAT DE FRANCE-KAHN WAS DOING?

THE DEPRAVITY OF LARISA DE FRANCE-KAHN.

THE WARNING SIGNS WERE THERE, NO ONE STOPPED HER

FAMOUS PRODUCER SPEAKS OUT IN DEFENSE OF DAUGHTER'S SCANDAL

LIFESTYLES OF THE RICH AND FAMOUS: FROM GLAMOROUS BRIDESMAID TO DIRTY DOMINATRIX

IS DE FRANCE-KAHN GOING TO JAIL?

IN THE LOCKED WARD: PATIENTS' RIGHTS IN PSYCHIATRIC FACILITIES

Chapter 32

The Silences of Yellow Dots

Three Months Later

The quiet had begun to take on a shape of its own. In the mornings, when the air was crisp and the lawn wet with the promise of a new day, the quiet in Larisa's room felt like isolation, a hard line between inside and outside, which resisted the invasion of birdsong. She liked to sleep through mornings in defiance of that promise, that innate avian cheer.

In the afternoons, the quiet shifted into the pockets of empty rooms around the house, stalking sound like the voids of small black holes. Even when the house was busy, Larisa could find a room or two so isolated from any other person's activity that the quiet felt artificial, like the dampening effect of plugged ears underwater, as removed from the energy of life as she was.

And at night, with her mother usually out at an event or her parents hosting guests in the entertaining wing, the quiet crawled with sharpened claws along the floors, the walls, the ceilings. It inflated with whispered taunts that echoed like ghosts down empty hallways. It became the dread anticipation of a collapsed ceiling, a fire, a flood, an unexpected death. Then Larisa would remember the dread she felt wasn't in anticipation, because the disaster had already taken place.

Never in her life had she lived without a schedule. To do nothing, to have no goals around which to structure her daily existence, only amplified the completeness of her collapse. One aspect of trauma recovery theory emphasized making small goals like cooking herself breakfast, exercising, or laying by the pool. But Larisa had never made goals for the sake of accomplishing trivial tasks. She derived no pleasure from making herself breakfast, as Estelle did it better and served it to her in bed promptly twenty minutes after Larisa called down to say she was awake. Laying by the pool made her restless. And she could only fill so many hours alternating between swimming and sunning.

Larisa found it easiest to sit in the glass-ceilinged sunroom in the family wing that opened on to the sculpture garden. She read vengeful true crime novels. She took naps with her kitten in the sun. She ordered scratching posts, cat towers, and an elaborate cat bed with the kitten's name embroidered around the edge. She'd named her Sabrina, the savior. Most of the time she ate regular meals. When Dansby's text messages stacked up to double digits, she summoned the energy to reply to some of them. Mostly they exchanged links to music videos. But even music had lost its power to move her.

On Thursdays she and Suzette had coffee in the garden, spending an hour working on Suzette's autumn masquerade. Sometime, usually during the ten o'clock hour on Fridays, a delivery person arrived with a bouquet of exotic flowers stolen from some remote tropical rainforest. Larisa wouldn't take Eddie's calls, so the flowers had become his apology, arriving every day in gaudy colors and sharp spines to reopen her wound.

Parish had live streamed the scene at Club D using Larisa's phone on a tripod set up on the audience side of the one-way window. By the time Larisa had been unmasked, several thousand people had been watching the grainy, poorly lit scene that lagged so many times the sound rarely matched the video. Several thousand more watched the pirated recordings and clips populating the internet like dandelions in the weeks that had followed.

Within twenty-four hours, intrepid reporters had identified Larisa's residency program. Dr. Bade had been fired. The program was now under review by ethics and accreditation boards. More than one journalist had faked a psychotic break in order to be admitted to the Sacred Heart psych ward and gain access to Larisa's cohorts, who'd said predictable things about her lack of dedication and unclear motivation for going into medicine when she had so many other options.

What fucking options?

Sophie had come forward, perhaps to give a balanced view of Larisa, the person, but her version of "nice but distracted Larisa" had been interpreted as a lie. Because no one who liked kinky sex could be a *nice girl*. What people thought she'd been doing with her patients in that dungeon was worse than evil. The only thing that might have been worse was if the patients had somehow been underage children she'd snuck into the club illegally.

After the initial surge dwindled, more reporters, desperate to keep the biggest scandal of the year humming, began to dredge up her past. The previous week the Internet had churned through her adolescence, the failed Hard Rock Café date, the years with braces, and going bra shopping for the first time. All of it archived on *Drama Queen*.

And then, the dreaded rehashing of Lucas started. So far, he was "the older man" she'd dated in college (she'd been twenty and Lucas twenty-seven), who'd sold the story of Larisa, the submissive schoolgirl, to *EW*, then been shocked when she'd dumped him. It was only a matter of time before speculation about their relationship began to draw connections to the current state of her sexuality.

Lucas had sent her one text each month since the live stream. Exactly three more than Quinn.

The day after the stream.

> Lucas: Shame you had so much clothing on
> for that camera.

A month later.

This morning.

For a few minutes she thought about saying yes. Reuniting with Lucas felt like cotton candy compared to the parade of supposed patients coming forward with their own damning tales. There were so many, Quinn, her only real patient who overlapped with the dungeon, had been forgotten. Even when he was mentioned in an article, it was only as an afterthought. The world seemed to have accepted he'd been caught between two controlling, jealous, and out-of-their-mind women. This had given him an unlikely sex appeal. "What's it about Quinn VanderVeer that drives women mad?" asked *The Hollywood Reporter* a week after the stream. When no one speculated on an answer, the question gradually faded away.

So, Quinn was safe, and Club D had become a tourist destination.

Two good things rising out of the catastrophe of Larisa's life.

"What's new with you?" asked Dr. Bade when she called for her usual Tuesday afternoon check-in.

"My mother thinks she's found me a husband."

"I didn't realize that was something you were trying for."

"Now that I'm the disgraced kinky, possibly sociopathic, unemployed daughter of famous people, our dating consultant says my metrics have improved within a certain demographic."

"Is that what you want?"

"Of course."

"You scare me sometimes with how believable you can be when you lie."

"I'm good at planning events and hosting parties."

"So become an event planner."

"He's coming in from Toronto this weekend. I'll let you know how it goes."

"What about Quinn?"

"Let's not talk about Quinn."

"Alright. Can we talk about something Quinn-adjacent?"

"I reserve the right to hang up."

"Parish has passed her psych evaluation," said Dr. Bade. "She's moving to a partial lockdown facility in the hills."

"Why would I visit the woman who ruined my life?"

"Have you noticed, in all this, no one has asked her why she did it? Why that weekend, after they'd been separated for months? Why target Quinn so publicly if her goal was to bring him back to her? It was a long game. She'd been watching you for weeks. She studied you well enough and long enough to know how she could do the most damage."

"I don't think about Parish," said Larisa.

"What do you think about?"

"Quinn's face when my mask came off."

"Anyone would've been shocked."

"It was more than that. I ruined his enchantment."

"In the moment, perhaps. But now? It might be worth talking."

"He hasn't called."

"Maybe he thinks you don't want to talk to him."

Larisa pressed her lips into a bloodless line. She watched as Sabrina submerged herself in the grass, then pounced on an unsuspecting cricket.

"I'm going to say one shrink thing and then hang up," said Dr. Bade.

"You're going to say I shouldn't settle."

"True, but I was going to say there's an open office in my new suite. You could pass a counseling licensure exam without even studying."

"Talk therapy?" Larisa shook her head even though Dr. Bade

couldn't see her. "Imagine what kind of patients I'd attract with my reputation."

"It's something to think about."

"Thanks for thinking of me."

"In the meantime, I do telehealth," hinted Dr. Bade.

"I'm not ready."

"What's stopping you?"

"The need to prolong denying that my career is over?"

"Is that what you're doing right now?"

"I'm not ready."

The Pacific Heights Clinic had once been a country club. Aside from the heightened security and locked medicine closets, much of it remained the same. Larisa followed a nurse disguised as a hostess along a thickly padded carpet to one of the several community rooms. She wondered how long it would take before someone with an authenticated socials platform knew she'd been there.

Parish looked older than she had before, which was to say, she finally looked her age. She was playing dominos with someone Larisa vaguely recognized as the current mayor's teenage son and a B-list actor. Larisa knew there hadn't been any news about the son checking into a clinic, which made his presence noteworthy. It was something she might've texted Kahleah to pass along to Cade to help with his campaign.

But Larisa and Kahleah weren't really speaking. "Cade doesn't want me involved in any scandals," had been her excuse via text message less than forty-eight hours after the live stream. Which was fair. But didn't make it hurt any less.

It didn't make it any easier that both Tate and Dev were involved in some capacity with Cade's campaign. So, the only friend left standing was Jaden, who was often traveling to Adrian's games or busy redecorating his house. Her support had been limited to baby animal memes and sadness over the loss of Quinn. She'd expressed so much sadness, Larisa had exploded one day and admitted to everyone Quinn had never really been hers; it had all been fake.

The group chat went strangely silent after that.

So, Larisa had no one to tell that the mayor's son was receiving in-patient psychiatric treatment, most likely for addiction, given the circles under his eyes and his general emaciation. Having this secret felt like a weapon. It made her feel confident about her decision to come, even though she was sure to regret it later. Just being in a care facility again brought up so many feelings she'd been holding back. The smells, the sounds, the people, were all so familiar even though she'd never worked in a private clinic. She couldn't help but eyeball the actor at Parish's table, and the two women at the adjacent table, and guess at their diagnoses. She also couldn't resist imagining their therapists were subpar, distracted, and prone to throwing drugs at problems needing specialized interventions.

Parish looked up from the dominos. She tracked Larisa as she skirted the edge of the room, then sat down in an empty chair by the window. Parish laid down two more dominos, declared herself the winner, then came to join Larisa at the window.

"It's you," she said. "Surprised."

"I thought we left some things unfinished."

"You're not a doctor anymore. You can't treat me."

Larisa shrugged. "Is it going well here?"

"It's boring. The food sucks." Parish paused. "My doctor thinks Quinn was only with me so I'd introduce him to my uncle."

"What do you think about that?"

"I hate it obviously. Why wouldn't he want me? I worked so hard to make him happy. And it didn't matter."

"Sometimes it helps to realize you could've been perfect and it still wouldn't have lasted."

"Is that how you feel?"

"About what?"

"About Quinn. That you could only be perfect for him in one way and the rest wasn't enough."

Larisa swallowed. Not for all the world was she going to react to Parish picking at her scabs. But that didn't make her internal space any easier to control.

"Quinn and I were playing our own game to get what we needed."

"Well, I got what I needed." Parish smiled dreamily out the window. "I don't care what people say about me. I took control from a worthless man. That counts for something doesn't it?"

Larisa shrugged, holding back her reaction because she sensed Parish wanted not just an answer, but her approval.

"He did the same thing to you." Parish's cheeks flushed. "No woman is enough for him. Seriously, I don't know why you aren't pissed."

I am pissed, but not at him.

"Do you ever feel guilty?" asked Larisa.

"Don't be boring."

Larisa held her ground. Parish only lasted through thirteen seconds of silence. "My doctor asks me that all the time. She's like fixated on it. How could I do what I did? Like it was some big deal."

"You drugged your ex-boyfriend."

"Who is an abusive, sex-addict asshole."

"No, he isn't," said Larisa softly.

"You're hardly unbiased."

"So, you don't feel guilty?"

"For bringing darkness into the light? For exposing you and your sadism?"

This was a mistake.

"I'm glad you got what you needed," Larisa said, as she stood to leave.

"Are you coming back?"

"Do you want me to?"

"If you do, you could bring chocolate ice cream. They only have vanilla here and I'm just dying for chocolate ice cream and pickles."

"No promises."

As she walked away, Larisa shook her head. *Chocolate ice cream and pickles?*

Quinn studied the painting on the wall across from his therapist's leather couch as he had at some point during every previous visit. He now knew the painting was a Kandinsky original from his early period. The maze of lines and geometric shapes contorting to make other shapes and other lines were an easy lure for his mind, which craved simple things. No doubt, this was one of the reasons his therapist had placed the painting opposite the couch.

"How's the movie going this week?" Dr. Edagwa wore a three-piece suit, shaved and oiled his head, and charged five hundred dollars an hour to ask Quinn these kinds of questions.

"We're doing test screenings on Thursday and Friday for the initial cut."

"No conflicts?"

"The executives don't like how sexual it is. They want a different ending. They asked for a stock shot of a giant American flag." Quinn shifted in his seat to try and ease the pinch in his right shoulder, which was still recovering from when he tore the labrum trying to get free of the chair in the Blue Room. "Eddie's handling it."

If anything good had come out of the scene at Club D it was that people now gave Quinn space. They didn't challenge him unless absolutely necessary. In return, Quinn found few reasons to be critical. If the suits wanted a different ending that could be pieced together from the footage already shot, he'd give it to them.

Giant American flags? Why not? So much felt like it no longer mattered.

"What else?" asked Dr. Edagwa.

The dreaded open-ended question. Quinn preferred sessions when Dr. Edagwa dragged out initial pleasantries for a while. He sometimes asked about Quinn's diet (narrowed down to as simple as possible, peanut butter and crackers, non-dairy vanilla milk-shakes, pre-plucked rotisserie chicken when Sid remembered to buy it.) He asked about the childhood Quinn had hidden from Larisa, the father who abandoned him as a toddler, the mother who left sixteen years later. Somewhere in another universe, he knew these traumas and their hidden truths were where therapists proved their worth, but Quinn couldn't have been less interested in such revelations.

Dr. Edagwa was smart enough he'd given up on this line of exploration after session five. Thus, the question, what else? Quinn was here voluntarily, which meant if he wanted his money to be well-spent, he needed to find an answer.

"I spent three hours online last night reading about Larisa."

"Did you find what you were looking for?"

"Eight years ago, *Entertainment Weekly* published a profile called, "Larisa Between the Covers: What's It Like to Date a Reality Star." Seven pages of pictures stolen from her personal camera or taken by paparazzi stalking her at UCLA."

Quinn paused, letting his eyes trace back over the lines in the Kandinsky. *Where am I going with this?*

"It seems someone close to her gave the reporter the details needed for the story. But it also felt like I was reading about a stranger."

"You're trying to understand why you didn't realize you were interacting with the same person in two contexts?"

"I want to know which one is the real Larisa."

"The two women you knew are so different that one must be a lie?"

Why did Kandinsky place a yellow dot there? wondered Quinn.

"I never thought about Larisa sexually until the wedding. Whenever we interacted, she was so professional, so removed from any hint of flirtation. Sometimes I think she tricked me into not seeing her as the Queen. Even now that I know, I can't draw them together."

"We know at some point she made a decision not to reveal her identity. What do you feel about that?"

Quinn squinted at the painting. What he'd thought was a rectangle looked like a slanted polygon on closer inspection. "I know why she did it."

"That isn't what I asked."

"I feel . . . like a fool. All those weeks I fought her because I thought she'd unmask me. I felt like I'd been forced to give her so much, but it was nothing compared to what she offered me."

"What comes next?"

That bit there looks like a cluster of stars, thought Quinn, *or maybe musical notes.*

"I'm doing a political ad," said Quinn.

Chapter 33

A Birthday Party

In August, Suzette and Larisa increased their masquerade planning to three hours twice a week. A reporter from *LA Today* came to the estate to do a piece on Suzette and marveled at how calm the two women were, piecing together an event for four hundred people as though it was nothing.

"You realize there's only so much you can control," said Suzette. "You plan three contingencies to adjust for the variability of humanity, the weather, and the fates. After that, you enjoy the ride."

The reporter directed her photographer to take several extra pictures of Larisa sitting at the planning table, then of her standing at the sunroom windows, calling to Sabrina to stop chasing birds.

"And what about you, Larisa?" asked the reporter. "Do you find party planning easier or harder than psychiatry?"

"Much easier." Larisa forced a smile. "Now that I've had time to reflect, I'm thankful for what happened this spring. I'd tricked myself into thinking I wanted to do something with my life entirely foreign to where I came from. Since that's been gone, I feel so at peace."

"So, you're ready to settle down and do some good in the world?"

When the article went live, two things happened. Krissy read it, burst into tears, then immediately called Larisa to apologize for being a bad friend. They scheduled a lunch together at the estate, and Larisa managed to not dwell on the fact it took her telling *LA Today* psychiatry was never a good fit before Krissy was brave enough to break ranks with Kahleah and to get back in touch.

The second thing was quieter. Sid shared the link with Quinn. He read the article on the backlot of the studio while stretching his legs; he was in the middle of what was shaping up to be a marathon session in the editing room after two lackluster test screenings.

He called Sid. "What the fuck trash did you send me?"

"I thought you'd be interested. Positive press and all that."

"This isn't her."

Quinn paced the lot, phone in hand, two finger strokes away from calling Larisa. *What the fuck is she doing?*

But he didn't call. There might have been a moment, hidden in those nightmarish first days after the stream, when he could have called. He might have said, "I didn't want it to be anyone else." He should have said it at Club D the moment he saw her instead of yelling her name in that bloody murder voice, as though seeing her true self had ruined him.

Maybe it had, though not in the way she thought.

When Anapurr had finally come in and released Quinn from the chair, he'd ignored the pain in his shoulder and tackled Parish to the ground. Not much was clear after that. The police had been involved. And then, ironically, he'd ended up staying in Larisa's psych ward for a few days zoned out on drugs he hadn't been allowed to keep once they released him.

So, Parish had robbed him of Larisa, the Queen, and the best possible moment of aligning himself with her. Once he was out of the hospital everything had felt different. The full weight of it had settled, an immobilizing cocoon, which made it easier for him to sit in his house and wait out the storm rather than go to her. He'd imagined the scene so many times. A phone call. A message.

Showing up unannounced, calling her from the front gate of her parents' house. As scenes, none of them worked. He never got past the opening line of dialogue. Now the silence had lasted so long, his abandonment so complete, it felt impossible to make contact.

Quinn was still fuming from the *LA Today* article when he returned to his seat in the editing room. Eddie and Tish sat with Lane, finishing off some Chinese takeout.

"You had to eat that in here," he muttered.

"You want some?" asked Tish.

"No, I don't fucking want your disgusting grease food."

Eddie and Tish exchanged looks. Eddie said, "Something wrong?"

"I'm angry," said Quinn, managing to exercise one of the practices his new therapist had recommended, to name his feelings as a statement of fact.

"Anything we can do to help?"

"Take the food out."

"You're angry about the food?" asked Tish.

"No." He forced himself to pause, breathe. "I'm angry Larisa is lying to reporters so people will like her."

Lane had the nerve to laugh. "I thought that was the whole idea. I mean, no one ever prints what *I* say, but—"

"What're you going to do about it?" Quinn asked Eddie.

Eddie threw up his hands. "What can I do? She doesn't want to see me."

"That's not good enough," growled Quinn.

"She broke the rules," said Tish, obviously confused. "I mean, it's terrible, but ethically—"

"Eddie didn't leave her a choice." Quinn's words snapped off his teeth. "That's the whole fucking thing, isn't it Eddie? You couldn't trust me. You had to have help. Private, confidential help."

Tish's mouth formed a small *O* of astonishment. "You were one of her patients. Oh God. But you were dating—"

"That happened later."

"This is so fucked up."

"What do you want me to say?" said Eddie. "I saved the movie. She came on board, she smoothed you and Dansby out, got everyone going. Best choice I've ever made." He motioned to the screens showing the takes of Dansby's prison sequence. "People were crying on Friday."

Quinn couldn't help but think they were crying because of the scene's music, a delicate piano melody gradually swelling to the climax of Dansby's emotional wreckage. The composer had wanted it, said it was important, and Quinn had given in, if only because he imagined Larisa would like it.

The days passed. Quinn attended marketing meetings. He paced in the dark, back row of a Malibu theater as another test audience watched his film. The exit polls improved enough Eddie gave him the green light to prep a final cut for the studio heads. He woke up at night from nightmares he couldn't remember, his face burning, and sweat coating his skin. He stopped being able to stomach milkshakes.

"There's a reporter that's been bothering me," said Sid.

"Why are you telling me?"

"Dunno. Thought you might . . ." Sid shrugged.

"Add my name to the list of Larisa's former patient exposés? She doesn't need that."

"Yours would be true."

"I have an NDA with the studio." Quinn paused as some stray corner of his mind took up the idea and briefly considered it. "No one cares about the truth. You saw what they did to that woman who worked with her at the hospital."

He took Friday morning before the final cut showing to drive to Cade's campaign headquarters and meet his ad production team. They weren't super thrilled by the hot shot movie director coming in and telling them how to do things, but he had good ideas and he managed to stand by them without yelling at anyone. Eventually, Cade arrived and listened to the plans. After it was all over Quinn was exhausted from being trapped in a room with people who saw him as an unworthy invader, but still allowed Cade to take him out to lunch.

"I don't suppose you're available to oversee this whole thing?"

"They'll do fine," said Quinn. "I'm an expert at making people look incompetent."

"I knew there was a reason I liked you."

You don't actually like me. Quinn considered the consistency of his salad dressing, then decided he'd eat his salad plain, one bite at a time, and see how it went.

"Well, it would still be nice to have you around. I could pay you a consulting fee."

"I have a movie coming out."

"Then how about coming to my daughter's birthday party Saturday?"

Quinn gave him a withering look. He made his silence expand, waiting for Cade to back down and admit he didn't want Quinn anywhere near his family. Cade twitched in his seat but didn't rescind the offer.

When Quinn looked away, Cade said, "It's Kahleah's idea, okay? She likes drama. And the sisters have convinced themselves Larisa needs to move on. So, just come and let her yell at you, or whatever needs to happen. I'll pay you if you want."

"Larisa is coming?"

"That's what I've been told, but she tends to cancel last minute."

"What does one wear to a kid's birthday?"

Cade and Kahleah's house was not a sprawling estate like Larisa's parent's place, but it was still impressive, elegant and slightly sleezy as all aspiring politician's houses should be. Quinn took a picture and sent it to Sid.

Sid: Be careful in there.

At this point, Quinn was pretty sure if he'd had any sense of self-preservation, he wouldn't have come. But Cade had said one thing that had felt true. Larisa deserved the chance to face him. Since he hadn't found the courage to offer himself to her, and she hadn't forced it, this was as good a chance as they were likely to get.

You'll know what she thinks as soon as you see her. Then the worst part will be over.

Inside the house, a man in a formal waitstaff uniform offered Quinn a glass of fizzy alcoholic punch, then directed him through the entryway to the back of the house where the expansive back lawn was covered in inflatables. A horse and carriage glided around a track at the fence line. More children than he'd seen since elementary school squirmed and screeched at each other on the second level of the pool deck. Up on the first deck, the adults sat or stood under umbrellas, guarding a tiered cake. He didn't see Larisa.

Still time to leave.

Quinn climbed the stairs, freezing in place on the landing to avoid colliding with two children chasing each other, then climbed the second set of stairs up to the first deck. Kahleah was waiting to slip her arm through his, holding him in place as though she knew how much he wanted to leave.

"Cade just loved what you did with those ad people this week. *I* told him you'd be able to see right away what wasn't working."

Quinn scanned the deck. He counted Larisa's four sisters, their husbands, minus Adrian the baseball player, various other adults who probably came with the children, and three grandparents. No Larisa.

"She's hiding inside," said Kahleah. "You know this is a big step for her. She hasn't left her parents' house for months."

"Does she know I was invited?"

Kahleah hesitated. "I thought you might just . . ."

These fucking people. Quinn took a breath. "I'm going to stand over there." He pointed to an empty space in the corner of the deck, behind the cake. "You tell her I'm here. If she wants to see me, you can come get me. If you lie to me and try to ambush her, I will know."

Kahleah's eyes widened. She ducked into the house. Quinn strode across the deck. He did not make eye contact. He did not say hello. He did not wave. They didn't deserve his courtesy even if they were Larisa's supposed friends. They probably thought he was a social climbing pariah who had taken advantage of Larisa's generosity, then ruined her with his ex-girlfriend. He wasn't going to waste energy trying to convince them otherwise.

Minutes passed. He occupied himself by taking note of the pool and its position in relation to the house. Though the front of the house had been pleasing, he disliked the back, which he thought came off as disorganized and chunky. The pool was over-large and too close to the house. The stairs were dangerous when wet.

The door to the house opened. Kahleah came out. Larisa followed. At first, he was shocked by how remarkably unchanged she appeared. After all that had happened, everything about her, from the gentle waves in her hair to the paint on her toenails, was perfectly curated. He studied her body, wrapped in a tight pastel sundress, and wondered for the hundredth time why he hadn't been able to recognize her as the Queen. It was so obvious to him now, the long line of her neck, her wide shoulders, the way she set her heels into the floor like she was trying to etch her footsteps into permanence.

"Sorry I'm late," she said to the group. "It's so good to be allowed back." Her gaze flicked towards Kahleah and Quinn wondered what had happened between them. Some kind of political ass covering, he thought. He held his breath as Larisa's gaze passed over him. "Hello Quinn, nice to see you again." As her eyes moved down his body, he could feel heat rising on his face. She didn't approach him, but instead went to a red cooler and pulled out a flavored spritzer. Her eyes kept moving as though she was afraid of looking too closely at any one thing. "Hello Krissy's Mama. I love your dress."

One of the grandparents rose to give Larisa a hug. "Such a lovely profile of you and Suzette in *Today*."

"So is she." Larisa's smile flickered.

Quinn felt sick.

"And we're so excited for the ball in October."

A ball in October was news to Quinn. He shifted his weight onto the balls of his feet and wondered what people would do if he made a mad dash for the door. Why did he want to leave? He felt like a spy, an invader. If he wasn't there she'd be more comfortable.

"I'm having my first dress fitting on Tuesday," said one of the other parents, approaching Larisa with timid little steps. "It's my favorite event of the season."

"Larisa, meet my new bestie, Annie Lu," said Krissy. "She and I are on the PTA together. That's her little Joon up on the slide."

"Nice to meet you." Larisa pressed a smile on her face. Quinn wondered if anyone else could see its strain.

"When will the call for volunteers go out?"

"In a few weeks. It would have gone out this week, but I've been distracted." Larisa's smile melted into something that looked like a smug secret. Annie Lu took the bait.

"Something else happening we should know about?"

"Well, it's not official yet, but I'm getting married."

Krissy squealed. From Quinn's side of the deck, Jaden screeched, "WHAT?"

"It's practically official. Just some paperwork to sign. Obviously, he's going to propose at the ball, then we'll set a date."

"Who is it?"

"Hasan bin Faisal Al Saud."

A fission of energy ran down Quinn's spine. He set his glass of punch on the deck railing so he wouldn't crush it.

"The Saudi prince?" Jaden was now out of her seat, shooting Rosa a worried look as she crossed to Larisa and edged into the circle around her. From their places leaning against the deck railing, Dev and Cade looked to Quinn for the reaction shot. His body was turned just enough he could keep looking down at the pool without appearing to be hiding from them. It had been a wrong move to choose this place to stand. Any exit meant he had to walk past everyone else. Larisa stood ahead of the door and just to the side of the stairs.

"Why so shocked?" she asked. "You knew we've been seeing each other here and there."

"Wow. Well, cheers to Larisa, who always has a surprise up her sleeve," said Krissy with a nervous giggle.

"But what about the weird sex thing?" asked Annie Lu.

Silence. The children screeching down below faded to the far distant background. Quinn's ears burned. He couldn't resist turning to look, to see Larisa frozen, her chin arched up out of her neck like she couldn't breathe. Their eyes met. He should charge across the deck, take her in his arms, and tell her to stop ruining her life. But too many people were watching, waiting for just that, or something like that.

"It's called bondage, Annie," said Kahleah.

"I did that once," said Krissy's mother. "So scary. But I came three times. We didn't even have sex."

"It's not a big deal," said Larisa

Quinn couldn't stand it anymore. If he didn't get out now,

he'd do something terrible. He crossed the deck, paused at the circle of women around Larisa, gazed at a spot on the door behind her right ear, and said, "Congratulations. I hope he's everything you want."

Then, before she had the chance to reply, he turned, jogged down one set of stairs then the other, into the main house, and across the atrium to the door. He fumbled in his pocket for his phone to call the car service, then thought better of it. The car came with a driver who would be a witness. He needed to be alone.

Where was he? Brenton Hills, where winding roads never ended up where they appeared to be going. He charged down the front walk, turned left, and began to run down the sidewalk.

Get away. Get away. Get away.

How could she seriously think of marrying Hasan? Of marrying anyone when she knew they were only saying yes now because they wouldn't have to compete with her other interests. She'd be a prisoner to a social calendar and endless children's birthdays with friends who knew nothing about her.

Your fault. Your fault. Your fault.

He stopped short, bent in half, and screamed into his knees.

"Quinn?"

His voice cut off midscream. He stood, all the blood in his head, and saw Larisa standing a few yards back, staring at him.

"You can't marry him."

"Why not?"

"He'll hurt you."

"I've known worse."

"Larisa."

Her name on his lips felt too large, like he didn't have permission to use it. When he did, she took a step backward. She held out her hand as though to block him.

"There has to be another way," he said. "Tell me what to do."

"Don't take this from me." The mask of Larisa's happy self shuddered as she shook her head. "Haven't you taken enough?"

She might as well have stabbed him in the chest. Of course, that's how she felt. She probably couldn't even look at him without thinking about what she'd lost.

But you chose me, he wanted to say. *I know it was real for you.*

A more selfish man might have said those things. Might have closed the distance between them and reached for her. That was all he needed to do.

You've taken enough.

Quinn began to back down the sidewalk. He wasn't the solution to her problems anymore. He was their source. And there was no going back from that.

Chapter 34

A Grand Gesture

"You have lunch yet?" asked Tish.

"If it's not about the film, leave me alone."

Tish ignored Quinn's warning and crossed the threshold into his office. She took one of the seats across from his desk and produced a tube of saltines from her purse.

"Please leave."

"You're wasting away." She opened the crackers, slid one across the desk toward him, then took a second for herself.

"I wanted to apologize for what I said about Larisa deserving what happened. I didn't have the full picture."

Quinn reluctantly picked up the cracker, broke it in half, and put one piece in his mouth. It tasted like sawdust. Almost immediately his stomach began to churn with revulsion.

"I thought I might reach out to her," said Tish. "With this big interview coming on Sunday, it seems like a good thing to do."

"What big interview?"

Tish handed him another cracker, waited until he chewed and swallowed it, then answered, "Dansby says it's with the parents of that patient who died this spring. Oprah's going to interview them for *60 Minutes*."

"What does Dansby know?"

"Apparently they text all the time."

Of course they do. Even with the film finished, the actor continued to haunt Quinn's life like a spotlight illuminating all his failings.

"Do you think she'd want to talk to me?" asked Tish.

"I have no idea." Quinn turned to his computer and looked up *60 Minutes*. The announcement for Sunday's show dominated the landing page: "Parents of Dr. Larisa de France-Kahn's last patient tell their story for the first time."

"How could they do this?"

"My brother says they're going to sue," said Tish. "He's a legal strategist. An interview is a good move to soften public perception before going after a public figure who might draw sympathy."

"Fuck."

"You'd be surprised how many legal decisions come down to public opinion and perception. We're all human after all."

"Is Eddie in his office?"

"Dunno." Tish handed him another cracker, which he ate without thinking, then accepted another one on his way out the door. He ran down the hall to Eddie's office.

"Get me on *The Late Show*," said Quinn.

Eddie sat behind his desk with a porn magazine open beside a Styrofoam takeout box. He barely glanced up from the spread. Two women in bondage play, Quinn couldn't help but notice.

When Eddie saw him noticing, he shrugged. "Your sexcapade made me curious. Do you know they have submissive auctions in New York?"

"Did you hear me?"

"Marketing will manage that schedule closer to launch."

"This week. Tomorrow."

"Not possible."

"You owe her."

Eddie looked up. "Sorry, what are we talking about here?"

"I want to talk about Larisa on *The Late Show*."

"No fucking way."

"Then I'll find a way to do it without you."

"You're out of your mind. You haven't been prepped. And

one could argue your front-of-the-camera persona falls some-where on the spectrum from dismal to dangerous."

"It's the right thing."

"Not for the film."

Quinn stood against the desk trembling from head to foot. The smell of Eddie's food was making him nauseous. He wanted to accept Eddie's rejection and give up. It would be so much easier to give up. The very idea of what he was thinking about doing turned his churning gut into a miasma of stabbing pain.

"You said it yourself, she saved the film."

Eddie turned the page of his magazine, gazing at it with unseeing eyes. Finally, he shook his head. "I'll call and see if it's even possible. But if you do this, the blowback is all on you."

"I understand."

Eddie swiveled in his chair, grabbing his desk phone to call his assistant. "See if you can get me Margie over at CBS." He glanced at Quinn. "Sit down before you fall over. Write me a pitch for this." He opened his drawer and fished out Post-its and a pen.

Writing with a pen proved impossible with Quinn's shaking hands, so he used his phone. He typed, deleted, then typed again. Putting his idea into words felt like a poor translation.

"Margie! Hey, it's Eddie over at Enterprise. What gives? You didn't take me with you to Iceland."

Quinn blinked at his phone as the words swam and reorga-nized themselves against his will. He stood up and wandered to the door where Tish stood holding the crackers. He took one, chewing as he typed.

"Next time then," said Eddie. "Look, I need a favor. No, it's a good one this time, I promise. You can scoop Oprah. I know, famous last words but trust me." Eddie waved at Quinn. Quinn reluctantly slid his phone across the desk. Eddie read it once, shook his head like this was beyond the kind of madness that could be diagnosed and said, "There was only one patient who went to the dungeon with Larisa de France-Kahn and it isn't the one *60 Minutes* found."

Silence. Then a woman's voice, indistinct. Quinn held his breath.

"Uh huh, I know. Sure, I can get him out there. When? Yes. Great. Next time, Iceland. I wanna see those glaciers before they melt!" Eddie let the phone drop in its cradle. "She said yes. You're taping the second session tomorrow for Friday's show."

"Thank you." The room was spinning and the breaths he took weren't satisfying. They felt too fast, then too slow. Eddie was on the phone with his assistant again.

"Have Phil draw up an NDA with flexible terms for a talk show appearance. And tell Ken to come over with some talking points for *The Key*." He hung up and answered Quinn's questioning look with a shrug. "If the studio is going to pay to send you to New York, you're going to plug the film. Margie will send us a draft set of questions. We'll choose the ones we want. Before Ken gets here, give me the first draft. What're you going to say?"

Quinn managed to get through three emergency meetings without vomiting or screaming obscenities at anyone. But it didn't stop him from wanting to. He felt as out of control as he had in those first days after being released from the hospital, sensory triggers coming at him from every direction, no safe space, not even in his mind. Especially not his mind. He thought of all the time he'd wasted being afraid of Larisa, resisting her best efforts to help him, accusing her of being Eddie's spy.

But one thing was different this time; at the center of the chaos there was a single grounding spike of purpose. He stood resolute in the face of a series of incensed executives, three questioning lawyers, and even with Sid, who was speechless for a full minute after receiving the news.

"What if she doesn't want you?" he asked.

"That's not the point," said Quinn.

On Thursday afternoon, after walking into the studio and seeing "*The Late Show* welcomes Quinn VanderVeer" on the door, Quinn's resolution faltered. Both Sid and Ken, the studio's marketing guy who'd come along to supervise, pounced on him.

"I can get you out of this," said Ken.

"She'll still marry that prince," said Sid.

Quinn barely heard them. He dove into the greenroom to puke in the bathroom sink. When only acid began to come up, he massaged his fist into his stomach until the force of his knuckles hurt more than the cramping. He wiped his mouth, looking at the stranger in the mirror. A severe face, the twin lines of his jaw and cheekbones, and the expanse of skin between them that he thought made him look, at best, like he had the head of a horse, at worse, the hollowed-out face of a serial killer drug addict. It wasn't a face someone like Larisa loved.

"Makeup is coming in ten," said Sid. "Want help getting dressed?" He held the Tom Ford bag from Jaden's wedding.

"She's going to hate me for this."

"Probably."

"I can't think of another way."

"So she'll hate you. But at least you'll look good." Sid unzipped the bag, came into the bathroom, and began pulling off Quinn's clothes.

"I should have called her. Afterward. I just . . ."

"Let's focus on the here and now. *The Late Show*, Quinn. Thousands of people are going to see your face on their screen tomorrow night. You're not an actor, you're not famous, and you're not pretty."

"You're not helping."

"What're you going to give them to remember you by?"

"My total humiliation?"

"What can we call that instead?"

"My story."

"Great. It will be over in twenty minutes. Anyone can survive anything for twenty minutes."

"Are you reminding him that he's supposed to smile?" called Ken from the couch.

"Fuck you," said Quinn.

The Late Show

Larisa: Do you have any interest in marrying me?

Hasan: . . .

Larisa: We could keep it simple.

Hasan: Marriage is never simple.

Larisa: How's your jaw?

Hasan: You're a mean woman.

Larisa stared at her phone, her gaze soft, not really seeing. The screen shifted with an incoming call. Krissy. Larisa watched it ring for several seconds before answering.

"My jacuzzi is broken," said Krissy. "Can I come over?"

Larisa looked at the time. Her parents were out. She and Sabrina were taking their third trip of the day over to the kitchen, this time to heat up dinner. She'd been wearing pajamas since lunch. She hadn't showered. Maybe they were friends again, but Larisa didn't feel like spending energy making Krissy feel better about their months of silence. And she definitely didn't want to talk about what had happened last weekend with Quinn at the party.

"Call Jaden. Isn't her jacuzzi industrial strength massage?"

"Jaden's here with me."

"So, you're both coming over."

"And Rosa and Kahleah."

They were having a girls' night without me. Larisa pressed her eyes closed and took a deep breath until the burn of unshed tears subsided.

"Fine. Whatever. But you're leaving by ten. I'm getting up early."

There really wasn't a reason for Larisa to get up early. She had some vague intention to go visit Parish. She'd worked with Estelle to construct a purse-like cooler to transport ice cream, but Larisa hadn't decided if she actually wanted to see Parish. When she thought of Parish, which was almost every hour of every day, Larisa almost always felt a spark of extra-sensory electricity at the back of her neck, the primordial warning of an encroaching predator. There was no question in her mind Parish was dangerous, but it was unclear if Larisa felt this based on the past or anticipation of the future. Perhaps the answer didn't matter. Both were equally stimulating. The only thing at this point that made her feel alive.

Her friends arrived wearing swimsuits and cover-ups, with their hair in high ponytails and their sunglasses stabbed into their hair like lawn ornaments. Rosa's new baby bump was on full display. She'd brought faux wine seltzer and the oil she used to massage her feet to help with swelling.

They flooded the house with their overly loud voices and giggles, shouting at each other. It felt scripted, as though they wanted no space left for possible conversations about Larisa's secret sex life, her lost career, her fake boyfriend, the doomsday clock counting down to *60 Minutes*, or how they'd left her alone for almost four months because Kahleah's husband wanted to protect his reputation. Larisa resentfully retreated out to the pool deck and sat on the edge of the jacuzzi.

Swirling her feet in the water reminded her of sitting on the side of the tub with Quinn in their Palisades hotel room. It still shocked her to realize that even then, in a window of time when they hadn't been fighting or insulting each other, he'd known he would see Parish the next day. He'd known he was trapped, and he hadn't told her. Not only that, but she hadn't been able to tell.

You were a wreck that night, Larisa. There was nothing you could've done. He doesn't know how to trust people.

Rosa's voice broke through her thoughts. "Can I eat this?" She was standing half in and half out of the kitchen doorway holding the carton of chocolate ice cream meant for Parish.

"Go for it," said Larisa.

"Do you have pickles?"

"Check the fridge."

A few minutes later, they began to file out armed with drinks and prosciutto on crackers with figs and cheese. Rosa sat beside Larisa, her feet in the water, a glowing pregnant woman with a bowl of chocolate ice cream decorated with pickle slices balanced on the orb of her stomach.

"That's disgusting," said Larisa.

"The doctor says follow the cravings, don't fight them. Being pregnant is too hard."

Larisa blinked.

"What?"

"Nothing," said Larisa, as she pictured Parish's smug face when she'd told Larisa she'd gotten what she needed from Quinn. *Oh,* thought Larisa. She suddenly felt very tired.

"I can't wait to have you over to the new house," Jaden was saying. "The countertops finally came in from Rome. They're beyond perfect. I thought we could host Toddie's birthday, then you don't have to be pregnant and host."

"I would owe you forever," said Rosa.

"Good news," said Larisa, mustering a smile. "I'll be there for this one. Absolutely no schedule conflicts. Maybe Hasan will come."

An uncomfortable moment, filled to bursting, followed before Krissy sloshed over to Larisa's side of the jacuzzi to give her a fist bump. "Three cheers for unemployment!"

Rosa patted Larisa's knee. "If you don't come, that's okay too."

It never felt okay not to come before, thought Larisa bitterly. Then, without warning, she was fighting down tears, *again*.

"What time is it?" said Krissy. "We can't ruin Suzette's couch with our chlorine butts."

"Ten minutes," said Kahleah.

"What's happening in ten minutes?"

"We're watching *The Late Show*."

Something fluttered in Larisa's chest. "When have we ever watched *The Late Show*?"

"That one time Harrison Ford—oops!" said Rosa, as she accidently dropped her spoon in the jacuzzi.

"I guess you'll have to wait and see," said Krissy, as she threw back the last of her wine and glanced at Kahleah.

"I'd like to be told now," said Larisa. "Then I'd like to know why you all know something about my life that's going to be on *The Late Show* and I don't."

"If we tell you, you have to promise not to back out."

"I promise absolutely nothing." Larisa kicked the water. "You think it's fun that the gossip has hit late night TV the same week I'm going to be the villain on Oprah?"

"It's just Quinn talking about his movie," said Jaden.

"I only know because he told Cade," said Kahleah. "He's consulting on Cade's ad campaign. I guess it was a last-minute thing."

"We thought you might—"

"I don't," snapped Larisa.

"But he's—"

Larisa pulled her feet up from the water and staggered to her feet, flushed, pain throbbing through her throat. "I'm going to my room. Stay and watch it if you want. The remote's in the side drawer."

Tears blurred her vision as she ran into the house, across the atrium to the stairs leading up to the family wing. She only made it to the top of the stairs before her legs gave out and she sat down, nearly banging her head on the railing as she sank against the wall.

What's he doing?

Four months of "no comment" to reporters and now this.

The studio sent him; it means nothing.

It's too early for the film. And they'd only send Quinn to a talk show if the rest of the cast had third degree burns or was in a coma. Even then, they'd find someone to send instead of Quinn.

Larisa, you're stronger than this.

It wasn't true. Maybe she'd been once, when she hadn't known how much could be lost. She was so tired of holding herself together. She was tired of getting up at a regular time each morning, of smiling to her parents and the staff, and sitting through weekly PR meetings strategizing what to do about the filth people were saying about her online. She wanted to lay in bed and sleep for a week. She wanted to go to the clinic the next morning and pull every strand of Parish's beautiful brown and purple hair from her head.

She wanted Quinn to be a bigger, braver version of himself that didn't exist.

Parish is pregnant, she thought. When he found out, he would take Parish back, set up a home with her and their baby, and become the fictional parents who loved the arts and wouldn't let their kids do sports, who saved up for a once-in-a-lifetime European vacation.

She's the one for him. After all she's done, she'll let him hide. I won't.

"He's on next!" called Krissy.

Larisa drew herself up out of the morass of her thoughts. She realized that Krissy's jacuzzi wasn't broken. Her friends had come here tonight so whatever Quinn said, she wouldn't be alone. She could honor that effort; they so rarely knew what to do for her. *He can't hurt me any worse than he already has,* she thought as she eased herself down the stairs and walked across the stone cosmos of the atrium floor back to the viewing room. Kahleah sat alone in the chaise, wearing her cover-up sans swimsuit. The others huddled together on the circular sofa. Krissy sat in the middle with a bowl of popcorn, while Rosa and Jaden sat on either side of her, scooping out greedy handfuls with their eyes glued to the screen.

"I'm so nervous," said Jaden.

"Me too," said Krissy.

On screen, Quinn was crossing the stage to sit on the end of the famous couch butted up against Letterman's desk. Quinn wore his Friday wedding outfit, a textured T-shirt and a tapered sports coat that somehow made him look even taller than he was.

He did not smile and wave at the crowd as they welcomed him. If anything, Larisa would have called his glance in their direction hawkish. When he looked into the camera (which was against the rules) he seemed outright resentful. His lips rested in an open position like a model posing. Given he wasn't a model, she thought this was probably a struggle to breathe.

An eternity seemed to slog past before he shook Letterman's hand and sat stiffly on the end of the couch. Larisa sat down beside Rosa. "The person who made him do this should be fired," she said.

On screen, the camera went wide to take in both host and guest, then shifted to only Letterman.

"So Quinn, people who follow film closely might know you from your independent films, but you've just wrapped production on your first big picture with Enterprise. What's it like in the fast lane?"

"Fast." Quinn's expression was a smooth line of the calculated disinterest Larisa knew so well. He didn't shift to acknowledge the audience's laughter. His gaze was slanted down from Letterman, perhaps toward the corner of the desk.

Rage rippled through Larisa like the aftershocks of an earthquake. The next time Eddie sent flowers she was going to send them back to him in pieces with a rejection written in blood. He should've protected Quinn from this.

"It seems like that's a big change, going from your own passion projects to a corporate production where lots of people have opinions you have to listen to."

"That's a strangely specific question," said Jaden, which was exactly what Larisa was thinking. *Where's this going?*

The camera shifted back to Quinn with his gaze still fixed on the corner of the desk. "I had a lot of trouble," said Quinn. "It became clear even before filming started that I needed help."

"Oh no." Larisa's hand flailed in the air for something to hang onto. Rosa caught it and pulled it into the warm space between her breasts and belly.

"Dr. Larisa de France-Kahn was recommended even though she wasn't out of school yet because she had experience in the industry."

Someone in the studio audience gasped at the same time as Krissy.

The camera shifted back to Letterman as he clarified, "Dr. de France-Kahn is the psychiatry resident you were dating this spring when your ex-girlfriend exposed the doctor's unusual therapy practices on her live stream."

"The only thing unusual about Dr. de France-Kahn's practice is how good she is at figuring out what people need." Quinn raised his eyes and looked, not at Letterman like he was supposed to, but at the camera. "I was overwhelmed in both my professional and personal life. I didn't know who I could trust. I did six sessions with her, and they saved my career. She changed how I work as a director. In fact, my producer was so impressed, he hired her to help the whole crew through a difficult part of the film."

"Mental health safety on a film set certainly seems important," said Letterman.

Quinn was back to studying the desk. "For all that people are talking about Larisa, no one has questioned Parish's claims. There hasn't been a moment to ask, is what we think we saw really what we saw?"

"The video quality was low."

Larisa heard discomfort creep into Letterman's voice. Quinn had gone off script.

"I started dating Larisa after I finished therapy. We'd met socially at a BDSM club and found we worked well together, better than I ever fit with Parish."

"So, you're saying Dr. de France-Kahn never used bondage techniques for therapy with you?"

"Never." Quinn once again shifted his gaze to the camera. His expression remained almost the same except for his eyes, which flickered with a tremor of barely constrained emotion as he said, "We've allowed someone who does so much good to be maligned because it made a good story. A lot has been lost. Our industry would be so different if everyone had someone like her on their side, fighting behind the scenes for them even when they're scared shitless she'll unmask them for the phony they are."

Letterman coughed. "That's some endorsement. And now I really want to see this film. It's out in December. What can we expect from *The Key*?"

"*The Key* is a spy thriller about a veteran CIA agent played by Vince Rocks and the hottest thief turned junior CIA agent you've ever seen, played by Dansby Vaast—he's doing a photo shoot that's going to release on our socials next week—and this question of how far people go for love of country and love for each other."

"Sounds amazing. Here's your holiday movie preview folks. Let's watch the trailer."

The camera cut to the applauding audience, then to the screen above the stage. The trailer lasted one minute and twenty seconds. Larisa counted every single beat. Afterward, the show cut to commercial. She knew when it returned Quinn would be gone, alone in a greenroom in New York probably having a panic attack.

No, she thought. This show is taped. He's already lived this.

"I think we should discuss what exactly Larisa meant when she said fake dating," said Krissy.

"I agree," said Jaden.

"That was more words than I heard him speak the whole weekend of the wedding," said Kahleah.

"This doesn't change anything," said Larisa. "I'm not what he . . . I can't . . . he doesn't love me."

"Oh honey," said Rosa. "For someone so smart, sometimes you act really stupid."

The sobs Larisa had been holding back rushed up and overtook her.

Chapter 36

An Autumn Masquerade

Larisa and Dansby leaned on the balcony railing, looking down on the atrium of her parents' estate. Each were watching as gala guests passed through the costume inspection. The dress codes for Suzette de France's events were infamous for their severity. When the invitation said red, tangerine, and ochre attire with minimal accents and half-face masks, that was what must be worn, or security would turn you away at the door.

"I don't understand," said Dansby, as he fiddled with his red leather mask for the umpteenth time. "Did you talk to him after *The Late Show* or not?"

"I sent him the invite."

"So, you didn't talk to him."

Larisa drummed her nails on the railing and watched a couple in matching gold silk suits pass security. Once inside, they stepped up to the gala banner to have their picture taken by the photographers who'd been granted special access to the event.

"I didn't want it to be over the phone."

"Remind me what 'it' is at this point?"

"I don't know."

"I'm confused."

"Can we go dance?"

"I thought we were watching to see if Quinn comes."

"Well, he hasn't, and I want to dance." As she spoke, Larisa struggled to keep the tremor out of her voice. What was she doing, really? She expected Quinn to magically become a real suitor just because he'd finally gone public and defended her? Did she think he loved her enough to take on everything that came with her life?

Technically, he's already done that.

At least as much as he knows about.

But Parish is pregnant.

"Maybe you don't know what you feel about him." Dansby motioned toward a figure cloaked in a long crimson cape. The hood was pulled up concealing the face. The figure carried a single long-stemmed rose in their hands. "That could be him."

"I don't care." Larisa pulled Dansby down the stairs, through the flow of people taking pictures, and into the estate's ballroom. She was about to plunge into the crowd on the dance floor, but Dansby pulled her back to the edge of the room.

"I don't want to do this with you," he said.

She glared at him. "You love dancing."

"But not right now. You're freaking me out."

Larisa felt tears begin to burn in her eyes. *Get a grip, Larisa.* "What do you want me to say? You think love is enough? You think he can look me in the eye without thinking about Parish, or how I lied to him, or how everyone thinks I'm a nymphomaniac?"

Dansby opened his mouth to answer, then closed it.

"You know what? I'll dance by myself." Larisa picked up the train of her orange Garibaldi dress and spun onto the dance floor. Masked faces swirled by in a blur as she drove her body to the pulse of the music.

Once or twice a male figure approached. They moved with ease in the crowd, imposing their bodies wherever they saw fit, hands moving with the confidence of possession.

Not Quinn.

Not Quinn.

Not Quinn.

After one of these men grabbed her and tried to pull her hips into his crotch, the allure of dancing diminished. Her feet ached.

On the periphery of the room, Larisa removed her shoes. She might have thrown them down with the various other discarded shoes, but they were her favorites and didn't want to risk someone taking them home accidently on purpose.

She decided she would drop them off in the sunroom and say hello to Sabrina before trying to catch a second wind. At the top of the hour, the rave beat in the ballroom would transition to more classical music in the style of a Venetian Carnivale ball, the section of the evening that Larisa had planned based on a ball she'd once attended in Italy. People would expect her to be present.

I would dance with him all night. Which was impossible. She wasn't even sure he knew how to waltz.

Larisa turned down a hallway, walking slowly toward the sunroom. As she passed the floor to ceiling windows lining the exterior wall, she reached out to rest her sweaty hand on the cool window frame. *This will pass,* she thought.

As Larisa continued to drift down the hallway, she was surprised to see a figure in the sunroom even though two different signs asked guests to stay out. The figure was the man Dansby had pointed out in the atrium, wearing a crimson cape with the hood pulled up and a long-stemmed rose in his hands.

"I'm sorry," she said, "You can't be in here tonight."

She watched as the figure bent over Sabrina's extravagant sunning bed. He set aside the rose and began to pet the kitten.

"Looks like you got yourself a name, little one," he said. "It's a good name. Lots to live up to."

Larisa froze. "I didn't think you'd come."

Quinn lowered his hood, pulling the string to release the cape so it ended up as a puddle around his feet. He reached up to untie his mask.

"Don't do that!" Panic rushed through Larisa. She wasn't ready. She couldn't face him.

Quinn dropped his hands and turned to her. He picked up

the rose, his fingers moving over the long stem in the same motion she'd seen him use on his prayer bead bracelet.

"I'm here to apologize," said Quinn. "For not seeing what should have been obvious. I didn't realize what you'd given me until it was too late. I've been pretending my entire adult life. Pretending I knew how to be a good person. Pretending I had money. Pretending my life mattered. You once asked me if I felt comfortable alone. I said something about feeling like I didn't have time to do what I wanted to do. The better answer is, when I'm alone I think about the family that should be with me and why they aren't. My entire life, I've been trying to compensate for that absence, to prove what my mother lost when she chose to keep me was worth it."

"Quinn—"

"I've been terrible to you. Every time we met I thought it would be the day you'd betray me. I've always hidden myself from people. Every relationship I have, one person knows some things, another knows other things. I fracture myself over and over so I'll never be forced to trust. I'm not sure I've ever been a whole person to anyone."

"You weren't hiding at Club D," said Larisa.

"I didn't have any other options left. The movie had completely overwhelmed me. I couldn't function. When I saw the Queen . . ." He paused. "When I saw you that night in the Blue Room, I thought maybe you had an answer. It was all instinct. I still don't know what I was thinking or why I was able to do it. But I knew I could trust you. It doesn't make sense, does it?"

Quinn turned from her, paced to the window, then came back. "I've spent months thinking about it, and I still don't know what it was. Fantasy? The feeling that whatever happened in the club didn't exist in real life? I don't know. I've spent a lot of time thinking about why you did what you did. What you saw in me. I think maybe that's why other guys have trouble. We look at you and can't see an obvious need. When we say a woman is intimidating, I think that's what we mean, or at least what I mean. I couldn't see what I'd be bringing to the table.

"Then, at the wedding, you kissed me."

Larisa felt the heat rise on her face remembering it. The sunset, how she had wanted to cling to him, the only thing that felt good. But she'd settled for a kiss, stolen under the guise of their charade.

"I couldn't make sense of it. Maybe in the beginning it was sex. I think you like taking care of people in a particular way and that brings you satisfaction. But at some point, you knew you'd . . ." He stopped as though he couldn't bring himself to say it. "You'd become interested. There was a future you were beginning to believe in. You weren't content to hide anymore. You started pushing me to see you, and I didn't know what to do with that. I'm sorry."

"Thank you." As a response, it felt inadequate, but Larisa didn't want to derail him. It felt like there was more to say. Or was she just wishing for more?

Quinn moved closer, his hands still nervous on the rose, his gaze steady as he stepped from shadow into a pool of moonlight.

"The thing is, we are both driven by the same quest for precision, to take the raw materials of our constructed existence and make them into something as close to perfect as possible. We become caught up in our work and miss the possibility of what's beyond the script."

He looked at her as he never had before, without need, without even desire, just a naked tenderness, as though he held his heart in his hands instead of the rose.

"Larisa." Her name in Quinn's throat cracked across his voice like shattering ice.

Her hand came up and pressed against her mouth to suppress a sob.

"I want the chance to know you as well as it feels you know me." He took another step forward so he was close enough to touch her. She looked down and saw the thorns had not been cut from the stem of the rose. His fingers had begun to bleed.

"I don't need you to love me," he said. "I think maybe you do, but I've realized that matters less than I used to think. We have more together than love would ever touch. Teach me. Break me. Put me back together. The only truth I want to know is you. All of you."

"What if I'm done with bondage?

"Are you?"

"I don't know. It feels . . . tainted. What we had at the club is gone."

"We might find something else."

"You didn't answer my question," she said.

"Even without Club D you'll still be able to break me open." He reached up and stroked a finger along the line of her neck. "I will never not want to kneel before you."

He knelt, first down to one knee, then to both. He sank back onto his heels, letting his bleeding hands rest in his lap. "Let me be your shield, and I'll make what you want possible."

Larisa released the strings of her mask and flung it away. Trembling, she reached out and cupped the crown of the head of the man who had shared with her his barest fears.

"You already are that man."

Her dress puffed up around her as she knelt in front of him and took the rose. Using her nails for leverage, she broke off the thorns before handing it back to him.

"Tell me what to do," he whispered.

She set her fingertips along the beautiful line of his jaw and pressed until he lifted his eyes to hers. "Kiss me."

Epilogue

In the luxury ward at Cedars-Sinai, Larisa sat in a recliner across from Anastacia Sinitsina, an actress she'd met multiple times but didn't really know, who was now in trouble. The well-appointed furnishings of the hospital room, as well as the flowers, which Larisa suspected the actress had sent herself, gave an illusion of agency she didn't have. She'd recently been arrested for attacking a studio executive at a lodge restaurant in the mountains.

"I'm so happy you came," said Anastacia, as though she was receiving Larisa in her home instead of a hospital room.

"You realize I'm not a licensed medical professional?" asked Larisa.

Anastacia wore Valentino resort wear marred with a coffee stain across her chest. Her mass of curly, red hair hung loose around her shoulders, and Larisa could see hints of glitter dusting her hair and clothes. She'd been attending a themed wedding at the lodge, though what theme involved glitter, Larisa couldn't guess. There was nothing reasonable about using glitter for anything. It was worse than sand and pine needles.

"Yes, but you did all the prep, right? You know how the system works." Anastacia lifted her mass of hair off her neck and waved fresh air at her exposed skin. "They said I was psychotic."

"What variety of psychotic?"

"It doesn't matter. My lawyer's working on it. I just wanted to talk to someone who understands."

"Alright. What do you want to talk about?"

"My husband has his eyes on my friend, and I need to stop him."

Last Larisa knew, Anastacia was divorced. She waited, allowing confusion to show on her face as she asked, "Duck Turkin?"

"Okay, ex-husband. But it's so ugly to say that. Anyway, we're not as separate as we should be, and this weekend . . ." Her hands made little fists against the fine fabric of her pants.

"I have some strategies for all those things," said Larisa, as she covertly checked the time on the wall clock. "We don't have time today for a full consultation. But why don't you tell me the short version, then we'll plan on something more formal at a later date?"

"Yes, that's exactly it. When I'm out of here. I just . . . it's so humiliating, you know? They won't let my dogs visit. The Internet thinks I've gone off the deep end. As if all the women in the world don't know how easy it is for a man to drive a woman to this. And really, the whole thing has been exaggerated. I didn't 'attack' him."

Larisa nodded. She could help Anastacia. She even felt disappointed she didn't have enough time to dig in right now. But when she'd agreed to take this appointment, she hadn't known what to expect. She'd thought it would be a prank. Some cruel joke to welcome her back into the world and remind her no one was going to forget what she'd done.

"Do you mind if I ask why you decided to call me?"

"Well, I'm between therapists as the moment—another thing I was sharing with Duck—and I heard about you on some talk show. Can't remember which. You're the shrink who saved that director."

Larisa stilled. Once she'd understood the meeting had been called in good faith, she'd thought the only explanation was Quinn's stunt on *The Late Show*, but it was still surprising to hear it confirmed.

"Don't you specialize in industry problems? Mental health consulting? Relationship mediation?"

Larisa swallowed back tears, pressing a smile on her face. "Yes, that's exactly correct."

Quinn was already at the West Hollywood parking lot two blocks from the soda fountain when Larisa arrived. Today, for their first real date, there were no tipped off paparazzi waiting. She hoped against hope she wouldn't be recognized. But it was hard to predict. It felt like her face had been everywhere the last few months, and she had no way to know how much that feeling lined up with reality.

She must have been sitting in her car staring at nothing as these thoughts tied themselves in knots because suddenly, Quinn was standing on the other side of her door, knocking on the window with his knuckle. She reluctantly opened it.

"Hi," he said.

"Hi," she echoed. It felt so new, and fresh, and strange to meet like this. To say hello, to have him smiling at her like everything was easy, like they were happy people.

"You ready to do this?"

She laughed as she stepped out, taking his offered hand.

They walked down the street as they had on their first fake date, holding hands, walking slowly, as though the goal was still to be seen.

"How was your meeting?" he asked.

"Strange. Good." Larisa felt the eyes of a pair of women sitting at the outside table of a coffee shop follow her, their expressions carefully neutral. She was sure they were thinking, *there's that doctor who made her patients act out her sexual fantasies.*

"Will there be more meetings?"

She drew her thoughts back to Quinn and took a moment to figure out what he was asking. "Yes, I think so. She heard about me from *The Late Show*."

"I'm glad it worked." He squeezed her hand. It felt like such a novelty for Quinn to be relaxed enough to do this regular-person thing. He was both exactly the same as he'd been before and also completely different. "But I'm never doing anything like that again. No matter how much trouble you're in. I came off stage and started hyperventilating, then I apparently wasn't actually breathing so I passed out, and Ken had to do CPR. I almost died for you."

He slanted his eyes toward her, the corners of his mouth turned up in a slight smile.

"Someday you'll be very angry at me, and you'll use that against me, won't you?"

"Naw. I'm not that petty. Besides, it was good for the film. Everyone wants to see the movie that kinky shrink saved."

They turned the corner and approached the soda fountain. There were more people here. The day was clear and warm. The boba shop across the street was full. Up ahead, a boutique worker was pulling a sandwich board out onto the sidewalk. Inside the soda fountain, they saw their window table was occupied with a pair of moon-eyed twenty-somethings.

"It's strange to be out," said Larisa.

"We only have to stay long enough for you to answer all my first date questions."

"How many do you have?"

"Thirteen."

"Fuck, Quinn. Can't we just stay as long as it takes us to eat?"

"Sure. But we're going to eat with those little sample spoons."

"Aren't you worried someone will recognize me?"

"I'm never not worried about everything. But I believe in you."

"I know."

"And I think, for reasons we're going to discover before leaving today, you also believe in me. So," he swung her hand through the air as he directed them to the back of the line to place their order, "let's see how far that takes us."

Please Leave a Review

So glad this book found you! If you enjoyed reading it, please leave a review on Goodreads and Amazon if you use them. Please also tell people about this book. Books are sold by people talking about them.

Cheers, Jaye

You're welcome to post about Elaborate Lives all you want on your own socials, but if you want a dedicated place to discuss this, and my other books, with your fellow readers, join my private, member-only reader group on Facebook.

Terrible Love

After Quinn's dramatic gesture at the Autumn Masquerade, Larisa and Quinn are finally dating for real, but it's not as easy as one would think. Larisa is hounded by the destruction of her reputation and continues to feel she needs to be the strong one by making decisions without consulting Quinn. For Quinn, the more he gets to know her, the less he feels he knows. In particular, the influence of Larisa's college boyfriend, Lucas, feels too present for Larisa to be telling Quinn the full truth.

As the couple prepares for the launch of Quinn's film, *The Key*, and the holiday season that follows, neither has any idea how Larisa's secrets will test them and what it will cost for them to stay together.

Sign up for my mailing list to receive early offers and announcements.

Acknowledgements

This is the second Larisa novel I've written. Someday, if the fates decide, you will be able to read the first one, but perhaps you will hate it because it is not quite a Larisa and Quinn story. Anyway, I wrote that first book and I began to ask those dangerous writerly questions about who this woman was before, why did she end up with Quinn? What was their relationship like in the beginning?

Elaborate Lives and its upcoming sequel, *Terrible Love*, are the answer to that question. Perhaps because I'd already spent so much time with the characters, the book came together quickly. I had already read a great deal on the film industry and Hollywood culture for my previous book, *Jane of Battery Park*, so my research for Elaborate Lives focused on the life of a psychiatry resident and mental health medicine. Oh, and I read books about how to write sex because I hadn't done that before.

- *Fifty Writers on Fifty Shades of Grey* edited by Lori Perkins
- *Swing* by Ashleigh Renard
- T*he Claiming of Sleeping Beauty* by A.N. Roquelaure
- *Committed: Dispatches from a Psychiatrist in Training* by Adam Stern
- *Good Morning, Monster: A Therapist Shares Five Heroic Stories of Emotional Recovery* by Catherine Gildiner
- *Whip Smart*: A Memoir by Melissa Febos
- *Body Work*: The Radical Power of Personal Narrative by Melissa Febos

- *Lessons: My Path to a Meaningful Life* by Gisele Bundchen
- *The Actor's Life: A Survival Guide* by Jenna Fischer
- *Falling into the Fire: A Psychiatrist's Encounters with the Mind in Crisis* by Christine Montross
- *Hollywood Ending: Harvey Weinstein and the Culture of Silence* by Ken Auletta
- *Kink*: Stories by R.O. Kwon
- *Making a Scene* by Constance Wu

Special thanks to my beta readers cd ybarra, Hannah Gage, and Meredith Alder who each gave particular feedback that ended up dramatically changing parts of this novel and making it better.

Thank you to Emily Ruth Verona for her feedback on my film industry research.

Thanks to Sarah McGuire my editor, and to Damonza Designs for the great cover and banner, and to Clara at Authortree for taking my Word doc and making it look like a book.

Thank you to my Clarion group, Anna, Cosmata, and Nichole for listening to my frustrations and fan-girling this book and my decision to publish alone.

Thank you to Christopher who said I have enough expertise to write a romance novel.

Lastly, thank you to the wonderful community of independent authors and book reviewers who shared so much knowledge and expertise with me as I went through the process of giving up on traditional publishing and took the future of this book into my own hands. Now, dear reader, its future has been passed onto you. Even if you hated this book, talk about it, complain about it, tell the world why you hated it, chances are someone will want to read it for those same reasons. But they can't read it unless they've heard about it. Your voice matters.

About the Author

Jaye Viner lives on what used to be the plains of eastern Nebraska with a tall human and three fur bombs. She knows just enough about a wide variety of things to embarrass herself at parties she never attends. Her short fiction has been published in Drabblecast, Everyday Fiction, The Rumpus, and Others. She is the author of *Jane of Battery Park* and *Elaborate Lives. Terrible Love* is forthcoming in 2023. Find her on Instagram @Jaye_Viner or her website JayeViner.com